continued . . .

BARELY BEWITCHED

"Frost's latest Southern Witch novel has all the fun, fast, entertaining action readers have come to expect from her . . . Populated with fairies, goblins, vampires, wizards, rampant plants, and a few nasty-tempered humans thrown in for good measure, there's no end to the things that can and do go hilariously wrong."
—*Monsters and Critics*

"What an amazing author! Kimberly Frost's Southern Witch series is fated for great things. *Barely Bewitched* was full of romance [and] magical havoc, and goes from one wild scenario to another. I was definitely hooked all throughout the book and couldn't put it down . . . I am definitely going to read Kimberly Frost's next novel!"
—*Romance Junkies*

"The author is on a roll with Tammy Jo. Book two has as much action as the first, if not more. Ms. Frost's sharp wit and interesting characters propel the story to a satisfying end."
—*A Romance Review*

"Kimberly Frost's Southern Witch series is destined for great things. Full of action, suspense, romance, and humor, this story had me hooked from the first page until the last."
—*Huntress' Book Reviews*

"*Barely Bewitched* is filled with humor, sass, and sizzle! Every page is a new adventure in a world of hilarious antics and smoking chemistry. I love this series and I am really looking forward to the next Tammy Jo fiasco . . . I mean, story!"
—*TRRC Reading*

"The amusing story line is fast-paced . . . Fans will enjoy the escapades of Tammy Jo in this jocular urban fantasy."
—*Genre Go Round Reviews*

"Kimberly Frost can tell a tale like no other . . . A can't-miss read."
—*Fang-tastic Books*

WOULD-BE WITCH

"Delivers a delicious buffet of supernatural creatures, served up Texas-style—hot, spicy, and with a bite!"
>—Kerrelyn Sparks, *New York Times* bestselling author of
>*How to Seduce a Vampire (Without Really Trying)*

"*Would-Be Witch* is an utter delight. Wickedly entertaining with a surprise on every page. Keeps you guessing until the end. Kimberly Frost is a talent to watch."
>—Annette Blair, *New York Times* bestselling author of
>*Tulle Death Do Us Part*

"Kimberly Frost makes a delightful debut with *Would-Be Witch*. It's witty, sexy, and wildly imaginative. Great fun to read. A terrific new series from a wonderful new author."
>—Nancy Pickard, Agatha Award–winning author of
>*The Blue Corn Murders*

"More magically delicious than Lucky Charms—Kimberly Frost's *Would-Be Witch* is bewitchingly fantastic!"
>—Dakota Cassidy, national bestselling author of
>the Accidental Werewolf novels

"A big, heaping helping of Southern-fried magical fun! If you like a lot of laughter with your paranormal fiction, you'll love Frost's series."
>—Alyssa Day, *New York Times* bestselling author of
>*The Cursed*

"Hilarious start to the new Southern Witch series that will keep you laughing long into the night! . . . Ms. Frost is an author to watch for in the future." —*Fresh Fiction*

"A wickedly funny romp . . . The story trips along at a perfect pace, keeping the reader guessing at the outcome, dropping clues here and there that might or might not pan out in the end. I highly recommend this debut and look forward with relish to the next installment in the Southern Witch series." —*Romance Junkies*

CASUALLY CURSED

KIMBERLY FROST

BERKLEY SENSATION, NEW YORK

THE BERKLEY PUBLISHING GROUP
Published by the Penguin Group
Penguin Group (USA) LLC
375 Hudson Street, New York, New York 10014

USA • Canada • UK • Ireland • Australia • New Zealand • India • South Africa • China

penguin.com

A Penguin Random House Company

CASUALLY CURSED

A Berkley Sensation Book / published by arrangement with the author

Berkley Sensation Books are published by The Berkley Publishing Group.
BERKLEY SENSATION® is a registered trademark of Penguin Group (USA) LLC.
The "B" design is a trademark of Penguin Group (USA) LLC.

For information, address: The Berkley Publishing Group,
a division of Penguin Group (USA) LLC,
375 Hudson Street, New York, New York 10014.

ISBN: 978-0-425-26783-7

PUBLISHING HISTORY
Berkley Sensation mass-market edition / February 2015

PRINTED IN THE UNITED STATES OF AMERICA

10 9 8 7 6 5 4 3 2 1

Cover art by Tony Mauro.
Cover design by Rita Frangie.
Interior text design by Kelly Lipovich.

PROLOGUE

FROM UNDER THE brim of a large straw hat, Melanie Trask glanced at her sister, Marlee, who tackled the weeds in their flower beds like they were vermin that might attack the house at any moment. Mar might not be interested in botany, but she did her part to keep their supply of witch's herbs healthy and flourishing.

"Tammy Jo, put your hat back on," Marlee said without looking up.

"Momma, I'm doing something," the little girl said, apparently oblivious to the blistering effects of the bright Texas sun, which was already blazing at nine in the morning.

"You can twirl around with your hat on," Marlee said.

"No, what I'm doing is giving the sun a chance to paint me some freckles so I'll be like a real redhead."

Melanie cocked her head. Tammy Jo's hair was the same flame-colored shade both she and Marlee had been born with. But Tammy Jo's tan skin was something neither of them could claim. They always burned and freckled if they weren't compulsive about hats and sunblock. It was a constant battle against nature to use creams to fade the light smattering of freckles, since freckles had never been "the thing" when they'd been growing up in England. When referring to red hair, *ginger* was a term applied with mild distaste or outright mocking.

"You don't freckle, my darling," Edie the family ghost said when she appeared. Their great-aunt Edie, who'd died in the 1920s, wore a dress with a sparkling Art Deco pattern and at least a foot of fringe on the bottom. Edie smiled when Tammy Jo clapped her hands and waved in excitement at her arrival. "Your skin goes from ivory to gold like Midas himself touched you."

"Hi, Aunt Edie! Look what I can do!" Tammy Jo said. She twirled with her arms overhead and then bolted to the ash tree and shimmied up its trunk. She hung upside down from a branch.

"Careful!" Mel said, rising.

"The twirl was nice, biscuit, but what are you playing at now? Monkey life?" Edie asked.

Tammy Jo giggled, letting her arms dangle beside her hair. "Kiss it," she said.

Melanie bent over and gave Tammy's upside-down lips a kiss, then reached out to lift her down from the branch.

Before she caught her, however, Tammy Jo had released the limb. Melanie gasped and lunged to break her fall, but Tammy Jo flipped in midair to land in the dirt in a crouch, like a tiny wildcat.

"Ta-da!" she said, throwing her arms out.

"Oh, my God! Mar, did you see that?" Mel asked.

Marlee glanced at Tammy Jo and then at Melanie and gave a small nod.

"Who taught you to do that? You shouldn't be flipping out of trees without someone to spot you," Melanie said.

"She's okay," Marlee murmured.

Melanie raised a brow. Both she and Marlee were extremely protective of Tammy Jo. Marlee had been excessively worried about the child being abducted from the time she'd been born.

Paranoid was the word Edie often used to describe Marlee's constant concern.

"Aunt Mel, your kiss tasted like watermelon lip gloss. Do you got it in your pocket? Can I have me some of that for my lips?" Tammy Jo puckered her pink lips. She was so cute with her impish face and quirky mannerisms.

"It's not 'do you got it.' It's 'do you have it,'" Melanie corrected. They might be raising the little girl in a small East Texas town, but she'd learn to speak the Queen's English properly if Melanie had her way. "And *you* tasted like chocolate. Did you get into the Hershey's Kisses? How did you find them? Were you spying on me when I hid the bag?"

Tammy Jo looked away guiltily and then charged into distraction tactics. "Um, you know what? You didn't hear me right. I wasn't asking for a kiss. I said Kissit 'cause I was telling you my faery name."

Melanie froze. "Your what?"

"My name from the faeries. It's how come I can flip so good. I learned it in fairyland. The trees taughted me. And know what else? Our trees like the new garden, but they don't think you gotta be so mean about the little weeds. Those plants got a right to live, too."

Melanie's jaw dropped; then she jerked her head to look at Marlee and Edie.

"I told you this town has all the signs of fae infestation," Edie said. "But you wouldn't listen. Faeries love boisterous children. And our little girl runs and dances from sunrise to sunset."

"Where did you see faeries, Tammy Jo? What did they say to you?" Melanie demanded.

"Um, I see them lots."

"But you know that when you see a faery you're supposed to pretend you don't. Remember? Because faeries sometimes steal children," Mel said.

"Yep, when I see them around town I pretend they're not even there. Just like the game Momma plays when that Boone who wants to kiss her tries to talk to her in the grocery store and she acts like he's not there."

Edie snorted and then said, "They fall at Melanie's feet and she scoops up the good-looking ones. When they fall at Marlee's feet, she leaves them there."

Marlee rolled her eyes at Edie and then looked at Tammy Jo. "If you haven't talked to any of the faeries, why did they give you a nickname?" Marlee asked.

"Oh, that's not from here. That's my name from when I lived with the faeries. When I was real little."

Marlee's brows pinched together.

"You never lived with any faeries, honey. You've been with us the whole time," Mel said.

Tammy Jo cocked her head. "Well, I lived there a few times in some dreams I had. That's when I got a special name. But in the faery town, I don't got no momma or aunties. I just live by myself with a big man who makes metal suits and horseshoes. Only he makes me nervous on account of he forgot how to smile."

Mel's stomach knotted. Were they just random dreams? Or had Tammy Jo's consciousness actually traveled under-hill? Had she perhaps crossed a fae path in bare feet and carried away its magic? Could it be clinging to her even now? "We should move," Melanie said to Marlee.

"Move?" Tammy Jo cried. "We can't move! I just got a real good kindergarten class!"

"We're not moving," Marlee said. "We'll brew her a tea to suppress astral projection in case that's what the dreams were. And we can give her some added protection against faeries. We'll soak her and her clothes in a bath of oatmeal, Saint-John's-wort, and four-leaf clovers."

Melanie frowned. If her sister thought Tammy Jo needed triple protection against faeries, Marlee was worried, too.

"Mar," Melanie said, her voice full of concern.

"Listen, Tammy Jo won't be able to see them for much longer. Another year at most," Marlee said, but Mel noticed the slight shift of Mar's eyes. Did she believe that whole-heartedly? Or was she just trying to make Mel feel better?

"But this did turn out to be fae territory! We're witches. We shouldn't be living in the middle of a town with such a strong fae presence," Melanie said. "Why were you so set on moving here? And staying here? It's never made sense."

"She's been keeping a secret," Edie said. "Haven't you, Marlee?"

"The trees can hear. And so can little ears," Marlee said. "We'll talk about it later."

"But we're not moving, right?" Tammy Jo asked.

"No," Mar said firmly. Melanie scowled.

"Hooray! It's real hot. I'll help," Tammy Jo said, grabbing the hose and unspooling it.

The summer heat baked the ground, and Tammy Jo haphazardly watered the plants.

"You don't have to water the stones," Marlee said. "Rocks don't get thirsty."

"We like to hear the sizzle," Tammy Jo said, glancing at the tree. "And it cools the dirt, too."

"Dirt doesn't need cooling," Melanie said.

"The ground likes it," Tammy countered, a twinkle in her eyes.

"Such unusual eyes. Most McKenna witches have green eyes. All three of us do," Edie said. "Tammy's eyes are hazel brown and golden. Like those of a great cat. Are you a little lioness?"

Tammy Jo roared.

"Tammy Jo, where are your garden clogs? Your feet are all dirty," Mel said.

Tammy's small feet sank into the muddy ground and she giggled. "My toes like it."

The laughter was another giveaway, Melanie thought, of the truth they'd suspected, but that Marlee wouldn't confirm. Even before the child started hearing the wind whisper and the brooks babble, Tammy's laughter sometimes sounded like wind chimes, musical and pretty, and vaguely unnatural. It sent an electric shock down Melanie's spine.

"Look at the mess you're making. You're dragging the hose right through the mud and getting it all over the cobbles. Hang that up, rinse your feet, and go inside. Edie will have a tea party with you," Marlee said.

Edie pursed her phantom lips. She hated tea. Of course, as a ghost she wouldn't actually be drinking it, but on principal she was disinclined to have tea parties. Tea reminded her of their time in England—the worst time in Edie's life or afterlife, which was saying something, since her life in her father's house had been no lollapalooza.

"Wanna have a tea party?" Tammy Jo asked, looking up at Edie hopefully.

A branch swayed toward the child, as if beckoning her closer. Edie narrowed her eyes jealously at the old ash tree.

"Yes, let's go inside," Edie said. Marlee had never said so, but Edie was certain Tammy Jo was half Seelie fae, likely the child of a warrior, from the hints Marlee had let slip about Tammy's father. It was the only explanation for why Marlee wanted to live in Texas on top of an underhill Unseelie stronghold. Duvall was the one place into which the Seelie wouldn't wander and discover Tammy Jo and recognize her as one of their own.

One of their own! Edie's great-great-niece, a half fae! Edie's lips curled in distaste. She almost couldn't bear the thought, but when she looked at the child she felt nothing but love for her. Tammy Jo's strange pointed features and vivacious urchin ways were appallingly irresistible.

She's ours. She's a McKenna witch, Edie thought savagely. *I won't share her with anyone, let alone the Folk.* Not that the fae would've been willing to share either. If they had known that a Halfling creature born of one of their knights lived with humans, they would have stolen her away. The Folk loved children and their juicy humanity. They also hated witches. How delicious would they find the theft of a bouncy little redheaded witch? Exceedingly so, Edie suspected. Oh, yes, the court would try to take her . . . if they knew.

Edie floated toward the sliding door with one last suspicious look at the ash tree. *That tree may know*, she thought bitterly.

None of them could understand treespeak. Only the fae and some young children could understand the oldest language of the Earth. Tammy Jo, who was both a faery and a child, heard the trees whisper. If Melanie and Marlee couldn't suppress Tammy Jo's fae abilities, Edie would convince the girls to burn the ash tree down.

Edie glanced over at Tammy's dirt- and chocolate-smudged little face and the small hands that hung the hose on its hook and then began braiding a vibrant green vine through her flame-colored locks.

"Tammy Jo, take that dirty weed out of your hair," Edie commanded. "Come and wash up. We're going to have a great party."

"With tea and red velvet cake?" Tammy Jo asked excitedly. "I love red velvet cake!"

"I know."

"And I love carrot cake. And chocolate cake. And vanilla cake. And pancakes with syrup and biscuits with honey . . ."

"Yes, you love sweets." *Just like the fae.* "Let's go inside," Edie repeated, and then lowered her voice to a whisper. "I know where the extra frosting is hidden."

Tammy Jo beamed, her perfect white teeth offset by rose-petal lips.

"And you and I will throw a real party," Edie added.

Tammy Jo clapped her hands excitedly, her golden brown eyes sparkling, and Edie couldn't help but smile. The child really was as sweet as the ghastly cakes she favored so much.

THE BEADS KEPT dangling over Tammy Jo's eyes, which made her laugh. In fact, she was giggling so hard the table shook. Aunt Edie laughed, too, and motioned for Tammy Jo to fix the strap of her dress that had fallen off her shoulder again. It was a lady's dress and much too big for her, but it sure was beautiful with its green and gold beads.

"I wore that dress to a party given by Tallulah Bankhead. A really wild affair. Do you know what she wore?"

Tammy Jo shook her head eagerly. She loved it when Aunt Edie smiled and laughed and told stories. Her stories were like faery tales, because everyone wore sparkly shoes and dresses, like Cinderella. Only the people in Aunt Edie's stories didn't end their parties at midnight. They ended only when the police came.

Folks in Duvall, Texas, Tammy Jo's hometown, never wore beaded headbands or made one curl lie flat to their cheek like a little vine pointing up to the sky. And they sure didn't live in buildings that scraped the sky. She wondered if the clouds got mad about all that scraping in New York City. The trees in Duvall sure got mad about the cement sidewalks blocking their roots.

"I'll have another," Edie said, tipping her fancy phantom glass toward Tammy Jo. Tammy pretended to pour some liquid into Edie's glass and then did pour a little more into the Velveteen Rabbit's glass and Winnie the Pooh's. Pooh was having so much fun, he kept falling out of his yellow chair.

Tammy Jo sat him upright again and adjusted his bow tie and the black jacket she'd borrowed from Momma's business suit. Momma didn't work for the bank anymore, so Tammy Jo didn't think it mattered that a little cranberry juice had gotten on it. Edie hadn't scolded her when she'd dripped, so it must be okay.

"Tallulah wore a double strand of pearls, a pair of high heels, and nothing else."

Tammy Jo choked a little. "Nudie Rudy?"

"Yes."

Tammy Jo slapped a bejeweled hand over her mouth and giggled like mad. "You're fibbing!"

"No. Flappers liked to be scandalous. We didn't let anyone tell us what to do. There was power in doing whatever we wanted. Especially in coming down a grand staircase naked. Everyone stopped to watch. No one spoke. No one breathed."

"They were so surprised, I bet. One time Georgia Sue's brother ran into the living room naked. Our dolls were dancing, and they fell right over when he came out. They were that surprised. But then we laughed, 'cause he doesn't know better. He's two. But I guess your friend probably knew better."

"She did."

"And she wasn't shy? Or afraid she'd get in trouble? At my school, if you don't wear clothes, they send you home and you don't get cookies."

"Tallulah got plenty of cookies."

"And nobody yelled at her or covered her up?"

"No, it was a different time."

"But I thought you said there was snow and ice by your house. If she was naked except for necklaces and shoes, wasn't she real cold? You said you wore fur coats over your dresses because of all that cold stuff. How could anybody go naked?"

"I imagine the gin warmed her up."

"The gin?" Tammy Jo echoed, chewing on her lip, which tasted funny on account of the bright red lipstick she'd applied. Tammy dipped a finger into Rabbit's glass. It was plenty cold. She gave Edie a skeptical look that made Edie laugh.

"It only works if you drink it," Aunt Edie said. "That's part of the magic."

Tammy Jo grabbed the glass and gulped it down and decided Aunt Edie was right about that warming-up effect, because it burned her throat. She exhaled, surprised that no flames came out.

Edie laughed, but shook her head. "You shouldn't have done that. You'll get us both in trouble."

"I don't care," Tammy Jo announced. "I'm Talulli Bankle. Let's do that dance again." Tammy Jo jumped up and started the old record player. The record was scratchy, but she liked the songs on it anyway.

She shimmied and knocked her knees together so the dress's beads and fringe danced, too.

Then the door opened, and Momma and Aunt Mel peered in.

"What are you listening to?" Aunt Melanie asked.

"What are you wearing?" Momma asked.

"What are you doing?" Momma and Aunt Mel asked at the same time.

Tammy Jo giggled uproariously. She laughed so hard she spun sideways and tripped over the bottom of the dress and fell onto a pile of pillows and stuffed toys.

"Tamara Josephine! Are those bottles from the liquor cabinet?" Momma asked.

Tammy Jo laughed harder, but then Aunt Melanie turned off the record player and Tammy Jo remembered that she was supposed to be the hostess.

She bolted up and returned to her position at the head of the table. "Welcome to my cocktail party, Momma, Aunt Melanie. Won't you sit down?"

They stared at her. The beaded headband sank forward, half covering her eyes like a blindfold. Tammy Jo shoved the headband up with determined fingers.

"A cocktail party? Edie, a cocktail party?" Momma demanded.

"That's right," Tammy Jo said, motioning to the bottles and empty juice boxes. "I'm a singular sensation, Momma. Nobody in town throws a decent cocktail party. This is the best one of the year. Aunt Mel, would you like a sidecar?"

"Oh, my God. A drunk flapper at five? That's the best alternative to gardening you could come up with?" Momma asked Aunt Edie.

Edie flashed a smile and sipped from her martini glass. "I have to go now, precious," Edie said, blowing Tammy Jo a kiss. "You were marvelous. Don't believe anything different."

Tammy Jo waved. "If you see Tabulli, tell her I said hi. And if she's naked and cold, loan her a coat!"

Edie disappeared, and Tammy smiled up at her momma and aunt Melanie. They were so pretty with their swirly magic and bouncy hair.

"If you don't like sidecars, Momma, I can make you a martini."

1

IF I INVITED a Hatfield to dinner, I wouldn't invite a McCoy. It's not something that most books on entertaining really talk much about, but it's common sense. Besides the basic gunfire and bloodshed that can result from having sworn enemies over to the house at the same time, there is also the problem that they'll be distracted by the company and won't be able to really appreciate what's being served. And if there is one thing that I care about, it's that people take the time to enjoy food prepared in my kitchen.

In small towns, there are always feuds. Sometimes long-standing and bitter ones. I try not to take sides, and I definitely try not to get in the middle of them by inviting the warring people to my house on the same night. But my current houseguests weren't neighbors or friends. They were a fae knight and a half-fae, half-witch girl. The Halfling girl was just like me . . . because she was the long-lost twin sister I hadn't even known I had!

Getting a twin for a Christmas present should've been cause for celebration, but there was a catch to my sister Kismet's arrival: She was being hunted. And if we didn't agree to go home to the Never, the knight who'd been hunting her said that our momma would be killed. I'd never been on an overseas vacation. I'd have been excited to go if there hadn't been the risk of imprisonment and death. To think, I'd once thought expensive plane tickets were the biggest obstacle to my traveling the world!

I glanced at the oven timer. Only three minutes before the biscuits would be ready. Kismet had asked if I knew how to make biscuits from scratch, which tickled me. My specialty is pastries, but I can cook pretty much anything. I'd been making biscuits since I was about seven years old. At twenty-three, I could make them without measuring the ingredients. I just shook and poured the items into a bowl and could tell by the color and texture as I stirred when the batter was right.

"I'll have another blended," Crux the Seelie knight said, his breath against the back of my neck.

I jumped, gooseflesh rising. I pointed a butter knife in his direction. "Don't sneak up on me."

He smirked. "It's impossible not to. You are completely unaware of your surroundings."

"I'm making strawberry compote and whipped cream for my sister's biscuits."

"That sounds good. I'll have biscuits, too."

"You had cake, pie, and an entire blender full of brandy Alexander ice-cream drinks. Now you want biscuits?" I asked skeptically.

"Don't forget the chocolate. I had six of those," he said.

Right, he'd eaten an entire tin of liquor-infused dark-chocolate truffles of the bourbon, coconut rum, and Frangelico varieties. I looked him over. He was tall, lean, and golden hued. There was no excess fat, only taut muscle and high cheekbones. He could have been a model in a fashion magazine. But I knew better than to let his nice looks distract me. He could be cunning and violent. He and I had had a couple of fights already, but since he wasn't holding that against me I was trying not to hold it against him either.

Kismet's reaction to Crux made me extra leery of him, though. She eyed him like he was a raptor who might move in a blur of speed at any moment to attack us. It had me on edge. But so far I couldn't think of a way to get rid of him. Also, if I did go to the land of the faeries I would need every ally I could get. So I hoped to win him over, which is why I said, "But if you're still hungry, you can have biscuits, too."

"And another blended?"

I had to smile at his calling the drinks "blendeds" instead of by their name, which I'd told him several times.

"Yes, sure," I said, dragging the blender to me.

He smiled. "Offer to bake for her first thing. She'll be intrigued, and when she tastes your sweets, you'll have value."

I peered closely at his face, which glowed more than usual. From the alcohol? I wondered. Were the fae susceptible to drunkenness? That would be useful to know.

"You mean the queen? I should offer to make pastries and candy for the Seelie queen?"

"Yes. The more value you bring underhill, the less likely she'll be to punish you if you make a mistake while there."

He talked like it was a sure thing that I'd be going to meet his queen, even though I'd told him that, being American, I don't recognize the authority of kings and queens, especially ones who aren't even part of my normal world.

I chewed the corner of my mouth. The trouble was that the queen had special leverage. Unfortunately, when Crux had announced that the fae monarch would execute momma if we didn't go underhill, my new sister had shrugged it off. She had escaped the Never and didn't intend to go back. That was one of the reasons I wasn't trying to kick Crux out of my house. I might need him to lead me into the Never. Of course if given a choice, I would much rather have had my sister's help.

I went out to the backyard. The bespelled bluebells that sounded an alarm when the fae were nearby rang, but not loudly. I looked around, then up. The light through the kitchen windows shone on the branches of the ash tree. My sister reclined on a tree limb with her back against the trunk.

"Hello. Are the biscuits ready then?" she asked in her lilting Irish accent.

"Just about," I said.

"You're an apple darling for making them," she said with a musical little laugh, and then rolled off the branch, flipping in the air to land on her feet in a crouch . . . like an acrobat. Or an ocelot. My feline companion and friend Mercutio made those kinds of moves.

I had a flash of memory . . . me as a little girl flipping from the tree in exactly the same way. Aunt Mel's surprised face. *Kissit*, I'd said. *Kismet*, I'd meant. I shivered.

"What's surprised you?" Kismet asked, rising from the crouch in a fluid movement, as if her spine were made of rubber and silk. Crux had that same grace.

"It's the way you have for getting down from a tree. People can't really do that . . . most can't. I think when I was little I could. I think . . . I felt you. Like we shared a connection back then where I could see through your eyes and learned things from you when you did them. The way I've been able to see and feel you lately."

When she passed by me, her pinkie caught mine and curled around it. My own pinkie curled too without my even thinking about it. Clasping her finger was like shaking hands or hugging: When the other person does it, you just automatically do it back.

For a couple months I'd had the feeling something was missing—until Kismet arrived. When her pinkie linked mine now, I felt like a missing piece of my soul returned to me. Joy rippled through my whole body, making me want to laugh and dance. Since I didn't want to startle Kismet, I just grinned at her.

She returned my smile and winked. "I'll teach you for real," she said. "To climb trees and to flip out of 'em and how to get them to lower a branch to swing you up. In return, you teach me to make biscuits and cakes."

"Deal!"

I didn't hear Crux approach, but I knew he was behind me by the change in her expression. The sunshine of her smile disappeared. Her head didn't turn. Only her eyes moved, and they were a cool, deadly green. She might look like me, but in the moments when she faced Crux, she reminded me of Mercutio, a natural-born hunter who would fight whatever needed fighting, no matter how big or how deadly. My sister was not intimidated by the famous Seelie knight, but she was wary of him. She moved between us, shielding me from him.

"You'd best go," she said to him in a low voice. "I won't be taken back alive. And you know that to kill me is no easy thing."

"Of course I do." He smiled at her over the top of his glass.

"I don't think she's kidding about being ready to have an all-out fight. My cat gets that exact same look, and when it comes to fighting, Merc doesn't play," I said, letting go of Kismet's pinkie so I could turn to face Crux.

"I remember," Crux said before he chugged the last of his shake.

"That's right. Mercutio took a bite out of your neck that one time."

"It's a wonder he didn't retch his stomach out at the taste," Kismet said with a little smirk.

Crux's smile never faltered. "I don't know why you say it's a wonder. You've tasted my blood. It didn't make you sick."

Her smile faded till it was gone. "I may yet, you know." She paused. "Kill you."

He shrugged. To me, he said, "If she planned to kill me, she'd have done it."

"I can change my mind. Free will," she said.

His smile finally disappeared. "You'd have to answer for it. You're Seelie fae. Inside the Never and out of it."

Kismet replied, "I don't bow to the queen's will anymore. And never shall again."

He sighed. "You're born of the blood. She'll always be your queen."

The oven timer rang. "Come on," I said. "Don't argue."

"My sister's a peacekeeper. She cares for people. Be glad her goodwill leaks all over me when I'm around her, or I might have challenged you to a death match."

She'd said it so casually, it was kind of unreal. I blinked, then swallowed.

"Um, well, death matches are illegal in the state of Texas, which is where we're standing. In fact, fighting to the death is illegal all over the United States. Canada, too, and probably Mexico. In the Old West, there were gunfights in the streets to settle disagreements and all, but that hasn't been allowed for a long time. At least a hundred years."

Crux cocked a brow. "A hundred years is a long time?"

"Yep. In human years that's a real long time. So c'mon. The biscuits are done. And everything will seem better with a belly full of biscuits."

Most times an announcement like that would be met with skeptical chuckles from people, but these two just turned and went inside, like they understood the truth about the fortifying power of biscuits. I frowned. There were moments when I felt my own Seelie roots.

I'd been raised by witches and hadn't known I was half fae until a couple months earlier. Momma, Aunt Mel, and my double-great-aunt Edie had all kept my magical mixed race a total secret, even from me, because the World Association of Magic was against the fae in every way.

It was possible that the Association would lock me up or kill me if they found out I'd used fae magic on occasion. It wouldn't even matter to them that I hadn't meant to or tried to. In some ways, that would make it worse. I had powers that I couldn't control and that they wouldn't be able to control either. They wouldn't like that. And when they didn't like something . . . well, they weren't nice about how they dealt with problems, or witches who caused them.

Inside, the house smelled like melted chocolate and spiced vanilla with just a faint note of pine needles from the tree. After putting the biscuits and fixings on the table, I raised the volume on the country Christmas music, hoping to put everyone in a festive and friendly mood. Kismet's shoulders bobbed in time to the beat as she broke her biscuit in half down the middle and dipped the right half in a circle of berry compote and then in a dollop of whipped cream. A jolt of recognition ran through me, leaving me tingling and smiling. I'd eaten biscuits that way a thousand times. When I'd been little, Momma and Aunt Mel told me over and over, "Use a knife and cut them in half the other way. Spread whatever you want on the bottom half and put the top back on, like a sandwich. When you dip, you make such a mess, and half the time the biscuit crumbles and you get your fingers sticky by going after the lost pieces. Little ladies have better table manners."

Little faeries apparently didn't. Neither did big ones.

A small chunk of biscuit fell onto the dish. Kismet retrieved it and dipped it and the tips of her fingers into the crushed berries. She dropped the morsel in her mouth and licked the sweetened fruit from her fingertips.

"That's delicious, delectable, and divine," she said.

I chuckled. "We're sisters, all right."

She grinned.

I ate a biscuit, dipping it into butter, then the fruit compote, and licking my fingertips in the bargain. Then a key in the door's lock announced that Aunt Mel had arrived. My shoulders stiffened and my smile dropped. I loved her dearly and couldn't wait to see her, but there was so much I had to tell her. And none of it would make her happy.

2

WHEN I WAS eleven years old, Edie told me that if we'd all been drinks, she'd have been a whiskey sour, I'd have been a gin fizz, Momma a maiden's prayer, and Aunt Mel, sangria. I hadn't understood her at the time, but now I did. Edie's sarcastic wit had a tart bite. I was bubbly. Momma was soulful and mysterious. And Aunt Mel loved exotic men and places, and she lived in pursuit of things that made music play in her head.

Upon entering, Aunt Mel called out my name and then strolled in wearing a fitted dress that had alternating indigo and mint-green horizontal stripes. She wore dark blue platform heels and a mint-colored scarf around her ponytail. She was thirty-nine, but looked twenty-nine, and her style was as young and fresh as springtime.

She'd come in with her hand outstretched to present me with a small wrapped present, but her arm dropped when she saw the visitors in the kitchen. Her lips parted slightly in surprise, her gaze jerking from Crux to Kismet and me and then back.

"What's going on?" she asked, moving slowly away from Crux. She clutched my forearm and looked at Kismet. "You're . . . Who are you?"

"You must be the mother's twin. Melanie, you're called," Kismet said.

"This is our aunt," I said, nodding. "Aunt Mel, you won't believe it, but I've got a twin sister, too. This is her. Her name's Kismarley, but she goes by Kismet. Isn't that pretty? I like it a ton."

There was a stunned silence, and Aunt Mel pursed her pale pink lips.

"I don't know how that's possible," Melanie said. She stared at us. I had dark red hair like Momma and Aunt Mel, while Kismet's was strawberry blond. I'd gotten hazel eyes that were mostly light brown and flecked with green and gold. Kismet's eyes were much greener, like theirs and Edie's. "She died," Melanie whispered. "You died. We had to—" Melanie swallowed.

"It was a changeling who died. I was taken underhill. I guess he decided one for the fae and one for the witches."

"He who? Caedrin? He made the swap? He stole you from Marlee? When? How?"

"I wouldn't know," Kismet said. "I was young at the time, being an infant."

Melanie looked at Crux, and her eyes narrowed. "What's he doing here? Why did you bring him? Can we count on him to keep Tammy Jo a secret now that he's seen her?"

"No, we can't count on him," Kismet said. "He's here to take me back. And he wants her, too. But he can't have us."

"No, he can't!" Melanie said, her voice rising.

A knock on the front door made my head jerk toward it. *Bryn?*

Bryn's my boyfriend. Actually he's more than that. A lot more.

Still, I didn't think he would come over without letting me know. I'd insisted I wanted to talk to Aunt Mel alone about some news that would shock her. Bryn agreed to wait at his place while I did. And since he and I had some big news of our own, I wasn't ready for him to arrive yet. One big surprise for Aunt Mel at a time.

"I don't know who that could be," I murmured. "But I'll check."

"Let's both go," Melanie said, hooking her arm through mine. When we reached the front hall, she whispered, "As soon as we get to the door, you run. I'll do whatever I can to slow Crux down. You go to Bryn Lyons's property. I'm sure his fortress of a house has some weapons you can use against the fae and—"

"Aunt Mel, we can't. And especially you can't go up against Crux with your magic not even working." Aunt Melanie had been in the land of the faeries looking for Momma, but later, when she'd come out, she'd gotten in trouble with the World Association of Magic. They'd bound her powers with a curse and she was supposed to stay in the United Kingdom and make amends. If she'd done as she'd been told, they would've given her magic back. But I'd been in trouble, and she'd come home to help. So if she didn't find a way to lift the curse, it would prevent her powers from working for seven whole years. It was a mess.

Melanie said, "Don't worry about me. If I don't attack him, Crux won't kill me without orders from the Seelie queen. You just go—" She pulled the front door open, but the path wasn't clear. Standing on the front step was the body of my friend Evangeline Rhodes. She reached for the knob, but paused when she saw us.

My jaw dropped. Vangie's looks had been transformed. Her former long, often disheveled hair had been cut to medium length, dyed from plain brown to sable, and smoothed until it shone like patent leather. Bright green eyes greeted us. The eyes of our aunt Edie.

"Melanie's home. Hello, darling," she said.

"Um . . ." I said, ready to explain that when Vangie got herself murdered, Aunt Edie's ghostly spirit inhabited Vangie's body to help me. When I killed the wizard we were fighting, Vangie's soul had been set free as a ghost, but Edie had stayed in the hijacked body and was still there. One look at Aunt Mel's slack-jawed expression, though, told me she recognized the sly tone and smile.

"Edie?" Aunt Mel finally whispered, cocking her head.

"In the flesh. Again," she said with a smirk. "Hello, biscuit," Edie said to me. "Did you tell her yet?"

"I didn't get a chance. She just got here and you showed up," I said.

"Not about me," Edie said with a wide sweep of her arm, dismissing her resurrection as though it weren't a hot topic. Edie strolled in. Her silky black coat swished behind her, as did the fabric of her dark purple dress. Her crystal-encrusted heels matched a beaded comb tucked elegantly into her hair.

"Where did you get that outfit?" I stammered.

"I bought it at a boutique. I'd admired it."

"The town's shops are closed. It's a holiday!"

"One thing you should understand," Edie said, nearly gliding into the room. "Any locked door can be opened with the right inducement. Charm, magic, money, or some combination therein always does the trick. This time it was charm and money."

"You can't spend Vangie's money! It's not yours!"

"What shall I do with it? Put it in an empty coffin and bury it in her body's place?"

"No," I said. "But it's not right for you to spend it. She might get back in her body sometime and then need her inheritance."

"There will still be plenty. She has a great deal of it in her accounts. I don't intend to spend it all. At least, not right away. Do we have champagne in the fridge?"

"Nope," I said. "Hang on." I reached for her as she sailed past, but I only caught rustling air.

"We should always have at least two bottles chilled. Reasons to celebrate and fabulous company can turn up at the most unexpected times. I'd have loved a glass tonight." Edie strode to the liquor cabinet and poured herself a gin and tonic. "To celebrate us all being together. If only Marlee were here, too. We need to get her home. Even if it calls for trickery. It would be for her own good, and she'd forgive us for deceiving her, because we're us, her precious family," Edie said. "Do we have lemons or limes?"

"We do have to bring Momma home," I said. "And sooner rather than later!"

"Why?" Edie asked, her green eyes turning sharply to my face at my raised voice.

"Because Crux the faery says that if I don't go to the Never, the Seelie queen will kill her."

"That bitch," Edie hissed.

"Crux is lying," Aunt Mel said. "Ghislaine won't kill Marlee. Mar and Caedrin have done everything imaginable to appease the queen. They—"

"Not everything. Caedrin's broken faith with our queen," Crux said, leaning against the kitchen door frame.

"Broken faith how?" Melanie demanded. "I don't believe it."

"He has. And at Marlee's urging."

"Never. She wouldn't risk the queen's wrath. The only thing she cares about is being allowed to stay with Caedrin," Melanie said.

"She would and did risk the queen's wrath. And she's brought it down upon them," Crux said.

"How?" Melanie snapped, incredulous.

"Ask your niece."

"For the love of Hershey, how would I know?" I demanded, throwing up my hands.

"Not that niece," Crux said, tilting his head toward the kitchen.

Kismet stepped into the doorway, shoving the golden knight aside. "Stop causing trouble."

Edie's glass slipped, but she caught it by tightening her grip. The liquor swished and a few drops splashed out onto her slim fingers. "Who's this?" Edie asked, her voice low and cool.

"She's my twin," I said, going over to Kismet. I tried to take her arm, but she pulled back. "It's okay," I told her. "That's our aunt Edie. She was a ghost, but now she's a girl again. Sort of."

"Witches by the houseful," Kismet whispered, wrinkling her nose.

"Well, yeah," I said. "Momma's people are all witches. You knew that, right?"

"I knew," Kismet said, her green eyes like tinted ice.

"What happened in the Never?" Edie asked, taking a slow swig of her gin and tonic. "You convinced Marlee to do something for you? Or she was forced to do something to protect you?"

"I don't need her protection," Kismet said.

"But she helped you," Edie said with a calculating look. "Didn't she?"

Kismet fell into a stony silence for several moments. I looked at Crux, but he didn't speak.

"If something happened, you can tell us about it. We're your family," I said, giving Kismet's arms a squeeze.

Kismet looked at me, ignoring everyone else. "I didn't ask that witch for her help. I wouldn't. She can't even help herself in there."

"But you might've needed help escaping," I whispered, looking into her eyes. "If you had to be sneaky about it?"

She bit the corner of her lip for a moment.

"She bites her lip like Tammy. See that?" Edie asked.

"Yes," Melanie said. "They're so much alike."

Kismet's expression flashed triumphant and then defiant when she looked at Aunt Melanie and Edie. "She and I are the same. Exactly. We're not like the faeries. And we're not like you either. We're our own breed. Just us. Just we two."

"Darling, really," Edie said. "You're sisters, not lovers. It's not like you can start your own tribe and populate the world with a mixed magical race. Calm down. Have some gin. We'll sort this out."

"We won't sort it out, and you won't want me to drink with you when you realize I'll never do what you want."

"What is it that you think we want?" Aunt Melanie asked.

"You want us to sacrifice ourselves to rescue her," Kismet said.

"No," Melanie said. "We don't want that. No."

Kismet's brows rose. "Even if the queen kills her because we won't go back?"

"Tammy Jo would not be going 'back.' She's never even been. And we don't expect either of you to go underhill.

There will be some other way to save Marlee. There's always a way. What does the queen want? There must be something she values more than Marlee's life," Aunt Mel said.

"Yes, there is. Me," Kismet said. "She values what I can do."

"What is it that you can do?" I asked.

"I can pass in and out of the Never, even with the witches sealing the gates closed."

"That's not all," Crux said.

"Why is that so important? You're a spy for the Seelie queen?"

"Sometimes," Kismet said quickly, and then glared at Crux, who grinned.

I glanced at him, hating the smirk on his handsome face.

"She's the queen's secret weapon against all foreign enemies. Kismarley is an assassin. She hunts her quarry all over the world. And a better killer you'll never see."

My stomach lurched, and my face fell. It was one thing to kill someone in self-defense or even to keep him from kidnapping you, but to track creatures down to kill them? To hunt people? That was totally different.

I turned to Kismet, hoping she would deny it.

She didn't.

3

TWIN SISTERS DON'T grow on trees, even if they do sometimes climb and flip from them. And my sister had helped me. She'd saved my life. That much I knew.

"You didn't have a choice? You had to kill people?" I asked softly.

She gave a sharp little nod.

"You don't have to anymore," I whispered, catching her hand and lacing our fingers together. "I'll help you get a job. You can live with me wherever I live."

The corners of her mouth turned up. "Let's live in the mountains, where the woods go on forever up one side and down the other."

I shivered. "Um, well, I bet that would be real pretty, too. But see, when I said wherever I live, I meant wherever I live in Duvall."

Her face leaned close to mine, her mouth by my ear. "We can't stay here. The fae will find us. I could kill Crux, but they'd send someone else after me eventually."

"No killing," I whispered back. "Not even Crux."

"Is there anyone you won't defend?" she asked with a

smirk. "I felt it halfway around the world. All those feelings! It's exhausting. But it's also—"

"Engaged!" Aunt Mel cried, making both Kismet and me jerk our heads in her direction.

I flushed as Edie saluted me with her glass. I frowned at her and then gave Aunt Mel a sheepish look. "It happened kind of unexpectedly, but yep. I'm gonna get married again."

Melanie sank down onto the couch. "He's really good-looking, Tammy Jo. And charming, but you know he's—"

"Yes, a Lyons. I'm aware. It wasn't my idea to get so involved with him, but love happens. Like a hurricane—"

"And other disasters," Edie said dryly. "Or like a dreaded disease, where this family's concerned."

"Not a dreaded disease! But it's true, love's kinda like a—what do you call it?—an affliction. There's no vaccine against it, and no cure for it." I shrugged with a small smile. "When you're completely in its grip and there's a marriage proposal, you gotta say yes."

"And suffer the consequences," Edie said.

I frowned at her, but nodded. "Yep. Maybe." There was a family prophecy that warned us not to get involved with a Lyons. "But I'm pretty sure the prophecy's already played out. Ninety to ninety-five percent sure."

"Didn't you nearly fail every math class you ever had?" Edie asked, mock curious.

I wanted to throttle her. Having a person know all your business when you're trying to argue something is a real problem.

"Bryn won't betray me on purpose. If he does it by accident, we'll cross that bridge when we come to it."

"If you survive," Edie said, mixing herself another drink. "He's nearly gotten you killed—"

"Wrong! I've nearly gotten him killed. Lots. He's saved my life. More than once."

Melanie clasped her hands together so tight her nails indented the skin, whitening it. "I chose the wrong man plenty of times, but never anyone from the list." She glanced up. "You met Incendio. You know that Marlee can't come home and might be in deadly trouble because she's tied herself to the wrong person. And those weren't even names with a prophecy of disaster attached. How much worse will your consequences be? Can't you learn from our mistakes?"

"Apparently not," I said with a shrug.

"Why should you rush into marrying him? Is he pressuring you?"

He had, yes. But I'd liked his pressuring me. I loved his earnest romantic side as much as his clever sarcastic side. "We both decided. We fell in love, and we can't stand to be apart too much, so it just makes sense. I'm not fixing to shack up with him, am I? You know what kind of gossip that would lead to." I'd already been married and divorced, and I was only twenty-three years old. That had set plenty of tongues to wagging. It was already a big enough shock for most people to see me moving on from one of the town's favorite sons. My ex, Zach, had been a much-beloved high school football star who'd gone on to play for the University of Texas. A terrible knee injury had ended his football career, so we'd come home to Duvall, where he became a sheriff's deputy who always helped anyone who needed it.

Bryn Lyons, on the other hand, was a lawyer, so of course anyone would have reservations about trusting him. Plus, he'd gone to school on the East Coast, was rich, and had originally come from a foreign country. That was a lot of *different* for a small town to swallow. But he'd been committed to a life in Duvall, and he'd put his time and money into helping the town develop into something even better than it had started out. He had people's respect for sure. They just didn't know him as well as they knew Zach. When you're born in a place and all your people live there . . . well, you're part of the town and it's part of you. With Bryn, there was always a nagging feeling that he might take off for somewhere else. He already had an office and a law practice in Dallas as well as Duvall. And people probably thought Dallas suited Bryn better. That place was as shiny and cosmopolitan as he was. But Duvall had two things that Bryn wanted: A magical tor. And me.

Of course, we would be able to settle down in town and build a life together only if I could make it back from the Never . . . assuming that I actually had to go.

"Kismet, did our dad help you escape the Never?"

Her face went blank, as if she were playing poker. She could've been holding a full house or nothing at all by that expression.

"C'mon. Tell me the truth."

"It doesn't matter. It was owed to me. Whatever effort he made was the least he could do. For so long he did nothing to help me."

"And why do you think he decided to help you now?"

She pursed her lips and then shrugged.

"Can't you guess?" I asked. "I bet Momma told him to. Don't you think? She saw you were unhappy, and she told him to help you get out even if they got caught. Even if it risked their own lives. Don't you think?" I asked.

She swallowed. "No, I don't think so. Whatever made him do it, it wasn't our mother. She doesn't care about me."

I clucked my tongue. "How can you say that?"

"I can say it easily, since I'm just repeating what she said."

"She would never have said that."

"She did. I heard her with my own ears," Kismet said bitterly. "I don't care. She's nothing to me. Just as I'm nothing to her. And if she's been blamed for my escape, well, she'll have to talk her own way out of it."

My jaw dropped, Aunt Mel gasped, and Edie rolled her eyes.

"This one is going to take some work," Edie murmured. "Melanie, give me Lenore's locket."

Aunt Mel put a hand over the front of her shirt, pressing the locket underneath. She paused for a moment and then lifted the chain. The antique locket that Edie's soul had been linked to from the time of her death in the 1920s appeared as Aunt Mel raised the locket over her head. She held it out and Edie took it. She smiled, admiring it.

"My twin sister wore this locket every day. We were

together. Always. Not even death could separate us. That's blood and loyalty," Edie announced.

Kismet leaned over Edie's shoulder to get a better look at the necklace. "That design was an interesting choice," Kismet said.

Edie arched a brow, glancing at the starburst pattern of diamonds on the front. "In what way interesting?" Edie asked.

"Front door," Kismet said. She flipped the locket over in Edie's palm. The smooth gold of the back was without a pattern. "Not there. On the inside?"

"What?" Edie asked.

"Open it."

The hinge of the locket had grown stiff over the years, and we'd always hesitated to oil it for fear of damaging the pictures inside.

Kismet reached over and tried to force it open. When it didn't budge, Kis pulled out a pin and started to jam it in, but Edie pulled the locket to her chest and closed her hands around it. "No. I'll do it. Or a jeweler will."

"Is there a pattern on the inside?"

"There are pictures inside. One of me and one of my sister."

"Under the pictures?"

"I don't remember. If I ever knew. The pictures were already inside when Lenore showed it to me. She gave me a matching locket. Mine was buried with my body."

"I never knew that," I said.

Edie shrugged. "There was no magic attached to mine, but I like that a little piece of Lenore's creativity and her image were buried with me. Together forever. Twins."

Kismet glanced at me. "Aboveground and below. Twins together, not allowing anyone to come between them. What do you think of that?"

"Sisters should be close," I said.

"Closer to each other than anyone else? Even than a parent? Or a lover?"

"Um, I don't think there's a reason to rank people by how much you love them. You can love lots of people."

"But someone has to be loved the most."

My phone chimed, telling me I had a text message from Bryn. Speaking of people I loved like crazy. I snatched the phone from the counter and opened the message.

How's it going?

I'd called Bryn earlier to tell him about my visitors and the possibility that I'd be going to the land of the faeries. He was understandably impatient to know what was going on. So was I, actually.

We both had concerns about my going into the Never, and not just because faeries were dangerous creatures. In the past, when my witch magic had been drained away by spells and I'd become more fully fae, I'd changed. My conscience—and my humanity, I guessed—had faded away, too. I'd become numb to my feelings and memories. Bryn loved me for my regular Tammy Jo self, who cared a lot about the town and everyone in it, especially him. He worried that one day I might change into full faery and not change back. I'd be lost to him then.

I didn't think that could ever happen while I lived in Duvall. I loved it too much. But inside the Never, who knew? I recognized the hard edges that I'd felt as a full fae in Kismet. A coolness emanated from her when she faced off with Crux. What if I entered the Never and stopped caring about rescuing Momma? I wouldn't do anyone any good if my heart turned to stone in my chest.

Glancing down at my phone, I thought, *That's why I need Bryn.* Once I'd stood on a faery path in full fae consciousness, and all I'd wanted in the world was to follow that path into the Never. Bryn, who'd been standing off the path, had reached out to me. Wanting him was the only thing that had drawn me back to the human world.

The corners of my mouth tipped down as I typed, *Things here sure are a mess. Come over if you want. I could use the help.*

4

BRYN ARRIVED WEARING trousers as black as his hair and a red shirt that made the blue of his eyes even more vibrant. For a moment I just stared at him, because he has the ability to stun a person with his good looks. Then I remembered that I was going to marry him and really needed to get over those looks, or who would keep him in line? Not that Bryn's the kind of guy who takes orders. But sometimes, when he gets ruthless with his enemies, he needs me to remind him not to go over-board. Just because someone tries to kill us doesn't mean they're all bad. And the good guys, which we are, can't go hog wild with revenge if they want to hold on to their white hats.

I glanced over my shoulder. Aunt Mel stood in the foyer, waiting to greet Bryn. Behind her, Edie opened drawers in the foyer chest, searching it.

"What are you looking for?" I asked Edie as Aunt Melanie stepped forward.

"Hi, Bryn. Merry Christmas," Aunt Mel said. She and Bryn exchanged a hug. "I'm surprised about the engagement. And worried. I hope you guys won't rush the wedding. . . ."

He remained silent.

"Getting married or even falling in love with you could be putting our girl at major risk. You know that, right?"

Being a good lawyer, Bryn never changed his expression. He wouldn't let her bait him into agreeing to a long engagement.

"You love each other so much there's nothing to do except get married?" Mel asked, raising her brows in question. "You're sure?"

"Absolutely sure," Bryn said.

Melanie sighed and shrugged. "All right. Then I'm behind you."

Edie glanced up. "I'm behind you, too, Lyons. With a club and bad intentions. Watch your back," she said in a saccharine whisper. Returning to her search of the chest, she added, "I'm looking for the extra bottles Marlee used to keep in here. Is there really not a single drop of brandy or cognac left in this house? For pity's sake, Melanie."

"I used up the brandy in the brandy Alexanders," I said.

"Well, what am I supposed to do for a sidecar then? Go to the Paris Ritz, where it was invented? We've got to keep this house better stocked. It's beyond the pale."

"Why do you need brandy?" I scoffed. "You're drinking gin and tonics."

"We're out of gin. There was only a splash left."

"There was more than a splash."

"Well, it went down like a splash," Edie said. "And I haven't had a sidecar since the week before I died. Don't you think ninety years is long enough to wait?"

"Ninety years isn't very long," Crux said, appearing at the end of the hall.

"Fae," Bryn said, narrowing his cobalt eyes. "Crux, I presume."

Crux inclined his head, saying, "Wizard." Crux stretched. "You're not wanted here. You should retrieve your rings and go."

I glanced at the canary-yellow diamond solitaire that sat big as an egg on my left ring finger. And the magical band on my right middle finger. Both were from Bryn, symbols of our romantic and magical connections.

Bryn's gaze assessed Crux for several long moments. Crux leaned against the wall.

"Don't tax your brain, wizard. Even full of sweetened

spirits, I could kill you with a motion so fast and smooth that the curtains would barely sway."

I glanced at the sheers hanging over the window next to Crux.

Crux added a couple words I didn't know. It sounded like Gaelic, and Bryn who speaks lots of languages, flicked his gaze past Crux.

"What did he say?" I asked.

"He said, 'Come out, deadly lovely.' I presume he wasn't talking to me."

I saw the fingertips then. It was all that showed of Kismet, and they twitched, beckoning me. I took Bryn's hand so that our rings connected. He wore a band on his left middle finger that reacted to the one on my right hand. Magic, which already flowed between us, spiked.

Kismet's face appeared then, her expression curious. She stared at Bryn for several long moments and he stared back.

"Hello," he said. "I'm Bryn. Tamara's fiancé."

Kismet's gaze flicked to my face. She whispered something, also in that foreign language.

"Yes," Bryn said, pleased. "I'm the love of her life. And she's mine."

Kismet's eyes never left mine. "You won't want to go without him. So wherever we go, he can come."

"I tire of this," Crux said. "The queen extended no invitation to this wizard, and there is nothing of his in the Never. He's not welcome."

"I'm—" I began, but Crux cut me off.

"No," he said with finality. "A man can't claim from the human world that which did not belong to it. You're fae."

Bryn was part fae himself, but we sure weren't going to admit that to Crux.

"If it will complicate things, I won't travel into the Never with her," Bryn said, lying to Crux so smoothly that for a second I was shocked that he'd changed his mind about letting me go alone. Lawyers! They're trickier than faeries sometimes.

"But Tamara's safety is important to me," Bryn said.

"She told me her sister's not convinced they should go. Let me listen to Kismet's reservations. Because if Tamara is traveling underhill without me, I want her sister with her."

I glanced at Kis, who was eyeing Bryn suspiciously. Exactly, I thought. What was Bryn up to?

I gave Kis a reassuring smile and nod, knowing that whatever Bryn did, it would be in the interest of trying to protect us.

Maybe he wanted to avoid a conflict with Crux so that he could get close enough to see his weaknesses? If so, that was a good idea. Except I wasn't sure that Crux had a lot of weaknesses. Even if Bryn had an iron weapon, Bryn couldn't take Crux in a hand-to-hand fight. Faeries can move like lightning. At their fastest, you can't catch them unless they want you to. But I presumed Bryn knew this. He wouldn't try any straightforward attack. Bryn was strategy . . . and magic. Bryn could wield power like a weapon. Would witch magic be strong enough to stop a faery knight's arrow? If the answer was no, I didn't want to find out.

Crux said nothing. He watched Bryn, and I wondered whether he was wondering the same things I was. Then Crux shrugged.

"By sunrise we'll be under way, or I'll send word that you're stalling. Your resistance is an insult to the queen's offered hospitality, and I'll suggest that your mother should pay the price for your insolence."

"He's lying," Kismet said.

Crux narrowed his eyes. "Test me. I'll let you hear the message I give to the nymph."

Kismet frowned.

"I'm in earnest. You'll both come, or there will be blood in payment."

All Crux's earlier cheer was gone. In his darkened mood, even his golden glow seemed burnished to bronze. I recognized this side of him. He'd used a rose stem as a switch on my back for defying him. The wounds had healed quickly, but not the nastiness of the attack.

"Let's sit and talk," I said. "One of us is better than none.

If Momma's in trouble, I'll go with you. The queen doesn't know yet that you found Kismet, does she? You can take me and then say you still have more looking to do."

"No!" Kismet said. "She could keep you prisoner. Don't you see? You can't go in alone. You won't know how to manage in there."

"But it's the best we can do."

"I won't let you go alone," Kismet said, her expression fierce. I didn't know if that meant that she was promising to go with me or promising to stop me from going.

"Kismet, if the queen makes a promise that she won't punish you for leaving, would you return home willingly?" Crux asked.

"She won't make that promise," Kismet said. "No defiance goes unpunished."

"If she promises, would you come?"

The silence seemed to stretch to oblivion. Then Kismet said, "Aye. If she makes that promise, I'll come."

Crux nodded. "Consider that her promise has been given."

Kismet narrowed her eyes.

"Don't think we'll fall for that!" I exclaimed.

"Before I left the Never, she said that if such a promise would shorten the hunt and I could return more quickly with my quarry, I could give the promise in her name."

"Well, why didn't you say so?" I snapped.

"He knows she won't be happy. She'd rather he brought me back without it." Kismet laughed. "You must have been angry when she told you that you could make that promise. You know what it means."

I glanced between them, my brows rising in question.

"The queen didn't believe he could bring her back against her will," Bryn murmured.

"It means that the queen believes this Halfling to be stubborn unto death," Crux said coldly. His gaze turned to Kismet. "She thought you might fight to the death rather than be brought back alive, which is exactly what you threatened tonight. You see how we anticipate your actions? We know you."

"Yes," she said. "When I fight, it is usually to the death. You know that because you taught me that."

We all studied Kismet. Her expression was so bland, she might have been talking about eating cake rather than the end of her life.

She is so like Mercutio, I thought again.

"Nobody wants to die. And no one wants to get punished. I'm glad we got that stuff settled. Come to the kitchen. Edie, you're looking a little tipsy," I said as she swayed while walking toward the living room couch. "How about some ham and mashed potatoes and gravy? Or some cocoa pecan cream cake. What are you in the mood for?"

"Not food, but thank you. I'll have a gasper." Edie pulled out a cigarette and lit it. "You go on negotiating. Lyons should at least be good in that capacity. He's proven he knows how to get what he doesn't deserve. Let's see him put that skill to some use."

"I may get what I don't deserve, but I've never stolen anyone else's body. Or life. That's the ultimate theft," Bryn said.

Edie chuckled. "It was accidental. I won't feel guilty about it. Besides, I've spoken to Vangie. She's happy as a clam. Much happier than I ever was as a ghost. And I'll be much happier alive than she ever was. Trust me—the girl was a tortured soul when she lived in this body."

Crux coughed at the smoke that wafted toward us from Edie. "Make more biscuits so she'll stop smoking. No one can resist biscuits."

"He's right, so it would seem. Irish wizards. Seelie queens. They all want a bite out of our little biscuit," Edie said before she sucked in another breath through her cigarette.

"Edie, don't cause trouble," I said.

She smiled. "You expect me to give that up? When it's a true talent of mine?" Then she winked.

"I like her," Kismet whispered. Then, to Edie, she said loudly, "I like you."

"It's mutual," Edie announced, then took another puff.

I couldn't decide whether to be pleased or terrified by this turn of events.

5

FOUR OF US sat at the table. I was across from Bryn. Crux faced Kismet. Edie lay on the couch smoking, sipping a sour-apple martini, and occasionally taking a bite of food from the plate I'd fixed her.

Melanie leaned against the counter, hovering near, listening. Occasionally she came up behind my chair and whispered that I shouldn't go with the fae into the Never. She swore that Caedrin and Momma could take care of themselves. She said they'd convinced her to leave for her own safety. And from the sounds of things, they'd helped Kismet escape. She said the last thing they would want was for another daughter they loved to come into the Never. I wasn't sure she was wrong. But I couldn't sit by and let them get tortured or killed because I wouldn't go.

Kismet glanced frequently at Edie.

"You keep looking at my earrings. Do you like them?" Edie asked, tucking her hair behind her ears. I realized she was wearing Aunt Melanie's magical Colombian emerald earrings.

"Yes. Green and gold are the best colors," Kis said.

"Here," Edie said, taking the earrings off. "A birthday

present. We owe you twenty-two more. Don't accept less."
Edie's eyes twinkled. Kismet didn't move. "Come take
them. You've got our green eyes. They'll be lovely on you."

"I don't have the holes for them," Kismet said, touching
her lobe.

"And they wouldn't suit you," Crux said. "Baubles are for
human good-time girls. Not warriors."

Kismet darted from her chair, taking a pin from the strap
of her quiver. She poked the pin through her lobe, making
me wince. She worked the pin back and forth and then took
the earring and shoved it into her newly pierced ear.

We all stared at her in shocked silence. She made a
matching hole in the other ear and put the second earring in.

"You're marvelous," Edie said, saluting Kismet with her
glass. "Every bit my niece."

Kismet shoved the bloody pin back into the strap of her
bag and returned to her seat with a small smile.

"Um, do you need a little ice? Or some aspirin? That was
kind of a rough way to pierce your ears," I said.

She shook her head.

"The right earring is higher than the left. Sloppily done,"
Crux said.

Kismet shrugged. "Maybe I'll fix it. Or maybe I'll like
them that way. It's no concern of yours."

Melanie frowned, whispering things in Bryn's ear. I
assumed she was trying to convince him to use his influence
over me to change my mind about joining these impulsive
warring faeries on their journey.

Bryn mostly listened, not saying much, but he was very
hospitable. He helped me bring hot food and then dessert to
the table, made spiked hot-cocoa drinks, and cleared plates
when Crux needed to draw a map. I wondered about Bryn's
movements, especially when I felt very faint threads of his
magic brush my skin.

"We'll take the trail to Quebec. Then across," Crux insisted.

"No. That goes into the Scottish woods. I don't go that
way anymore," Kismet said.

"Of course it goes to Scotch woods. It's the easiest way to enter."

"It's easiest to enter, but the woods aren't safe. I take the trail from here to the woods near the Great Lakes and then to Ireland. It's a better way."

"It isn't," Crux said. "She's mostly witch," he added, nodding at me. "She's never been underhill. Witch magic is much thicker in Ireland, and forests are scarce. Harder for me to pass unnoticed."

"Difficult for you, maybe, but the fact that Tammy Jo's never been underhill makes no difference to getting her in. She's my exact flesh and blood. She can pass into the Never wherever there's a gate. Now, if you agree to go by way of Ireland, I'll help you avoid witches' traps."

"What's in Scotland that you don't want us near?" Crux asked.

For a second, a guilty look passed over Kismet's face before her expression went blank. "The trails in Scotland have become dangerous."

"Who's more dangerous than we two?" Crux demanded fiercely.

"Which of us walks the roads of men and wizards dozens of times in a human year? I'm telling you that I don't go by way of Scotland. Ireland's best," Kismet said impatiently.

"There are barely any woods left in Ireland. It's all cities and farms, I'm told."

"I know the way to go, and I'll show you."

That settled things for me. Kismet hadn't denied that Momma and Caedrin could be in trouble for helping her. She'd never tried to convince me Momma was fine, and Kismet and Crux knew better than Aunt Mel what the faery queen was capable of. Now Kismet was talking about re-entering the Never along with me. There was no doubt anymore. I was going underhill.

Crackling music filled the rooms, and we all looked into the living room. Edie had brought out the old record player and albums. We hadn't played them in years.

She started to dance the Charleston, kicking up her heels. She managed to look cool, despite the fast steps.

"Tammy Jo knows this one." To me, Edie said, "Do you remember?"

I put my hands out and moved them in time, kicking my heels up a few inches from the floor, but keeping my butt firmly on the seat of my chair. Bryn watched me with a smile.

"We used to dance five or ten times a day when I was little," I said. "I had a record player in my room. They'd bought it at a flea market."

Crux and Kismet had not looked at anyone but Edie since she'd started dancing.

"I don't know that one. I must learn it," Kismet said.

"Let's settle this first. Then Edie and Tamara can give us all a lesson," Bryn said, surprising me.

"I'm going into the Never," I said firmly. "I have to check on Momma and help her if she's in trouble."

"The route is settled as well," Kismet said. "I won't go through Scotland. Besides, I left my horse in Michigan. I have to go by way of the Great Lakes trail." She rose without a look at them. Crux pushed his chair back.

"Crux, may I have a word?" Bryn asked. "Tamara, go show your sister how to do that dance."

"I'm still healing. Edie will teach her."

"Go talk to Melanie then. She's worried. Feed her cake. There's very little in life that doesn't get better with a mouthful of something you've baked."

I flashed him a smile at the compliment, silently wondering what he wanted to talk to Crux about alone. I went over to Aunt Mel.

A moment later I heard Bryn say, "Let me show you this." His chair scraped and then there was the soft ping of something small and hard hitting the floor. I turned as I felt the magic rise like a hot wave.

Crux jerked to his feet, sending the chair flying back, but even Crux wasn't fast enough. The wall of magic closed around the table.

"Wizard!" Crux roared.

I saw for the first time the five stones that Bryn had obviously put in position on the floor when he'd delivered and removed plates from the table. Except for the last one, they hadn't made a sound when they'd dropped. Apparently they'd floated down on woven magic meant to conceal them.

He's so clever and talented, I thought. *And a little bit diabolical.*

Edie had stopped dancing. She and Kismet stared at us.

Bryn licked the tip of his thumb where he'd cut it to use his blood to close the circle.

"Lift the spell now, or I will kill you," Crux said.

"No, I don't trust you enough to travel with you." Bryn turned to me. "If it's possible, we should try to get into the Never and out again with as few fae knowing as possible," he said.

"That's a wise idea," Kismet agreed. As she approached, Bryn held out a hand.

"Be careful. I've closed the circle so that more than one witch's magic can open it."

"Kismet, break the circle. Do it now," Crux said.

"Kismet, you can go wherever you want. You'll have a head start. When he's eventually freed, he'll have to choose whether to come after us or after you," Bryn said.

"Since you've trapped him, you'll need me to show you the way underhill," Kismet said.

"We'll find our way in," Bryn said. "The faery trails in Ireland are well-known, and Tamara has felt the one here in Duvall. She'll lead us to the entrance."

"She'll find her way in, but you're human. You'll need the right gateway."

"I'm an Association wizard. I know how to weaken the magic that seals the gates. We'll manage."

She grinned. "Go straight into the belly of the beast for her, wouldn't you? Well-done." Her lilt was irresistibly charming, especially when she smiled. She walked to me and leaned close, taking my hands. "I'll meet you in Dublin and take you the rest of the way. Don't go in without me. He's brave, but you'll need more than bravery in there. To get you out again, you'll need me. Don't go in without me," she repeated.

"Okay," I whispered.

"Are you sure you don't want to leave your wizard here, where it's safe? We can go along the trails faster than sound travels. With him you'd have to go by plane, because he can't pass the trails like we could alone."

"No, he'd never forgive me. If the worst happens and I can't get out, he'd rather us be trapped together than for him to be safe here alone."

"All right, but you're my other half. We'll do things together no one expects. Don't go in without me. Swear it."

"Do you swear to come?"

"Yes. Go on the literary pub crawl in Dublin. I'll find you there. I have to go by the college anyway. If I'm going back I'll need to steal a book to give her as a gift. She likes when I do that."

"Steal a book? What college? What are you talking about?"

"Never mind. Just be sure to go on the pub crawl."

"How will I find it?" I asked.

"You'll find it. See you on the Seelie side of the ocean," she whispered, and kissed me on the cheek. Then she turned and lunged to grab her bow from the counter. She was out the back door before I even had a chance to say good-bye.

"She moves like a faery," Bryn said.

"That's because she is one," Crux growled.

6

OUTSIDE OF TEXAS, I have been to New Orleans, Nashville, and Puerto Vallarta, Mexico. The airplane that took Zach and me to Mexico was small and packed with people. He's tall, and his knees hit the seat in front of him the whole way. And when the people in front of us leaned back, they were almost in our laps. Being so smashed together, I knew how the marshmallows in a s'more must feel. So I wasn't looking forward to a whole workday's worth of time on a plane. Being trapped on a bus in the sky for more than nine hours would be nerve-racking.

But when I saw the airplane to take us from Dallas to London, England, my mouth fell open. It was Texas-size! The seats in first class were like giant recliners. They were practically twin beds.

I was astounded and took a quick walk to the back of the cabin to have a look at the coach seats. "There's a lot more room even in the regular seats. I don't think your knees would've hit the seat in front of you."

"Hmmm," Bryn said, handing the flight attendant a bag that got hung in a closet, just like we were at a house.

"Would you like a drink?" she asked.

"I'll have whiskey on the rocks. Tamara, what do you want to drink?"

"Me? I'm good. I have that giant bottle of water, remember? And the whole box of pralines, two magazines, and the little bag of Hershey's miniatures. I'm so glad the magazine store had miniatures, since my bags of kisses are in the big suitcase. I put them there so I wouldn't start eating them on the flight. I've gotta ration. Don't wanna run out of Hershey's all the way across the ocean!"

"They may have Hershey's in Ireland. I can't recall. They certainly have Cadbury, which is just as good," Bryn said.

"Yeah, Cadbury is good. Really smooth. But there might not be any chocolate at all underhill," I whispered, shuddering at the thought. I should've asked Kismet about that.

"Come sit down, sweetheart."

I sank into my seat with wide eyes. It was as comfortable as the couches at home. "How much did it cost to sit up here?" I whispered.

"Food and drinks are complimentary. So you should think of it as being at a buffet. We've already paid. Have whatever you want."

I bit my lip and looked at my giant diamond ring. I wondered if I would get used to living rich, because it seemed like Bryn did not believe in living any other way.

"Would you like something to drink other than your bottled water?" he asked.

"I already told her I didn't. And she's trying to help people get in their seats. Let's not bother her."

Bryn kissed me on the forehead. "I love you."

"I love you, too. And I would've loved you the same if we'd been sitting in coach. Maybe more."

He laughed. "Why more?"

I tucked a loose strand of hair behind my ears. "Because you'd be more like a regular person I could relate to."

His grin widened. "You can't relate to me, huh? We don't have anything in common?"

"Nope."

"Other than being part witch and part fae?" he whispered.

"Right, other than that."

"That hardly counts, it being such a common thing. There are what . . . maybe a couple dozen of us in the world?"

I smirked. "You don't know that it's rare. Maybe there are whole mixed-race tribes of merrows living underwater. Maybe it's where all the 'mermaids who get legs on land' stories come from. Just because we don't know them personally . . . Look at that ghost from Victorian times that we met. She was part witch and part fae. For all we know there could be hundreds, maybe thousands. We should start a club."

"Right," he said, laughing. "With a Web site. Let's make it easy for WAM. We'll include a pdf of our members, so the association can print the names for a hit list with one click."

I frowned. "The fae want to claim anyone with faery blood. The witches want to eliminate anyone with faery blood. Even though I'm scared of going into the Never, I think the faeries may be nicer than a lot of witches I've met."

"I wouldn't count on that."

"You know your wizard magic won't work underhill. Aunt Mel said she and Momma couldn't do a single spell. Are you really sure you want to go in there?"

"The only thing I'm sure of is that I don't want you going anywhere without me. For life and longer, remember?"

"You're the craziest sane person I know, to tie yourself to a woman who is on the most-wanted list of so many scary supernatural creatures. You should've gotten engaged to a nice lady lawyer with no magic at all. If you'd been smart that's what you would've done."

"I got the woman I wanted. If we live fifty more years or fifty more hours," he said, repeating part of what he'd said when he'd proposed.

"Crazy," I murmured, but gave him a kiss, feeling the magic curl into me, warm and silky like melted caramel. "I hope it's fifty more years. But don't say I didn't warn you if it's fifty more hours."

"Kiss me again, and I won't care if it's fifty more seconds."

Yep. Crazy.

*   *   *

FOR PART OF the flight we slept, but when we were awake
Bryn read secret WAM files sent by his friend Andre. The
electronic documents contained the most up-to-date intelli-
gence on the Seelie fae. Unfortunately there was no information about getting into the Never or getting out of it.
Several operatives had breached the gates, but they were
either found dazed and confused in the woods, unable to
give any information about what had happened, or they were
never seen or heard from again. Not encouraging.

"You should never let it slip to anyone that your aunt
Melanie has been underhill and returned with her memory
intact."

"You're right. WAM would send someone from the Conclave to get her, so they could question her," I said grimly.
The World Association of Magic was the organization of
witches and wizards worldwide. Its leaders had an agency
that reported to them called the Conclave, which was made
up of killers and spies. It was hard to tell who was the most
dangerous . . . the operatives sent by WAM or the leaders
who sent them.

I rubbed my tired eyes. I didn't know why I'd bothered to
buy *Saveur* and *Fine Cooking* magazines. I hadn't really
looked at them. I'd spent most of the time whispering back
and forth with Bryn about the trip, and regretting that the
first time I'd see his home country was just to pass through
on the way to the Never.

"I wish we had time to see where you grew up," I said.

"Next time," Bryn promised.

"Maybe on our honeymoon."

He smiled. "Ireland would be great for our honeymoon, but then, I'd be happy just about anywhere celebrat-
ing that."

I smiled. "Sweet-talking candylegger."

He laughed. Candylegger was what Edie called him. It
was slang from the 1920s and supposed to be an insult, but
I'd turned it into a pet name.

* * *

HEATHROW AIRPORT IN London, England, is four-point-six square miles, and I think we walked at least half of that. I was so tired I used a pillar to hold me up while we waited for our luggage.

I noticed Bryn go still and then look around sharply. I felt his magic gather. Suddenly alert, I felt my spine stiffen, and my gaze darted side to side.

"What is it?"

"I sense magic from at least three different practitioners. It's all around us."

I bit my lip. "I wish Merc were here," I said.

Mercutio is my ocelot companion and pretty much my best friend. I'd had to leave him in Duvall, because Merc's a jungle cat and there are no jungles in the United Kingdom, and it was going to be really cold. Also, I didn't trust the faeries. What if they locked us up? Mercutio roams all night. He has to be free to go wherever he wants or he's not happy.

"I wish I had a gun," I whispered. Being unarmed made me feel vulnerable. For weeks I'd kept a gun in a kitchen drawer with other occasionally used utensils. "Wait, look. It's okay—there's Andre!"

Bryn's friend Andre is as cute as a cupcake. He's chubby and has thinning light brown hair and wire-rimmed glasses. He looks like a baker for Pillsbury, but really he's a wizard and physicist.

"I didn't tell Andre to meet us," Bryn said.

My smile drooped a little. "Well, he probably wanted to surprise us."

"I never told him what time we were arriving. I planned for us to go straight to Dublin after collecting a pair of reference books on the fae from a London bookshop."

Andre hurried to us. "My friend," he said, embracing Bryn. "My dear," he said, kissing and hugging me.

"What's going on?" Bryn asked.

Andre is Swiss, but he speaks German as his first language, and he lapsed into it, speaking rapidly.

Bryn glanced around and then nodded. I gave him a questioning look.

"We have to go to WAM headquarters."

I tensed. "Why?"

"Andre wasn't told," Bryn said.

We'd gotten into trouble with WAM pretty often. They'd sent operatives to train me for a magical challenge, and those guys had ended up dead. But they'd been bad guys. Then the Association had sent more representatives, including the president and his superspy bodyguard. Three out of the four people they'd sent on that trip—including the superspy, who turned out to be my great-aunt—had wound up getting killed.

A lot of what had happened had been their own doing, meaning sometimes they'd killed one another. Assassin-spies, go figure! But Bryn and I had played a role in the demise of every WAM entourage that came to Duvall. We'd been acting in self-defense and in the defense of others, but even though we'd given proof of criminal conspiracies and wrongdoing, I didn't think the Association was particularly pleased with us. Their operatives had been trying to secure Duvall and its magical tor for WAM; Bryn and I had prevented it. We just kept rebelling against everything the powers that be wanted us to do.

"How does the Association know we're in London?" I asked, glancing around. I still hadn't seen anyone who looked like a magical assassin. And Andre certainly wouldn't have told his bosses about our plans.

"I don't know," Bryn said; then he leaned close. His voice in my ear was low. "Remember which things to keep secret."

"I'll remember!" I whispered fiercely. "Listen," I said, grabbing his arm. "We're in the airport. They won't try to take us from here by force. There are too many people and cameras. We can just get on our plane to Ireland."

"Getting to Ireland wouldn't do us any good."

"Why not?"

"Because Andre's given us the message. If we don't comply, they'll have operatives waiting to take us by force in Ireland the minute we step out of the airport in Dublin."

I frowned. "That's not fair."

"I know. Take a minute. Remember the practice interviews we did to prepare for the interrogations last time? Go through those in your mind."

I took a deep breath and nodded. I sat on top of my suitcase and closed my eyes to concentrate. I ran through the practice question-and-answer sessions I'd had with Bryn until I heard him say, "Christ. You've got to be kidding."

My lids popped up, and then my mouth fell open.

Dressed in a fur-cuffed coat in dusty rose and a short burgundy beaded dress and matching booties, Edie strode toward us. Next to her, on a leash that was attached to a jeweled collar, came Mercutio. And bringing up the rear in a cowboy hat, jeans, a dark sweater, and boots was my buff ex-husband, Zach. He had a coat under his arm and a duffel in his hand. People turned to stare at the trio. It's not every day that you see an heiress in flapper wear with an ocelot and a cowboy in tow. In fact, I'm pretty sure no one had seen that combination before. Ever.

Mercutio darted forward and, rather than being pulled by the leash, Edie let it go. The leash slapped the ground and slithered behind him.

I put my arms out and hugged him when he got to me.

"Thank goodness you're here, Merc! We've just landed, and we're already in trouble!"

"Hello, biscuit," Edie said to me.

"Edie, how—"

"First of all," she said, leaning forward to whisper, "let's remember that we are in the land of tea and treachery. My name is Evangeline Rhodes. My friends call me Evie, which is short for Evangeline, of course."

"Oh. Right. That's good thinking. *Evie*. I'll try to remember that."

"Luckily Edie and Evie are very close. If you slip, it may go unnoticed."

Zach nodded briefly at Bryn and then joined Edie and me.

"But I don't understand how you got Mercutio here."

"It's called money," Edie said.

"Edie," I hissed.

Evie, I corrected in my mind. *Think of her as Evie.*

"I chartered a plane, paid some fees, and arranged for some powerful people to smooth the way. One exotic animal arriving in London for an ad campaign and commercial shoot with his owner," she said, touching her chest. "And his trainer," she said, nodding at Zach.

My eyes widened.

"Lyons could've managed it if he'd bothered to try. Remember that, darling," she said. "Who best takes care of you? Fiancé or family?"

"Hello," Bryn said, and bent to stroke Merc's fur. "I'm not even going to ask."

Edie looked around. "There's a lot of magic here," she observed.

"Yes," Bryn said. "It belongs to the Conclave, and it's here for us."

"Oh," she said, frowning.

Andre stepped forward and extended a hand. "The beautiful Ms. Rhodes, I believe."

"The very one," Edie said, turning to Andre. "And men who call me beautiful may also call me Evie."

Andre blushed. "Evie, I'm Andre Knobel. I'm very pleased to meet you. I wish the circumstances were better." His brow crinkled. "I'm afraid the Association sent me to greet you and to extend an invitation for you to come to headquarters."

"Just when I thought I'd made a friend," Edie said.

"Do you still think it was a good idea to blow into town on a pile of cash and flash?" Bryn asked.

"You tried to sneak through, and that didn't work. So why not flash and cash? If we are going down, at least we can do it in style."

For the love of Hershey!

I took a deep breath and stood up straight, giving each of them a stern look.

"Everybody needs to remember his and her manners, and that we"—I gestured to the group of us and continued—"are all on the same team. Rule number one is no fighting with each other in front of the bad guys. And here comes one."

7

THE WIZARD WHO'D come up to us in the terminal was our driver. We'd been taken from the airport to a London neighborhood that featured stately old buildings on big lots of property.

Our destination was a building of beige-brown brick that made it look bronze as we approached. We emerged, and I looked up. Gargoyles perched on stones three stories above us. My eyes widened. Were the creatures real? Did they turn from stone to flesh at sunset? Or were they just decorative? At the headquarters of magic, you never knew.

At the window of a corner turret, someone held back dark curtains. I tried to figure out whether the figure was a man or a woman, but the person stepped back and the curtains swung closed. Another wave of unease rolled through me.

The morning air had an icy grip, frosting the steps and making me pull my new emerald-green wool coat closed around me. Bryn had ordered it for me over the Internet. When I'd tried it on in Texas, I'd thought there was no way the United Kingdom would be cold enough for me to need something so heavy and hot. It wasn't like we were going to

Alaska or the arctic, after all. But luckily I'd trusted Bryn and hadn't exchanged it for something lighter.

I quickly found that I don't appreciate it when the weather's cold enough to make my breath look like smoke. Breath should be invisible.

Andre held the door for us, but I paused on the steps to look at the black sedans that sidled up the street. Those cars with the darkly tinted windows had followed us all the way from the airport. They stopped in the street next to where the van we'd ridden in was parked.

"Tamara," Bryn said, nodding to the open door.

"They're watching. Waiting to make sure we go inside," I said.

"Then let's give them something interesting to watch," Edie said, sashaying up the stairs as if her hips were maracas to shake.

"Wow," Bryn said. "Is she for real?"

I couldn't help but smile. "I guess so. For now, at least."

Zach's narrowed gaze never left the sedans until we were inside and could no longer see them. I wondered if they would stay there, double-parked, to be sure we didn't bolt out.

The lobby's tapestries depicted the seasons. One had the four elements with spring flowers, one had the night sky with a witch in a sundress, one showed a storm with blowing leaves, and the last one had an elderly man reclining and a woman holding a bundled baby in the falling snow. I realized they represented the major kinds of magic: elemental, celestial, weather, and blood and bones.

Edie's shoes clicked across the parquet floor as she followed Andre to the elevator. The elevator doors were brass with square-framed images on the right and left. The right side looked familiar, and in an instant I recognized it.

"It's the sunburst from the locket," I said, pointing to the panel. "That looks familiar, too," I murmured. On the left the pattern was a diamond shape, bigger on top than bottom. There was a large gold gem at its peak, two black stones of equal sizes on the sides, and then a small white gem on bottom. "Where's that picture from?" I asked.

"I don't know," Bryn said. "It's an image one sees in different mystical art representations, but it's not a constellation or pattern that's historically meaningful."

"Edie, have you seen that picture before?"

"I suppose so," Edie said, shrugging. "I've been here before."

I held the heavy brass rail inside the elevator and wondered why it was there. Would the thing lurch as it went up? But no, the ride was perfectly smooth. We exited on the fifth floor. The corridor was painted burgundy with rose and gold trim, but the door to the office of the president was simple oak, and when it opened there was a whole different decor inside: glass and steel, very cold, very modern.

A fit, tall man in his middle forties stood at a raised workstation of smoky colored glass and metal, typing quickly. He wore trousers and a thick sweater, and had honey-brown hair and wide-set eyes with fine lines around them. If someone gave him a jacket and goggles, he could've advertised a ski vacation in the Alps.

He finished typing and lowered the screen to close the laptop.

"Hello," he said, coming forward. He shook Bryn's hand first and then mine, introducing himself as Lars Anderson, the interim president of WAM. "I understand that I owe my current position to you."

I flushed. "Well, you're welcome, I guess. Though we didn't mean to get John Barrett fired—or thrown in jail. Is he in jail?" Or had he been tried and executed?

Anderson said, "You have no cause to apologize. His fate was of his own making, yes?" He smiled, stopping in front of Edie, who looked bored. He took her hand and held it for a long moment. She favored him with a smoldering green-eyed look. I cleared my throat.

"Um, Evie, do you have any gum in your purse?"

"No," she said.

"How about chocolate? Or mints? Can you check?" I asked, wanting to separate her from the president.

She ignored me, but Zach, who appeared to be looking

around, hooked a finger in her pearl necklace and tugged. She took a step back to ease the pressure of the necklace on her throat.

"This is Mr. Sutton," Edie said, adjusting her pearls. Zach's finger slipped out.

"What are you?" Anderson asked Zach. They were the same height, but Zach had bigger muscles, which was almost always the case.

"I'm just the animal trainer," Zach said, nodding toward Merc.

That'll be the day! Merc and Zach weren't even friends.

Mercutio prowled around the office, stopping to look at his reflection in the window.

The door opened, and my jaw dropped. It was the Winterhawk, with upswept hair and dressed in tweed. But of course it couldn't be the Winterhawk, because I'd killed her.

So this was her twin sister, Josephine, my grandma. The one I'd never known about growing up.

While I was little I thought Granny Justine had had Momma and Aunt Mel late in life, but it turned out that she was my great-granny. Momma and Aunt Mel had pretended their own momma didn't exist. And so far, no one had told me why.

Her hair, a mix of silver and steel gray, was pulled and sprayed into submission in her bun. Her hands were tucked into the pockets of her tweed blazer, making me wonder if she had a weapon. This was the Winterhawk's twin, after all. But her hands stayed hidden away, not doing anything aggressive. She wore a three-quarter-length wool skirt and black boots. I remembered I'd been told she was a teacher at a school for witches. I could see that. She looked very professorial. She also looked stern, like she might break and breed horses in her spare time.

I hesitated for a moment. I'd killed my grandma's twin sister, Margaret. If someone had killed Aunt Melanie, Momma would never have forgiven that person. Same for Aunt Mel. Sisters, especially twins, were as close as people could be.

Her light green eyes swept over me. She didn't smile, but she didn't frown either.

I stepped forward. "Hi. I mean, hello." I thrust out a hand. "I'm Tamara Josephine Trask. I'm real sorry about what happened to your sister. I didn't want it to turn out that way."

"Yes, well, I can't say I approve of your choosing to protect a Lyons to the death, but I understand that you owed him a debt. He'd saved your life in the past?"

I nodded.

"Debt discharged, then. Maggie understood duty. As do I." She cleared her throat, and then glanced at Bryn. "He's a Granville prizewinner. An asset to the world of magic that it would be a shame to lose."

Was there a little threat in her tone? Or was I just imagining it because her voice was a lot like her sister's?

"Except for the eyes, you look just like your mother," my grandmother said. "You inherited my grandfather's bright red hair."

"But not his personality, thankfully," Edie murmured.

My grandma's gaze, cool green and sharp, turned to Edie. My stomach dropped. The locket that had held Edie's soul had been passed down through the family. For a time, this lady and her sister would've been the keepers of the heirloom. She knew Edie. If she recognized her in Vangie's body, would Grandma reveal her identity?

I moved closer to the president's desk and put myself between him and them. "So, um, what did you want to talk to us about, Mr. President?" I asked, trying to turn the focus back to our WAM visit and away from my double-great-aunt the body snatcher.

"The first order of business is to discuss a rumor we've heard that's raised some concerns." He extended his arms toward me. "May I have your hands, please?"

I hesitated and felt Bryn's magic as he approached. The power current was restrained, but readying itself. The heart of WAM was probably the last place a wizard should start a magical fight, and I knew Bryn wouldn't do anything that wasn't smart unless it became absolutely necessary. So his readying magic made every muscle in my body tighten.

"Sure, okay," I said, putting my hands into Anderson's palms.

Mercutio brushed against my legs. Zach, too, walked casually closer.

"A ring to bind you to Mr. Lyons?" he asked, brushing a thumb over the band on my right hand.

"We have magical synergy. That's such an incredibly rare phenomenon, I'm sure the Association wouldn't want its potential to be neglected," Bryn said, a note of challenge in his voice.

"My predecessor made it clear that your involvement with Ms. Trask was to have its limits until formally assessed by the association. Our caution is understandable, yes? You've proven a volatile combination."

"We've brought justice to bear," Bryn said.

"You also blocked Association efforts to secure a powerful tor in a town whose magical significance has long been kept hidden from us."

Bryn shrugged. "There is no legal mandate requiring WAM members to report sources of power outside the U.K."

"No. But if the Association has stated an objective, for an individual wizard to counter that objective *is* against the law."

"Prior to attempting to create an overseas magical colony, the Association should have announced its intent to do so, and there should have been a vote by the general membership. If the original action was illegal, our efforts to circumvent that illegal act can't be considered illegal. I cite Whalley, 1543."

"You looked up your defense."

"My caution is understandable, wouldn't you say? Conclave activities in the U.S. have proven volatile," Bryn said, echoing what the leader had said to us earlier.

Mr. Anderson studied Bryn for a moment in silence. Then he said, "Would you have interfered with a magical colonization of Duvall, Texas, if this young witch had not so strongly objected to the idea of her friends and neighbors being relocated?"

"The residents of Duvall have a long history in the town."

"That was not the question," Anderson said with a smile. He raised my left hand and looked at the ring that I'd mostly been trying to keep out of sight. The giant yellow diamond sparkled. "Are you now engaged to this man?" Anderson asked me.

My cheeks flushed, and I barely kept myself from looking apologetically at Zach. Not that I owed him an apology. Our marriage had been over a long time ago. And our romantic relationship was finished, too, though recently enough for things to be real awkward.

"Yes, I'm going to marry him."

Anderson gave my hands a brief squeeze and returned them to me. "Your grandmother, Mrs. Josephine Hurley, has made a formal objection to the match."

"No disrespect," I said, giving my grandma a sharp look. "But she doesn't even know me or Bryn. This is the first time we've met her. And actually, even if she'd raised me, that wouldn't give her or anybody the right to interfere. Who Bryn and I decide to marry is our business and nobody else's."

"That's not true," Anderson said with an apologetic expression. He took a file from his desk and handed it to Bryn. "There is legal precedent. For magical lines that are ten generations or older, and in which mixing with a different magical line could damage the integrity of the power of future generations, family members may petition for dissolution of a match."

My jaw dropped. "Um, we're not breeding stock. We're people."

"Nevertheless, we have two very important magical legacies to consider. The Lyons magic is an excellent blend thus far. We want to cultivate that power in future generations. And you are sixteenth-generation McKenna with exceptional earth magic. You may not realize, but we've seen several lines of earth magic die out in the past sixty years. If you and Mr. Lyons marry and his magic were to force yours into recession, we could, in another fifty years, see earth magic become extinct. It's been completely unexpected, as it used to be the most common. It's the legacy not just of your family, but of the entire Association."

Bryn tossed the folder on the desk. "Our magic is synergistic. There's no reason to think our children would have dominant celestial magic. Earth magic would likely be strong in some of them," Bryn said.

Some of them! Just how many was he thinking we'd have?

Not that it mattered yet what he had planned, since I wasn't even sure I could have babies with anybody. After Zach and I had gotten married, we'd never used birth control. We'd made love a lot, and I'd never gotten pregnant. I'd slept with Bryn a few times without protection, too, and so far nothing. Maybe my lady parts were broken like my magic.

"But there is a risk that one magic or the other would be sacrificed. If you each married and had children with someone of similar or compatible magic, or married someone nonmagical, the integrity of each line would be assured," Anderson said.

"No magic could be considered more compatible when we have synergy."

"The synergy can be explored, and I would personally support that. I would be negligent in my duties as president, however, if I ignored a legitimate concern raised by a learned member of the Association about the fate of future generations of members."

"But my magic is already—" I began.

"Spoken for," Bryn interjected, giving me a pointed look. I'd been about to blurt that my magic was already mixed-race and messed-up. Which would've been disastrous! I had to keep that secret at all costs, and I'd almost let it slip out.

"There's also a prophecy and some other considerations. Put your emotions aside for a moment. In my position, what course of action would you consider the most prudent?"

Bryn scowled. "I wouldn't insert myself into a deeply personal matter of any Association member. If there was matchmaking to be done, it should've already taken place."

"I didn't deem matchmaking necessary. She made a good choice once before," Mrs. Hurley said. "A healthy, strong, handsome young man whose family wasn't magical. Despite the unfortunate divorce, she continued to be involved with him. There was every reason to believe they would settle and remarry. There was no reason to suspect she would choose someone inappropriate."

Did my grandma know my first husband was in the room?

Zach stood with his arms folded across his chest. He was everything she'd said. And yet we couldn't make our relationship work. Bryn and I could, even against terrible odds. In times of trouble, Bryn and I had gotten closer and closer. I hooked my pinkie around his and gave it a squeeze of support.

His hard blue gaze swiveled from the president and softened when it met mine. "For life or longer," he whispered.

"Yep. That's the deal, and we're sticking to it."

He smiled and his magic poured over me.

I love you, too, I mouthed.

"I think you'll find that it's impossible to effectively separate us," Bryn said, turning his attention back to the president.

"Perhaps that will be the case. But although I don't condone some of the methods used by the Conclave in the past, I believe you know they are often quite effective. Naysayers have many times been proven wrong when they've claimed they could withstand Conclave persuasion."

"If your objective is to preserve the magical legacy of both lines, it would be a mistake to attack people who have proven they're willing to defend each other to the death," Bryn said.

Lars Anderson tapped his fingertips lightly on the desk. "Well, your concerns have been explained, Mrs. Hurley. There will be more time for private discussion later, but I'll ask you to excuse us while I speak to Mr. Lyons and Miss Trask about a different matter."

My grandma nodded, but held up a hand. "Mr. Anderson, may I have a private word with you before I leave?"

"Of course. Excuse me," he said to us, and walked to her. They retreated to the other side of the room and spoke in lowered voices with their backs to us. He nodded, touching her elbow as she turned to leave.

"Mr. Sutton, Ms. Rhodes, would you and your cat like to take refreshments in the private dining room? Mr. Knobel, will you make them welcome and see to their every comfort while they wait? This conversation won't take long, and then Ms. Trask and Mr. Lyons will be free to continue their travels."

Edie scooped Merc up, giving the top of his head a kiss.

"Come on, darling. Let's see whether the wretched reputation of English food is exaggerated or deserved."

The door closed, and we were alone with the most powerful man in the world of magic. I took a deep breath and braced myself, hoping that things would go smoothly and peacefully. My body was still healing, so it would be inconvenient for me to have to tackle a politician.

8

ANDERSON EXTENDED A hand to indicate that we should sit in the chairs across from his desk. They were steel framed with white leather cushions. To me they looked like they belonged on a patio.

We sat. The chairs weren't uncomfortable, but they would never be cozy. I suppose people meeting with the president of WAM weren't meant to feel relaxed.

Bryn moved his chair closer to mine, and I rested my hand on his forearm. His magic thrummed under my palm, familiar and reassuring.

"Mrs. Hurley intends to make things difficult for you. There are plenty of people who've heard about what occurred in Texas and would like to see your partnership, both magical and otherwise, put to an end. There are those who feel that if the Association doesn't take some action, it'll open the door for others to defy this governing body. 'A path to anarchy' was the phrase put forth at one point in the discussions."

"Um, we're not trying to rebel. We just want to be left alone," I said.

"For that to happen, you would have to disappear. Are you prepared to go underground?"

Yep, in many ways we are. Only not for good, I thought.

"Duvall, Texas, is our home. We may be away from there for a time, and if it allows frustrations to die down, all the better. But we don't intend to live off the magical grid," Bryn said.

"I'm not interested in extinguishing a magical union that's synergistic, nor in seeing a Granville prizewinner destroyed for protecting the witch with whom he fell in love. But there are obstacles, and I suspect that if the issue were forced today, Mrs. Hurley would win. Miss Trask would be ordered to live in Revelworth to be trained as an earth witch and you, Mr. Lyons, would be banned from visiting."

"I'm not moving to England to learn magic! Who do you people think you are?"

"We are your government, a sovereign body over the nation of magical practitioners. The only nation that truly matters," he said with a calm that was infuriating. He looked at Bryn. "She can be taken by force. There are seventeen members of the Conclave ready to act. You could fight, but it would be no contest and you know it."

I stiffened. "You don't have any right! If you kidnap me, I'll escape. I've done it before!" I snapped, my hair falling around my face from the force of my jerking forward.

"Tamara," Bryn said, putting a hand on my arm to keep me from standing.

"What? I'm not moving here. And they are not going to break us up. Not just because we love each other, but also because it's not right. They can't just go around—"

"Hang on, sweetheart. Let's hear the rest of what he wanted to say to us in private. Plenty of time to fight later, if that's what it comes to," Bryn said.

Fury and adrenaline had me ready to pounce. I trembled as I forced myself to be still. I folded my arms across my chest.

"So," Bryn said. "What do you want?"

"One of the Trasks, Marlee or Melanie, it's not clear which, was in the Scottish Highlands and knows the location of a certain valuable artifact that rightly belongs to the Association.

Melanie denied knowledge of the object, but the Conclave was not convinced she was telling the truth. She was barred from leaving England because we intended for her to retrieve it herself, or to contact her sister to do so. But she left, despite her magic being bound. The fact that she fled makes it likely . . . Well, it's not relevant." His gaze turned from Bryn to me. "Find out from your mother or aunt where the artifact is hidden, retrieve it, and turn it over to the Association. If you do so, I will convey to everyone that you've performed a valuable service to the Association, and I'll block any actions Mrs. Hurley takes to prevent your marriage."

"What are you talking about? My aunt Melanie wasn't here about artifacts. She came over to see my momma. And Momma came to see an old flame."

"Regardless of why they came originally, one of them stumbled onto the location of this valuable object."

"I don't know anything about that. And listen, we don't really have time to go looking for treasure. We've got our own plans," I said, thinking that WAM didn't know what it was talking about. Momma had been in the Never for more than a year, and Aunt Mel had just come from there, too. Neither of them was romping around in Scotland discovering WAM artifacts.

"Mr. Lyons, can I count on your cooperation?"

Bryn tipped his head back to look at the ceiling. Silence stretched through the room. I fidgeted.

Bryn's gaze returned to Anderson. "If the Conclave operatives haven't found the artifact, it would be foolish of us to agree to take on the assignment. And by accepting your proposal, the implication would be that we acknowledge that you have legal grounds to force us into a negotiation. No, I'll fight you in open court. I'll put our conduct up against that of your operatives and trust my peers to decide in my favor."

"Would you make this a public battle?" Anderson asked.

"Yes!" I said. "Let's let people hear the truth and see what they think."

"If that's what you're determined to do, the price will be high. And not just for the two of you," Anderson said.

I froze. "What are you talking about?"

"Andre Knobel has accessed top-security files without clearance. To assist you, I think. He'll be prosecuted. And Mrs. Hurley believes that your friend Ms. Rhodes is not who she claims to be. A ghost may be sharing her body. Knobel and Rhodes have been taken into custody. We'll launch a full-scale investigation—"

I jerked out of my seat and dived across the desk. Bryn grabbed me and pulled me back, but not before I socked the president of the World Association of Magic in the face.

"Let me go!" I yelled. "He tricked them into leaving the office so we couldn't help them! I—Let go of me, Bryn!"

Bryn wrapped his arms around me, and I felt his furious magic vibrate around us. "Wait," Bryn whispered. "Just wait." Even when really angry, he's able to control himself. Me, not so much.

My breath came harsh and fast, but I stopped struggling. "What am I waiting for? Are you going to zap him with some magic?"

"We can't win a fight here."

"I was winning. See that bruise on his cheek that he's rubbing?" I whispered fiercely.

"Show us the artifact," Bryn told Anderson. "It costs us nothing to ask Melanie and Marlee about it."

"He has to let Andre and Edie go, or we're not going to talk to anyone about anything. They have to leave here with us."

"No," Anderson said. "They stay. But no investigation will be started. They'll be treated as guests of the Association until you return. If you have the artifact, you will have my goodwill and so will your friends. If you make an effort, but the artifact can't be recovered for reasons that can be verified by the Conclave, I'll still release your friends and will remain neutral toward your marriage. But if you attempt to mislead us . . . if the item is not recovered by lack of effort or by some design of yours or your family's, then you and all you care about will be considered enemies of the Association."

I glared at him.

Anderson slid a paper across the table. There was a drawing

of a pendant with a smooth golden-brownish center and a setting that had small gold slats pointing outward.

"The stone is amber," Anderson said.

I peered at the picture. The amber wasn't uniform in color. Parts were lighter, others more shadowed. As I studied it, I realized that the geometric spikes of gold were rays. The pattern was shaped like the sun.

"You may take the sketch. We have others."

"Does it do anything we should be worried about?" I asked.

"Excellent question," Bryn said, looking at Anderson.

"Its value makes it dangerous for a person to have it in his possession, but not because of its magical properties. You should be very discreet in your inquiries and, once you find it, keep it hidden until it's safely here at headquarters. There are those who would kill for it."

"Like your operatives?" I asked, glancing again at the sketch. It was pretty, but it was no canary-yellow diamond ring. What made it so valuable? Was it because the amber was really old? Did it have some history to it that made people sentimental about it? That's the way art worked sometimes. But no. These people dealt in magic. This little chunk of amber must do something. *What?*

I folded the sketch and handed it to Bryn, who put it in his pocket.

"I want to talk to Evie and Andre before we go," I said.

Bryn and I stared at Anderson, who nodded. "They're in the dining room. You may talk with them and eat if you like. I'll get some ice for this," he said, touching his cheek. He looked more amused than annoyed. I probably should've punched him harder.

"Um, yeah, sorry about that," I said. "I've got kind of a bad temper sometimes."

He smiled. "A lot of passion. Engaging, but dangerous. I worry that you won't live a long life, but I think you'll make something spectacular of it nonetheless."

"Well, thanks . . . I guess." I glanced to see what Bryn thought. He looked like he'd just popped a lemon drop. He reached a hand out and corralled me, putting me on the other side of him so he was between me and Anderson as we left the office.

"Does the WAM dining room serve dessert?" I asked.

"Of course."

"Finally some good news!"

Bryn smiled, and Anderson laughed. I'm not sure why they thought that was funny. I was being completely serious.

CLASSICAL MUSIC PLAYED in the wood-paneled dining room. My grandma talked to Zach, while Edie and Andre sat half a table away, with Edie giving Grandma the occasional dirty look. I couldn't blame her. My grandma had sold her out to give WAM more leverage over Bryn and me. I was beginning to understand why Momma and Aunt Mel had run away from home at a young age and never looked back.

I grabbed a fruit parfait and a slice of chocolate cake from the buffet, along with a spoon. Bryn poured coffee for himself, but didn't get any food. Bad news kills some people's appetites. Not mine.

Bryn quietly explained to Edie and Andre what had happened with Anderson. The color drained from Andre's face, and I thought he might faint. Bryn put a hand on his shoulder and spoke to him earnestly in German. I smiled and nodded, even though I had no idea what Bryn was telling him.

Edie, however, never paled. There might have been a little extra color in her cheeks, but mostly she looked completely unruffled, even a little smug.

"Are you all right?" I whispered.

"Yes, darling. I'm fine. Lady Hurley went on the offensive. Not surprising. That's our Josephine. You know, I always felt that Josephine was too romantic a name for her. She should've been a Katherine or an Elizabeth. Regal and ruthless, that's her nature."

"Do you think you can be okay here for a little while? Bryn says we don't stand a chance of successfully fighting our way out right now." I leaned so close my lips touched her ear, and I whispered so no one else would hear, "But if we can't find what they want, you know I'll come back anyway. And I'll be back armed and ready to bust you out. No matter what it takes."

"I know," she said, and her hand pressed the side of my cheek to hold my face in place while she kissed the other side. "Let me see the artifact they want."

Anderson had said to be discreet. Would he think Evangeline Rhodes should be told the mission's details? I wasn't sure. I turned and gave Bryn a hug, reaching inside his pocket and slipping the sketch out. I unfolded it on my lap so that it was hidden by the table.

Edie glanced down.

"Recognize it?" I asked.

"No, but from the look of it, the pendant is amber, which brings to mind the Hebrides Amber. It wasn't actually from there, but the Scottish ghosts called it that because there was a battle in the Hebrides between wizards and faeries, and it was said to have been over a small chunk of amber with a dragonfly fossilized inside. The ghosts never found out what was so special about the fossil, but at the end of the battle there were dead witchfolk and even more dead fae. The faeries had been outnumbered, but fought anyway."

Edie's lashes fluttered as she recalled the story. "When the wizards won, they didn't even stop to bury or collect their dead. Instead they raced south. Selkies came for the fallen fae and pulled them into the sea, but it was several days before witches and wizards came to claim the bodies of their people. It happened three hundred years ago, but the ghosts still discuss it because they'd never seen that kind of battle fought among the ruins."

I chewed on my lip. President Anderson had said that anyone holding the artifact would be in danger. Was the danger from the faeries? If the artifact had something to do with the fae, maybe Momma or Aunt Melanie had come across it when trying to enter the Never. Was that possibly its purpose? To allow a human being to go underhill?

Or could the artifact have actually been found there in the Never? Maybe Aunt Mel had discovered it and recognized it as a witch artifact and brought it out with her. But wouldn't she have mentioned that? And if she hadn't turned it over to the World Association, wouldn't she have brought it home to Duvall? Of course, she could've brought it to Texas and not told me; she and Momma had a habit of keeping secrets from me for my own protection.

I needed to talk to Aunt Mel right away. She had been working in her garden a lot since returning. Was the artifact buried there now? As a tin of pixie dust had once been?

"What's going on?" Zach asked, standing over us. I looked up.

"Hey, there," I said, slipping my left hand under the table.

"No point hiding the ring now. That cat's out of the bag," he said grimly.

"Sorry I didn't warn you," I said softly.

"Ain't no big thing." He shrugged and turned to Edie. "So I hear you're gonna stay here, Beads, to do some research?"

Edie snorted. "Research? That's rich." Then she shrugged as if she didn't care. "Let them say what they like. Yes, I'm staying. The biscuit and her candylegger can fill you in."

"Nah, I'll stay, too. We'll catch up with them."

Edie shook her head. "No, you might be needed."

"So might you," he said.

I felt like a third wheel, which I never had with Zach before. It was so strange to see Edie and Zach talking like old friends, or like partners. Once upon a time Edie had been a ghost Zach didn't even believe in, and his denial of her existence is what had been part of the cause of our marriage ending. That made it feel twice as peculiar for them to have become close friends.

"Let's hope I won't be needed," Edie said. "I have to stay here. But I trust I'll see you both again soon. Godspeed, Cowboy."

Zach's eyes narrowed, and he glanced around the dining room.

"The president of WAM didn't give us a choice about who stays and who goes," I said.

Zach glanced at me and nodded slowly. "We don't have to

buckle under as easy as all that. Could show him what we're made of."

Bryn shook his head and spoke in a low voice. "This place has enough accumulated magic to level the twenty surrounding city blocks, and there are Conclave wizards who can unleash worse. You don't see the operatives, but they are inside and around the building. We wouldn't even reach the front door."

Zach didn't bother to look at Bryn. "You never know how something will turn out. It ain't the size of the dog in the fight; it's the size of the fight in the dog. Tammy Jo's proof of that. Little slip of a girl who's survived against werewolves, faeries, and powerfully trained Conclave operatives to boot."

"Do what you want, Sutton," Bryn said dismissively as he stood. "We won't join you. There's a more sensible option to try first."

Zach looked at Bryn and they locked eyes, Bryn's sapphire, Zach's the color of denim. Neither blinked.

I rolled the sketch and kept it next to my body as I shot to my feet and pushed between them.

"Whatever we do, we're going to do it together. Right now that means we're leaving here. Come on, Zach," I said, putting my free hand on his upper arm. He jerked away and stepped back.

My stomach gave a lurch, surprise and regret coursing through my veins. Zach didn't want me touching him. I understood, but it was still a shock. I'd been touching him for years.

"Let's go," I said softly to Bryn. "Mercutio, we're heading out. C'mon."

Merc padded over and joined us as we left the dining room. I didn't look over my shoulder to see whether Zach had accompanied us. But I did realize that I'd left something behind. I should've finished my cake, I thought as my stomach growled. Who knew when I would get a chance to eat chocolate cake again?

9

THE SILVER MERCEDES van that had brought us from the airport stood outside the front entry of WAM headquarters, waiting to shuttle us, but I walked away from it and to the building next door. We had to decide where to go first, but before we did anything, I wanted to talk to Aunt Melanie. And while I spoke with her, I didn't want any WAM operatives eavesdropping. I huddled near the corner of the building with my back to the street. Bryn stood behind me. Mercutio prowled the space between buildings. Zach waited several feet away, watching the street and likely estimating the potential number of operatives in the pair of sedans that were parked at the front and back of the van.

Aunt Mel's cell rang and rang and then went to voice mail. I left a message and then called again.

She answered, "Tammy Jo, thank God. I was just about to call you. Crux escaped."

I grimaced. *For the love of Hershey!*

"I let Johnny and his boyfriend in, but my phone rang before I had the chance to warn them, and—"

"It doesn't matter what happened. I need to ask you something real important."

"Sure. I'm really sorry about Crux!"

"It's okay. He couldn't live in the kitchen forever. I was hoping we would have a bigger head start, but what can we do? Now, the thing I need to know is whether you know anything about a valuable piece of magical amber."

"A what?"

"A magic artifact made of amber."

"No. Why?"

"Are you sure? Because it's real important."

"Of course I'm sure. This is the second time I've been asked about this recently. When I got to England, a pair of high-ranking WAM members came to see me at the Savoy, asking about an amber relic. I told them the only amber jewelry I've seen in the past five years was at a shop in Houston. Pretty, but definitely not magical in nature. They asked permission to search my hotel room. I let them. They even patted me down."

"What about Momma? I know she's been visiting that . . . guy she loves in his hometown. Is it possible that she left there and was running around Scotland, treasure hunting?"

"No, I don't think so. As far as I know, she's been with him inside his homeland ever since she arrived there. She definitely didn't leave when I visited. What's going on? Why are you asking about amber artifacts? You won't need one to get into the Nev—to get through the gates around the city you're going to. You just need to find the main gate."

"I know. Something's happened is all."

"Government business?" she asked.

"Exactly."

"I don't know what makes them think we know anything about whatever they're looking for."

"I guess someone told them you or Momma know something about this thing's location. It's pretty valuable, and I've got to find it for them or there will be problems."

"You? Why? They have plenty of people to go on search-and-recovery missions. What do you know about finding artifacts?"

"Less than I know about trigonometry, so nothing at all

to brag about. But that doesn't seem to matter too much." I sighed. "I'll tell you the details later. We've gotta go. If you think of anything, call me."

"All right. Be careful, honey."

"I will."

"I love you," she said.

"Love you back," I replied, and made a kiss sound. "I'll call again as soon as I can."

I turned to Bryn, shaking my head as I ended the call. "Crux is loose, and she doesn't know anything about the Scottish amber." I gestured for Zach to join us. We filled him in and discussed what to do next.

Bryn suggested that we go to Scotland to look for the amber first, since we didn't know how long we'd get stuck in the Never.

"We don't even know where to start looking. And if Aunt Mel doesn't know anything about it, then it must've been Momma. Doesn't it make more sense to go to talk to Momma first?" I said.

Zach nodded his agreement.

"Plus, we have to meet up with Kismet in Ireland. I don't want her hanging around waiting for us when Crux knows where she was headed and will probably try to track her down. He might force her to go back inside without us. Or worse, if he tries and she escapes, maybe she'll just take off."

Bryn's frown deepened. "Andre's at risk because he helped us. He accessed restricted information when we needed it. The Association says it will wait until we return to take action against him, but if we completely disappear, they might think we've gone underground. By all accounts, time moves differently in the Never. We might be inside for what seems a short time to us, while a lot more time is passing for the imprisoned people we care about."

I sighed, chewing my lip. Bryn had a point. Edie had been a free-roaming ghost for years and years. And she'd always had a restless spirit. She wasn't likely to stay locked up for long without trying to escape, or causing such a fuss that she got herself in more trouble.

"What if the reason the trained spies from the Association can't find what they're looking for is because Tammy Jo's momma found it and took it with her when she went inside to see that guy?" Zach said.

Bryn and I exchanged looks, and Bryn nodded. "All right." He glanced back at the building. "I hope they can hold on while we're gone."

We walked back to the van. The driver was a wiry man with sunken eyes, a crooked nose, and brackets around his mouth. They called those smile lines, but he didn't look the type to have smiled too much in his life.

"Hey, there," I said, putting out a hand. "I'm Tammy Jo Trask. From Texas. In America."

The driver quirked a brow, but didn't extend a hand.

"What's your name?"

"You can call me *driver.*"

"No, I can't. That's, um, well, it seems a little rude, Mr. . . . ?"

The driver guy slid the back door open.

"Speaking of being a little rude," I murmured.

He didn't look like he cared about manners in the least. It's a problem with the Conclave members, along with their tendency to shoot and bespell people.

"Thanks for the lift to headquarters from the airport. We can find our own ride from here on out," I said, walking to the rear of the van. "Wanna open the back so we can get our suitcases?"

"I'm your driver. I'll take you wherever you'd like to go."

"We're going back to the airport," I said. "Did the WAM president tell you we're on a mission?"

"Tamara," Bryn warned.

"I'm not gonna say anything about the particulars," I said.

"No," the driver said.

"Well, we've got some business to take care of. And to begin with, we need to go back to the airport."

The driver nodded. "Wherever you'd like to go," he repeated.

None of us moved. I could tell by Zach's stance and the feel of Bryn's magic that they hesitated to get in, but it came back down to the same question we'd faced inside: Resist by starting a fight, or go along and hope for the best?

I climbed into the van.

Zach and Bryn joined me. I glanced at the divider that was made of smoke-colored glass. I'd never seen a van with one like it, and both the guys had been eyeing it suspiciously on the drive to headquarters.

"I don't like that. Kinda feels like a prisoner transport van, huh?" I said.

"Nailed what I was thinkin'," Zach agreed.

Bryn was silent.

The driver closed the doors and got in front, and then we were under way.

Looking over his shoulder, Zach said, "The black sedans are still keeping us company."

After we'd driven for ten minutes, Bryn stared out the window, then frowned and shook his head.

"What?" I asked as we got on the expressway.

"This isn't the way to Heathrow."

I unbuckled my belt and jumped up, slamming my palms against the glass. "I knew it!" I banged my fists on the divider. The driver didn't even turn around. *Jerk!*

"Didn't have the nerve to shake my hand when you were going to abduct us, huh?" I pointed my finger at him, trying to catch his eye. He stared straight ahead.

"That doesn't make it any less rude," I snapped, and then turned back to Bryn and Zach. "What do you think? Should we bust the glass?"

"We'd never reach the driver before he did something to prevent us from getting control of the car. And the Conclave members in the sedans would be on top of us."

I scowled, but nodded. I really wanted to break that darn divider. Vandalism seemed the least I could do to annoy Driver. My fist stayed clenched for several minutes; then my temper finally cooled.

Bryn sensed the change in my mood. "Ready to talk?" he asked.

I gave a jerk of a nod. "Got a plan?"

"Working on it," he said with a small smile. Zach swiveled

his chair to face us, and he leaned forward so it was like we were in a football huddle.

"I assume the driver is taking us to Scotland. Anderson said the amber was discovered in the highlands. If we can't escape before we reach the destination the Conclave has in mind, at least we'll have an idea where to begin looking for the artifact when we return from seeing your mother, assuming that she doesn't have it or know where it is."

"But the president has Edie and Andre. We said we'd try to get the artifact. How come they're kidnapping us?"

"The Conclave doesn't trust us. Or anyone. They likely want to hold on to us until they have the amber."

We spent the entire ride whispering to each other, with Bryn's magic swirling around us to muffle the things we said from any devices or spells that might be trying to listen in. Yeah, wizards are tricky like that.

Since we'd already flown for eight hours, it was really annoying to have to drive for another eight. If we'd flown from London to Dublin like we'd planned, we could've been there with seven hours to spare, I thought bitterly. So far my international adventure didn't have a lot of sights to recommend it.

I shuffled between the seats and kicked the small cooler that the driver had directed us to earlier, when he'd turned the intercom on to respond to my complaint that I was hungry. The cooler just had sandwiches. No cookies. No brownies. No Cadbury bars. I tried to get him to make a stop so I could get my Hershey's out of my suitcase in the back, but nothing doing.

Huge jerk! Actually, he was much worse than a jerk probably, but I was reserving judgment until I saw what his reaction would be to our escape attempt.

I'M NOT SURE what I expected when we turned into the woods, but the road was rough and the trees were thick around us.

"Now we're talking," I said. "We must be getting close."

We finally pulled up alongside a small cabin. The two sedans that had followed us the entire way flanked our vehicle. When the driver got out and unlocked the back door, sliding it open to let us out, we found five Conclave operatives dressed in cat-burglar black, with automatic pistols pointed at us.

The driver had a rifle slung over his shoulder and nodded for us to go inside the cabin.

I glared at him, but we followed him in. We took turns using the restroom, and I washed my face, which made me feel a little better. I would've liked to shower and change clothes. And we all needed sleep, but that wasn't possible.

A female operative with short brown hair stepped forward. I guessed she was the leader.

"President Anderson said you claim to have no knowledge of the artifact," she said. "You made phone calls outside Association headquarters. I assume if your mother or aunt was willing to disclose the location of the amber, you'd have traded the information for the release of your friends."

Bryn and I exchanged glances, but didn't disagree.

"We have reason to believe the artifact wasn't taken far from the location of its original discovery."

"How come?" I asked.

"That's not your concern."

"Does President Anderson know you kidnapped us?" I demanded. "Because he acted like we could find the amber on our own."

A couple of the operatives smirked.

"A good Association president allows the Conclave to work at its own discretion on matters of national importance, which this is," the leader said. She held out a hand. "Do you know the location of the artifact?"

"I couldn't reach all the people I needed to reach," I said.

"Well, until you do, we'll go ahead with our own plans. But anytime your aunt or mother wants to rendezvous with us to turn over the stone, we'll be happy to accommodate them."

I frowned, but didn't argue. What could I say? That I couldn't reach Momma by cell phone because there were no cell towers in the Never?

"I'm hungry," I muttered.

"I'd imagine everyone is," the leader said, nodding at the team.

One of the operatives, a tall man with buzzed brown hair, laid out food from a cooler while the driver tacked a map to the wall. We ate standing up.

"Pay attention," the leader said, waving me over. "You're the key here. This is the pub. You'll go in alone and order a hard cider. You'll spend at least an hour drinking, and be sure they know you're an American looking for a member of your family. If no one approaches you, this is the route you take back," she said, pointing.

Mercutio, who'd slept the entire drive, was climbing on the furniture and doing his feline acrobatics.

"Hear that, Merc?" I asked.

Mercutio meowed.

"He's got it."

"He's not going with you. You're going alone," the woman said.

Try to stop him, I thought. Mercutio was as slippery as a fish when he wanted to be. "So I'm supposed to drink for an hour and walk back here. Then what?"

"Then we wait. Hopefully the contact will come to the pub when he hears you're there or will track you back here. If no one does, then tomorrow you'll go back and have another pint."

"And then?" Bryn asked. "If no contact approaches her tomorrow?"

"Drink, walk, repeat," the operative said.

My jaw dropped. "That's your whole plan? What the Sam Houston?"

"In the meantime, Lyons can walk through the woods with a couple agents. He's from your hometown. If there are traces of your family magic out here, he should be able to recognize them."

"You're as able to detect magic as I am," Bryn said. "Why don't you just investigate any traces of magic you find?"

"These woods are old. There are lots of whispers of magic rolling through the place."

Bryn shrugged and remained silent. I felt the tension in the room build. None of the Conclave members took a step, but it felt like they crowded us nonetheless.

"No harm in taking a walk," Bryn finally said.

The room seemed to exhale. Except for Zach and me.

I didn't like the idea of being separated from the guys. All our escape plans depended on our being together, of course.

"Van Noten, this is quite the team you've put together," Bryn said to the woman with the spiky hair. "Fire, water, wind, and weather magic. I don't recognize your fifth," Bryn said, looking at the chubby blond girl who was about my age. She stared at him. Women often did.

"Don't get clever," Van Noten said.

"Blood and bones," the little blonde said. She offered Bryn a cheeky smile.

"You? Blood and bones?" Bryn said.

"Too right. Wanna see?" she asked with a little smirk, and glanced at me.

"No," Bryn said, stepping between us.

"Poppy, why don't you clear this stuff away so we can use the table," Van Noten said.

"I'm not maid service," the girl said.

I glanced at all the other operatives, who were at least twenty years older than she looked to be. She must've been pretty powerful to have been so confident.

"I'll take my dish, but no one else's," she said coolly.

Van Noten glared at the girl as she walked away.

"Always good to have a group of team players," Bryn remarked.

"Poppy's better at making messes than cleaning them up, but it doesn't matter. Cohesiveness isn't this team's strength. Talent is. She could, as an example, flay the skin from your body with a six-word spell. Not bad for a little blond babe," Van Noten said.

Bryn nodded. "I suspected she was more than a cute smile."

The girl beamed as she walked back in. "If you think my smile is cute, you should see my arse," she said, wagging her round butt.

I gave Bryn a sideways glance, but he didn't drop his gaze. He only smiled. If Zach had been the one flirting, I would've thought he really was in danger of falling for some foreign girl witch, but a newly engaged and newly abducted Bryn wasn't going to be distracted by a sexy witch, especially not in front of me.

"Kato, you take Ms. Trask to the pub," Van Noten said. "And wait in the blind."

A scruffy wizard who reminded me of Shaggy from the *Scooby-Doo* cartoons nodded toward the door.

I glanced at Bryn and Zach. "So, I'm going to the pub. Anybody need anything?" I asked.

"Get going," Van Noten said.

I rolled my eyes. "You know, I heard a lot about English people being real polite. So far I haven't seen too many examples of that."

"I'm Dutch," Van Noten said.

"Hmm. And Dutch people are naturally rude? I didn't know that."

Kato held the door open, and Mercutio streaked out.

"For God's sake," Van Noten cursed.

"Want me to get the cat?" a small man with a sharp goatee and impeccably tailored clothes asked in a French accent.

"Good luck catching him," I murmured.

"No, leave him, Mouclier. But if the cat interferes with the op, Kato, he's expendable."

"To hurt my cat you'll have to go through me," I said. "You've been warned, Mr. Kato."

Kato smiled.

"So have you," I announced with a pointed look at Van Noten, who just rolled her eyes. It made me mad, but it was probably a good thing. Being underestimated had often worked in my favor in the past.

10

THE WOODS WERE thick with trees that whispered to me. I didn't speak treespeak fluently, but sometimes I got the gist of what the trees were trying to tell me. These were as old as the dirt, and they welcomed me.

"Hey, there, Scottish trees," I whispered, and put my hand out to let my fingers trail over their bark as I passed. "Excuse me, Mr. Kato, we're in Scotland, right?"

"Right," he said.

My boots seemed to tighten, which happened pretty frequently to me in the woods at home. It meant my feet wanted to be turned loose from boots and shoes. It wasn't their fault. It was nature calling to my fae side. The squeezing sensation became more intense until my toes started to curl and cramp.

"Hang on," I said, dropping down to sit on a log. I pulled off my boots and socks. I rolled my socks and put them inside my left boot for later.

"What are you doing?"

"I'm a witch with earth magic. Sometimes I like to get in touch with the Earth."

"If you try to conjure against me, I'll flatten you. Now put your boots back on."

"No, no. I'm not trying to raise power to cast attack spells," I said, standing. "I just like to go barefoot."

"Put the boots back on."

"I can't. They're hurting my feet."

"Do you really want to test me?" All the friendliness drained from his face. I took a step back as he muttered a few words. A light breeze ruffled the leaves and then shifted and seemed to flow to Kato. He inhaled like he'd suck the breeze right into him.

The trees whispered more urgently.

I know there's about to be trouble, I thought, but I didn't try to talk to them in case he thought it was some sort of spell.

"Listen, I swear I'm not planning to do anything bad to you out here. But if I try to put my boots on again, I won't be able to walk very far," I said, digging my toes into the dirt. The more connected I am to the earth, the stronger I am. I glanced around, trying to decide which direction I would dive to get myself out of the line of fire if he cast a vicious spell at me.

His hand snapped up, fingers outstretched.

"Don't!" I yelled as I dived to the right and rolled away from the blast of magic. "Stop!" A branch swept down and whacked him in the back. He fell forward, his next spell coughing up clumps of dirt where his palms hit the ground. He landed facedown, and I sprinted into the woods.

Mercutio's meow made me jerk my head to look his way. He ran with me.

"We've got to get out of here, Merc," I said, panting. "But I don't know which way to go. Do you?"

Mercutio can sense magic and has the best instincts a cat can be born with, so when he darted forward, I followed him.

"Hey, Merc, we should still probably go to the pub to see if I can meet up with whoever Momma's contact was. If she really even had a contact!"

Mercutio raced through the woods, sleek and spotted, lightning made flesh.

"Did you hear me, Merc? About going to the pub?"

Behind me, the slap of shoes against the ground warned me that we hadn't lost Kato. Mercutio looked back, slowing down.

"Merc! Come on!" I hissed, running past him. Mercutio turned and backed into some bushes, crouching.

"No! No attacking. Let's go!"

Mercutio likes to run, but he doesn't like to run away from a fight. Ever.

I hid behind a big tree and tried to catch my breath. I wanted to keep going, but I wouldn't desert Mercutio. I looked around and spotted a long fallen branch. I grabbed it and dragged it, putting it between a pair of trees and then lying down on my belly.

"Merc, get him to chase you, and I'll trip him," I whispered.

Mercutio cocked his head. He much prefers to attack and does that from behind. "Come on! I want to get his gun."

The footfalls approached, and Mercutio shot out of the bushes. Kato raced forward. I held my breath and lifted the branch as he reached the pair of trees.

He tripped and flew forward. I dived on top of him and snatched his gun from its holster. I rolled away and had it pointed at him by the time I was on my feet.

He rolled on his back and stared at me with his arms out in a gesture of surrender.

"Who trained you?" he asked with narrowed eyes.

"Nobody," I said.

Mercutio sauntered over and gave a soft yowl.

"Yep, we did it. We got him," I said, keeping the gun trained on Kato. "Okay, get up. You're going to come with me to the pub."

"If you planned to go to the pub, which is what we want you to do, why attack me?"

"I didn't attack you. You attacked me," I corrected. "Now, here's what's going to happen. You're going to go in before me and sit at the farthest table inside the place. If you try to leave the pub, to call anybody, or to cast any spells, I'll take off and you can forget about me cooperating with any more Conclave plans."

"You don't need to hold me at gunpoint," he said as I took his cell phone and pocketed it.

"Yeah, sure. As a Conclave operative, you're totally trustworthy." I rolled my eyes. "Not my first rodeo, Slick. Get moving," I said, nodding for him to walk.

He rose to his feet, glanced at the compass strapped to his wrist, and strode through the forest. The trees whispered their approval.

"Yep. And thanks for the help," I whispered back.

"You and your cat work well together."

"We sure do. Unfortunately, we've had lots of practice fighting for our lives."

"I wasn't planning to kill you."

"I suppose not, since you still need me. But after that, I wouldn't be surprised a bit if your orders are to see that I don't leave Scotland alive."

He didn't deny it, which made me shake my head. So maybe they planned to murder us after we helped them? The worst manners ever!

THE GREY WOLF pub smelled like beer, seasoned meat, and mountain men. The tables were crowded with guys who all shared a certain lumberjack quality. There wasn't a single girl in the entire place.

I wouldn't have to worry about getting noticed. There I was with flaming red hair and a blue sweater with faux fur and silver trim around the top and bottom. It had seemed like a pretty choice for Christmastime traveling, but it was totally out of place for the rough, rustic world of this pub in the woods. They were workingmen; I was a party favor.

I sat on the bar stool, glancing around. I didn't like to have my back to the room, but Van Noten had specifically said I should sit at the bar. Besides, there were no open tables anyway.

Kato sat at the other end. I didn't make eye contact, but kept him in view. If he tried to leave, I would follow.

A pair of young men with long hair and thick, trimmed beards stared at me. Was one of them Momma's contact? Or were they just checking me out because I didn't belong?

The bartender spoke to me, but I didn't understand him.

"Um, hello. Do you speak English?"

He threw his head back and laughed. More men turned to look at me, and I flushed.

He spoke again, more slowly, and I recognized a couple of words. *Welcome* and *now*. As for the rest of what he said, he might as well have been speaking Greek. My brows furrowed.

"I'd like hard cider," I said, hoping he understood me better than I did him. He quirked a brow and poured me a pint, then went into a room behind the bar. A minute later he returned with a bowl of stew, a slice of warm bread, and a small jar of honey. He set utensils, butter, and a napkin on the bar with the food and nodded.

I gaped for a moment.

Someone brushed my arm, and I looked up to find that one of the bearded young men had come to stand next to me. He was too close, given the amount of space available, but I sat still and waited. He smelled like wood smoke, dogs, and pine needles.

He inclined his head toward me, or maybe toward my stew—I couldn't tell which—and then inhaled deeply.

"Hello," I said, but he'd already started to walk away by the time I got the word out.

I buttered my bread and added heaping teaspoons of honey and then ate it with bites of the savory venison stew. After a few minutes I glanced over my shoulder to see if the young men were still staring, but they'd gone. Maybe they'd left to go and tell someone that an American girl who looked like Marlee Trask was having a fantastic snack in the pub.

I complimented the bartender on the stew as I drank my cider. For as long as we were in Scotland, I'd try to eat in pubs rather than having cold sandwiches standing up in a cabin full of Conclave operatives. I'd try to find a bakery, too, I thought, wondering what the local desserts and pastries would be like.

After the meal, I paid with European money. I spent a few minutes looking at the bills. It was so strange to have a pocket full of foreign money.

I didn't understand what the bartender said when he gave me my change, but his smile was real friendly, so I just smiled back and waved good-bye.

I rounded the pub and signaled Kato to leave. When we walked out, I didn't want him behind me. He stood and exited, with me following closely.

I looked around for Mercutio, hoping he hadn't wandered too far away. Now that I was armed, I could help us get the upper hand against the other Conclave operatives. I would likely need Merc's help. Also, I wanted Mercutio ready to jump in the van with us so we could drive away in a hurry.

I slowed, wanting Kato to get farther ahead, but he slowed when I did. I'd expected him to start down the path from the woods that we'd walked to arrive at the pub, but he didn't.

Where's he going?

He turned suddenly. I dropped just in time to avoid being hit in the head with the doorstop he was carrying. I shoved the gun against his chest and he froze.

I shook my head.

He cursed and dropped it.

"You shouldn't just take a pub's doorstop. Didn't your momma teach you it's wrong to steal?"

"Who trained you? Not Maldaron. He was never that smooth. And Perth was mostly clerical," he said, referring to the first Conclave operatives who'd been sent to Duvall.

"If anybody trained me it was my cat, Mercutio. Now get going. I want you to stay ten feet in front of me until the cabin's in sight. If you shout or try to warn them that I got your gun, I'll shoot you in the leg."

"It would be smarter to kill me."

"Yep, but I'm not a bad guy like you."

He smirked. "You live by a code, huh?"

"Not one that I've written down, but yes, I guess I do."

He shook his head. "I like you."

"I wish I could say the same, but as a general rule, I'm

not friends with people who abduct me." I paused. "Except once I fell in love with a guy who kind of did," I added, because when I'd lost my normal mind while under a spell, Bryn had trapped me in a circle to keep me out of trouble. Sometimes a kidnapping is for a person's own good, but not usually, in my experience.

"Been abducted often, have you?" Kato asked with a smirk.

"Yeah, pretty often. Twice in one day one time."

"By Conclave operatives?"

"Most often, but not always."

He grinned. "You're a regular escape artist then, are you?"

"I don't know about being artistic, but I get the job done."

We walked through the woods at a quick steady pace until Mercutio flew out of the foliage and head-butted my calf. I knew that move. My gaze darted right and left as I hurried forward.

"Get moving," I told Kato. "There's a problem."

He stopped. "What sort of problem?"

Mercutio zipped past with a soft yowl.

"I don't know," I said, waving the gun. "Just get going. Jog! I'll tell you when it's okay to stop running."

Kato looked skeptical.

"I'm not kidding," I snapped. "My cat only makes me run when my life's at stake. Otherwise we saunter." I cocked my head, listening. I didn't hear anything, but the trees were buzzing with unease. Mercutio stopped about twenty feet in front of me and crouched.

Uh-oh.

The growl was so low I almost missed it.

"Run!" I yelled at Kato, and shoved past him. I sprinted along the path until it reached the woods. I rushed into them.

Mercutio yowled and herded me to the left, and I hopped over fallen trees and raced forward, but Kato was noisy as he ran with me, and in the distance I heard small noises made by whoever pursued us.

Mercutio jerked to a stop and yowled.

I froze. "What, Merc?" I asked, looking over my shoulder.

Merc pawed the ground.

"He's probably just scenting other animals. He could be hunting," Kato said.

"I know the difference between hunting and being hunted," I whispered.

Then I spotted them: a pair of yellow eyes, watching us. I jumped back. Kato jerked. Mercutio stood his ground.

Within seconds we were surrounded by four huge wolves. Not natural wolves. Unfortunately I had enough experience to recognize a pack of werewolves when I saw them. And I could feel their impression of me.

Prey.

11

ONE OF THE wolves charged forward. I whipped up the gun, but the wolf who knocked Kato to the ground pinned him, but didn't maul him. I released the pressure on the trigger that I'd almost pulled.

"What do you want?" I asked as the three remaining wolves inched closer. I shook my head and bobbed the gun in warning.

Mercutio hissed, ready with teeth and claws to defend us to the death.

Branches swayed, and the trees murmured their displeasure. The wolves looked around sharply. I wasn't sure whether they understood the trees' language, but they must have felt the mood of the forest.

The wolves stayed as they were, waiting for something, I realized. Kato struggled under the wolf's weight on his chest, and wind began to flow through the trees. He was calling the air to him, gathering power.

The wolf on Kato growled and then grabbed Kato's throat in his jaws. He didn't clamp down or tear flesh, but the warning was obvious. Kato's words trailed off into silence.

"What are you doing? What do you want with us?" I asked.

"We haven't done anything to you, and you're starting trouble you probably don't want."

They prowled circles around us. I wasn't sure how much these men could understand in wolf form. They'd seemed to know that Kato was preparing to cast a spell, but they didn't look at me or change into human form to explain what was going on, so I couldn't be sure they understood my questions.

As seconds ticked by, Mercutio and the wolves grew restless, and their crouches deepened. Merc's gaze turned away from the circle and then quickly back. I realized the wolves' attention was partially focused there, too, on some distant point.

"What is it, Merc?" I asked, looking to the north the way he had. The woods loomed dark and sinister. A shiver of fear raced down my spine. Whatever or whoever the wolves waited for wasn't likely to be a welcome sight for me and Mercutio.

I placed a hand against the bark of the nearest tree. Its branches had curled toward me protectively when the wolves had first surrounded us. My right foot rested against a tree root; the left burrowed its toes into the dirt.

My muscles tightened. I didn't look at Merc. His reflexes didn't need to be primed. He was already at the ready, like always.

I gripped the rough bark. A warm pulse from within the tree greeted my fingertips. "Help me," I whispered, and then darted around it.

The wolves lunged forward. Sharp nails grazed my back as I leapt. A branch swung down, and my outstretched hands caught it. The woody limb snapped upward, dragging me into the air.

Mercutio darted to the trunk, barely evading snapping jaws that tried to catch him. He ascended in a spiral of blistering speed, avoiding the paws that scrabbled and slammed the bark trying to reach him.

Merc came to stand on the crook of the branch I dangled from. He cocked his head and meowed.

"Yep," I said, pulling myself up. My arm muscles shook from the effort. I really needed to add chin-ups to my fitness routine. I also needed to add a fitness routine. I bet Kismet would've just swung up and flipped into the air and landed on her toes on the branch like a gymnast. Yeah, I had to work on that.

I put my leg over so I sat straddling the branch, facing the tree trunk and Mercutio. "Made it. Thank you, tree," I said, patting the branch.

Twenty feet below, the wolves growled and circled us. In a whisper, I said, "Someone's coming, huh, Merc? So it's not a good idea to sit waiting for the wolves to give up and go away."

The tilt of Merc's head and his stance told me he agreed that we weren't in the clear. I looked around. This wasn't the jungle, so there were no vines to swing from. Plus, not being Tarzan, I wouldn't know how to do that anyway. I'd probably just crash into a tree trunk and fall down. It would have to be a more normal plan.

"Kato," I said.

He looked up.

"When I start shooting, get up and run back to the cabin."

Kato nodded.

I pointed the gun at the wolves. "Let him go," I shouted.

The wolves didn't budge.

Animals can sense a person's nature. I reached deep into myself for my fae side. That side of me didn't have much conscience. She was ruled by instinct, impulse, and a lust for tasty things, like honey and Bryn. Calmness washed over me, and for a moment I was flying down a faery path on horseback, the air a tunnel of flashing colors and wind.

I jerked on the reins, and my horse's thundering hooves planted to a stop.

I blinked and was back on the branch, my connection to Kismet broken. I felt her, though—in the distance and in myself.

I looked down at the wolves, calculating my chances of killing them all before they scattered. They stiffened, sensing the change.

Wait, I thought. *They're men in wolf form. I won't murder them.*

A voice in my head whispered that if my intent was to get away, my best chance would be if the wolves around the tree couldn't chase me.

My heart thumped.

Mercutio made a small sound of warning. He likes me as regular Tammy Jo, not the detached faery version of me.

Right, I thought with a shiver. I pushed my inner faery aside and took careful aim. I squeezed the trigger. The bullet skimmed through the fur of the wolf holding Kato. The wolves scattered.

Kato rose, flung spells over his shoulder, and tore off through the woods. The wolves didn't pursue him. They all stayed with me. *Good grief!*

At least Kato could bring help back. Would it be in time?

I looked around, wondering what Kismet would've done in my place. Would she have been able to hop from tree to tree? I might miss an outstretched branch and fall to the ground. That would be especially painful, since I was still healing from deep wounds that I'd gotten the week before.

I pulled out my cell and Kato's. Neither had a signal. Typical! In places with lots of magic, electronics often didn't work right. Or perhaps it wasn't the magic. Maybe there just wasn't one of those cell towers near enough to penetrate the deep woods.

Unless I was prepared to shoot and incapacitate the wolves, I couldn't climb down and make a run for the cabin, because there was no doubt they'd catch me within a few feet of the tree.

Getting bolder, the wolves returned to the tree's base, watching us from the ground.

"You know, Merc, there's no telling what will happen once Kato goes to the cabin. Maybe they'll come armed with silver bullets and kill these wolves," I said, looking at the gun I held.

Realization dawned. I removed the clip of Kato's gun and checked the ammunition. It wasn't silver. The wolves should be able to recover from the wounds made by regular bullets. They'd have to live with the pain of being shot, but they would live.

I grimaced. The pain from deep wounds was no picnic.

But it might be better in the long run, because knowing the Conclave wizards, they'd do whatever was the most efficient thing, which might be killing the werewolves.

"Hey, listen," I called down. "That wizard is from the Conclave. You know the Conclave, right? It's like the magical

CIA. Um, that's American. You know what the CIA is, right?" Was there a British version? Of course—James Bond worked for it. What was the name of it? I sure didn't know.

"So the Conclave operatives are like James Bond, except way less charming. If they come, I don't know what will happen. It'd be better if you let me go before they show up. Safer for you," I said.

They didn't leave. I wasn't sure if they understood me.

Mercutio made a skeptical sound.

"What? I shouldn't have given away about Kato being with the Conclave and going for reinforcements? You're right. Probably giving away strategy's not a good idea, especially since it didn't make an impression on them."

I chewed my lip, trying to think of a way to distract the wolves so I could get down and run. If I'd known a spell to create a diversion . . . Of course, my spells usually went hopelessly wrong, and this might not be the best time to experiment. On the other hand, I needed to try something.

"What are you doing?" a little voice said.

I jumped, nearly falling off the branch. I grabbed it to brace myself as Merc swiped a paw at a pudgy winged creature who could've sat cross-legged in my palm. He wore a small leaf on his head and fuzzy pants that might have been made of squirrel fur. Another winged creature who was thinner with a long nose zipped up next to him.

"What's she doing?" the thinner faery asked.

"Is there something wrong with your eyes? She's sitting here."

"But why? She must know he's coming. Is she hurt?"

"Of course she's hurt, or she would've already gone, wouldn't she?" Chubby snapped. "You can see she doesn't even have her bow. It must have been a terrible fight."

"I don't see blood. Who's this cat?" Thin demanded, darting out of Merc's reach. "Is this cat bothering her? Why hasn't she thrown this cat out of the tree if he's bothering her?"

"I don't know!" Chubby shouted. "I'm trying to find out."

I grabbed Merc's paw to keep him from batting Chubby through the air.

"I like her humanside hair. Very bright," Thin said.

"You have to get out of here," Chubby said to me. "The wolf lord is coming. He's two miles away, and you know how fast he can run. When you don't give him what he wants, he could lose his temper and tear you apart."

My stomach tightened. "I don't know how to escape. They have us surrounded."

"And you're too hurt to try to outrun them? You need a fast horse," Chubby said, looking around.

"The horse is not here," Thin said. "The wolves would've caught his scent if he was humanside and nearby."

"And he's not on the path. We've just come from the path," Chubby said, scrunching his round face. "Where is the pony?"

"I think you have me—"

"Don't get distracted, Royal!" Thin shouted. "We have to help get her out of here."

Royal jerked to attention. "I know!"

"Torch the tails," Thin said.

"And get eaten? That's getting too close!"

"Torch the tails!" Thin shouted louder.

"They'll crush us in those jaws. They'll eat us alive!"

"They'll try," Thin said, poking Royal in the belly. "You've gotten too fat. You're slower than a drunk fly."

Royal glowered. "I could thrash you, Shakes."

"Not if you had to catch me first."

"Oh, I'll catch you. After we torch those tails, you'll see."

Shakes grinned. "We'll help. Wait and see," Shakes said to me. "I told you you'd be glad you saved us."

Shakes and Royal swooped down. Within moments they were flying around the wolves with tiny flaming spears, trying to set the wolves' tails on fire. The wolves spun in circles, snapping at the faeries.

Merc and I climbed partway down and then jumped to the ground. Then I ran as if my life depended on it—which, if the faeries were to be believed, it did.

12

THE WOLVES WERE gaining on me when I heard Zach shout, "Get down."

I dived to the ground and covered the back of my neck with my hands, expecting to feel a wolf land on me, but instead a gunshot rang out, and a wolf landed heavily on the ground next to me.

He shifted into human form, gasping for breath.

"Oh, God," I said as blood bubbled from a hole in his chest. He must've been leaping when the bullet hit him. I crawled to him and pressed my hand over the wound. "Hang on."

He gripped my upper arms tight, his eyes wild with fear. "Silver."

The raging howls of the other wolves echoed around us as they crashed into the woods. I heard more shots and explosive sounds as magic was wielded, and then a scream and growls.

"My son . . ." the werewolf lying next to me whispered in his accented English. "He's three. He won't understand."

Tears sprang into my eyes. "Then you have to hang on so you can see him again. Werewolves are the strongest of all the supernatural creatures. You can make it," I said.

His large brown eyes squeezed shut, causing crinkles around them. "Can't breathe," he said.

"We need help here!" I yelled. "Stop fighting! He needs a hospital."

The man's eyes opened, and he stared at me. "You're not her."

"Who?"

"Not a disguise to trick us. Who are you?"

"I'm Tammy Jo from Texas. That's in America."

A ghost of a smile appeared on his face for a moment. "Wait!" he yelled, his expression startled as he looked over my head.

I turned just in time to see the muzzle of another wolf, who leapt at me. I got my arm up, but the force of him slamming into me toppled me over the fallen guy. Sharp teeth sank into my flesh.

I screamed.

The wolf dragged me behind a tree, holding my arm and shaking me by the trapped arm when I tried to fight.

"Stop!" I yelled, the pain like a lance driving into me.

Another wolf raced up, and then transformed. He was short, but powerful. His dark hair skimmed his shoulders, and he glared at me as he put his hand on my throat and squeezed.

"Where is it?" he demanded.

"Let her go," Bryn said.

Yes! Get off! I wailed in my head.

I tried not to struggle, which only sent piercing pain through me, but lack of air made me feel panicked.

Neither werewolf released me.

"Let her go now," Bryn said, pointing a gun at the wolf who had my arm. "This gun is loaded with silver."

"I can crush her throat before you have time to shoot us both."

"I can save her from a crushed throat, but nothing can save you if a silver bullet rips through your skull. I won't miss."

"You're wasting your time. Leave her to us. She'll never give it to your kind," the werewolf said.

I clawed at his fingers with my free hand. I was starting to see spots.

Bryn narrowed his eyes. "She's not who you think. This is the first time she's ever been in Scotland. You've confused her with her mother or someone else."

The werewolf bared his teeth in a snarl, but he dipped his head and smelled my hair. "She's the one," he said with a sneer. "She's disguised her scent with magic, but underneath it's the same."

Bryn shook his head. "She's not the one you're looking for. Let her go or I will kill you." The deadly calm of Bryn's voice sent a chill through me. The wolves must've been able to feel how serious he was.

The man's grip on my throat slackened and then released. He shifted into wolf form, made a low growling sound, and then he and the other wolf turned and melted into the forest.

"Are you all right?" Bryn said, extending his free hand to help me up. I rose and looked around.

"I'm okay," I said, dabbing my arm carefully. The teeth punctures weren't nearly as deep as they might have been, but they throbbed. Blood seeped from the wounds, but luckily didn't spurt or gush.

"This way," Bryn said, hurrying through the woods, glancing at the night sky occasionally.

"Where's Zach?"

"I don't know. We got separated. But he'll know to double back to the cars as soon as he gets the chance."

"He won't leave the woods if he thinks we're out here and in trouble."

"If I hadn't gotten to you after ten minutes, I would've lit the night sky at five-minute intervals to let him know not to return to the cabin."

"What if he'd found me rather than you?"

"He'd have signaled with a double shot into the rotten tree near the site where we confronted the wolves."

We spoke and jogged as quietly as we could.

"I'm surprised the Conclave gave you guns."

"They didn't give them to us," Bryn said. "The wolves killed Van Noten, the driver, and the Frenchman, Mouclier."

I shuddered.

"Van Noten had a lot of power, but she was too slow when casting. She wanted to sweep the area with a big spell. There's no time to get complicated with werewolves. Mouclier was taken by surprise. He was shooting and spelling at two in front of him that kept weaving in and out of view. Then a third flanked him. He was blindsided and taken down, his throat torn so deeply there was nothing but—" Bryn clenched his teeth. "Sorry. You don't need to picture that. I didn't see the attack on the driver, but passed his body. We got separated from Poppy, Kato, and Lundqvist, the operative with the brown buzz cut. I'm not sure whether they're alive or not."

He swallowed and frowned. "These werewolves attack with more precision than most. Almost military or paramilitary. Sutton noticed immediately," Bryn said with admiration in his voice. "That's why I decided to try to reason with the leader. Normally with attacking werewolves, you just have to shoot them. I don't have to tell you. You saw what the pack in Texas was like."

I nodded.

We emerged from the woods at the cabin to find Zach and Mercutio running toward us.

"Wolves or wizards?" Bryn asked, yanking the van door open.

"Both," Zach said, shooting holes in the tires of the other cars. "Keys?"

"I've got them. Van Noten had them on her."

Once we were locked in the van, Bryn started it and slammed his foot down on the gas pedal. I heard the soft pop of gunfire from the woods. The sound was muffled by the heartbeat pounding in my ears. I held my breath, bracing for a tire to be blown out.

As we barreled down the narrow road, kicking up gravel and dirt, I spotted two pairs of yellow eyes just behind the tree line. The wolves were running with us. If our car was incapacitated, they'd get to us before the wizards. I had no doubt they'd tear the van open as if it were made of tin.

I bit the inside of my mouth, sitting rigidly still and holding the armrest. We turned onto a wider road. I looked back, finally exhaling, when I saw that we were out of range for the wizards.

I unbuckled myself and went to the window, peering into the trees. Mercutio joined me, standing on a seat with his paws on the window.

I spotted a blur of dark fur and saw it stop. I watched the wolf's yellow eyes, stationary now. The wolves were done chasing us. At least for the moment.

Did that mean they'd given up? Or would they track us? Werewolves, like Mercutio, can track anything, including magic. I had a sinking feeling that we hadn't seen the last of them.

"WE NEED TO change vehicles," Bryn said.

"Tracking device?" Zach asked, leaning forward. He was in the back behind the divider, but Bryn had turned on the intercom to allow us to talk together.

"I assume. It's standard on Association cars."

I stared out the passenger window. "That werewolf who got shot, he had a little boy. Three years old."

"Kato shot him. Not Zach or I."

I pursed my lips, frowning. "They didn't try to kill Kato and me when they had the chance. They were holding us for the leader to come and question us. If I'd had the chance to convince them I wasn't whoever they wanted, nobody had to get shot."

"I'm sorry, sweetheart."

My gaze turned to Bryn. "Did Kato tell the other Conclave members that they didn't hurt us?"

"No," Bryn said. "He just said that werewolves had chased you, that he'd gotten away using gunfire to slow their pursuit, and that he'd left you up a tree with them circling, ready to attack."

I folded my arms across my chest and looked back out the window. "Do you think it's possible a werewolf shot in the chest with a silver bullet could survive? If they got him to a surgeon who could take the silver out and fix whatever things in his chest had gotten hurt?"

"Yes," Bryn said. "They have an amazing capacity to heal. If they got him to help in time, he could recover."

I didn't know if Bryn was just saying that to make me feel better, but it worked. That werewolf had still been talking and breathing when I'd left him. I'd recently survived a wound that would have killed any regular person, so the power of supernatural healing could never be counted out. I rubbed the breastbone in the middle of my chest, which still ached on and off, especially when I jarred it.

The difference was that I hadn't been stabbed with a metal that was poisonous to my supernatural healing. Still, he'd been in the heart of his homeland. The other wolves would know right where to take him for help.

I ran a hand through my hair. "I don't think it was Momma they were looking for."

"Let's not talk about that right now," Bryn said, cutting me off.

"Why not?" I asked, glancing back at him.

"There could be recording devices or bugs in the van."

"Oh," I said. I pursed my lips and shook my head. "You know what? I'm sick to death of the Conclave. They can go to hell."

Bryn's brows rose, but that didn't stop my flapping jaws.

"President Anderson, if you're listening," I said loudly, "I know that you just took over, but you should really worry less about artifacts and more about what your assassins are doing. Because sooner or later it's going to come back to bite you in the butt. And speaking from experience, I can tell you, werewolves have real sharp teeth."

13

AFTER WE STOPPED so I could wash and bandage my arm, we drove from the northern part of Scotland back down to one of its main cities. Bryn looked up car rental agencies in Edinburgh, and we dropped him off there, parking the van a block away. He joined us with a different van and we transferred our luggage and ourselves to the new vehicle. Then we left the Conclave van and drove south into England. We weren't going to bother going back to London to fly to Dublin, since London was the heart of the Association and Conclave operations. Instead we stopped for the night, sleeping in the van. It was more comfortable than I expected, but that might've been only because I was so exhausted.

I dreamed that the wounded werewolf was okay and reunited with his little boy and werewolf wife; then I dreamed I was eating carrot cake in a fancy hotel room that looked out over a city full of skyscrapers, and finally I dreamed that I was standing on the banks of a river petting a palomino pony who drank from it. I bent and cupped some water and drank, too. It was fresh, not salty, and tasted of earthy silt. Strands of strawberry-blond hair fell over my shoulders.

Not my hair, I realized, but I wasn't startled awake by the realization.

Green eyes rose, and Kismet's lips, rosy with cold, whispered, "You've gotten hurt again, twinheart. Don't let that trouble you. I think it's naught but a scratch." Her lilting Irish voice made me smile. My arm tingled, my body growing feverish in the dream.

"It was a werewolf that bit me like I was honey and apples," I said.

"Like you were a stag, you mean," she said.

"He thought I was someone else. You, I think."

"That's as may be. Where were you, Tammy?"

"We were in Scotland. In the woods."

"What did I say about the Scotch woods?" she said, frowning. "I don't warn you just to hear my pretty voice. Heed me."

"I got kidnapped."

"Are you still?"

"No, I escaped."

"Good. Next time escape sooner, so you don't end up in places I've told you not to go."

I made an exasperated noise.

She looked over her shoulder. "I have to get back on the path. Rest now, Tammy love. I'll see you soon. Don't forget our meeting place."

I jerked awake, sweat sprouting on my forehead. Bryn slept in a reclined seat across from me. Zach lay sprawled on the floor, perpendicular to the bench seat he'd started the night on. It had been way too short for him.

I wiped my face with my sleeve, then pulled the fabric up to examine my arm. The puncture wounds had been scabbed over, red and sore when I'd gone to sleep. Now, however, the scabs were gone and small pink scars were all that was left behind. I touched them, but they didn't hurt. The scars would likely fade, too.

It was lucky for me that I was born of supernatural creatures. When regular folks were bitten by werewolves, the wounds never healed. They just kept bleeding and festering until the person either became a werewolf or, more frequently, died.

I studied Zach, so full of muscles and robust health. Hard to believe it had been only a few months since he'd nearly died of a werewolf bite.

I lifted my wool coat that I'd been using for a blanket. I stood and slipped my arms into the sleeves, then took Kato's gun from the pocket in the back of the passenger seat where I'd put it. I tucked it into my pocket and got out of the van.

I closed the door and shivered in the cold, misty air.

"Mercutio," I called.

We were parked on a village lane in Northern England. Mercutio's nocturnal, so he was outside hunting. He might find some rodents to eat, I supposed, wondering if the time change was affecting him. Did he realize that we were on the other side of the Atlantic Ocean? Did he even know about the Atlantic Ocean? He was a jungle cat, maybe from South America originally, since he understood Spanish as well as English.

I stretched and then rested my hands on top of my head, watching my breath fog past the cold tip of my nose.

A soft purr near my leg made me smile and bend down to stroke Mercutio's fur.

"You know what, Merc? Remember that pair of tiny fae I met while we were on the branch? They thought I was Kismet. They warned me the werewolf leader was coming. Just now I saw Kismet in my dreams. When I told her I thought the werewolves had bitten me thinking I was her, she said that was possible. The Association doesn't know about Kismet. If someone from the Conclave spotted Kismet or were brought a picture or a sketch of her and her hair looked redder than it is, she might have been confused for Momma or Aunt Mel. We all look a lot alike."

Merc cocked his head.

"The leader of the werewolves said that *I* would never give *it* to Bryn's kind. They knew Bryn was a wizard. The wolf suggested that Bryn leave me to them. If the wolves know Kismet's a faery, they certainly wouldn't expect her to give anything valuable to the witches' association." I licked my lips. "How likely do you think it is that Kismet's

the one who knows what happened to the Association's stolen artifact?"

Merc's soft meow rose into the cool air.

"Yeah, I think so, too. This artifact, whatever it does, is
probably like the Hebrides Amber that the faeries and witches
fought to the death over. If we had it, and if the Seelie queen
wanted it pretty bad, that might be all the leverage we'd need
to buy Kismet's freedom from the Never and to get Momma
and Daddy out of trouble for helping Kismet escape. The only
trouble is that we need that artifact to trade for Andre and
Aunt Edie." When I looked down at Mercutio, hair fell into
my eyes. I shoved it back and held it off my face. "What do
you think, Merc?"

Mercutio meowed softly.

"I know," I said. "I'm not sure either."

In the distance, the sun was starting to rise.

"I know one thing: If we find the amber artifact, before
we give it to anyone, we've got to figure out what it does and
why everyone wants it."

Merc didn't disagree.

THE WATER CROSSING from England to Ireland was as
rough as cake batter full of nuts. The choppiness made Zach
and me feel sick. Bryn convinced me not to stay belowdeck,
and he was right; it was better standing at the rail with wind
in my face and my eyes closed.

Zach was sick over the side once. He went down to brush
his teeth and wash his face, but he came back up and then
lay on a bench with his eyes closed and the sun on his face,
the sea air blowing around us.

Bryn stayed close to me, bringing me a scone and jam that
made me feel better. Zach refused to eat until we reached
land.

In Dublin, we checked into a hotel in Temple Bar. We'd all
agreed not to unload the van. We each just took in a small bag
with a change of clothes and toiletries. After Bryn and I show-
ered and dressed, we met Zach in the lobby, which was decked

out with lime-green couches and chocolate-brown and white accent pillows. Adele's voice belted from the speakers as we exited to the street.

I liked the way that some of the streets were just for pedestrians. There were lots of shops and tourists taking pictures and having fun. It felt almost like a Duvall street festival. We found the literary pub crawl online and booked tickets and then went to a restaurant for lunch. We each had a bowl of Irish stew. Zach had a shepherd's pie, too, making up for not having eaten much since leaving America. I ate dessert to keep him company.

I told Bryn and Zach about the small faeries and my dream where I'd talked to Kismet. I wasn't sure if the dream had been a real conversation or just my imagination getting carried away.

"She's younger and her hair's quite a bit lighter. I'd be surprised if the Conclave mistook her for your mother or aunt," Bryn said. "They don't usually make those kinds of mistakes."

"I don't suppose they do."

"We know she's traveled through Scotland over the years when she's left home on various missions that were unrelated to the amber artifact, right?" Bryn said. "She's been sent to spy and assassinate fae enemies?"

"Right." I licked my lips.

"And werewolves wouldn't have any use for a magical relic. They can't perform magic."

I nodded. "So she's probably got something else they want, because don't you agree that the werewolf leader thought I was her?"

Bryn nodded.

"Yes, and those little faeries thought so, too. They mentioned a horse and a bow, and that my hair was darker red from being humanside."

"When we see her, you can ask her," Bryn said, taking the bill.

He was the only one with Irish money, and he insisted on paying for lunch. He didn't want us using credit cards until we were ready to leave Dublin, in case the Conclave had arranged to track us electronically.

We had a couple hours before the pub crawl. On the street, we stopped to listen to a band of young guys playing for the crowd. I rubbed my hands together to keep them warm.

"Here," Bryn said, holding out his.

"I'm okay," I said. "I've got pockets." I didn't want to hold hands with Bryn in front of Zach. It seemed too soon for that, when things between Zach and me had just ended for good.

When I looked his way, though, Zach wasn't watching us. He squinted, and I tilted my head.

"Move," Zach said, grabbing my arm and pulling me back into the crowd.

"What?" I asked as Bryn ducked into a doorway with us.

"The girl from the Conclave, Poppy, was at a jewelry stand."

"Christ. You're sure?" Bryn asked.

Zach just looked at him. Zach was a sheriff's deputy. Even though he worked in a small town, his powers of observation had been honed with training and practice. I thought maybe playing football had helped too. He was used to noting the location of an entire field of guys with a quick glance.

"Let's get off the street," Bryn said.

"What if they found our hotel? Mercutio's asleep in the van. I should get him," I said.

"He'll be too conspicuous," Bryn said.

I chewed my lip.

"He's right," Zach said, waving us into a men's clothing shop. Bryn pretended to shop while Zach stood at the window, watching.

I paced until Bryn told me not to. "Sweetheart, try not to draw attention to yourself," he said.

I folded my arms across my chest as he moved to the corner of the shop. I followed him, and he said, "Pick something out for me to buy. I need to think about what sort of distraction I can create," Bryn said. His Irish accent had thickened since we'd gotten to Dublin.

I flipped through racks absently and made my way to Zach's side.

"How are you?" I asked.

He didn't answer.

"Zach?" I waited.

He didn't turn his head, but when he realized I would wait there until he responded, he said in a low voice, "Other than the knife in my heart, I'm right as rain."

I winced. "I'm sorry I didn't have a chance to tell you I got engaged. It happened all of a sudden, and I—"

"The only thing I'm trying to care about right now is keeping us alive. Leave me alone so I can concentrate."

I nodded, though he wasn't even looking at me. I should've walked away, but I couldn't make myself do it. We'd be traveling together for a while and into a dangerous place. We couldn't afford to be distracted by personal stuff. For that reason, and for my peace of mind, I really wanted to clear the air.

"You and I will get through this," I said. "I know you don't think we can be friends, but we can. We've known each other since the days of wearing party hats at birthday parties. I'm not fixin' to give up on us as friends. Not ever."

Zach's denim-colored eyes turned to me. "If you let me in, I'll wreck your engagement."

I took a step back. "No one can do that."

"I know you're not ready to let me go," he said.

I blinked, surprised by the sudden appearance of Zach's smile, which I hadn't seen in quite a while.

"Is that right?" Bryn asked.

I jumped and turned. "Oh, hello. I was just telling Zach that we can be friends."

"She was also telling me she'll never give up on having a relationship with me. *Not ever.* So I guess we're going to be a threesome on this side of the ocean and the other. Forever," Zach said, still smirking as he locked eyes with Bryn.

"As long as she's sharing my bed and not yours, I suppose I'll be able to tolerate it better than you will." Bryn's voice was dead cool, his gaze steely.

Zach looked back at the street, the corners of his mouth still curved up, but there was a tightness to his expression, and the set of his shoulders told the real story. He'd have liked to knock Bryn's head off his shoulders.

"Got a plan?" I asked, taking Bryn's hand and walking him away from Zach.

"Not completely. The Conclave operatives are well trained. Diversionary tactics will have to be good to fool them. I think I'm going to ask for some assistance."

He put up a finger to have me wait. He made some calls, often speaking Gaelic. When he finished, he said, "I hope it's not a mistake to involve the friends I have here. I won't ask them to come out right now. They're too likely to be spotted by the operatives. But tonight I've asked them to cast some spells, to fill the air with magic that will hopefully make it harder for the Conclave operatives to track us. I'll cloak us as best I can as soon as we put some distance between us and them."

I looked up at the sound of rain striking the window. Bryn frowned and muttered, "Hell."

"What is it?" I asked.

"Kato uses wind magic, and this storm is gusting. Lundqvist is weather magic, so storms will add to his power. Clouds and city lights will make it more challenging for me to see and draw power from the heavens tonight. Assuming that it's still Van Noten's original team that's tracking us, a rainstorm with brisk winds is the last thing we want."

"Well, we'll cut through a park and I'll put my toes in the dirt. I'm earth magic, and you can draw power from me. Plus, I've got a gun. You know what a good shot I am. And Zach's got his amulet and a gun. There are three of them and three of us. To my mind, it's an even match."

"We've got company," Zach said.

Poppy pulled the door open and flounced in. She wore a tight black sweater with a cartoon skull on it, and she'd paired it with a black-and-fuchsia tutu skirt of layered lace that hit her midthigh and made her an extra couple feet wide. Her blond curls bobbed around her face, tighter and frizzier after having been rained on.

"Hello, loves. Fancy meeting you here," she said cheerfully.

"C'mon over here, darlin'," Zach said. "Lemme bend your ear."

Her smile widened, causing a deep dimple in each cheek. "I like it right here near the door, so no one can slip out. But you can bring that big buff body to me."

Zach nodded for Bryn to take over watching the window, and Zach walked to her. He bent forward and his blond curls nearly matched hers for color. When she cocked her head, though, I thought I spotted darker roots. Not her natural color then, which, of course, didn't matter. Her magic was the only thing I should've cared about. I couldn't help but notice the way she pressed her big boobs against Zach as he leaned in, talking to her. He was at least a foot taller, so they hit him around his six-pack. I scowled. When he put a hand on her back, I'd had enough. She was the enemy, after all.

"Um, what are you guys talking about?" I asked, giving her a little shove to widen the space between them.

"Nothing much," Zach said. "I was just telling her I like her style." Zach pulled Poppy against him and turned her like they were going to twirl right around the store doing a two-step.

My jaw dropped as they moved across the aisle. Then her smile disappeared, and she jerked her arm. When she couldn't raise it, I darted over to have a better look. I hadn't heard the click, but apparently he'd handcuffed her to a rack.

"You can't be serious," she snapped. "I may be blood-and-bones magic, but I can certainly cast a rudimentary spell to get myself out of a pair of human handcuffs."

He grinned. "I really do you like your style, darlin'. Stay out of trouble. Tammy Jo, Lyons, let's go."

Poppy murmured a spell, and then her face scrunched. "What is this? What?"

"Move it," Zach said, shoving me out the door.

She raised her free arm and started to cast. Bryn thrust me out the doorway, and the three of us ducked around the side of the building.

"Those weren't regular handcuffs, huh?" I asked.

"Nah. Special issue," he said, shrugging his brows.

Bryn led the way between buildings, casting a spell to cloak us, but it bent away from Zach, who'd taken out his amulet. After he'd learned that there was an underground of supernatural creatures and magic was real, he'd gone to train as a human champion. I didn't know what the training had been like; he kept the details secret, whether by his choice or because the people who'd trained him told him to. One thing that I had become acquainted with was a gold amulet with a purple stone that defended him against magic.

Unfortunately, the amulet's power was strong and aggressive. It gave me a headache to be near it, and when it was activated it could even burn my skin.

"You don't have to bring that out yet," I said, shielding my eyes from its bright reflection.

"Walk ahead of me if it's too close," Zach said.

I frowned, but did as he suggested. It seemed the distance between Zach and me was getting bigger in every way. I caught Bryn watching me out of the corner of his eye and decided that, maybe for the moment, some distance was for the best.

14

WHEN WE SLIPPED into the Duke pub on Duke Street, where the literary pub crawl would begin, Zach put the amulet away. Bryn had Guinness, Zach had a beer I'd never heard of, and I had a half a pint of hard cider.

Zach ignored us, his eyes trained on the window. Bryn cast glances out, but split his attention between me, the window, and the surroundings. When the back of his hand brushed mine, I laced our fingers together under the table.

"Thank you," he whispered without looking at me.

I smiled and squeezed his hand. "Welcome," I whispered back, stealing a glance at Zach, who seemed not to even know we were there anymore. It was an act, of course. I wished Edie were there to distract him. And to distract us and anyone else who might be in hearing distance.

"I wonder how Edie and Andre are doing," I said.

"I'm sure they're all right," Bryn said absently. "Those are the pub crawl actors." Bryn nodded to a pair of men in black bowler hats. "Let's go upstairs."

"I'll wait here," Zach said.

"Don't forget that the window's glass works both ways," Bryn said to Zach. "You can see out. They can see in."

"Thanks for the tip," Zach said in a pancake-flat tone.

"Maybe we should all stay down here. If the Conclave members come up the stairs, we'll be stuck," I said.

"I'm thinking of Kismet," Bryn said. "We haven't seen her. She might be upstairs already. She likes that vantage point. Up above," he said, glancing at the ceiling.

"She does like being up high, but that's in trees," I mused. "Can't hurt to check if she's there, though."

Upstairs, the cozy room was already nearly full, and the two men in hats were greeting people and telling jokes. I smiled. "This would be lots of fun if we weren't having to hide out from the Conclave and such," I said.

Bryn nodded with a slight smile. "This is not exactly the Irish vacation I planned to show you."

"Yeah, seems like something unexpected is always happening. I suppose we should expect it."

He laughed softly. "I guess."

Kismet wasn't upstairs, but Bryn bought our tickets.

"I want one of those," I whispered, pointing to a souvenir program. He raised his brows. "Yes," I said emphatically. "On account of the fact that I'm a visitor in Ireland, and this might be the only tour I get to go on. Maybe we'll get hung up in the Nev—you know where—and these guys in hats will have retired by the time we come back."

Bryn frowned. "Let's try not to think that way," he said, but he bought me a booklet anyway. I couldn't resist flipping through it as they ushered us downstairs to have a drink and be on our way.

I'd never been on a pub crawl before, let alone one about writers. I wasn't sure why they called it a crawl. Maybe it was because some people had to crawl home after drinking in every pub along the way. I wasn't fixing to get drunk. We needed to keep our wits about us.

At each stop, the actors did a skit and gave a little talk, sharing stories about famous Irish writers. Then we went inside for a pint of beer or cider. In my case, I stuck with half pints. Zach followed the group, but stayed back from us, his gaze constantly scanning. Bryn had a different style. I knew he was also vigilant, but he was subtle about it. Every few moments I'd feel a thread of his magic drift outward, searching for signs of other magic that might be closing around us.

The actors were sure funny. Pretty soon I was only half paying attention to the street, because I was laughing and watching their performance. Bryn, it turned out, already knew all about the writers they were mentioning, and he joined in with quick, funny comments when the actors asked the audience questions.

When we reached Trinity College, Bryn led me away from the group. They stood out front while we slipped into a quiet, dark square. There were grand old buildings, and I bet in daylight it was even more impressive to see.

"If I'd lived in Ireland in my teens and twenties, this is where I would've gone to school," he said. "We visited here often when I spent summers in Dublin. And members of the W.U., including me, have left things in the square."

My mouth dropped open. The W.U. was the Wizard's Underground, a secret organization dedicated to stopping WAM from doing unethical things to its members.

Bryn led me to a bike rack. He glanced at the sky and then around before twisting one of the rungs on the rack. I felt dozens of tendrils of magic emerge. My eyes widened.

"Hello, there, Tammy, darlin'," Kismet's voice called. I turned as she emerged from the shadows with a book tucked under her arm.

"Hi! There you are," I said. "I was starting to worry."

"No need for that. I can take care of myself."

"What have you got there?" I asked, nodding at her book. It wasn't a little souvenir program like what I had, that was for sure. It was a hardcover that looked older than both of us put together.

"Oh, this is a little gift for Her selfish Highness."

"Did you steal it?" I asked, frowning. It was pretty late, and I doubted my sister, the fae assassin, had a library card for a human school.

"No. Mind you, I could have." She shrugged her brows. "No security's good enough to keep me out, do I want to get in."

I cocked my head and realized that when she said, "do I want to get in," she meant "if I want to get in." She had a funny way of talking sometimes.

"But," she continued breezily, "I don't steal from students. And I won't take their valuables for her if there's just one copy of something. I make sure I only get the double of something, and the lesser one. Don't tell her, though. She thinks I only bring her the best."

"I definitely won't tell her. I don't think she should be getting copies of rare books, even the lesser copies. Those belong to the school."

"Aye, well, she wants what she wants. And usually gets what she wants. And remember, it's you who insisted we go in there. I can't come empty-handed."

Bryn was walking along one of the buildings, running his hand over the brick wall.

"What are you doing, Bryn?" I asked.

"Looking for a mark we left," he said softly. "Here." He scraped off some loose cement between bricks, and I smelled his magic and tasted something sweet and strong.

"Sealed with whiskey cream," he said with a smile when I licked my lips.

"Two things you can count on the Irish for . . . drunkenness and rebellion," a voice said.

We spun as Kato stepped into the courtyard, a gun pointed at us. I jerked my head toward where Kismet had been, but she'd melted into the shadows. I bit my lip. Where was she?

"We heard the Wizard's Underground had concealed magic on the grounds of Trinity College," Kato continued.

"I stored magic here when I was a teenager training in magic," Bryn said. "Nothing to do with an underground, if one exists."

Gusts of wind blew around Kato, and I shivered. "Don't point that gun at us," I said. "It's wet out. Your finger might slip."

"It might," he agreed. "On your knees, Lyons. I'm taking the girl."

In a blink, Kismet came from behind him and put a dagger to his throat. "Hello, wizard," she said in a soft voice that could barely be heard above the wind. "Drop your arms and your weapon, or I'll drop your whole body." Her eyes shone a tawny green in the darkness, with flecks of gold that glowed. She'd never looked more catlike than at that moment, all grace and deadly purpose.

"Who and what are you, girly?" Kato asked, lowering his arms as he tried to see her over his shoulder.

"Kis!" I said, spotting fuzzy curls bouncing up behind her.

"What have we here?" Poppy said with a giggle.

Bryn raised a hand at the same time Poppy did. He pushed me aside, and I felt a barrier of Bryn's magic slide in front of us, but not before Bryn sucked in a sharp breath that told me he'd felt her blast of magic. Her assault spell had been meant for me. My head jerked to look at him, and he clutched his throat. I felt a slight burning in my own throat.

"What's wrong? What happened?"

Zach rushed into the courtyard, his shirt open, amulet blazing. "Trouble's coming down the street," he called, but stopped when he saw Poppy and Kato. She whirled toward him, raising an arm.

"Don't—" Zach warned, but she flung magic.

It bounced off the amulet and boomeranged back toward her. She was seized by a fit of coughing that brought her to her knees.

"Come on," Zach said, waving for us to move.

Bryn and I jogged to Zach.

"Good night," Kismet said, making a thin slice on Kato's neck. He sucked in a breath, but no blood gushed. There were just a few small beads that welled on his skin.

A moment later his eyes rolled back, and his body crumpled to a heap at Kismet's feet. Without missing a beat, she slid her dagger into a sheath on her small leather backpack and walked away from the fallen Kato.

"Is he—?"

She shook her head. "Just unconscious. A sedative poison on the knife. I introduced it with a nick from the blade."

"Are you okay?" I asked Bryn, who cleared his throat as we all left the Trinity grounds.

"Yes," Bryn said, then swallowed. I swallowed, too, but my throat felt okay.

"Stay close to the wall," Zach said, guiding us so the crowd with the pub crawl blocked the view of us from the street.

The drizzle worsened, prompting the group's umbrellas to whoosh open.

Bryn looked over his shoulder as we hurried around a corner. A streak of lightning lit the sky for a moment, and Bryn's eyes narrowed. "I can feel his power from here, so he can probably feel ours, too."

"Another wizard? Wait here for me," Kismet said, pulling her bow out from under the back of the long black oversize sweater she wore over her T-shirt and skirt.

"Hang on," I said, clutching her arm. "Let's just go."

"Why would we run from a lone wizard?"

"Because we don't want to kill him. Or for him to kill us. We just want to get away."

She scowled. "When people chase me through a city, I stop them." She glanced around. "There aren't enough trees to make it a fun game."

"The hotel's this way," Zach said.

I nodded. "Come on, Kismet. Let's stay together." I hooked my arm through hers and pulled her against my side. "Sisters stick with each other."

A smile stretched her mouth toward her ears. "Yes, all right." She gave a little nod. "Sisters," she whispered, still smiling.

I smiled, too, feeling happier than was logical. We were being chased by Conclave operatives, and if we managed to escape them, we were going out of the frying pan into the fire in the form of the Never. The last thing I should be doing was smiling, but when you've got friends and family close at your side, things don't feel as bad.

WE RETURNED TO the van. When I slid the door open, I had to shake my head at Mercutio, who wanted to hop out.

"Sorry, Merc. We loaded our stuff earlier so that we could get right out of town when we found Kismet."

Mercutio made a dissatisfied noise, but eased back inside.

"Where are we heading?" Bryn asked, climbing into the driver's seat.

"Do you know the way to Killarney?"

"Of course," Bryn said. "I'm Irish."

She grinned. "All right there, candy man. Stay sweet."

"Candy man?" I asked.

"Well, no one's got candy legs, have they? Where is she, by the way? I thought our aunt meant to come along," Kismet said as she and I climbed into the back and Zach got in the front passenger seat.

"Edie told you that?" I demanded. "She didn't tell me."

Kismet shrugged. "Maybe she thought you'd tell her to stay home."

"I might have. And if she'd been smart, she would have. Now she's been captured by the World Association of Magic, and she's a prisoner."

"What's that you say?" Kis said, grabbing the handle of the door that she'd just closed.

"She's in London. Eventually we have to go back there to get her, but we're going to the Never first."

Kismet tilted her head thoughtfully. "Easier to get her out of a human stronghold than the Never. She's safe there, do you think? Till we can come back for her?"

"I think so," I said. "They want us to get this artifact for them. We're supposed to trade it."

Kismet nodded. "So she'll be all right till you come then. Good enough."

"But we haven't got the relic they want."

Kismet waved this detail away. "I like her. I'll get her."

I blinked. "Getting into WAM headquarters won't be like sneaking into a college library. They have a lot of safeguards against all kinds of magical creatures. Right, Bryn?"

"Definitely," he said, sounding a little hoarse.

I felt a tickle in my own throat. "Does your throat hurt?" I asked.

"A little," he admitted. "I may stop by an A and E in Killarney."

"What's an A and E?"

"Accident and emergency."

"Oh." I nodded. "Will medicine work on a magical illness?"

"It will work on something like an infected throat. This may even just be laryngitis, which would get better without intervention. Poppy didn't panic when the spell she cast at Zach came back and hit her. She went to her knees coughing, but she didn't look scared, so the spell must not have been too dangerous."

"Why would she be scared? Even if it was a deadly spell, she could just heal herself with her blood-and-bones magic."

Bryn shook his head. "That's usually easier said than done. Most blood-and-bones witches can't cast on themselves. It's thought that it's a protective thing. That way they don't accidently hurt themselves while developing their powers. The ones who could cast on themselves likely died out years ago."

"Huh," I said. "So far, as Conclave members go, Poppy's not so bad. She hasn't betrayed us or tried to kill us. According to Van Noten, she's really powerful, but she didn't hit us with any really nasty spells. She's a little too flirty with guys, in my opinion, but of all the Conclave operatives I've met, she's my favorite. If I see her again, I may tell her so."

Bryn laughed and then rubbed his throat. "You are one of a kind."

"Actually no. Two of a kind," I said, pointing at Kismet.

Bryn winked at us in the rearview mirror and looked cute doing it.

"Kismet, I have to ask you a couple of things. Do you know anything about a magical amber relic that the government of witches is desperate to find?"

"Can't say that I do."

"We heard a story about faeries and witches fighting over an amber years ago. Have you ever heard a story like that?"

"Can't say that I have."

I frowned. I'd really hoped she'd know something

helpful—like where the amber artifact was hidden and what its magical power was.

"We ran into some werewolves in the Scottish woods."

"Did you? I told you not to go to the Scotch woods."

"Yes, I know. We didn't have a choice, being kidnapped."

"You ought not let yourself be kidnapped. I'll teach you to fight so you can stop that from happening again."

"I know how to fight. But the thing is, those wolves mistook me for you, I think. And they wanted something from you."

She smiled. "My blood, no doubt."

"An object," I said.

She glanced away, shrugging.

"Can't you tell me?" I whispered.

She shook her head. "It's nothing."

"This is important, Kis."

"If something is important, I'll attend to it. You needn't worry."

"I want to help. We're in this together."

She smiled and glanced at me. "If I find I need help, I may ask for it. But trouble should be more afraid of me than me of it," she said with a wink.

So confident. Hopefully not overly so.

I sighed. She was used to being completely on her own. I'd have to keep working on her to convince her she could trust us.

Bryn watched her in the rearview mirror, and he and I shared a look.

He looked so healthy and normal, the last thing I expected was for him to run us off the road two hours later.

15

I TOLD KISMET stories about growing up in Duvall. She laughed and asked a lot of questions. Zach, who'd started out quiet, gradually warmed up. When I told the story of our stealing Barney the bulldog, mascot of our biggest football rival, Zach commented, "That was a move we'd live to regret."

"Not a smooth abduction then?" Kis asked, laughing.

"That dog was fifty pounds of muscle and another fifty pounds of attitude. Still got the scars on my forearm where he tried to tear off a piece of me."

"Let's see," she said, hopping up from her seat and leaning over his.

He flicked on the small light near him and extended his arm.

"Where? Oh, yes," she said, running her finger over the faint marks. "Beauties. I've only two that haven't faded completely. Iron scars last the longest—they can even become permanent if it's just the right temperature when it breaks the skin. But the queen won't let us keep our battle scars. She has the healer cut away the injured flesh so fresh skin will grow in. I had a tattoo on my foot done with a little iron in the ink to make it last. It was to mark my surviving a ten-vampire attack." Kismet pulled her slipper shoe off and extended her leg. She was just like a ballerina, the way she could extend her foot so perfectly. "It's fading," she said. "But not so quickly as it would in the Never." The green-and-gold vines were still a lovely color, but had obviously been more vibrant initially.

"Seelie skin is supposed to be perfect, yeah? So the queen considers it an insult to her kingdom if our bodies hold the marks of war. We're to be pretty as part of our tribute." Kismet bent to put her shoe on.

"But you tattooed your foot. She must not have liked that," I said.

She looked up at me through her lashes, green eyes sparkling. "No, she didn't." A brief smile flashed.

"Did you get in trouble?"

"Aye, I did. But I'm in trouble most of the time these days. At least this was trouble I chose outright. Not trouble I backed into without meaning to."

"What kind of trouble have you gotten into accidentally?"

She waved a hand. "It's all in the past. Nothing to dredge up like the bottom of a ditch. Tell me more about your battles with the rival school. Did they retaliate against you for stealing their dog? And who kept this Barney?"

"Oh, we returned him after the game! We took good care of him, too, while we had him."

"He dined on steak every night, like a canine kingpin. Ate better than we did and knew it. That dog didn't want to go back. Had to drag him out of the truck," Zach said.

I laughed. "It's true. That dog," I said, shaking my head. "First he didn't want to come. Then he didn't want to leave."

"You fed him those sausage dog biscuits you made," Zach said. "That's what did it as much as the steak, I think."

I pulled my jacket tighter around me and leaned closer to the vent blowing heat onto me.

"Are we to be greenhouse flowers?" Kismet said, dropping her sweater on her seat. "I know you're used to hot weather, but this is—"

"Yeah, man. It's gotta be eighty-five in here. Wanna turn the heat down?" Zach, who was down to his T-shirt, said.

Bryn didn't answer.

"It doesn't feel hot to me," I argued. "I'm chilly." I clasped my hands together and put them in my lap, closing my thighs against them to conserve warmth.

"Chilled?" Kismet asked, dropping to her knees in front of me and grabbing my face.

"Actually I feel a little strange. Like we're drifting—"

"Lyons!" Zach yelled.

The tires rammed the curb, and we bounced off, swerving into the opposite lane and then running up onto the grass. The van listed to the right, but didn't tip all the way over. We landed back on all four wheels with a thump and came to a stop.

Mercutio yowled a complaint and then darted forward to look out the front window.

"What happened?" I asked, unbuckling my seat belt. I wobbled, feeling unsteady.

Zach stood next to Bryn's seat. "He's out cold," Zach said, shaking his head.

I put a hand on Bryn's forehead. "Feel his head. Does he seem hot?"

"As a stovetop burner on full. I can feel it from here," Zach said.

Bryn's breathing turned noisy.

"Hey," I said, shaking his shoulders. My own throat ached. I swallowed and grimaced at the pain.

"She hit you both with her spell? That little cream puff! I'll give her a pain in the throat when next our paths cross," Kismet said.

"She did more damage than I thought," I said in a raspy voice.

Kismet clutched her own throat, massaging it. "Why can't I feel this sickness magic? Whenever you're gravely injured I feel it when I try."

"I don't think she hit me with the spell. Bryn and I are

linked magically. When one of us is the victim of injurious magic, the other is affected, too."

"Let me help you," she said, closing her eyes. She'd helped me heal in the past. Both she and Bryn had been able to at different times. It was the way I'd survived several very deadly and damaging attacks. Now, though, I didn't feel better.

"Feel anything?" she asked.

"Nope."

"Me either," she said.

"What happened?" Bryn croaked. His voice sounded like he was part frog.

"You passed out," I said.

"And ran us off the road. Why the hell didn't you say you felt dizzy?" Zach asked, hauling Bryn from the driver's seat.

Bryn glared at Zach, but allowed himself to be helped to the back bench. "I didn't feel dizzy. I felt cold and—"

"But you felt sick, right? You can't tell when you're gonna pass out?"

"Truthfully I . . ." Bryn swallowed with trouble, then continued in a faint rasp. "Can't talk. Just . . . fuck off."

At that, Zach grinned. "Hell, getting a lawyer to shut up? That girl's magic is all right."

Bryn's middle finger popped up.

Zach laughed.

"Leave him alone," I said, giving Zach a shove. "He doesn't need you giving him a hard time when he's sick."

"He's all right," Zach said. "How 'bout you, darlin'?" he asked, turning to Kismet. "You're from these parts. You any good at driving on the wrong side of the road?"

"I don't drive at all. I have a horse, two legs, and a Tube pass."

"Great," Zach said, glancing out the window and looking around. He sat in the driver's seat and fastened his belt. "Better buckle up."

"Hey, Kis, where is your horse?" I asked, sitting next to Bryn.

"Left him on the path. There's nothing for him in Dublin."

"So he'll wait for you, huh?"

"He wanders as he pleases, but though he's a horse, he could be part hound. He finds me wherever I am."

"That sounds like someone I know," I said, glancing at Mercutio, who had come back to the bench seat and pawed Bryn's neck.

"Benvolio chose me for his friend when I was but seven. Everyone wanted him, including a fae knight who keeps all the best horses. Benny was beautiful, but wild. Like me," she said, flashing a smile. "I raced off Magnus Cliff to swim with the selkies, and Ben did too. From a colt he was fearless. And a bit reckless, aye? The queen said he should go to the knight, who'd train him to behave. But he was too wild for the straps they tied him with. He would've hurt himself."

"You let him out?"

"Cut him loose, aye," she said. "They tied him up again, but I taught him how to work the buckle to unhook it. By the time he was a year, none could catch him. And I was the only one he let ride him."

"His full name? Benvolio?" Bryn asked in a strained voice.

"Yes. Why?" she asked.

Bryn smiled, shaking his head. "Half a supernatural world away . . . still connected."

"What do you mean?" I asked.

"Benvolio is a character's name in one of the Bard's plays. We don't like that playwright as much as you do humanside, but we like him well enough," Kismet said.

"Hmm."

"Mercutio. Benvolio. Both Shakespeare characters," Bryn murmured.

"Oh!" I said. "You rest now," I told him, stroking a finger over his temple. He closed his eyes.

"I'll help the cowboy navigate," Kismet said, making me smile. That was what Edie called Zach.

"He's not really a cowboy, you know," I said.

Kismet grinned. "He's like one. With his hat and boots, right? Just as they are in the movies and books."

"Kind of," I said as she moved to the front of the van.

Mercutio sat with Bryn and me. Whenever Bryn woke, I

tried to get him to drink sips of cold water, but by the end he couldn't swallow or talk.

"Will he be cured if we go to the Never? Aunt Mel said witch magic doesn't work there."

"That's true. He might instantly be cured. Or he might die as he tries to cross over. During the transition, the path accelerates life and death for those few seconds. Then everything slows. Some people who are more dead than alive simply drop and fall off the path. How sick is he?" Kismet asked.

I frowned. "Too sick to risk that. We'll have to go to a hospital." I pushed Bryn's black hair back. Heat radiated from his skin. He'd been injured by dangerous magic too many times because of me. But being with me was his choice. And I'd never let bad magic take him. "Zach, you heard me, right? Find a hospital."

"Yeah," he said.

I fidgeted nervously. "Kismet, talk to me. I'm worried. Distract me."

She tilted her head. "What should I talk about?"

"Tell me why the werewolves are after you."

She smiled. "I embarrassed their leader. They think the woods are their territory, but I pass through them when I decide to, even though I've been warned not to. Also, I freed some prisoners and threatened the wolf lord. The pack leader can't afford to be seen as weak. He'll kill me, does he get the chance."

"*If* he gets the chance."

"Aye, if he gets the chance." She snapped her fingers. "Sometimes the old way of talking English comes out. My foster da taught me the English way of talking, but he'd not been humanside in a few hundred years."

"What prisoners did you free? Witches?"

"Nah. I don't care much for witches. A pair of small forest fae. A pair of mixed-breeds—half brownie, half pixie."

"Royal and Shakes?" I asked.

"You know them?" she asked, her brows shooting up.

"They thought I was you. They helped me escape the wolves."

"Ah. Well, the wolves have cause to be angry with that

pair, I guess. They're free fae, those two, but all fae in the isles have to pay a tithe to the Seelie queen. The wolves have antique coins. And those two steal a few each year to pay their tithe. The wolves finally caught them. They had them in a glass case, pinned down with iron pins through the wings and wrists so they couldn't use faery magic to disappear. To pierce a faery's wrist with iron is bad enough, but a pixie's wings are as delicate as spiderwebs. It's a brutal punishment to poke anything through their wings." She frowned. "They aren't mine to protect. Not Seelie. Just minor creatures the queen wouldn't pay for with even copper coin," she said, shrugging. "But they're fae just the same. And only small." She tilted her head. "I'm not a knight, but sometimes I get a notion to protect creatures as can't protect themselves. It's a weakness. Like the heel of Achilles. You'll know that story?"

I nodded. "I have that same Achilles' heel, and there's nothing wrong with us. It's how folks should be. It's the bullies who are in the wrong. You did right saving those little faeries."

She smiled, a little shyly, then shrugged. "We used to be protectors way, way back. The Seelie were. But not anymore." She shook her head. "None can be trusted in the Never. Not now."

"That's maybe true until we get there. But once we're inside, it'll be different. You can trust me. And Momma. Hopefully Caedrin, too. It'll be all right."

"Don't pledge to her. That's the one thing you must not do. You ken?"

I tilted my head. "Ken?"

"Sorry. Do you understand me? Don't pledge your loyalty to the queen. If you do, she'll never let you leave. And she could command you to betray anyone."

My brows shot up. "I won't betray my people for her or anybody. Not ever."

Kismet nodded with a slowly spreading smile. "You're softer than me on the outside. But inside, we're just the same. Don't let her know it. Not till it's too late."

"Too late?" I asked, but Kismet had turned back to face the road and was directing Zach into the Irish town of Killarney.

He found Kerry General Hospital, and we took Bryn to the accident-and-emergency unit. The lady doctor there said Bryn's throat was so infected he needed to stay in the hospital in case he got an abscess that needed surgery. But he agreed only to take a shot of antibiotics, some fluids, and a shot for the swelling and inflammation. He could hardly talk, so he wrote a note saying he wouldn't stay, but would come back if he wasn't better by morning. She argued with him, and both Zach and I thought he should just stay overnight, but Bryn can be really stubborn.

"How come you won't stay?" I said, frowning at him.

He just shook his head.

"Why not?" I demanded.

He wrote, *Don't like hospitals.*

"You don't have to be scared. I'll stay right with you," I said.

That made him smile and put an arm around my shoulders. He gave me a squeeze, but shook his head.

I rolled my eyes at Zach. "He's not staying."

"If he stops breathing from that swollen throat, he'll be sorry there's no professional to make a neat hole in his neck," Zach said. "'Cause if you and I have to do it, it'll be a bloody mess."

"Don't talk like that!" I snapped. "He's not going to need any holes in his neck." I gave Bryn a sideways glance. He couldn't even swallow his own spit at the moment. And when he breathed it caused a whistling sound that made the doctor's hair stand up. My own throat felt tight, too, like something was caught in it. Like it was closing and by morning I wouldn't be able to breathe.

I ran a hand through my hair nervously.

"You heard what that doctor said," Zach said.

"Just hush. His throat doesn't need to get ideas about closing up. He's got medicine now." I frowned at Bryn and whispered, "If your throat tries to choke you, and Zach has to use his pocketknife to save you, I'm gonna be really mad."

Bryn shook his head.

"You'd better be okay. That's all I'm saying."

Bryn pressed a kiss to the side of my head, but I noticed the way he held the rail tight to get down the steps. He was pretty weak. I thought about Kismet saying she'd shoot Poppy if she saw her again. I decided maybe I wouldn't stop her. Poppy wasn't my favorite Conclave member anymore.

WE WENT TO a very nice hotel on the lake. The girl at the front desk was so sweet. Bryn pressed a credit card into my hand and wrote me a note to get three rooms. Normally Bryn takes care of things, but he looked pale and tired when he sat on a bench. And he was still having trouble talking.

I started to get three rooms, but Zach came up behind me and said in his low drawl, "One room. Strength in numbers."

I grimaced, knowing Bryn wouldn't want them in our room, but also knowing Zach was right. And it was only for a few hours. I got a suite with two big beds and a couch. My jaw dropped at the price, but I bit my lip and slid the card across the desk.

"May I see your ID? And can you sign your card, please?"

I pulled the card back to me and flipped it over. I walked to Bryn with a pen. "New card, huh? You forgot to sign the back."

"Your card. You sign," he said, then closed his eyes.

"My . . . " I stared at him. He'd picked this moment to give me the card. A time when he was sick and probably knew I wouldn't argue. Bryn's real rich. And I've told him I don't plan on spending his money. But we kind of disagree about that. He wants me to feel like we're together in every-thing. Only he made all his millions before he met me, so that doesn't exactly seem fair to me. And I don't want people thinking I got together with him for his loot.

"Sneaky timing. You are such a lawyer sometimes," I whispered in my own raspy voice. "We're gonna have a fight about this later. Just so you know."

Bryn gave me a thumbs-up, which struck me as absurd, so

I laughed. He smiled, too, without opening his eyes. I went back to the desk and signed the back and showed my passport and driver's license. The girl checked, and I was authorized to use the account, so she gave me keys with a smile.

I glanced up, right into Zach's shrewd eyes.

"I'm not keeping this card. It's just practical tonight."

"I didn't say a thing."

"But you thought something."

"If you're gonna take his name, might as well take his money and anything else he's got. What's the difference?"

"Here's a key," I said, holding it out.

Zach shook his head and walked to the bench. "Lyons, can you stand or what?"

Bryn shrugged, but opened his eyes and put a hand on the arm of the bench and forced himself up. He stood, steady enough, and nodded.

"Lead the way," Zach said to me. I noticed that he stayed close to Bryn, and I had to give Zach credit. A part of him would've liked to beat Bryn to a pulp for getting engaged to me. But another part of him was man enough to hold back that urge and even put our personal stuff aside while we were facing greater threats.

"I'm proud of you, Zach," I said when we got into the room.

"If I were going to kill your asshole fiancé, do you think I'd let you see me do it?" he asked when Bryn was lying on his back on the bed. Bryn flipped his middle finger up. Presumably it was meant to be directed at Zach, but Zach had moved, so Bryn just flipped off the bathroom door. I didn't tell him.

I got a cool washcloth and put it over Bryn's brows and eyes. I knew to do it because my forehead ached and my eyes burned. When sweat popped up on the back of my neck, at least I knew our fever had broken.

Zach took a pack of cards from his bag, and he and Kismet played poker until Bryn's breathing got easier and he fell asleep. Then Kismet ordered Zach to take the bed, since it was bigger, like him.

On his way to the bed, he stopped by her pack.

"Fancy arrows," he said, peering inside. That made me walk over.

Kismet took out an arrow and handed it to him to examine.

"It's oak with silver wrapping around it and an iron tip," she said.

"What are these symbols?" Zach asked, pointing to the shallow carvings on the shaft near the tip.

"There's a different type of poison painted in each mark. When the arrow enters, the poison mixes with the target's blood and gets absorbed. These arrows will kill witches, banshees, vampires, fae, werewolves, and merrows. There is very little that it won't kill. Only zombies and a few mostly dead creatures wouldn't be felled by this type of arrow from my bow."

She ran a finger along the silver. "My first foster da was a smithy. He made me one hundred of these assassin's arrows. He gifted me the first ten when the queen sent me out on my first mission alone. He said, 'In every battle to the death, may you be the survivor. These are for that . . . to protect your life. Be worthy of them, Kismet. Be deadly, lest you be the one lying dead.'"

She took the arrow and tucked it back into the quiver.

"He must love you a lot," I said.

"No, but I think he's proud of me now. Finally. As a little one I was a burden. Rebellious. He was paid to keep me, but even gold and magic weren't payment enough early on. He tried to get rid of the responsibility. Eventually he did give me away to foster with another. I've laid my head many places."

"He gave you away?" I asked, suddenly furious. "And what were you doing with him, anyway? Why didn't you live with our dad?"

"The golden knight?" She clucked her tongue. "Not good enough for him. He didn't claim me. Never has. Even now that I know who I am to him."

My fists balled. How must Kismet have felt growing up? Unclaimed and unwanted? How could he do that to a little girl? His own flesh and blood!

"He wants only her. Our mother. No one else means

anything to him. Except perhaps the queen. But even that is just duty, I think." She shrugged. "I don't care."

Of course you do, I thought. "Well, I do care. Shame on him. Shame on all of them." I bit down on my lip to keep tears from welling up in my eyes. "You should've been with us," I whispered fiercely.

She smiled. "I've heard tell of the bond between twins. It's why I looked for you. So I wouldn't be alone anymore. So I'd be half of two."

I nodded. "Yep," I said, squeezing her arm. "There are two of us now. For as long as we live."

Her smile faded. "Those that hunt you should be wary. I don't miss my target except by choice. And I'll prize your life above any other."

A shadow passed behind her eyes. I saw the savage child and the cold assassin. I recognized her. Many times when my fae nature had taken over, there had been a cool calculation to it. Its conscience had felt numb and unformed. I saw a glimpse of that remorseless nature in Kismet. She wouldn't protect me out of love. She didn't know me well enough yet to love me. What she knew was that she didn't want to be alone. She would kill to keep the sister she wanted. I shivered, feeling I should explain to her that she'd understand about love eventually, but she walked away. She dropped onto the couch, fluffed the pillow beneath her head, and closed her eyes to sleep. The threats she made didn't trouble her. Would they ever? I hoped so. It would be hard to keep her from killing people if she didn't learn to care about them.

"What do you think, Merc?" I asked softly as he paced the room. I opened the balcony door. "Wanna go have a look around?"

Merc meowed but didn't go out. That made me uneasy. Was he staying close because an outside threat was on its way . . . or did he sense trouble in our midst? Zach and Bryn could certainly end up at each other's throats if they weren't watched. The peace between them wasn't easy by any means. But it was Kismet, willowy and slight on the couch, who worried me the most.

Still, she was my own sister. For better or worse, we were family forever. I bent and kissed her forehead.

Mercutio eyed me curiously.

"So you're gonna stay here, huh?" I ran a hand through my hair. "Wake me then, if there's trouble."

Merc meowed that he would.

I sighed and lay down. I tried to stay awake, but I'd had so little sleep since leaving Duvall that I couldn't.

I don't know how long I was out before Merc's yowl woke me and everyone in the room.

Bryn sat up, his damp hair flat on one side and pushed up on the other. His eyes were unnaturally bright as he looked around.

Mercutio meowed and padded back and forth near the door.

"What?" Zach demanded, putting a hand on his chest over the amulet under his T-shirt.

"You're right, Mercutio. I feel it," Bryn said. His voice had returned to normal strength, though it was still a bit hoarse. He glanced at Zach, then looked at me. "There are at least five wizards. They have the hotel surrounded."

16

I WAS USED to fighting with only Mercutio for company and often against terrible odds. Having a whole group to face the current trouble amazed me. I had a gun and some magic, albeit broken; Zach had a gun and his protective amulet; Bryn can wield his magic as a weapon; and Kismet had her bow and dagger and a wealth of experience.

We divided so that Zach went out the front, Kismet went out the back toward the lake, and Bryn and I took the west side.

The steady drizzle blew against us, drenching our clothes. It was dark enough that I didn't spot Lundqvist, the weather wizard, when we approached him.

Bryn grabbed my arm, and I felt his magic gather and pulse. The blast of magic from Lundqvist seared my skin. It would blister, but the frigid wind and rain took away the burn's bite. Despite his having just been down with fever and dehydration, Bryn's magic was sharp and strong. He flung it at Lundqvist, who scowled and shouted curses and spells.

Bryn defended us with magic, putting up barriers, but the storm fueled Lundqvist, and eventually small cracks in the shield allowed the scalding magic to get through. He'd heated the rain so that it struck like boiling water popping from a pot.

I didn't want to kill Lundqvist, but twice we'd escaped the Conclave operatives, only to have them chase us some more. What if they pursued us right to the Never? Or prevented us from getting inside?

Another bucketful of water without the bucket flew toward us. Bryn flung up an invisible wall of magic, and the water splashed against it, steam rising. Scattered droplets made it through to scald our skin.

Bryn shook his head. "He's feeding off the storm, and I'm not at my strongest. We need cover."

"Take power from me," I said, grabbing his neck and pulling him in for a kiss. Bryn's mouth didn't taste like him. I could still taste infection on his breath, which made me gag. He drew magic into him in a sharp intake and then spun to cast more spells. Under Lundqvist's constant assault, we didn't have much time to smooch so Bryn could draw power.

The flying rain's temperature changed. Instead of heat, Lundqvist worked with the weather. Hail pelted us. One ball of ice struck my skull hard enough to raise a knot on my head.

"Damn it!" I yelled. I dived forward under the edge of Bryn's barrier. Popping up onto one knee, I whipped out my gun and squeezed off two rounds.

Lundqvist yelled and went down. I'd shot in the middle of each thigh. I could tell by his screams that at least one, probably both bullets had broken through bone. He wouldn't be chasing anyone for a while. Midthigh wounds don't usually bleed too much, so hopefully they wouldn't be fatal, no matter how long it took for help to reach him.

"In high winds and near dark, with water and hail making it almost impossible to see, you hit a moving target. Twice." He shook his head. "They talk about training you, Tamara, but why would you need it?"

I smiled. Bryn is impressive, so I love when I impress him.

I grabbed his arm and pulled him in a wide arc so we

could reach the back of the hotel without passing close to Lundqvist, who was casting spells with wild fury.

Bryn licked his lips as we hurried across the grass. "You're a natural with a weapon. I wonder if that's spillover."

I cocked my head. "What do you mean?"

"I think you have some synergy with your sister. Her skills spill over into you."

"Wonder if it'll be the same for her. Imagine if she could make cherries jubilee or a chocolate mocha soufflé without ever reading a recipe. Now, those are skills to be proud of," I said, and winked.

Bryn laughed, but the humor drained away when we spotted a figure down on the ground. She lay about thirty feet in front of half-crumbled rock ruins that edged the lake at the very back of the property.

I spotted Zach, sprinting across the grass. He skidded to a stop on his knees next to her. Bryn and I rushed to them.

Poppy writhed on the ground, mud covered, with an arrow sticking out of her chest just under the collarbone.

"Can't breathe," she said with a breathless gasp.

Zach grabbed the shaft of the arrow and tugged it gently. Poppy screeched.

"Hang on, darlin'," Zach said in a soothing voice. "This thing's poison. It's got to come out." He looked up. "C'mere, Tammy Jo. Hold her arms."

I knelt on the ground and grabbed Poppy's hands. Looking at Bryn, I asked, "Can you do anything? To help ease her pain?"

Bryn glanced around. "We may need the magic I have left."

"For Christ's sake, Lyons!" Zach yelled.

Poppy was whimpering as Zach manipulated the arrow.

"Bryn, we have to help her," I said.

"Healing's not my area of expertise," Bryn said with a grim expression, but he extended a hand and whispered a spell. Warm magic flowed over us, and Poppy seemed to struggle less.

"You can't pull it out toward you. The barbed tip will tear

her flesh and do even more damage," I said. "You'll have to push it out the back first and then cut off the tip."

"Got some experience with arrows?" Zach asked, putting steady pressure on the shaft. Poppy gasped in pain.

"Unfortunately, yeah, I do."

"Hold her," Zach said. With one hand he raised her up and with the other he shoved the arrow through. She screamed as the tip pierced the skin and came out her back.

"Careful of that tip," Bryn cautioned as I tried to break it off.

"Here," Zach said, brushing my hand away. He pulled his magical amulet out from under his shirt. It blazed purple and gold, making me shield my eyes.

Zach held the end of the arrow and brought his knife down against the shaft. After a few moments it cracked. He unwound the silver on the end to get the tip off and then tossed the arrowhead aside.

"Almost there, baby girl. Hang on," Zach whispered.

Poppy braced herself with a hand on the side of Zach's chest.

With a sharp yank, he pulled the arrow out of her chest from the front.

She moaned and fell back to the ground. Zach bent his head and listened against her chest.

"I can't tell if her lung's deflated on the injured side," Zach said.

"I feel cold," she murmured, holding up a hand to block the rain from hitting her face. Blood stained her hand and ran down her arm.

Poppy looked at Zach and said, "You're wounded."

"Just a scratch."

"Can't help myself. Gar, wish I could. Bloody unfair. But can help you," she said. Her lips had taken on a bluish-purple color that could only mean bad things.

"I'm all right. Conserve your strength," Zach said.

"I can do it. Last act ought to be a good one," she said through ragged breaths.

"Hang on. Your magic won't—"

Poppy whispered a spell and the magic burst forth, but it hit the amulet. It sparked and reflected backward onto her. She howled as a blinding light lit the area for a moment, burning our eyes. I fell back, throwing an arm across my face. Finally the magic faded, and Poppy lay still with wide eyes and raised brows.

"I can breathe," she said, surprised. She took a tentative breath, then a deeper one.

"Your spell reflected off his amulet back onto you. It healed your worst injuries," I said.

She felt the wound in her chest. "Gar, that still hurts. But I don't think I'm dying."

"C'mon. Let's get the wounded to the van. We can take them to the hospital," Zach said, picking Poppy up.

"Leave them. Let the hotel call for aid and they can be transported by local emergency services. We need to go," Bryn said.

They argued as I stood. "Where is Kismet?" I asked, looking around. I started toward the trees, but froze when I spotted a pair of glowing eyes. Two werewolves burst from the woods, the smaller one with an off-kilter gait, favoring one side, I realized. I sucked in a breath and raised my gun, but both wolves stopped several feet from me.

They snarled, but didn't attack. My finger trembled against the trigger. I didn't want to shoot unless it was necessary, but they weren't very far from me. If they leapt, a bullet might not stop them in time.

My heart beat loudly in my ears. The larger dark brown wolf's mouth closed. He raised his face and seemed to scent the air. Then he looked up in the direction of the ruins. His head and shoulders turned and he walked away. The other wolf watched the first for a moment but didn't follow. He turned a circle and went back toward the trees, looking over his shoulder twice at me, as though he wanted me to follow.

I glanced back at my group. Poppy stood with Bryn and Zach. They were deep in discussion. I inched forward to the forest's edge.

The wolf's body was obscured by a tree when he shifted.

A moment later he stepped forward with some scattered bushes between us. It was the man who'd been gravely injured in the Scottish woods.

I smiled when I saw him. "You made it."

He nodded.

"I'm glad."

"My family was as well," he said in that rumbling accent. "She's your sister? Or cousin?"

"Who?"

"The archer. The fae girl."

I nodded. "We just met each other, but yes. She's my family."

"She's done things. You don't—"

A short howl made us both turn toward the ruins. I wasn't sure what the structure had originally been. Some small primitive dwelling? The dark gray stone walls stood, but there was no roof anymore.

The dark brown wolf walked along the top toward—

I gasped.

Kismet lay on the wall, her hair and leg dangling over the blocks of stone. My breath caught, coming to an abrupt halt.

My feet understood before my mind, because even as I wondered whether she was dead, my legs carried me to the wall. He howled, and I opened my mouth to scream, but he didn't pounce on her.

She'd been still as a statue, but in an instant her arms came up and a nocked arrow pointed at the wolf's neck.

He reared up and transformed, shifting from animal to man within a haze of shadow. He threw his arms wide, his chest exposed.

"Go ahead," he growled, his voice guttural, as if the animal still reigned in his throat.

Her arms were as steady as oak branches on a still day. Water pelted her skin and dripped from her, running in rivulets down the stone.

"Don't cower from it. Kill me outright," he yelled, his voice as powerful as the storm.

Her lips curved. "If it's death you're after, come and get it."

He crouched, and my breath caught again.

Zach raised his gun and Bryn a hand, but no one moved except the young man. His shoulder-length hair fell forward as he leaned over her. The tip of her arrow pressed against his chest as he spoke to her. He'd lowered his voice, so we couldn't hear what he said.

Her eyes never left his face. "Then run," she said, her voice cool as the drizzling rain.

He pushed the bow aside and lowered his head farther. I thought he would kiss her. That's what it seemed he would do . . . bring their bodies together. But his nose pressed against the fabric of her shirt and nuzzled her skin. When he lifted his face, darkness stained it.

Blood!

"She's hurt! Bryn!" I called, running to the ruins.

The walls were slick. I tried to climb, but slipped and landed hard on the ground, my knees thumping and sinking into muddy earth.

I yanked off my shoes and dug my fingers and toes into the cracks. I fell a second time before I managed to scale the wall. The wolf man turned. He was tall, well over six feet. His eyes scanned my face; then he turned and stepped off the wall. He dropped with almost no sound into the wreck of an enclosure. I glanced down. He shifted into a wolf and bolted out.

I crawled to her. "Kis, how bad are you hurt?"

"Bad enough," she said, tilting her face to the sky and closing her eyes against the falling rain.

I crawled forward as the wolf had done. I lifted her shirt and gasped. There was a jagged gash where the skin had been torn open. I could see a marble-white rib between lines of muscle.

"Oh, my God! Oh, no!"

"Go away," she said, giving my shoulder a shove.

"We'll get you down." I turned and yelled to Bryn and Zach, "She's badly hurt. I'm going to help her slide over the edge. Zach, you have to catch her. Bryn, use your magic to slow her fall. Get ready!" I said. Each of her legs dangled on a different side of the wall. I grabbed the one hanging down the inner wall and lifted it. She kicked me. Not hard, but I was so startled I fell backward, nearly toppling off the wall.

"I said leave me alone," she snapped.

I sat up, holding the slick stones to steady myself.

"What are you talking about? I'm not leaving you. I have to help you get down so we can take you to the hospital."

"I don't need your help, which is a lucky thing for me."

"What's wrong?" I asked, leaning toward her. "Why are you acting like this?"

"While I lay here bleeding, you tended the witch who gave me my wounds. You walked away with a wolf to the woods."

"I didn't know you were hurt."

"Exactly."

"You could have called out. I didn't see you."

"You didn't try to. After all the times I reached for you across the miles and helped you tap fae power to heal. After the times when your magic was drained away, leaving you empty and I filled you with half my spirit. Could you not seek to help me first just once?"

She held her side and sat up. We faced each other. "You're no different than the rest of them." She swung her leg over so she faced the inside of the enclosure. She looked back at my face for a moment, then said, "If I'm nothing special to you, then you're nothing special to me either."

I opened my mouth, but she slid off the wall and dropped down. She landed on the mud with a grunt of pain.

"Kismet, wait!" I said, but she strode to her wet pack, which lay in the corner. She grabbed it and climbed out of the ruins. "Kis!"

She didn't answer or even look back.

17

AFTER I GOT down from the wall, I searched for Kismet, calling her name in the darkness until Zach picked me up and carried me back to the hotel by force.

Poppy tried to argue in her cockney accent, which I learned is a kind of English hillbilly accent, that she'd caught us and that we'd have to come with her. She claimed she was in charge because she could cast the most dangerous spells. I was so mad about her giving Bryn the throat infection and hurting Kismet and being the cause of the rift between Kismet and me that I told her that if she tried to cast a spell, I'd sock her in the nose and then shoot her in the legs so she couldn't chase us anymore.

She'd seen Lundqvist, so I suppose she knew I was serious. But I also suspected that it was Zach telling her he'd take offense if she tried to cast spells on us again that really kept her from getting aggressive.

Zach wrapped Lundqvist in a carpet, and we took him to the hospital. There were two dead wizards, one courtesy of the wolves, from the look of his torn flesh, and one who'd died of blood loss from a dagger slice through his left groin artery, which was probably Kismet's work.

We found Kato in a coma with one of Kismet's arrows next to him. He'd been shot through his spell-casting arm. It wouldn't have been too bad a wound if the arrow had been removed properly, but he'd torn it out, leaving a lot of damage. Also, I guess he'd absorbed too much of the poison, since he ended up in that coma. We dropped him at the hospital, too.

Lundqvist played dirty by hollering that we'd attacked him. We got out fast, with Bryn casting a spell to short out the security cameras. I hoped it had worked. I sure didn't want to be on any of Ireland's most-wanted lists.

"That Lundqvist isn't much of a spy, yelling like that. What's he going to say? That we were trying to mug him? He'll have to make a report. It's kind of crazy to try to get us detained that way," I said.

"We heard a rumor that you were planning to go underground," Poppy said. She'd fully recovered and followed us out of the hospital, threatening us with another toxic spell if we didn't give her a ride back to the hotel. Rather than have a scene in the parking lot when we were trying to leave quickly, we'd brought her along.

In the van, she rummaged around and started to unzip a suitcase, saying, "Do you have any biscuits? Spelling like that leaves me starving!"

"Biscuits? Those would be all crumbled and dried out by now," I said.

"By biscuits she means cookies," Bryn said.

"Why didn't she say cookies then?" I asked. "There are no cookies. Get out of our bags," I said, giving her a shove. I couldn't believe the nerve of the woman.

She shrugged, completely oblivious. I was going to knock her over the head the first chance I got.

"Sun's up. Now it'll be easier to follow Kismet's footprints to find her," I said to Bryn.

Zach and Bryn exchanged looks, but didn't say a word. Poppy found some Hershey's minatures that had fallen out of my purse. She unwrapped them and swallowed a mouthful of chocolate. "Any wine to go with the chocolate?"

Wine at dawn?

"Nope," I said. "Bryn, we have to look for Kismet. She might be waiting to see how long I search. And we need her, remember?"

"Need her for what? And who is this Kismet? A witch from America? We've not heard about her before. And what's she doing shooting arrows? Some kind of Yank fad?" Poppy huffed a sigh at our silence. "Come on. You know I'm going to find out."

"You want more chocolate?" I asked, to distract Poppy. I wouldn't mention Kismet again in front of her. I was just so worried about Kis that I couldn't stop thinking about finding her.

"No, but we could duck into a market for a bottle of dry merlot."

"Um, you're from England, right?"

"Right," she said.

"So this is morning time where you live, right?"

She laughed, tossing her head back so her fuzzy ringlets danced. "Gar, do you really think I'd hold with convention after the night we've just had? I'm bloody Conclave! You're American outlaws. And we all could've died last night. If we want chocolates and wine for breakfast, that's what we'll bloody well have. Come on; let's just get pissed. It'll give your friend a chance to cool off and come back. And if we have to fight, we can always do that later in the day. Let's say noon or half past two."

Even though I wanted to throttle Poppy, that almost made me smile. Despite the fact that we'd had a terrible fight the night before, she didn't see us as enemies. She was just doing her job. "Um, how long have you been working for WAM?"

She grinned. "Not long enough for them to have cut off my bollocks, if I had them, which I don't. Though he's welcome to check me for them," she said with a wink at Zach.

"No checking necessary, darlin'," Zach said. "You're about as female as they come."

Her smile widened. "Certainly got a nice pair, haven't I?" she asked, thrusting up her giant boobs.

Good grief.

I glanced at Bryn, who rolled his eyes.

When we got back to the hotel, Zach said, "You guys check out back for our girl who's gone missing. I'll come down and help you look in a little while. I'm gonna take a shower to wash my cuts. You need to do the same," Zach told Poppy.

"I do," she agreed. "Though I'm not sure I can reach the one on my back."

Zach smiled. "If you need a hand, all you have to do is ask."

She beamed and wiggled her way down the hall.

Bryn turned and led me toward the stairs. "If he's planning to cuff her to something, he'd better be ready with more than his charming-country-boy routine. She fell for that once. No Conclave operative would fall for it twice," Bryn said.

"If he's planning to handcuff her to something, I don't suppose he'll give her a choice about it. He'll just outmuscle her."

"She packs quite a punch with her magic."

"His amulet didn't seem to have too much trouble deflecting it."

"Let's hope he's smart enough to keep it on."

I scowled. There was no way Zach was going to strip down and fall into bed with a foreign witch, no matter how big her boobs were.

At least, he'd better not.

THE DAY BLOSSOMED clear and cold. The soggy ground didn't show many tracks; it just hardened and crunched beneath our feet. We explored the grounds and a little part of the woods, but there was no sign of Kismet. I made sure to scan the tops of the trees in case she was up in one of them waiting for me to find her. No such luck.

In the woods where the ground had been protected by the tree canopy, we came across wolf tracks leading away from the hotel and followed them for a while, but for all we knew they'd lead all the way back to Scotland, so we eventually stopped and doubled back.

Zach waited for us. He rubbed his left arm and I raised my brows.

"You okay?"

"Right as rain. Any sign of Kismet?"

"Nope."

"So now what?" Zach asked.

"Let's go to the Gap," Bryn said. "There's supposed to be a faery gate within it. Either she'll be waiting for us there or she won't, but no matter what, we're going in, right?" Bryn asked me.

I sighed and nodded. "I really want to find her, though. Not just so she can come with us, but also because I want to prove that I haven't given up looking. She thinks I don't care."

"She was too quick to jump to that conclusion," Zach said. "I'm not sure you're the one who should have something to prove. Seems to me she owes you an apology, not the other way around."

"Agreed," Bryn said.

I held out my hands to ward off any more advice. "It's sure nice of you both to side with me. But I'm not the person who needs people on her side right now."

"Tamara—" Bryn said, shaking his head. "You may not be able to fix what's broken with her."

"She's not broken. She's just lonely. And that I can fix."

Zach took a deep breath and gave Bryn a look that said, *I'm glad Tammy Jo's your problem now. Good luck with that.*

Bryn put an arm around my shoulders and gave me a squeeze. "Let's go into the park. Maybe she's waiting for you there."

18

FINDING A FAERY path is tricky, even for me, who's part faery. I had Bryn draw off some of my witch magic to make me more fae. That was always a dicey proposition, though, because when I'm more fae, I don't have as many feelings. I thought about what Kismet had said the night before. She'd said when I was drained of magic, she'd sent me part of herself. Was that why I lacked feelings? Because she had gotten so numb to them? Now that she wasn't trying to connect with me, would I just be myself when drained? Or a shell of myself?

As we walked toward the entry to Killarney National Park's Gap of Dunloe, I held tight to Bryn's hand. He gave me the kiss I asked for and drew my magic into him.

I lost my breath for a second, but then eased against him. He was well again and tasted delicious: warm toffee with a hint of salted caramel.

Zach walked ahead and stopped next to a four-seat open carriage with a horse attached. When Bryn and I reached it, he'd made the arrangements for our passage.

The horse was initially skittish about Mercutio joining

us, but settled down when Merc, who was pretty sleepy, ignored him.

A horse-drawn cart that takes people through the Gap is called a jarvey. I liked that name and it seemed to fit, being a jaunty little vehicle. Because it was cold, the driver, a deeply suntanned lady with a cute accent, put a smelly horse blanket over our legs.

I noticed Zach was still rubbing his arm. "What did Poppy do to you?" I whispered.

Zach smiled. "She got a couple good licks in. Managed to nearly twist the amulet off my neck. When that didn't work, she blocked it with a pillow, and then she hit me with a spell hot enough to burn my skin," he whispered back.

"Gotta be careful of strange witches."

"Careful doesn't always do much good. She's a real fire-cracker," he said with a smile that made me frown. Zach might not be mine anymore, but our breakup wasn't ancient history either.

We moved along at a slow pace, which was helpful. It meant I could look for Kismet and also try to catch a glimpse of the entry to the Never.

"Where are your cameras?" the driver asked.

"Um, we're just going to use our phones," I said, giving Bryn's foot a subtle kick.

"I've got a lot of pictures of the Gap from prior trips," he told the lady, letting his accent come out strong. "I told her to just enjoy the view."

The lady launched into a lot of questions for Bryn about where he was from, how long he'd lived in America, and what it was like. She was so friendly she would've fit right in in Duvall. I told her so, which made her laugh.

When we wound around a particular bend in the road, I spotted a shimmer and caught the scent of something famil-iar . . . honey, dandelions, and apples.

The tip of my nose was half-frozen from cold, so I was impressed I could still sniff out anything useful.

I leaned close to Bryn. "I think I found it. We should get out of the carriage here."

Bryn paid the driver. We'd told her earlier that we would pay the full fare, but would be traveling only partway in the cart. We said we wanted to do some walking and hiking. We had backpacks with us, so we looked the part.

I wondered if she thought we were crazy. Both Zach and I were shivering almost uncontrollably. It was probably obvious that we would've preferred to stay huddled together under the moldy blanket.

Even though Bryn had lived for years in Texas, he was oblivious to the cold, and hopped down as if he'd just had a refreshing mojito.

We waved to the driver, who was all smiles after her big tip. She headed back toward the front of the park, where she'd probably have time to get another group of travelers and double her money for the day.

We waited until we were alone on the road and then I waved stiff fingers for the guys to follow me. The terrain was rocky, but covered with vegetation. I jumped over a stream that was burbling past. The weight of my pack nearly toppled me over, but Bryn's hand steadied me.

Mercutio explored the nooks around the rocks, but stopped when I said, "Here."

A small circular patch of grass tucked between a pair of big sharp slate-colored rocks shone a little brighter in the sunlight than the grass around it.

I slid down between the rocks and rested my boots on the center of the spot. Though it felt vaguely familiar, it didn't open a path to anywhere.

I leaned against a rock so I could lift one leg to get to my foot. I hated to do it in the cold, but I pulled off my boot and my sock. I lowered my foot to the grass, which felt as soft as moss. A tingle started against the sole of my foot and spread up my leg.

"Yeah," I said, exhaling an excited breath. I quickly pulled off my other boot and sock and stood in the circle. The smell of heather and honey wafted toward me. I crouched down and knelt like a runner about to spring from the blocks. I rested my palms on the grass, and the green ripened to a summer color. Soft light streamed like water, curving around rocks and over fallen trees.

Home, I thought. That's the way it felt to be on the path.

Mercutio yowled, backing away, but Zach scooped him up. Merc twisted, snagging Zach's jacket, but Zach held fast to him.

"C'mon, wildcat. You're not gonna let her go alone, are ya?" Zach demanded.

Mercutio settled, but remained stiff, like a coiled spring. Zach swung his legs over and landed in the hollow between the rocks. He looked around.

"Feel the difference?" I asked.

"No."

"This way."

"You forgot your boots," Zach said, grabbing them from their place next to one of the rocks.

"I don't need them."

"You damn well might. It's colder than hell out here."

For the first time all morning, I'd forgotten about the cold. The goose bumps on my arms were from exhilaration, not the winter's bite.

"See?" Zach demanded as snow began to fall on either side of the path.

"Yeah, but do you see how it doesn't blow onto the path?" I said, moving forward, weaving around the rocks and over bumpy ground.

"What are you talking about?" Zach asked, his breath still fogging the air when I looked over my shoulder.

Bryn stood behind him in the circle.

"Bryn, do you feel the difference?"

"I think so," Bryn said, looking around. "It's a little brighter and a little warmer in this spot."

I nodded, smiling. "Exactly."

Zach reached down and brought his hand up. His open palm was dusted with snow until it melted. "How is this spot warmer?" he demanded. "It's snowy."

Uh-oh. "I don't know if we're going to be able to get you inside. Maybe you're not on the path," I said.

"I'm standing right here," Zach argued.

"Um, maybe so. Maybe not."

He scowled.

"Let's get going, Tamara. We don't want to be seen," Bryn said.

"Why not?" Zach asked.

"Because we don't want hikers to think this is a path they should explore. What if they followed us? Or what if Poppy or some other Association witches are tracking us? The fae won't appreciate our leading others to their gate. The paths are kept hidden for a reason."

I turned and hurried onward. I crossed a stream, climbed over a rock, and dropped to the grass, feeling the path dip sharply. A warm breeze rose up to greet me, smelling of honeysuckle and baking bread. I raced down the slope. At the bottom there were wildflowers as tall as me.

They swayed and parted.

"We're almost there!" I called, then burst into laughter. I tripped and rolled through a patch of dandelions and daisies. Sprawled in front of a trellis of twisted vines, I stared up at an archway of roses.

I inched my foot into the opening. Petals rained down, shimmering pink, purple, and red. I rose and stepped inside. The scent of a thousand roses surrounded me, more petals falling like snow. Warm wind and beams of sunshine came through the lattice of the vines.

I skipped forward to the end, and there was a wall of trees as far as I could see in either direction. Their crossed branches blocked the center of the path, and there was a gold lock hanging from a branch.

"I'll be damned," Zach said.

I looked over my shoulder to find my three companions standing just behind me.

"Did you see the rose petals?" I asked.

"Kind of hard to miss them. It was like a rose storm. Couldn't even see where I was going." Zach rubbed his wrist, coming away with blood.

"What happened?" I asked.

"Got sliced by the business end of some long stems."

"Thorns?" I said, surprised.

"All those swinging flowers. Not like we could avoid it."

The flowers, of course, had not even swayed across my path. They knew me for fae, I thought with a ripple of pleasure.

"Easier to pass if you're part fae, I guess," Zach said. He looked past me at the trees. "How are we going to get through?"

"I have to open the lock."

"What lock?" Zach asked.

The sun shone brightly as it reflected off the lock, making my eyes sting. How was it possible that he couldn't see it? The longer I stood there, the harder it was to look at anything else.

The trees whispered, "Sing with me and find the key."

"What do I sing?" I asked.

"What?" Zach asked.

"Don't talk," Bryn said.

"She asked a question."

"She's not talking to us. Be quiet so she can listen to the trees."

"The trees," Zach muttered, but then he closed his mouth.

"Sing with me. Find the key," they said.

"Sing anything?" I asked. "Even a country song? From America?"

They didn't answer.

"It'll have to be that, I guess. Those are the songs I know." I cleared my throat, closing my eyes before the light practically blinded me. "I'm not the best singer. Just so you know. But if you really want me to sing, okay." I hummed an old song I hadn't heard in years—"Wide Open Spaces" by the Dixie Chicks.

The trees hummed, too.

"Hey! How do Irish trees know the Dixie Chicks' music?" I asked, and laughed. I started at the beginning, my voice rising as I sang, "She needs wide open spaces! Room to make a big mistake!" I twirled in circles, fresh air rushing around me.

When I finished the last chorus, I fell over laughing from so much spinning.

Music echoed in my ears, and when I opened my eyes at last, a pinkish-gold key dangled above my face. I plucked it from the branch that held it out to me.

"Thank you very much," I said, touching my finger to the tip of the branch. "And thanks for the backup music." I rolled onto my side and got up, clutching the key to me. I wobbled on unsteady legs to the lock. I squinted, humming "Cowboy Take Me Away." I held the lock and pushed the key into it.

I sang softly as I turned the key. With a loud creak the branches swung up. Sunshine spilled out, drenching us in light and warmth.

"How 'bout that? It's summertime!" I hopped forward like a rabbit. Then I threw my arms wide and spun in a circle. "Hello, faery world! Welcome home, Tammy Jo!" I sang some more, then fell over, giggling so hard my eyes watered.

"Hell," Zach said, then laughed. "Haven't seen her this drunk since she polished off most of a bottle of champagne the first New Year's Eve we were married."

"Kismet," someone said. I barely heard the voice over the music ringing in my ears. "Kismet, what are you doing here?"

19

I SHIELDED MY eyes and turned my head toward the voice. He looked like a column of sunshine. He came slowly into focus.

Oh, my gosh!

His skin was lightly tanned to a tawny golden brown that was just the color my own turned. And his eyes . . . I'd gotten his eyes, both the shape and the color.

He cocked his head. "Your hair . . . this is the darkest red it's ever turned."

I stared at his face, which was really handsome and very young. He looked my own age.

"Your eyes are changed." He pushed his hair back from his forehead as if to see me better. Then he tucked a longer strand behind his ear. That was familiar, too. It was a gesture I made a lot.

He lowered his voice, glancing around as if the trees might be listening. Maybe they were. "Are you my human daughter?"

I smiled. *This is him. Caedrin!*

He smiled back and put a hand out. He had long fingers. Kismet had gotten his hands. I had gotten human hands from Momma. His fingers brushed the hair back from my face. "I have wanted to meet you for such a long time. You got Marlee's hair. Very dark red. If you stayed here for long, it would fade. Your fae sister's hair darkens when she's humanside for weeks. Where is she? I can't believe she allowed you to come alone. Or at all." He looked up and around.

"I had to come," I said, sitting up.

"No, you didn't. It's fortunate I'm the one who found you. I've been monitoring the gate she likes to use. I hoped to talk with her. You'll go back the way you came before you're seen."

"How can I go? Crux said if I didn't come, they'd execute Momma."

"Crux said that?" He scowled. "He overstepped. Badly." He looked at Zach and Bryn, then back at me. "Where is Crux? Still pursuing Kismet?"

"No. Well, I don't know. Maybe. We sort of trapped him to give ourselves a head start. She was going to come back. On her own terms. But she got angry."

"As she often does." The fingers of his outstretched hand moved, beckoning me. I set my hand in his, and he closed his around it. "You managed to trap Crux? Would that I had been there to see that," he said with a smirk.

"Is Momma in trouble?"

His smile faded. "I know her mind well on certain subjects. And one is that she would not want you here under any circumstances."

"But Crux said the queen expects me to come, or she'll retaliate. He said you and Momma are in trouble for helping Kismet leave the Never, and that Ghislaine will hurt Momma."

"He overstated things. The queen knows nothing of you, and I endeavor to keep it that way. Come," he said, waving Bryn and Zach along with us as he led me toward the branches that had crisscrossed again to block the exit. "I won't say I'm sorry you came, because I've wished to meet you for a long time. For the whole of your life, truth be told. But this is no place for you. Especially now."

We stood in front of the wall of trees. He raised my hand and touched it to his jaw, then released it.

"I wish you wind at your back, and the speed of sunlight."

I smiled. "It was really nice to meet you. And you're sure you guys will be okay if I go? You and Momma?"

"If you stayed, it would provide no advantage to us. It would only create more risk."

"What about Kismet? Do you need her to come back?"

He took a deep breath and then exhaled. "Don't concern yourself. Live happily."

"I won't be able to be happy if I'm worried about you guys or her."

"Wind at your back," he said with a gesture to the branch gate.

I glanced at it. "We'll go for now. Where's the lock?" I asked.

He shoved a hand through his hair, tucking some of it back. "I can't see the lock. Full fae won't see it. We can't get out easily because of the magic on the other side of the gate. But you should be able to see the latch, whatever it is. Sometimes it's a lock and key. Sometimes it's a bolt or lever. The look of the magical latch changes. But if you search for it, you'll see it. You've the special skill because of your mixed blood."

I turned and looked at the gate. "On the outside, I saw the lock to get in. But there's no lock here."

"Look carefully," he said.

I walked along the branches, running my fingers over them. "Hey, there, trees. I'd like to leave. Need me to sing?"

The trees didn't answer. I listened hard. With concentration I could hear the wildflowers sway in the breeze, and voices and laughter in the distance, and ringing bells.

I narrowed my eyes, following the patterns of the interwoven limbs. I shook my head. "There's no latch."

Caedrin put his palms on a tree trunk and whispered. He paused and then cocked his head. "Come with me now," he said, turning and striding away from the trees. "She's had them block Kismet's exit after entry. Our lady Highness didn't want Kis to be able to turn and bolt out. She'd assumed that Crux would be dragging her through the gate. The exit will reappear, but I don't know when. Colis has silenced the trees so we can't ask."

We had to jog to keep up with him. He ducked into a field

of sunflowers. We threaded through it. Music and voices became louder as we progressed.

"This way," he said, cutting away from the sounds of celebration. "Wait—" Caedrin held out a hand and made a motion for us to crouch. Zach and I dropped down with Caedrin, but Bryn remained standing.

I grabbed his arm and pulled. He hesitated, and time slowed even though my heart raced. The sun gleamed off his hair. He seemed even taller and stronger than usual. And yet I felt the urge to protect him since we were underhill and he'd come because of me. Actually, if I were being honest, it went farther back than our arrival in the Never. He'd saved my life often enough, and I'd saved his. But of the two of us, I healed more quickly. And that knowledge, plus the fact that I loved him, made me want to get between him and danger.

My grip on his arm tightened until I knew I might leave a mark. Then I jerked. He bent down near me.

"What's wrong?" I asked.

He put his mouth near my ear and whispered, "The sea is calling me."

My brows rose. We'd believed for a long time that Bryn was part fae, one quarter selkie, but there had never been proof. Excitement made my heart race faster. Despite the fact that I didn't want him recklessly ignoring a warning from Caedrin, I was thrilled that the evidence of his fae nature might show itself.

"Do you hear the water?" Bryn asked, his eyes sparkling like the blue Caribbean Sea that I'd only ever seen in pictures. Bryn's eyes were usually cobalt or sapphire blue, but now they were blue-green. His gaze wasn't on me, but was turned to stare out into a distance beyond what I could see.

"What does the sea sound like?" I asked. "And what's it saying to you?"

Caedrin put his palm over his mouth to signal us to be quiet. I covered my mouth with one hand and Bryn's lips with the other.

Caedrin turned and moved back the way we'd come.

I'd have thought that a crawling man would look weakened,

brought to his knees, but not so in the case of a golden faery knight. It might have been the long reach of Caedrin's arms and the way his broad shoulders dipped. He didn't move like a man. He moved like a lion, as though made to stalk and hunt through tall grass. He paused and then sprang forward.

There was a yelp and a thud that happened almost simultaneously. Grass swayed as someone thrashed.

"Do you think it's wise to mirror my steps? Am I prey?" Caedrin's voice demanded.

"Dude!" a young voice said. "Get off me. Is she here? I heard she's here."

I crawled, though not with the feline elegance of my dad. Or sister. Or an ocelot. I peeked through the tall grass.

Caedrin's forearm pressed against the throat of a young man with strands of blond dreadlocks with actual gold dusted on them. There were vine tattoos on his neck, and he wore a vintage Rolling Stones T-shirt.

"Listen, dude, I didn't know it was you! Colis asked me to watch the wall. The trees said someone came in from outside. I thought it was our fleet-footed traitor. I wanted to talk to her."

"Who says she's a traitor? That's not been proven."

"She left without an order. She snuck out."

The pressure of Caedrin's arm increased, making the young man's face redden.

"Dude, it's what we heard," he rasped.

"Stop calling me *dude*. You've never been humanside. Last I was out there, I didn't hear a single person call another dude. Be on your way," Caedrin said, giving the guy a shove.

The faery rubbed his throat. Caedrin reached out and grabbed the guy's skin and pulled. The tattoo—or what I'd thought was a tattoo—peeled away like plastic, leaving a pinkish mark, which quickly faded.

"Hey!" the guy cried. "I paid a hundred seeds for that."

"Go," Caedrin said with an impatient jerk of his head. "Don't follow me again."

The dreadlocked stranger rose. He was taller than I'd thought, perhaps six feet.

"I didn't know I was following you. I thought it was her."

"More foolish that," Caedrin said. "Who has a more impulsive temper? She or I?"

"Her for sure, but she and I aren't enemies. She brings me shirts," he said, flicking a finger against his T-shirt. "And I give her Oz art to sell and trade out there. This time she's paying me for a special order and—"

"I'm not interested. But I warn you to be careful if you do see her," Caedrin said. He was a couple inches taller than the guy, and broader across the shoulders. "If she thought herself labeled a traitor, and someone tried to corner her so that she might be captured and punished, then she might kill. Humanside, they try to take her every time she goes out. Escape is instinct, like taking a breath. Don't doubt it."

"I wouldn't be fool enough to try to restrain her," the young man said before he bolted through the grass.

Caedrin waited for several long moments, watching the other faery disappear.

"They know you're here, but think it's Kismet. They'll be careful about whom they send to find her, but Our lady Highness won't hesitate to send a force. We must get you out quickly."

Zach stood and so did Bryn, but I didn't move. I stayed kneeling, looking down at the shoots of grass rising from the ground. Kismet had been willing at first to come back into the Never. Had she known they were calling her a traitor? What did the queen really have in mind for Kis when she returned? If Crux had lied about the queen wanting me to come to the Never, what else had he lied about? Had he lied about the queen's promise not to punish Kis when she returned?

For the first time since Kismet had left, I was glad she had.

"Come," Caedrin said.

Mercutio pressed his head against the side of my leg. I didn't know what he thought of the Never, but he clearly wanted me to get a move on. I got to my feet and we all marched through the grass.

20

WE EACH WANTED something different. My stomach had begun to growl, and I started to mention being hungry every few minutes. Bryn asked several times how far it was to the ocean and whether we could pass by it on the way to the next exit. Zach was interested in the queen's castle. We'd seen it in the distance. It was covered in rose gold and trimmed in pale yellow and salmon pink, and studded with pink quartz and pearls. Zach tried to steer us that way, asking about exits near it and suggesting that no one would expect Kismet to head toward it. Mercutio wanted to wander, and twice Caedrin retrieved him and told me to hook a leash to his collar.

"Um, that collar's for decoration only. It's like a necklace."

"Or it could be a collar that functions as a collar," Caedrin said impatiently. "You put it on him."

"No, I didn't. He had it on when I met him."

"When you found him and took him as a pet," Caedrin said.

"When I met him and became his friend," I corrected. "He's never acted like he wants the collar off, but if he did, I'd take it off him."

"You'd take it off him because he can't take it off himself. Because he's an animal. He can be a pet or livestock or an exhibit in a menagerie—"

"If someone put me in handcuffs, I might not be able to get them off myself. That wouldn't make me anybody's pet."

Bryn smirked. "That cat's as smart as a person. Smarter than some."

"Yep," I said.

Caedrin glanced at Mercutio, who didn't seem to take offense at the conversation. I was never sure how much Merc understood of human conversation, but I was convinced he understood some. In fact, he understood phrases in both English and Spanish, which was one more language than I was fluent in.

"There are no cats like him in the Never. We had a zebra-tiger once—" Caedrin said.

"Zebra-tiger?" I asked.

"Zebra colored," he said.

"A white tiger with black stripes?" Bryn asked.

"Yes, like the exotic horses that are black and white. They're called zebras and they—"

"We know what zebras are," Bryn said.

"What happened to the tiger?" I asked.

"It broke free of its cage and killed a hundred livestock. We have no more bison. It's hard to bring animals in. So cats are banned, because they are always predators."

"No cats at all in the Never? Not even a few tabby cats?"

"Not now. Not for years."

My stomach rumbled. "I'm really hungry. Mercutio probably is by now, too. If it's not safe for him to hunt, then we'd better get him some meat to eat soon."

"There's no meat where I'm taking you. He'll have to wait until he's humanside to eat."

I frowned. "Well, let's hurry then."

THE SECOND EXIT was closed, too. Caedrin had been worried about the trees talking to the tree keeper about us, so he'd taken us to a gate of iron. It made my skin break out when I got close, but I saw the key, and Zach had no trouble with iron, so he climbed up the rock wall to fetch the key from the hook it hung from. When he climbed to the lock, however, he shook his head.

"What?" I demanded. "It's a lock. I can see that even from here."

"Yeah, but there's a problem you obviously can't see," Zach said. He turned it one way and then the other. "There's no keyhole."

"That's not possible!" Caedrin yelled. "None could get close enough to damage the lock. How—"

"It looks like someone poured molten metal into the lock, and it cooled and hardened."

Caedrin put a hand to his forehead, which made him look entirely human for a moment. "Someone used an endless flame to make the tip of an arrow turn molten. When the wood finally burned away, the shaft would drop and be extinguished. Clever."

Zach swung down so he dangled, then dropped to the ground. He walked along the gate and then crouched, touching a bald spot on the earth where there was no grass. "Sounds about right. There's a charred spot here and some ash and dots of metal."

"I'm so hungry," I said, chewing on the inside of my cheek. Merc paced, too, in circles.

"I'm pretty hungry myself," Bryn said. "We could fish."

"Yeah, we've gotta eat," Zach said. "It's something about this place, isn't it? For the past half hour, food's practically all I can think about."

"It's the smell of food from the festival," Caedrin said. "The spices enlarge the appetite so the celebration feast will be grander and more satisfying."

"Do they have meat there?" I said, bending to give Mercutio a hug when he looked like he might bolt away. "We have to give Mercutio something to eat or he's going to go hunting for it himself."

Caedrin rubbed his chin. "I'll have to get it from the castle. It's the only place I have access to meat that won't be missed."

"Great. Let's go," Zach said.

"You're not coming. None of you can be seen." He tucked a strand of gold hair behind his ear and nodded, mostly it seemed to agree with himself. "I'll see what can be learned about where the open exits out of the Never are. There will be gossip. Some of it will be reliable."

"Faeries gossip?" I asked.

"For many it's a great talent," he said with a rueful smile.

"This place will feel just like home," I said, exchanging a look with Bryn and Zach.

We walked down a dirt trail that was three feet wide and shouldered on each side by wildflowers taller than me. A clearing popped up, and in its center was a small house.

I cocked my head and asked, "Is that . . . ?"

"Gingerbread?" Bryn said.

"It is. Our Highness likes the human faery stories. There are little tributes here and there created for her pleasure."

Merc sprinted forward and licked a swirl of white trim that looked like icing.

"Is that frosting?" I asked, hurrying over for a closer look.

"Don't eat the house," Caedrin said when I pinched off a tiny piece to taste.

"Right, sweetheart. Don't eat that. It's been exposed to the elements."

I rubbed my fingers together and dropped the crumbs, but bent my head and touched my finger to my tongue. Definitely gingerbread!

"What are the roof shingles made of?" Zach asked.

We all looked up. There were small rounded shingles in red or green.

"Apple skins. They used frosting to glue them in place."

"So clever! And water-resistant! I love it," I said. I opened the heavy door and walked inside. The floor was made of candy tiles. "Let's not get the floor here wet or it'll be as sticky as flypaper," I said.

"The kitchen is operational, but I don't know what supplies there are. This is more of a showplace, meant for brief visits and for the young to play in. But it's one of the few houses not surrounded by woods. You have to avoid the trees, since the queen has had Colis convince them to report on activities at the entries and to block the exits." He jerked his head to get the hair off his face. "I'll be back as soon as I'm able."

"Bring Momma," I said. "I wanna see her. At least for a few minutes."

"She won't be near where I'm going."

"I'd like to see her," I repeated.

"Agreed," Zach said. "We want to hear from her that she's all right." Zach's expression was all business. He'd been a sheriff's deputy for quite a while and was used to having his authority respected.

"You are free to want whatever you like. The same as every creature in the Never," Caedrin said to Zach. "But being entitled to that which you want . . . not the same circumstance. Don't mistake things. Your safety concerns me only in that it is tied to my daughter's." Caedrin gestured to me and then looked back at Zach. "Have a care whom you challenge. Words and actions carry different consequences here than humanside." Caedrin looked at me, offered a half smile. "Don't wander from here—for your safety. If possible, I will bring Marlee."

He strode out without a look back.

"I don't trust him," Zach said.

"You don't trust many people," I said, my stomach rumbling loudly. "Who's hungry?"

"I am," Bryn said.

"I'm starvin', darlin'. Cook like I'm still in college and comin' home from football practice."

Mercutio walked around the small living room and then followed me to the kitchen. The framed windows looked out at a lawn that was trimmed with lollipop lanterns. The flower borders looked like gumdrops. It was as cute as Candy Land.

Beyond the lawn there was a tall row of hedges, and behind them fields of enormous wildflowers.

I quickly took stock of the supplies. Most of the ingredients would be good for making sweet things, but there were also some herbs and spices, salted meats, and root vegetables. I found the pots and pans and went to work.

When I'd been cooking for a while, Bryn said, "Tamara?"

I looked over my shoulder at him. "I'll have some things ready in a few minutes. Assuming the stoves here work the same as the stoves in Texas. But a few things—"

Bryn clenched and unclenched his fists and shifted his weight from foot to foot. He had plenty of energy normally, but he didn't waste it fidgeting.

"What's wrong?"

"I'm going to see the water. I'll avoid the woods."

"I don't think you should go alone. Or before we've eaten. We're all famished."

His gaze moved to my lips, then my throat, then lower. He drew in a shaky breath. "I want a thousand things at once. To eat. To make love to you. To go to the festival and take in the sights and sounds. But roaring louder than anything is the call of the Irish ocean. I can't be still. I can't wait."

My brows rose and I set down the dough I'd been rolling. I rubbed my hands on a hand towel embroidered with playing children. "Here, eat some bits of salted meat and dried fruit while we walk," I said, smoothing the towel out and then dumping things onto it.

"No," Bryn said, catching my hands and stilling them. "Sweetheart, I should go alone. The water's going to be frigid, and I feel like I'll be diving deep. Too deep for you to come with me."

"But I can walk you to the water. And guard the area if you—"

"You should wait here. The fewer of us wandering around out there, the better. If I didn't feel so bloody compelled, I'd stay myself." A troubled expression crossed his face. "I just need to go."

"It's all right." I stood for a moment, torn between the need for food and the desire to go with Bryn. I chewed on my lip and glanced at Mercutio. "What do you think, Merc?"

Mercutio hopped onto the table and began to eat the bits of meat and probably some of the dried fruit that got in the way.

"You also need to wait for Caedrin to get back. If we all leave, he won't know where we've gone. And if he's able to bring your mother, I want you to have as much time with her as possible," Bryn said.

That made me settle back against the counter. I did want to see Momma. I wouldn't admit it out loud, but I was worried that the trouble for Momma and Caedrin was worse than my father was letting on.

Maybe if I asked her, she'd want to leave the Never with me when I left. She'd come in to be with him, but sometimes anticipating going somewhere was better than actually being there. That was how my culinary school and apprenticeship in Dallas had been. I'd sure learned a lot, but I'd been so homesick and lonely I'd probably cried enough tears to fill a gallon container.

"How will you find your way back after you go for your swim?" I asked.

Bryn smiled. "That won't be a problem. There's no other magic to distract me. No witch magic. My connection to you burns brighter than anything."

"So you feel my faery magic?"

"Yes."

"Does it feel different than my witch magic did?" I asked in surprise. He'd always been able to feel my magic and I could feel his. But here I didn't feel that wizard's magic of his anymore. I felt the magic of the Never humming around us, but none of it was loud or distracting, not the way the siren song of the sea apparently was for him.

"It does feel different. The taste of honey and apples is stronger. The cocoa and ginger has faded. The silkiness has become crushed velvet. Still soft, but richer and earthier."

"Hmmm. That sounds good."

"It's all good with you." He put his hands on my cheeks and tilted my face up. But then he clenched his jaw and shook his head. "I can't start something I'll feel compelled to finish. I'll kiss you when I return."

I was tempted to send Mercutio with him, but I worried that the cat might get a big urge to go exploring and end up in the woods. None of us were used to the Never yet. It seemed to be pulling us in a bunch of directions at once. My toes twitched to walk barefoot in the grass, and my fingers ached to bury themselves back in the pie dough or to run through Bryn's hair and pull him close for a kiss. A lightning bolt of lust made my belly tighten. I wanted to grab Bryn and drag him down to the floor on top of me, to wrap my legs—

I sucked in a startled breath and forced my feet to take a step back. "Yeah, go ahead." I tucked my hair behind my ear, glancing at the doorway to the room where Zach was standing.

"What were you just thinking?" Bryn asked, the corners of his mouth inching up into a smirk.

"None of your business."

"I beg to differ."

I waved a hand, urging him away. "Go on now."

His smile broadened. "You're pretty when you blush."

"Uh-huh."

"And when you don't."

"All right, Casanova. Go on now."

Bryn kissed his fingertips and blew on them to send the kiss to me. I swear I felt the heat of his breath against my skin. I shivered, retreating until the counter pressed against my lower back.

"See you soon," he said.

I turned and leaned over the counter, exhaling and then taking another deep breath in. The Never was dangerous in ways I hadn't realized. I pulled the bowl of dough to me and sank my hands into it. The soft lump swallowed my fingers, and I felt a rush of anticipation. I was still hungry for more than a blue-eyed selkie man.

I worked steadily with Mercutio weaving around me and through the legs of the table. I was too focused on my work to stop and try to figure out what was driving his endless circling, until he hopped onto a chair and leapt across to the top of the counter. He darted to a window and looked out.

A flash of dark blue and green bustled by. I stopped. It was a peacock's plume, attached to a plump peacock. I reacted too late.

Bird! I thought, reaching. My fingers brushed the end of Merc's tail, but by the time my fist closed, he and his tail were out the open window.

"Merc, hang on!" I called, turning and running out of the kitchen. "Zach, Mercutio's gone out the window."

An empty living room greeted me as I rushed through it. *Where's Zach?*

I pushed the door open and burst outside. "Mercutio, don't kill that bird."

Zach wasn't standing on the front walk, but someone was.

It was a woman—a female faery—the likes of which I'd never seen. And she had a dangerous question for me.

21

THE FAERY'S LAVENDER eyes narrowed, a thin smile fixed on her thin face. "Who have you brought home with you?" she asked. "And why would he kill a bird?"

I froze, my gaze darting left and right.

Cats are banned from the Never. I can't let her see Merc.

"Um, hi." I stepped down onto the walkway.

She tilted her head, her upswept pink-and-yellow hair swaying when her head moved. Her throat and collarbones were decorated with green and gold vines. And her body was encased in a dress that had a lavender corset top cinched tight with gold ribbons. The skirt was layers of gathered satin falling in scallops to skim the tops of her crystal-encrusted dark green slipper shoes. She looked like a cross between a princess doll and an Easter egg.

"Hello," I said.

"Who is this Mercutio of whom you spoke?" she asked, resting her long-fingered hands against the fabric of her skirt. The nails were filed to points and painted dark green. The pointed nails looked sinister . . . and strange, considering her springlike getup.

She had pretty, delicate features. Like a porcelain doll. Or a bird.

Was this the queen of the Seelie fae?

I pressed my lips closed. Probably the less I said to anyone the better. I glanced around again. Zach still hadn't appeared.

"Cat got your tongue?" she whispered, and her tone sent the hair on my arms straight up, like soldiers at attention. "Isn't that what they say humanside?"

The mention of cats made my spine tingle, but I forced myself to keep still and not look toward the back of the gingerbread house.

"Your hair is very red-orange. As a ruby in a flame. It's gotten darker when you've been humanside before, but never as dark as that. Did you touch it with dye? To look more like Witch Marlee?"

She poked at a hairpin with a pointy fingernail. "You stand so silent and still, looking a little—don't take offense—a little startled. . . ." She waited. "And even a little . . ." She hesitated again, assessing me. Finally she whispered, "Slouched and scared."

My spine stiffened, and I stood up straight. "You did surprise me, but I'm not scared." Sure, I was worried. All my men were missing. But that was none of her business. "Speaking of hair, that's sure an interesting style you've got there."

Her brows rose. "You're not yourself, are you?"

My mouth opened, but I closed it again. What should I say?

"Aren't I?"

"No, you're not. Do you know me? I'm Roseblade. Do you remember our friendship?"

I hesitated before shaking my head. She thought I was Kismet, didn't she? And that Kismet had lost her memory. I wasn't sure whether it was safer to pretend to be my sister or if it would be better to admit who I really was. One thing was certain: I didn't trust this Easter egg–headed girl.

"You've been bespelled. I'm all curiosity over how that might have happened. Witch magic should have washed off you when you returned to the Never. And how could you have found your way home if your memory was lost to you? No, it must have happened after you arrived. Did you drink a potion? Or do you have a wound somewhere? It could be as small as a pinprick."

"Nope."

"Take off your humanside clothes. Let's look closely. It might be very, very small. Just a poison splinter or the tip of a thorn sticking into your skin."

Realization dawned. Her hair was fashioned into the shape of a rose bloom and her skirt was like satin flower petals. Her nails were shaped like thorns.

"Roseblade. That's an unusual name."

"It is? I've had it the whole of my life."

"Rare."

"It's true that I'm the only one there's been or will be." She smiled. "Unique. You're unique as well. Do you recall your name?"

The smell of food turned my head. "Oh! I forgot I've got stuff in the oven!" I hurried back inside. I grabbed the hot pads that were embroidered to match the dish towels, and I removed the pies from the stove.

"By the golden sunrise," she exclaimed.

I waved the hot pad over the smoking piecrust. There was a tiny bit of char I'd scrape off. I closed the oven and glanced over my shoulder at the lavender-eyed woman. Her gaze moved slowly around the kitchen, and my own followed it. The table and counter were covered with dishes of freshly made food, ready to be eaten. It was a feast fit to feed an army. Had I made it all? I rubbed my palms together. Yes, I had.

For a moment I pictured my hands working furiously in almost a blur of speed. I hadn't thought it was strange at the time, but I didn't think I'd ever worked so fast in my life.

I took a plate down and held it out to her. "Here. Won't you eat something?" I didn't want her to stay and couldn't afford to spend time with someone I suspected might be trouble, but my mouth moved before my brain could stop it.

"I'd be so pleased if you tried everything. Won't you sit?" I asked, extending a hand.

She laughed. "So charming! I'm charmed," she said with a broad smile. "I believe Witch Marlee bakes. I think you're afflicted with the same spell as she. Maybe it's one that encompassed her talents."

My momma could cook and bake pretty well, from what I remembered, but by the time I was thirteen I'd taken over the kitchen.

I spooned hearty vegetable stew into a bowl, putting a buttered biscuit with it. Then I filled another dish with apple cobbler, adding a dollop of berry compote and whipped cream to the cobbler. I was sorry I hadn't made ice cream.

"May I dress up your biscuit with honey?"

"Please!" she said.

I drizzled honey onto the biscuit and then added other little bits of food and garnishes to her dish until it was ready to overflow.

"Go ahead," I said, my own hunger secondary. I waited breathlessly.

"Sunbeams and rose petals! Crystals and coins! Ambers and gemstones!" she exclaimed between bites. "Fantastic!"

Happiness and pride washed over me. More than food, this was what I'd craved—praise.

Only when I'd served her another plateful of food—roast vegetables with spiced meat and herbs, croissants, warm gingerbread cookies, and cinnamon rolls with white icing—did I make myself a dish. I sat across from her while she ate and smiled and waved her free hand enthusiastically.

"I'm going to tell you something secretly," she whispered. "I won't be sorry if you never remember that which came before. I won't be sorry if you never have to leave again. You can stay and make these dishes. We'll have garden parties that everyone will want to attend. With my blooming flower arrangements, the table set for royalty, and these magnificent foods, everyone will want to come. I will make them wait. I'll make them court our favor. We'll be as popular as any, and more than many." Her eyes twinkled.

"Our lady Highness will be the only one who doesn't need a card of invitation. Everyone else, even the golden knights, will wait for our invitation. And in some cases, wait and wait, if we wish it."

"Um, I don't—" My voice dropped off when Caedrin appeared in the doorway.

Seeing my expression, Roseblade looked over her shoulder.

Caedrin's brow rose, as he seemed to question her presence.

"So she's come back on her own," Roseblade said. "Not by force, as some expected."

"So it seems. How did you come to be here?"

"I surmised it. Am I not clever?" Roseblade said, licking icing off her fingers. "Did I see Osmet? I did. Someone had entered the Never from humanside, he thought. If it was Kismet and if it was known that the trees were telling tales, where might she go to remain undiscovered until ready to reveal herself? This place avoids the trees' notice. Am I not clever? As clever as a knight or the queen's first assassin?"

"You are cunning. None could dispute that," he said, his expression hard.

A blush stained her cheeks. "Kismet, why don't you wrap some food? We'll take it to Our Highness."

"She's not accompanying you."

"Why not? I've discovered her. Why shouldn't I take her?"

"You're not her friend."

"I was once, which is more than can be said of you. You were never her friend—as she's said herself to many in the past. I wish to be her friend. Can you say the same?"

Caedrin's eyes narrowed. "Leave now."

"Have you a claim to her? If so, make it. Not by general proclamation, but here, in front of her and her oldest friend. Call her your daughter."

Caedrin stood stone-faced.

"You won't." Roseblade rose, smoothing her flower-petal skirt. She folded her hands together and looked at me. "Some whisper that he's a relation to you, but he's never said so. He's wanted nothing to do with you for your—"

"Your tongue is as pointed as your nails, Rosebet."

"Don't call me that," she snapped, darting forward to slap him.

He caught her arm before her hand made contact. She grabbed his forearm with her free hand, sinking her nails into it.

"Let go! I'm not afraid of you," she said.

"Nor I you," he said with an amused expression.

Roseblade's face turned blotchy red with fury. He didn't release her arm until she let go of his. Reddish-gold blood welled in his wounds and spilled over. Drops rained down onto the floor.

I handed him a cloth, watching the pair of them warily.

"You don't outrank me, Caedrin. The queen's made me her first maiden. I'm in her favor. More so than you." She cleared her throat. "More so than you," she repeated, hissing the words.

"And yet if I killed you, she'd forgive me."

Roseblade paled, stepping back. "You wouldn't dare."

"I have dared to do many things none expected. No doubt I will do some again. Push me if you will, and we will both find out."

Roseblade clutched her skirt, raising it enough for me to see her ankles clad in dark green tights.

Legs dressed up as flower stems, I thought.

"Kismet, let me be your friend. This queen's knight has never been your protector or adviser. If you allow me, I'll claim you as dear as a sister. In front of the entire Never."

"That's sure a nice offer," I said, glancing at the marks on Caedrin's arm. "Let me think it over."

"What I did . . . it was never a betrayal. No matter what he says," she said, scowling at Caedrin. "I'll wait for you at my house, Kismet. It's on the way. Follow the roses." She flounced out of the kitchen. Caedrin watched her exit through the front door, which she left wide-open.

He was so still. I wondered whether he needed to breathe at all. Finally he inhaled and then exhaled. I mirrored the action, realizing for the first time that I could take a deep breath without pain. I looked at Caedrin's arm. His wounds had already closed. I pressed a hand to the middle of my chest. There was no soreness, let alone pain, from the terrible wound I'd gotten the week before. Upon entering the Never, I'd healed.

"Where are your companions?" he asked.

"I don't exactly know. Bryn's gone swimming," I said absently.

"Swimming?" Caedrin echoed, his brows practically touching each other.

"Um, yeah, more or less," I said hastily. I didn't want any of the faeries to know that Bryn was part fae. "Zach left without saying a word, which surprises me." I chewed my lip. "I need to figure out where he's at. Merc took off after a bird, which doesn't surprise me, him being a cat and all."

"What bird?"

"A peacock."

"One of the queen's birds," he said, shaking his head.

"Is she the only one who has peacocks?"

"Yes."

I sighed. "Of course. What's the penalty for eating one of the queen's birds?"

"How could we know, when no one sane would dare? If an animal were to kill a pet of the queen's, that animal's owner would slaughter it immediately."

I felt the blood drain from my face, but clenched my teeth. "Chasing birds is in his nature. Can't blame him for being an ocelot. He was born one."

"If he's found, you must deny all knowledge of him."

"No way."

"You can't protect that cat in here. You can't even protect yourself," he said.

"Maybe not. And it seems like you won't protect us either. You left Kismet to fend for herself, huh?"

His tawny-brown eyes narrowed. "You know nothing of the situation here. You should leave while you still can."

He didn't even bother to offer an explanation about why he'd never tried to help Kismet.

Fae don't have human consciences. They don't feel things

the same way, I reminded myself, recalling how it felt to have my humanity drained away.

That was another thing I hadn't realized when we'd entered the Never. I was underhill and still myself, full of Tammy Jo feelings. So it seemed like I had been channeling Kismet's emotions or lack of them when I'd been drained of witch magic in Duvall.

It made me sad to think of how deadened Kismet's emotions were. She was half human; caring about people was at the heart of being a person. Her instincts about wanting to get the hell out of the Never were right. She needed to be among normal folks.

"Roseblade wasn't Kismet's friend. When she learned that Kismet was a Halfling, she pretended not to care. But she spied and bided her time until she gained information she could use. Kismet entrusted her with the secret of her ability to pass in and out of the Never. Roseblade connived to get the queen's ear and told her. If not for Roseblade, the queen might not have forced Kismet to become an assassin."

I scowled. *That rotten—*

"Kismet calls her former friend Rosebet. *Bet* is short for *betrayer.* Kismet doesn't trust her. You shouldn't either."

"Kismet doesn't trust anyone. I'm starting to figure out why that is. And just so you know, you broke Kismet's heart by letting her be an orphan. How could you do that?"

His face looked pained, but then he recovered, and his expression hardened again. "Your chances of escaping are narrowing. Delay is dangerous. I'll draw you a map. You have to run. Roseblade will wait a little to see if you come to her. She'd like to present you to the queen in person for the most dramatic effect. But she won't wait long before she sends word to the castle that you're here."

"Where is Momma?"

"She's here in the Never."

"Is she okay?"

"She's not hurt."

"That's not what I asked."

"It's the only answer I'll offer. As I said before, if she

knew you were here, she would advise you strongly to leave this place while you can."

In that instant, I wouldn't have taken his word about anything. If he'd said the sky was blue, I'd have looked up to check for myself.

"I'll go when I'm satisfied my momma is okay. And not a minute sooner."

"If she wanted to be with you, she wouldn't have come to be with me," he said.

I sucked in a breath. "What exactly are you sayin'?"

"You had your time with her. She raised you until you could live on your own. And then she left your world. As soon as she could, she came to me."

My brows shot up and my stomach tightened. "She came looking for you, yeah. And I'm sure she knew it was risky. But since then, maybe she's changed her mind about you and about being here. Sometimes feelings change. As a faery you should know that, since you guys are supposed to be the most fair-weather creatures of all."

He scowled. "Marlee is not fae. Her feelings haven't changed."

"Well, I'll hear that from her."

"I won't take you to her. It's useless and dangerous."

"It's not useless."

"It is! Because she won't recognize you. She doesn't remember the second half of the life she's lived."

"What?" I yelled.

"She's under a curse."

"What curse? Who cursed her?"

"The only one who could."

"That bitch of a queen?"

He shot forward and covered my mouth, looking around. "Never say that again whilst in this place."

I shouted against his hand, doing my own version of cursing someone.

"She's not suffering. It's not a punishment for her. If anything she's happier. She doesn't have to miss what she left outside."

I relaxed my shoulders and spoke calmly against his hand. He drew it back tentatively.

"Then why did the queen put the curse on her? If it's not to punish her?"

"It's not her punishment. It's mine."

"How? What do you care whether she remembers the second half of her life?"

He tipped his head back, and I saw that his eyes shone unnaturally bright. Maybe Kismet didn't feel strong emotions, but our daddy apparently did.

"What?" I whispered.

"Her memories of us after the first summer have been taken away."

"What memories? Are you saying you saw her again after that first summer?"

He nodded.

"When?" I demanded.

"Whenever I could."

My jaw dropped. "How many times?"

"Five." He shoved his hair back behind his ear and looked at me. "There are words I spoke to her, things I confided, which can't be confided again. Do you understand? I risked the wrath of my queen. I gambled with my life just as Marlee gambled with hers to come here. We were united in our sacrifices and our commitment. I laid out the contents of my mind and heart so she could be my closest friend. That's lost."

"A curse can be undone."

"Yes, but that won't be soon. The queen's punishments are never short."

"You shouldn't have kept this a secret from me. I came here to help."

"You can't help."

"Yeah, I can."

"How?"

"I don't know yet. That's what we've got to figure out. Sit down and tell me everything you know about this curse."

"You don't have the magic to undo it. Even if you had the

full power of the fae in you, you couldn't undo a queen's curse. Your fae magic is only half, if that."

"Kismet is half, like me. The queen couldn't keep her from leaving. And so far she hasn't been able to make her come back."

"Eventually Kismet will be caught," he said grimly.

"Maybe so. But she's already proven the most important thing: A half-faery girl can defy a queen and get away with it. At least for a while. And that's all I need. Just a chance."

The pain in his expression drained away, replaced by surprise. He caught my face in his hands and kissed the top of my head. He pulled me toward him and whispered, "I can't conspire against the queen. An oath I've made prevents it."

"So I shouldn't tell you anything that I plan to do? Or even that I plan to do something?"

"Right."

"Well, that would've been nice to know earlier!"

He grinned.

"What are you smiling about? This could be a problem!"

He shrugged. "It's just that you're like us. Marlee and I never gave up. Stubborn and unflinching. Kismet has that fire. So do you. At the core, even on the darkest days and nights, we seek sunlight and have faith we'll see it again. Within that common ground are the hidden roots of our small family."

I cocked my head, my eyes widening with a dawning understanding. "You can't claim Kismet, can you? That's some other oath you had to make, right?"

He looked at me pointedly.

"As soon as you met me, you said right off I was your daughter. It's not like you're trying to keep being a dad a big secret. But you never told her or anyone about her being your daughter. It's because you're not allowed to tell anyone, isn't it?"

His expression was carefully blank. "Kismet can shoot an arrow straight in high wind. When others cower at the cliffs, she leaps. No matter how deadly a target or how guarded the encampment she's sent to, she returns alive. There is greatness in her, and all the Never knows it."

"You're proud of her."

"I can't express pride in her. I don't claim the girl."

I took a big breath in and then sighed, shaking my head. "You shouldn't have made that deal. Whatever it was, you should never have agreed to it. You know that now, right?"

He opened his mouth and closed it again.

I put a hand on his chest over his heart. "Maybe you didn't think you had a choice. And maybe you didn't. I wasn't there. And I'm not one to judge. Sometimes I've had to decide things on the spur of the moment and then see how things turned out. Life can be kind of unpredictable."

He hugged me to him.

"Was that one of the things you got to tell Momma? Was there some loophole in the rules about what you could tell? And the queen closed it?"

He held me so tight he practically crushed my bones.

"Don't worry," I said, my eyes stinging with tears. I sniffed and bit my lip until I got hold of myself. "Don't worry," I repeated firmly. "You know what's a secret weapon for finding loopholes? A lawyer. Luckily, I brought one with me."

I started to speak, but stopped as magic flowed over me like a wave, salty and cool. I licked my lips, knowing Bryn had found his place in the sea.

I stilled, holding my breath. *There's my lawyer. Here's hoping I can get him back from the deep end of the ocean.*

22

CAEDRIN AND I talked it over, and we—well, I—decided that it would be best for Roseblade to take me to the castle to meet the queen, for several reasons. First, because I wanted Caedrin to find Zach and Mercutio, and possibly Bryn if he didn't get back soon, so my guys would be seen by as few fae as possible. I wanted them together, too, if we needed to leave on the run. Second, I thought it would be better if Caedrin and I weren't together when I met the queen, since she was prone to jealousy when it came to her knights. Or so I'd heard and sensed. Maybe she wouldn't be angry to find that Caedrin had a new daughter that he'd kept hidden from her, and that I liked him and vice versa, but I thought I'd better not take a chance.

I bundled up pastries and loaded myself down with them. Caedrin gave me directions, but they weren't as helpful as they'd have been in Duvall or even a place that I was vaguely familiar with. "Veer left at the tallest oak along the way" just didn't do me much good. But I had a plan. And the plan was to be friendly and ask directions in a stealthy way. "Have you seen Roseblade? Which way?" In my experience asking directions can be better than a map, because the best way to get to know a place is to get to know the people.

I walked what felt like a long way, following the sound of music and voices. There was singing, shouting, and laughter. When I emerged from the path to a clearing of rolling lawns, I'd found the faery festival. There were hundreds and hundreds of faeries scattered over the lawn, eating and drinking, joking and playing, dancing and performing. Some of their clothes were natural fabrics in earth tones like what the Native Americans had on in pictures you see in books. But then there were also those dressed in vibrant, bright outfits and costumes.

I followed a trail of rose petals and it led me to a booth with Roseblade's picture painted on it. The young man who had followed us through the field of flowers was standing behind the counter, decorating straw hats and woven floral crowns with bits of carved bark and leaves that had been dipped in gold. He strung vines like boas and lengths of garland. Roses of every style and color seemed to be bursting from buckets in corners and on tables. It was more incredible than any flower shop I'd ever seen.

"Hi," I said, taking out a cinnamon roll and offering it to him.

"Kismet! You are back." He grabbed the pastry and took a bite. "Wow, which booth had these? Hey, I finished it. Did you get me the stones we talked about? And that headband, what's it called again?"

"Osmet, I'm having a little problem with my memory. Kinda got zapped with a curse."

"Bogus!" he said, which made me laugh. "And don't call me Osmet. It's Oz. Out there, there's an entire storyland named after me, remember?"

I stared at him.

"The Wizard of Oz."

I laughed. "That's not named for you."

"Yes, it is. You talked to a bard about me, and he wrote a whole story inspired by me."

"Do you know what that story's about?"

"A tree keeper's son who goes on an adventure and saves a band of rebels from an evil wizard."

I grinned. "Um, okay."

"The story's obviously about me. And where else would a bard have gotten the name Oz from?"

"If my momma had named me Star, it wouldn't mean *Star Wars* was inspired by me, especially since I came after that was already written. And so did you, probably—come after *The Wizard of Oz* got made up."

He frowned. "This problem with your memory sucks. Sucks is right, right? Yeah, it is. I probably remember better than you. Listen, have you got a small pouch on you? Full of five emeralds from that place . . . Colonia? The really hot, spicy place. Colombia! That's it."

"Why do you want Colombian emeralds?" I asked.

"To decorate my bandmanah."

"Your what?"

"Bandmanah. The headband tough bikers wear." He reached inside the pocket of his calfskin pants and unfolded a faded newspaper picture of a man on a Harley wearing a bandanna.

I giggled. "How come you want to dress like a biker? There are no motorcycles underhill, right?"

"No, not yet. Maybe there won't be ever. But one day I'll get out there, humanside, and I want to fit in. I want an American girlfriend, or one from London. Someone cool like you. Or like you usually are when you remember yourself."

"Uh-huh."

"Listen, I have Ozart for you. Come and see me when you remember. I have a special piece you wanted. You know, I'm not sure I like Ozart as the name for my stuff. It's not very imaginative. Oz art. I'm thinking of calling them Fozzels. Understand?"

"No."

He shook his head. "Never mind."

"Hey," he said. "Are you playing with me right now? Practicing? You trick people with accents and clothes to fit in out there, humanside. Or so we've heard. But in here you've never performed." He tore off another piece of cinnamon roll, a bite with lots of white icing. He chewed it and moaned. "Marbles and coins, that's fantastic. Which booth is trading these?" he asked. "Hey, Rosebee!" he called. "Look who's come to your stand!"

I turned, and Roseblade hurried over. She'd shortened her skirt somehow so that her dark green tights were displayed from the knees down. Her thin legs really did look like the stems of a rose.

"Hello! So, Kismet, you've met my cousin." She looked at Oz. "Did you introduce yourself?"

"No, she knows me. Sort of."

Roseblade tilted her head. I worried the weight of her swollen hair might tip her over, but her neck must've been used to the workout, because she didn't wobble.

"Has her memory come back?"

"Definitely not."

Roseblade looked at me. "Say something."

"What should I say?"

She laughed. "That's plenty. She's so good at humanside voices, isn't she? Like a chameleon. Or Gobus. He's the best of the Seelie actors. He can do the talk of any people in any time! What's in your sack? More pastries? May I have another?"

"Yep," I said, reaching in. I gave her a chewy molasses walnut bar.

"They're brilliant! Which is wonderful. Now the queen will have to consider letting you change your occupation, which is what you've wanted for a while," Roseblade said in a conspiratorial whisper. "Or so we've heard it said."

"The pastry was great. But don't change professions, Kis. Then you wouldn't have leave to go out there. You know you wouldn't like being stuck inside the Never all the time. Or maybe you don't know, with your damaged memory. But trust me, you wouldn't. Humanside is the explosion!"

"The bomb," I said.

He laughed. "She remembers a little."

"Don't interfere, Osmet!" Roseblade said. "We're going to have grand parties. I've spoken to MagpieMeadow. She's the queen's tea maker. She's said that if Kismet's pastries are as good as I've proclaimed, she will blend and brew the tea for our first party. It will be so grand!" Roseblade threw her arms wide, and I couldn't help but crack up. Even though I couldn't trust her and didn't plan to stay in the Never long enough to throw parties, a part of me felt like that was too bad, because her enthusiasm was fun.

"I've picked out the paper for the invitations! Gorwrit has the best new stock and ink. It really—"

"Before all that, shouldn't I go and see the queen?" I asked.

"Sunrise sunblind! Yes! In my excitement, I almost forgot. We should go before too many words have been carried about your return. We won't want her to feel she's been kept waiting!"

I nodded.

Roseblade glanced around the stand. "Give me the queen's crystal white, Osmet. This instant."

Oz reached under the fabric covering the table, and rose with a box. Roseblade peeked in and smiled.

"All right. Off we go."

I licked my lips and wondered what would happen when the queen saw me. Would she know that I wasn't Kismet returned with amnesia? Crux said he'd sent word about finding Kismet's twin. But Caedrin didn't think the queen knew about me. Was it because she really didn't? Or because she'd kept that news a secret for some dark purpose of her own?

THE PATH TO the castle was paved with dark and light pebbles arranged in perfect patterns like mosaic tile, except they hadn't been glued down. When we walked over them, our feet kicked up some of the stones and knocked them out of place.

"Uh-oh," I said, starting to turn to fix the design.

"No, no," Roseblade said as a buzzing insect flew in. An instant later the pebbles were back in place.

I squinted and realized the insects were actually tiny pixies. "Wow."

"Keepers of the queen's path," Roseblade said. "You shouldn't handle their stones. They don't like it. Small fae are very touchy. They can't lift boulders or so much as a cabbage, but they can do the most amazing detail work, and it infuriates them when a large fae tries to do it, too. They want to think none can do intricate designs as well as they."

"Oh. Okay. I won't mess with their rocks. And they sure did do a pretty job."

"Wait until we get to the welcome way," Roseblade crowed. "When it was announced that I would be made queen's first maiden, they—No, I won't say. Just wait."

We walked on and eventually the path widened and revealed the front of the castle. The pebbles in the border as we neared the entry were tiny chips of marble and tiny nuggets of gold.

The section closest to the door had pastels, but the pieces weren't heavy like rock. When we walked, they floated up and drifted down.

I paused, skidding my foot forward to watch the soft, feathery wafers rise.

"They're rose petals! They requested two hundred roses, which I provided, and they cut tiny petals. See the design pattern? Crowns of roses."

My jaw dropped. "It really is the most amazing thing."

When we stood on the castle steps, I turned and watched the tiny pixies, whose features were too small to make out from a few feet away, buzz back and forth.

"There's an amusement park called Disney World where there are no trash Dumpsters. Or so I've heard. They keep everything spotless and take the trash underneath so everything looks pretty and nice. But even the Disney team never had a crew like this. The Never is like Disney World. Only more incredible."

"I've heard of Disney," Roseblade said, wrinkling her nose. "His picture plays are famous, right? And his festival lands? But you can't expect anything humanside to be more impressive than the Never. We're the original, after all. The inspiration for everything he's ever done."

I smiled. I couldn't dispute that Mr. Disney had been inspired by faery tales, but to say fae like Roseblade were the inspiration for all he did was taking a crazy amount of credit for things. I doubted Mr. Disney had ever even met a real faery.

"Did Mr. Disney visit the Never?"

"Of course not. We welcome human children, but human adults? Ugh." She frowned.

"Could he have visited as a boy?"

"No. Once they come, they're ours. We don't send them back, especially since they never want to leave without a piece of the Never." She brightened. "And there's no place for them out there anyway. We leave a changeling in their place that grows up. Their parents grow old and die. Humans die so fast, I'm told! It's shocking. Lucky, lucky are the children who get to live here with us."

Oh, sure, lucky! I thought furiously. Stolen from parents who love them more than anything. Brought to live with the faeries, who were ruled by a jealous queen who forced a young girl to be an orphan and an assassin. Kidnapped children living underhill, so lucky!

Roseblade leaned near a round grate at eye level next to the door. She spoke softly into the grate, saying, "Roseblade, queen's first maiden. And Kismet, queen's first assassin." She said the last triumphantly.

I had to stop myself from rolling my eyes.

A lively tune played. And then a darker-edged one. After the music, the door latch clicked, and Roseblade depressed the handle. The door swung open and the light flashed over a carved pattern in the door that I hadn't initially noticed. It was the sunburst pattern from the front of Lenore's locket and the elevator door from WAM headquarters.

I stared at the door. "That pattern," I said, pointing at the front door. "What does it mean?"

"It's sunlight. This is the original door."

"The original door?"

"Yes, from the first fae castle. Anytime there is a new castle built, the door is moved to it. For tradition's sake."

"Is there a diamond pattern on the back door?"

"A triangle with an added nasty spike on the bottom," she said, pursing her lips. "Yes, the original magical triangle."

"What is that? The original triangle? And why is the bottom point bad?" I asked.

"Never mind," she hissed in a whisper. A falsely cheerful smile spread over her face. "We're inside the castle now. Smile."

"Um, actually my face only smiles when it feels like smiling," I said, which wasn't completely true, but I didn't like being ordered to fake a grin.

The inside of the castle was so opulent and dazzling it left a person half-blind. White light poured in through cut-glass windows. Crystals studded the walls in mosaic patterns trimmed in yellow and rose gold. Rails and grates of gold and silver were so polished that reflections of light bounced off every twist of metal. I blinked. Several times.

"This way. She'll receive us in the great hall. If she's really pleased, she'll ask us to stay and accompany her upstairs." Roseblade clapped her small hands together, clearly excited and hopeful.

We passed through a double golden archway, and I thought of McDonald's, which made me chuckle. Had the human side of the world actually taken inspiration from the land of faeries, as Osmet and Roseblade claimed? Nah, I thought. It was just a coincidence.

The great hall looked like a giant room in an English castle. There were fancy couches and chairs, parquet wood floors, and oak-paneled walls covered with enormous paintings. The room had to be ten thousand square feet.

A ballroom and then some, I thought.

I walked to the closest couch, which was pink with white legs trimmed in—what else?—gold, of course.

"I lost her, but I have reason to think she'll return," a man's voice said.

"Yes, I have reason to believe that as well," a woman said.

I spun toward their voices, startled to have heard them. When we walked in I'd thought the room was empty, but in a corner, standing in front of a painting, were three figures: A tall woman with cascades of white-blond waves and a voluptuous figure that could've landed her in a *Playboy* centerfold if she'd been willing. The faery knight Crux. And, in his faded Levi's and orange-and-white Longhorns T-shirt, Zach.

I stared at the three of them. How had Zach ended up here? He didn't seem to be under arrest, so had he come on his own? And why?

And what about Crux? Had he told the queen about our trapping him in a circle in my kitchen? Were Bryn and I in danger of being arrested?

"My lady Highness, hello!" Roseblade said, her voice projecting across the room like an actor's onstage. She made an elaborate curtsy and bobbed up, her rose-shaped hair swaying.

The queen turned, and she was every bit as pretty as a porcelain figurine. She had creamy white skin with rose-colored cheeks, golden-brown eyes, and pink lips. She wore a pistachio-colored gown that floated around her curves. She was tall—nearly six feet, I'd have guessed.

"Yes, I have every reason to believe that Kismet will return as well," she murmured slyly to Crux. Then she looked at me. "Your hair is very dark, Kismet. I hope you've come back in time for it to return all the way to its natural shade."

I touched a lock of my red hair. Could she really not tell I wasn't Kismet?

I glanced at Crux, who leaned casually against the wall between two paintings. One of them seemed to depict a fight between vampires and faery knights. The other showed a dead woman, possibly a witch, dressed in a black lace dress. A blade impaled her chest, and a knight—Crux, I realized—stood over the fallen woman. Her lips were bloodred, like the circle of blood around the dagger. I shivered. Yeah, the faery artwork was just as gruesome as a lot of human paintings of war and executions. They were pretty, if you could get past the violence. Which I couldn't. I liked water lilies and sunflowers. The Impressionists, Bryn said.

He had nice art in his house. Seaside landscapes, green hills, rainy streets, and starlit skies. There weren't any dead bodies in his paintings. Thank goodness.

"Hello," Crux said. "It's good to see you again."

My eyes widened, but I quickly looked away.

The queen laughed. "She's still angry with you. Are you still angry with me, too, deadly girl?"

"I brought you pastries," I said, gesturing to the sack I'd fashioned from the tablecloth.

"A different sort of gift. No book? Still, it's generous of you, Kismet. And you're such a fine mimic. You've taken an accent and are still using it? Is that to entertain me?"

"Not exactly, but if it does, I'm okay with that."

"Your friend wanted to hear our stories," Ghislaine said, motioning to the pictures. "And he told me a story for each that I told him. We've only begun, but he's a very good storyteller." She glanced at Zach. "And very golden." She said *golden* like someone human might say *gorgeous* or *handsome*.

I frowned. The last thing we needed was for the Seelie queen to develop a crush on Zach.

"He says he's been inside the headquarters of the witches. You'll want to listen to him tell of that. You may go there one day on a mission. It could be where the second is kept."

"Second what?" Roseblade asked, which was exactly what I wondered.

"Not your business, flower maiden, but I'm pleased with you for keeping Kismet company on her walk to the castle. A friendship between you, that's new . . . or rather a return to the old. Yes, I'm pleased. We want her to feel at home in her homeland."

"Let's lay out the food. Is MagpieMeadow at the clearing?" Roseblade asked.

"I am in the castle. So Mags is in the castle," the queen said. "Of course."

"You may call for tea if you wish it," the queen added in a more generous tone.

"There's something you should know, my lady," Roseblade said. "Kismet's lost her memory."

"What?" the queen said, her perfect brows drawing together. "Is this true?"

I shrugged.

"Do you have your memories or not?" Ghislaine demanded impatiently.

"I don't remember this place. It's like it's my first time underhill ever." I shrugged again. "I don't remember you."

"How could this have happened?" Ghislaine's eyes turned to Zach. "Are you aware of how my assassin became bespelled?"

Zach shook his head.

"Crux, what do you know of Kismet having amnesia?"

"I know nothing of Kismet having amnesia."

"If she was spelled by witches or another humanside caster, the spell would've fallen away when she entered the Never."

"I thought the same thing, my lady," Roseblade said quickly, clearly anxious to chime in before anyone else. She didn't need to worry—nobody except her wanted to talk anyway.

"And, Roseblade? Have you any theory about it?"

"Well, there have been rumors that she's the natural daughter of—"

"Quiet!" the queen commanded.

Roseblade's mouth snapped shut.

"Crux, take Zachary to the silver hall. Ask Mags to show him the art there. Call Colis and Caedrin to the castle. I want them here as quick as legs can carry them."

Crux inclined his head and strode out with Zach.

"Now, First Maiden, approach and tell me your theory."

Roseblade, pale and hesitant, walked stiffly to the queen and whispered.

"No," the queen said, not in a whisper. "Unlikely." She shook her head, looking at me thoughtfully. "Improbable." The queen's long fingers gestured to the door.

"What's your preference, my lady Highness? Shall I remain in the castle? Or return to the festival?" Roseblade asked.

"I have no preference. Do what pleases you. But don't come upstairs. And don't gather gossip from my halls."

"I believe I'll return to the festival. I brought you a gift," Roseblade said, holding up the small box.

The queen didn't reach for it. She ignored Roseblade, continuing to stare at me.

Roseblade's gaze followed the queen's, and all the triumph and excitement from earlier was gone. Pure venom lit her eyes, and her fingers twitched as though she'd like to sink those thorn nails into me. I sighed. It didn't look like we'd be throwing grand parties together after all.

"You've been cross with everyone, Kis. You don't recall that?" the queen asked. She glided across the floor. Did she have roller skates on under her gown? I looked down, but couldn't see her footwear.

She stopped a couple feet from me and studied my face. "You're transformed in more ways than one. Those eyes are more fae. They suit you."

Obviously Crux hadn't told her Kismet had a twin. Why not?

"Come upstairs," Ghislaine said.

An invitation upstairs was supposed to be a good thing, according to Roseblade, but despite the Never's summer weather and the lightness of Ghislaine's coloring, she and her castle seemed cold to me. I had the urge to bolt out, dragging Zach with me. I wanted to find everyone I loved and flee the Never as soon as possible.

Instead, I followed the beautiful Seelie queen up her long stairwell and down what felt like endless hallways until we reached an unusual room that we could see into from the hall. The room reminded me of an opulent jail cell; there was a lattice of metalwork that made up the front wall and doors. The queen pulled a lever. Exposed bronze gears turned, sliding the doors into pockets. Sitting in the far corner, looking out a barred window, was a woman. Her dark red ponytail sat high on her head.

That had better not be . . .

Her clothes were odd, some sort of costume. The black back had tiny stripes of white, and the front was solid white. She turned her head and of course it was. Sitting in the fancy cell of the fancy castle of the fancy fae queen was my very own momma. Not only had her memory been stolen, but she was being kept caged.

If we'd been standing at the top of that long stairwell, I would've given the Seelie queen a shove and pushed her right down it.

23

THE QUEEN WATCHED us carefully. When Momma spotted me, recognition flashed in her eyes, followed by confusion and concern.

I couldn't move, because I didn't know what to do or say. I wanted to hug her and shout for joy that we were reunited. But I was also furious that anyone was keeping her prisoner. Why hadn't Caedrin said so?

Only a few seconds passed before she took a single step forward and spoke.

"Hi. For a moment I thought you were my sister, Melanie." Momma touched her hair. "It's the red. Yours is almost the same color." She smiled and walked to the doorway. She extended a hand to me. "I'm Marlee."

My throat tightened. I was a stranger to her. I don't know how to describe how sad it made me feel. It turns out that of all the things a momma does, recognizing and being excited to see her child is the most important thing of all.

In that moment I understood the depth of the queen's punishment. Momma knew Caedrin, but not the way she once had. She no longer knew how close they'd become. The loss of memory . . . was there anything more terrible?

"Hey, there," I managed to say. I took her hand and squeezed it. "It's real nice to meet you." I didn't let go of her hand. I told myself to, but what I really wanted to do was tell her who I was. I looked at the queen. "What's she doing in a room with a wall and doors made of bars?"

"Isn't it pretty?" the queen said.

"It looks like a cage."

"Yes, doesn't it? Like a lovely gilded cage. And isn't she a pretty bird?"

I glanced at Momma and realized what the costume was. She was a woodpecker. I scowled.

"Come out of there, Mo-arlee." I tugged on Momma's hand. "People don't belong in birdcages. Neither do birds, for that matter. I think birds ought to be able to fly around the world, if that's what they want to do. Not get stuck in a cell like a common criminal. Everybody should be free. Except for common criminals. And uncommon ones."

I pulled her through the opening, but she withdrew her hand and stepped back.

"I have letters to write," Momma said, nodding toward a desk that was made of blown glass. It was swirly and beautiful, like everything in the infernal castle.

"Oh, yeah? Well, come on out of there. I bet we can find a lot of other pretty desks and tables for you to write at."

"So obsessed with being able to come and go," the queen said. "Even without your memory." She shook her head at me, then looked at Marlee. "Kismet likes to roam. The thing she can't stand is to be enclosed in small spaces. Crux and I suspect that her need to wander comes from having found she can enter and leave most places, even the Never, at will." The queen glanced at the window of Momma's cell.

"I'd never put you in a bird costume, Kismet. It would be too cruel a reminder that you can't fly." To Momma she said, "Kismet's magic is crude and flawed. But she has a rare and valuable skill. My knights spent a lot of time training her to make great use of it. She doesn't remember that now. Or even when she has her memory. Her recollection is always somewhat selective."

"Hmm," I said. "Sometimes a person gets training in one thing, but then changes her mind and decides to pursue a different career. That's the way people are."

The queen's lovely eyes narrowed.

"Now, where is there another nice desk or table for Marlee to write her letters?" I asked.

"It pleases me to have her in that room. And she doesn't mind. Do you, dear heart?"

"No," Marlee said with a shrug, but the smile that played on her lips was one I recognized. It was the one she used when she was just being polite. I studied her face and saw the smallest hint of defiance flash in her clear green eyes. My lips curved. My momma was still in there.

I was surprised she didn't speak up and contradict the queen. Aunt Mel tried to please people, but when things weren't right or fair, Momma got fed up pretty quickly and she let people know. I supposed things were different when a person lost her memories.

My hands balled into fists. It took a lot of will for me to unclench them and let them hang limp at my sides.

"The room's very comfortable," the queen said. "Join her in there for a bit of time and see. You seem to be sharing so much these days."

I looked at the queen blankly.

"Your memory, dear heart. Marlee has had some problems with her memory as well. Roseblade thought that perhaps her affliction had somehow affected you. But it's not likely. I would say it's not possible, but impossible isn't something that applies here. Impossible fails to hold its ground against magic. Or against the will of a queen."

"Determination does work wonders," I said.

"If you're too fearful to go in," the queen said, making it a question and a challenge, "we can retire to the dressing room."

I had no intention of going anywhere without Momma, but getting locked in a room was exactly counter to my plans. I intended to get her and everyone I loved out of the Never as quickly as possible.

"Why don't we all—"

"No," the queen said, pulling the control for the door. It started to close.

I darted through the opening, my shirt catching between the gatelike metal doors. The fabric ripped as I wrenched it free.

The queen smiled. "I shall have to get you a costume, too."

"That's real sweet of you, but I pick out my own clothes."

"You'll wear a costume if it pleases me to see you wear one."

The cool steel in her voice stiffened my spine.

I will knock your block off, Your Highness, I thought furiously.

"Is that some kind of crazy law in here? That you get to tell people what to wear?"

Her smile faltered. "Don't be contrary. This is the way you always get yourself into trouble." The queen cleared her throat. "Because of your memory loss, you forgot to bow when we met. Of course, you forgot to ask permission before you left the Never the last time, even with your memory still intact. You seem to forget your place whether you're cursed or not. That's especially offensive in a Halfling. Despite being bespelled with memory loss, Witch Marlee has been exceptionally compliant. Learn from her example."

Exceptionally compliant? I thought. That didn't sound like Momma at all. The spell's memory loss had regressed her to her younger self. But had she really been so different as a teenager? How young did she think she was?

I turned to Momma. "How long have you been here? How old are you?" I whispered.

The corners of her mouth turned down. "It doesn't matter," she said, not whispering.

"It does," I said.

"Technically sixteen, but I'm emancipated."

I cocked my head. "Doesn't that word mean free?" I asked, gesturing to the bars.

She laughed, and it made me smile even though nothing seemed funny about being stuck in a birdcage. I glanced at the queen, who had stepped back a couple feet, but stood watching us.

"They don't let witches wander around the Never," Momma

said. "I traveled underhill for a specific reason, and I've gotten what I wanted. This is just"—she shrugged—"temporary. They have to be sure of me."

"You came to be with Caedrin?"

Momma nodded.

"Because you're in love with him?"

"Well," she said, and paused. She walked to the window. "It's personal."

To me, too! I wanted to say. She'd gotten imprisoned for him. I sure hoped they loved each other. "How did you meet?" I asked, so curious I didn't move an inch while I waited for her to answer.

A small smirk returned. "I saved his life . . . or thought I did. He thought that was cool. I guess no girl ever tried to protect him before."

From the corner of my eye I saw the queen become as still as a statue. Her expression could've frozen a raging river to solid ice.

"But it turned out he didn't need saving," Momma said. "In fact, he'd been coming to rescue me." She grinned. "My sister and I were on South Padre for spring break. One day on the beach, Caedrin came up to me to ask directions, which made no sense, since there were better people—locals—to ask. He wore tan pants that had a drawstring that looked made of twine. He was shirtless, but carried this brown pack, like he'd been camping."

Her ponytail swung as she glanced at the bars. The queen was still there, within earshot.

"Do you want to wait until we're alone?"

Momma shook her head. "The queen's heard the story."

"Go on then. You said you saved him?"

"When we met on the beach, Caedrin and I talked, and there was something between us." She shrugged. "One of those things where you like a guy and know he likes you, but more intense. After a while, he said good-bye and left. By his questions and the way he looked when he left, I decided he was on the island looking for something other than a spring fling."

Momma sat down on a cushioned bench and crossed one

long leg over the other. She rested her folded hands on her lap. She didn't look much like a bird, more like a dancer playing one. She and Aunt Mel were graceful. I'd heard people say so more than once, and had always been proud to hear it. Too bad I hadn't inherited that. I was small boned and slim, even more so than they were, but when our gym class learned different kinds of dances, my teacher always shook her head and put me in the back. I could do a Texas two-step without treading on Zach's toes, but that was the best I could claim. I thought about Kismet, so light-footed and able to flip out of trees. Was she graceful? Yes, in an athletic sort of way. But I didn't think she'd necessarily have been good ballerina material either. I smiled. For some reason, every time I found some little way that we were alike, it made me happy.

Momma tipped her head slightly. "Later that night, Melanie and I were at a bar. She was flirting like crazy, and we were surrounded by random guys. If boys were a major, that's what my sister would study in college," Momma said, rolling her eyes.

My grin widened. She seemed younger than usual, but also worldly-wise.

"I spotted Caedrin leaning against a palm tree a few feet from the patio. I wanted to speak to him, but Mel had gone to the bathroom, so I waited for her."

She made a casual gesture with her hand. "Meanwhile, I'd seen this other group standing in a cluster between the beachfront bars. They loitered near the place that led to the road and parking lots. I'd noticed them because they looked too dressed up for spring break on the island. Black lace and hooker heels? The guys in silk shirts and trousers? Come on. A couple times, one or two would peel off from the group a few minutes after a good-looking girl or guy passed them. Then one laughed, and I caught a flash of fangs. Normal people wouldn't have seen them, but witch eyes," she said, touching her temple. "A gaggle of bloodsuckers, looking for easy prey. A couple of them had begun to stare at Caedrin, which wasn't a surprise. He's tall and gorgeous, and the light catches him more than it does a regular guy. I don't know why I didn't realize he was fae when I talked

to him. I guess because I'd never met a faery before. Even the
smell of honey and apple cider didn't register. So close to the
ocean, the smell of fishy salt water had been too strong. Anyway, he walked past the patio and went down the dark path
toward the street. Four of the vampires went right after him. So
did I." She smiled. "I carry a spring-loaded stake in my purse.
Don't ask me how I thought I'd use that one weapon against
four bloodsuckers." She rolled her eyes, her smile widening.
"In those moments, you don't really think."

With a roll of her wrist, her hand made an "and then"
gesture that Edie sometimes made. "I did kill one of them.
But the others would've dined on witch blood if he hadn't
been what he was. You've never seen anyone move like that.
He took them by surprise. In an instant he'd double-loaded
his bow and sent arrows through the hearts of two vampires
at once. The other was so stunned he was clumsy in his
lunge. He opened his mouth to call out, but barely made a
sound before Caedrin shoved an arrow into his chest."
Momma shook her head. "'What are you?' I asked him."
She licked her lips. "He said, 'Did you know they were
throat rippers when you followed them?' I nodded. He
laughed and then said, 'I wanted to draw them away so I
could deal with them before they targeted you.'" She tilted
her head, and her red ponytail swayed to the side. "I asked
him, 'What makes you think they would've come after me?'
He said, 'How could they have resisted?'"

I smiled.

"That made me laugh," Momma continued. "'They probably would've because of my sister. She draws attention wherever she goes,' I told him. He asked, 'Is she very like you? I
couldn't tell from where I was. It's hard to notice anything other
than you.' I asked if he was serious, and he said, 'Certainly.'"

Momma shrugged. "My sister and I are identical twins.
But Caedrin sees something more than what's on the surface.
From the beginning he came straight for me. And I went
straight for him."

I thought about that. I'd known that feeling—initially
with Zach, who'd been my first love, and later with Bryn. In

a room full of people, there was an awareness of where that one guy was, and an invisible force pulling me to him. "Go that way," something inside me would say.

"Did you spend the rest of the spring break with him?" I asked.

"I met up with him on and off. He didn't want to meet my sister or my friends. He had stuff to do, but he wanted to see me. On my last night I told him I had to go home to Houston the next day. He wasn't happy. He said he'd been sent on a mission by his queen and would have to return underhill when he finished it. But he wanted to see me again. I told him I'd be out of school for the summer. He wanted to know when I'd be free. I told him the date that summer break started. I'd been planning to get a job and take a vacation in Mexico with Melanie. But he said he'd come for me when school ended. He told me to plan to go away with him. And that's what I did."

"Was . . . Did your sister get mad that you decided to leave?"

"Maybe a little. But Melanie can fall in love in five minutes. And if she's going to meet a boyfriend, Timbuktu's around the corner, you know? So she couldn't exactly give me a hard time. I told Momma Just that I was going on an exchange program for the summer, and Melanie played along."

"You call your momma 'Momma Just'?" I asked. This was the other thing I really wanted to ask about. Now that I knew that my granny Justine Trask in Houston had been my great grandmother, I wanted to find out what had happened between Momma and Mrs. Hurley. When I'd asked Aunt Melanie about Josephine, Aunt Mel had gotten tears in her eyes and said her momma was someone she never talked about. She said she couldn't.

Momma glanced at me. "Just is short for Justine. It's her first name. It's also short for *justice*. She always treats people fairly."

"Most girls would simply call her Momma. Is there a story there?" I asked.

Momma's gaze settled on my face. She seemed to reach past my eyes right into my head. She couldn't actually do that with her magic, especially in the Never, where her powers didn't work, but when I was a little girl she'd always known when I was fibbing or angling for something. She could read me like a book.

"I was born in London, but I live with my grandmother in Houston. She's the mother of my heart."

My mouth opened, but it took me a few moments to come up with any words. "How come?" I asked.

"My mother and her sister did things I couldn't forgive. So my sister and I ran away from home when we were thirteen."

"All by yourself? From England to Texas?" I asked with wide eyes.

She nodded. "We had company."

Aunt Edie, I thought. But she couldn't have helped them if they'd been kidnapped or hurt.

"What did your momma do to make you leave like that?"

"We have a family ghost. They forced her to spy for them. If she didn't do exactly what she was told, they punished her. They trapped her in increasingly small spaces, stealing her energy so she couldn't wander and travel to places she loved. Her closest friends in New York were gone by the time she was able to return there; the place they'd haunted was demolished, and our ghost still doesn't know what happened to them. We hope they crossed over."

"They kept her a prisoner?" I asked, shocked.

"My mother's highest priority is the community of witches. The future of witchcraft in general is the most important thing in the world to her. More important than her own family. When she was really strict, our ghostly aunt encouraged us to rebel. I suppose my mother resented that. She began to keep us apart from our aunt Edie. My sister and I accepted that when we were small, but then Melanie found out what they were doing to Edie, and we couldn't stand it. I decided to protect our aunt from them. I decided to take her out of their reach."

"It was your idea to leave?"

Momma nodded.

"That must've been a hard decision."

"No, it wasn't. Not for me. My sister was the one who wasn't sure about leaving our life in England."

"How did you convince her?"

"There was no real debate or discussion. I just said I was leaving and would never be back. I didn't consider Josephine Hurley my mother anymore. Melanie chose me. She chose to help rescue our aunt from forced servitude and cruel punishments. It was the right thing to do. That's what got us through. You see, we didn't get away clean. We were caught and put in shackles and held in a dungeon by the witches' association." Momma smirked. "Our mother tried to make us too terrified to run again. It did scare us, but it made us mad as well. Melanie became very determined. We were both good at sleight of hand and glamours. Our aunt was great at them and had helped us master them. We put a death glamour on ourselves. When our captors checked on us, they were shocked and terrified that our mother and her sister would hold them responsible for our deaths. I lifted the key from one of the witches who was guarding us. They left us alone while they tried to decide how to handle things. We escaped."

I stared at her. "Who were the people who captured you?"

"Members of the Conclave. Our aunt Margaret's colleagues."

"They sent the Conclave after you? When you were thirteen?"

"I'm glad they did. It convinced Melanie they were capable of anything. She was sure that if our mother got us home, she'd lock us up for months. Or do the worst thing imaginable: She might separate us. When we got to Houston and told our grandmother Justine what happened, she called England and told her daughters that if they set foot in Texas, she'd consider it an act of aggression. It could've turned into an all-out war. Momma Justine has powerful friends who don't like answering to the World Association in England. They consider American witches independent. They wouldn't let English witches come for us without putting up a fight. We're American witches now."

"But you're underhill in Great Britain. With the Seelie."

"No one hates the World Association of Magic more than the Seelie court. So we have that in common."

"Um, have you told them that? Because right now you're dressed up like a cartoon and living in a birdcage room."

"That's a little thing." She paused and added in a low voice, "I never did mind about the little things."

I froze. I knew that line.

Momma shrugged her brows, and my mouth went dry.

That sentence was from an action movie where the girl with strawberry-blond hair was a spy and assassin. I wasn't supposed to watch it, because I was too little. But I'd snuck into the room and hidden under the couch. They'd caught me when they heard my wrappers crinkle. I'd been eating Hershey's miniatures.

Before I'd gotten caught, I'd seen the way they trained the girl to pretend everything was okay even when it really wasn't. I'd had a lot of questions about that. Edie had explained how a person sometimes had to hide what she really thought so she could get the chance to escape. I hadn't understood at the time, but I'd never forgotten the way the girl had pretended not to be scared or sad about the violence all around her.

I never did mind about the little things, the girl had said. And in the end, she'd gotten away and was free.

By saying that line, I knew what Momma telling me: She was pretending not to mind the birdcage and costume, even though she did. She was biding her time.

Without saying so, she also told me something else, something that made my heart slam against my ribs in excitement.

Momma watched that movie after I was born. If she remembered it, my momma didn't have amnesia at all.

24

I DRAGGED MY eyes from her face. Obviously she had her reasons for pretending that she'd lost her memory. I looked over my shoulder toward the bars. The queen had backed up.

The sound of something being dragged over the floor made Momma walk to the bars. A moment later a stone wall began to slide into place, blocking our view through the bars.

"What the hell?" I yelled, rushing forward.

"You want privacy, don't you, Kismet? Well, this should give you plenty."

I shoved my hands through the bars, trying to push the wall away, but it was too heavy. Someone—or likely more than one strong creature—was putting it in position. The room fell into shadow, with the only light coming from the one small window.

I continued to try to dislodge the huge stone barrier, but I'd have needed bigger muscles and more leverage to shift that mammoth thing. After a few moments I slapped my hands against it in frustration, panting from the effort.

I looked over my shoulder. Momma folded her arms across her chest as she stared at the sand-colored stone.

Then she muttered, "For fuck's sake."

My brows shot up.

Glancing at my surprised face, she gave a sheepish smirk. "Sometimes a four-letter word is the only one that really fits."

I smiled. Then I laughed, and she chuckled, too.

She walked to the desk and lifted the glass sitting on it. She offered it to me. I drank the water while she lit a candle. She stood near the flame, as if waiting for it to do something besides burn. The candle seemed to be handmade and smelled of earth and herbs. An insect buzzed near it, and Momma made a sharp move, slamming the overturned cup down, capturing the insect under it.

My jaw dropped.

"A bug, but not the usual sort," she said. "One of her spies," Momma whispered.

I strode to the desk and peered through the glass. Sure enough, there was a tiny pixie flying in circles in the small enclosure.

The pixie flew toward me, bumping against the glass and shaking her fist furiously.

"Well, if you weren't spying, you wouldn't be in there," I said with a shrug. "We have to get out of here," I said to Momma, looking around for something long and heavy to wedge against the wall. Zach and Bryn would eventually come looking for us, but I didn't want the false wall to make us impossible to find.

"She must have figured out that I palmed a key," Momma said, pulling the band off her ponytail. Hooked to the band was a brass key that had been tucked into her hair, hidden from view.

"Where—"

"All witches need to be good at sleight of hand. I would've made a great pickpocket," she said with a wink. "Do you remember me teaching you?"

"Yes," I said, recalling it suddenly. I'd been able to palm things. I'd used it to cheat at cards. I remembered showing off for Zach's daddy when we were little. He'd gotten a big kick out of me.

"Show me," she said.

I only looked at her.

"You have magic now. It's important to have fast hands and to show you can use them for tricks, so that your real power can be concealed," she said.

I did as she asked, taking the key from her several times. At first I was rusty, but after a few moments, my light-fingered technique returned.

"It's not just important out there. Even in here, that skill may do you good," she said as she put the key into the gate's lock. She turned the key and the gate slid open, but of course that wasn't a help, since there was a giant slab of stone blocking the way.

"How come you didn't use that key before?"

She opened a drawer and pulled out a pair of black stretch pants and a green V-neck T-shirt. "There was no point," she said as she changed clothes. "As long as we're underhill, wherever we go she'll eventually find us."

"So you have to get out of the Never."

Momma lifted the mattress of her bed, and I gaped. There was an iron mallet and a metal pickax. "He smuggled them in for me."

"As what? A Valentine's Day present? Anniversary gift?" I scoffed.

She grinned.

"What he should have done is taken you out of the Never for good."

Her smile faltered. "If only it were that simple."

"Why isn't it? He can live humanside. He's done it plenty of times."

"He's sworn his allegiance to her. He can't leave unless she gives her permission."

I froze.

"Which she will never do."

"Momma, you can't stay here. You must see that. She thinks she poisoned you into losing your memory. When she finds out—And, hey, how come her curse didn't work?"

Momma rolled her pretty eyes. "She's so vain. She loves

the human faery tales. She considers them a tribute. So she tried to poison me with a magic apple."

"Like you were Snow White?" I asked.

"Exactly," Momma said, smiling. Momma tipped her head and drew a hand quickly across her mouth. "I pretended to swallow a few bites, but didn't."

"I never knew you could be so sneaky."

"Well, now you do," she said.

I laughed. I couldn't help myself.

"See if you can lift that mallet," she said, taking the pickax.

I hoisted it. It was really heavy. I started toward the stone wall, but she went the other way. My eyes widened as she swung the ax, puncturing the bricks under the window with the sharp edge.

"The mortar between the bricks is old. This side faces the back of the castle."

"But we're upstairs. How far is the drop?"

"We'll soon find out," she said, nodding toward the wall she'd damaged.

I swung the mallet and pounded open a big hole. Bricks spewed outward and the wall under the window crumbled.

"That should do it," Momma said, taking the candle in her hand and looking through the opening. "It's a big drop. Too far to jump." She took the linens from the bed.

"Momma, you're not thinking we're gonna tie those sheets together and climb down, are you?"

She looked at me through her lashes.

"Seriously? Knotted sheets? You think they'll hold?" I asked.

"Do you have a better plan?"

I opened my mouth, but since I didn't have any helpful suggestions I shut it again and shook my head. "Here, gimme one of those," I said.

She smiled as she handed me a sheet. "That's my girl."

AS WE RAPPELLED down the side of the castle, I told her Zach and I had broken up for good and that I'd gotten involved with Bryn.

She paused, and my feet nearly bumped into her head.

"Despite the prophecy?" she asked, and then proceeded on the downward climb.

"Yep."

"Falling for the wrong guy is risky."

"I know. It's the whole reason I'm climbing down the side of a castle. My momma got involved with the *wrong* guy."

She laughed.

"It's all right. Falling for the wrong guys is getting to be a family tradition, I guess. I met one of Aunt Mel's exes, who was a killer fire warlock. Nearly got murdered by him."

"Oh. I remember him. I never met Incendio, but she told me about him."

"Anyway, Bryn's a lot nicer than a fire warlock. He's saved my life instead of trying to end it. So he's got that going for him."

She didn't answer, which made me frown.

"Try to keep an open mind, Momma. You were gone for over a year. You can't expect everything at home to stay the same when you're gone that long," I said. Of course, almost all the changes had happened in the past couple of months. It had been a real whirlwind. But she didn't need to know that. "And by the way, I kind of got engaged."

"Kind of?"

"Bryn got down on one knee and made the prettiest speech you ever heard."

"Did you give him an answer?"

"Yeah. I said yes."

"So you're engaged to a Lyons."

"Edie hates him. And she's alive again."

"Pardon me?"

I explained, and she laughed until I thought she'd lose her grip and fall. When I told her that Mrs. Hurley and Edie were together at WAM Headquarters, she shook her head. "My money's on Edie." She licked her lips. "But mostly for sentimental reasons. Josephine's like those prophecies of Lenore's: You never want to get on the wrong side of one."

We reached the ground, and she pointed to the path we should take.

"We need to avoid the trees," I said, explaining the way they'd been spying.

"It's impossible to do that. The trees are everywhere," she said, striking out through the woods. "But the ones near Caedrin's won't be loyal to anyone but him."

We walked for a while in silence, and I found it hard to judge time and distance. Finally she said, "It's okay to talk now."

"We won't be overheard?"

"There's always a risk, but it's safer here."

"It's good to see you, Momma. I missed you."

She turned and hugged me. She held me real tight and whispered, "I missed you, too, baby. Every day."

"You should come on home. He knows it's not safe for you here. If he really wants to be with you, he should find a way to do so out there."

"It's not possible. The laws that govern the world of the Never are complicated."

"Even if he can't come out, you have to leave here. You see that, right? No matter how much you love him. You can't be locked up behind a giant stone wall in some castle."

She looked over her shoulder at the castle cloaked in clouds and sunlight. "It's been bad here since Kismet left and Ghislaine heard that we helped her."

"Did you guys help her?"

"In a roundabout way we did. It's not easy. There are restrictions on what Caedrin can do."

"So you care about Kismet?"

"Of course."

"She thought you said you didn't."

Momma gave me a sharp look. "She said that? You've talked to her?"

"Yes."

"How is she?"

"Um, she's a real good assassin. She can flip out of trees like an acrobat and shoot an—"

"That's not what I meant. How is she? Really?"

"Kind of sad and lonely, I think. She got mad at me over something. . . . I think she gets mad pretty easily. So about saying that you didn't care about her, she made a mistake about that, right?"

"No, I said it." Momma shook her head with a pained look. "She wasn't supposed to hear that. I told Ghislaine I didn't care about Kismet because Ghislaine is so jealous. I didn't want to add fuel to the fire. Though it's hard to imagine things getting worse."

"Why does Ghislaine care what you think of Kismet?"

"Kismet is supposed to be Ghislaine's. Caedrin brought her here and gave her to the queen. He thought it would cool Ghislaine's fury. Caedrin was once Ghislaine's lover, and she hates that he fell in love with anyone else, especially a witch."

I clucked my tongue. "There's a lot of supernatural prejudice here. And out there. It's a problem." I bit my lip and shrugged. "I'll maybe have to work on that, being half-and-half. Start a group or something. I'll think on it. Now, back to Ghislaine and Kismet. If Ghislaine doesn't think much of Halflings, why did Caedrin think she'd want Kismet at all?"

"Because she wanted a tribute . . . repayment for the slight. Ghislaine assumed there was one daughter and that she had her. A child was the biggest apology gift he could've given her. But she didn't raise Kismet in the castle. She put her out and forbade Caedrin from ever revealing that she was his child."

"How did you forgive him for that?" I said, my voice louder and sharper than I'd intended. "He took one of your babies and gave it to some jealous psycho faery. How are you even talking to him, let alone living in this place with him?"

"He had to do it."

"He did not!"

"You don't understand. The law made it impossible for him to leave Kismet with me. He had to take her into Never and to offer her to the queen."

"There are some messed-up laws here. Someone should change them."

"Yes, but the person who benefits from the laws isn't likely to alter them, is she?"

"Maybe somebody should force her to."

"Easier said than done," Momma said, crossing a stream.

A pretty house shimmered into view. A silvery mist hung all around it, but I could see its archways and windows.

Momma put a hand on the door. "I'm home," she said, and like magic, it opened.

In an instant I knew there was trouble, because I heard raised voices, and one of them was Bryn's.

25

I HUSTLED INSIDE and found Caedrin and Bryn in a
room that had a collection of furniture that could've doubled
as a swing set. Everything was hooked to wires on the ceiling or walls. It made you want to hop on and take a ride.

Bryn was shirtless and wet, his black hair slick and shiny.
He wore black pants that started below his navel and ended at
his ankles. They were as glossy and dark as his hair.

He walked to me, smelling like salted caramel.

"Hey," I said.

He caught my face in his hands and gave me a kiss that
could've doubled for foreplay. When he let go, I flushed and
took a deep breath. Then I murmured a little dazedly, "I'm
fine. So are you. Really fine. That's good."

I glanced at Momma, who arched a brow and said, "So
it's like that."

Bryn took a step toward her. "It's nice to see you, Ms.
Trask. I know you'll have reservations about my involvement with Tamara, but I intend to put your fears to rest."

She studied his face. "Even if your intentions are good,
that prophecy might be about things outside your control."

"I don't accept that anything to do with us is out of our control."

Momma laughed softly. "Not even here?" She glanced down at his legs.

Was it my imagination or had the pants gotten lower and higher at the same time, exposing his hip bones and calves?

"Hey! What's wrong with your clothes? Salt water shrinks them?" I demanded, putting a hand out to touch his thigh. It wasn't like any fabric I'd ever felt. It was soft, sleek, and attached to his flesh. My brows shot up.

"He's fae," Caedrin said with a smile.

"Is that sealskin?"

"In the water it covered my entire body like a wetsuit. Only my hands and face stayed human."

"Wow! And how was swimming?"

"Amazing."

My smile widened.

"I need to talk to you about that, though. I found something out," he said, glancing around.

Momma looked past us at Caedrin. "And how about you, lover boy? Doing all right?"

The corners of his mouth curved up, and he looked at her like she was a biscuit covered in honey. "As well as the world allows. Better still if your memory's restored."

"My memory's fine."

"So the queen released you from the curse and the castle because she believes she has her first assassin back? She'll be twice as angry when Tammy Jo leaves again. Or if she finds out she's not who she's been pretending to be."

Momma shook her head. "Ghislaine didn't release me. In fact, she tried to trap Tammy Jo in the cage room with me."

He frowned and then covered his mouth thoughtfully. "You broke her out of the castle," he said, looking at me. "Without negotiating for your freedom?" He shook his head gravely.

"I didn't break her out. She broke me out!" I exclaimed, then thought about that mallet I'd swung. "Well, I guess it was fifty-fifty on the breakout."

Momma made a gesture to wave off the trouble we'd probably started. "Ghislaine went too far."

"What will you do? Leave with them?" Caedrin asked in a low voice, like he almost couldn't bear to say the words.

"Yes, Momma. You should get out. Actually, you ought to go right now. Bryn and I will be right behind you. After we collect Zach and Mercutio."

"Mercutio?"

"He's my friend. An ocelot. That's a jungle cat." I turned to Bryn. "But speaking of Zach, guess where he's at? Can't guess?" I demanded, not really giving him time to. "He's at the castle," I said. "Don't ask me why. But I'd sure like to know what he thinks he's doing spying in there. Makes me wonder whether he had his own reasons for coming here besides just protecting me." I glanced at the skin of Bryn's hips and thighs where the black was fading. "Hey! You need some real pants right now." I stepped in front of him to block Momma's view.

"Come with me, selkie," Caedrin said.

I joined them in Caedrin's room. The bed had four wooden posts and was covered by a mossy green quilted silk spread that was as soft as a cloud. I sat on the edge of the bed as Bryn dressed in tan pants and a white pullover shirt. He looked like a pirate. A sexy one.

"Can you give us a few minutes alone?" Bryn asked.

Caedrin nodded and left.

"Have you noticed your hair?" Bryn said, lifting a strand and showing me the end.

It had grown lighter by several shades.

"Wow," I said. It wasn't strawberry blond like Kismet's yet, but the color was somewhere between my normal color and hers. "The sun here must be pretty powerful."

"Or the magic must." Bryn laid the hair down thoughtfully. "When Kismet's out there off the faery trails, her hair may get almost as red as yours."

"Yeah, I think maybe it does."

"I heard something interesting. I met other selkies in the surf. They sent me down to find a treasure chest that's buried.

It's a test for young selkies, to see how deep they can dive and whether they're drawn to the chest's magic. Anyway—"

"Did you find it?"

"Yes."

"What was in it?" I couldn't help asking. I loved the idea of buried treasure.

"Gold and pearls mostly, but also a few handmade pieces of jewelry brought from the human world."

"That must have been amazing. Now that you've been a selkie here, I wonder if you'll be able to dive way underwater in the regular world. You could find shipwrecks and buried treasure all over the place. Although you'd have to watch out for merrows," I said, frowning. The fae mermen and merwomen were vicious, and they lived in the waters of the Gulf of Mexico.

"Tamara," Bryn said.

"Yes?"

"There's another piece of sunken treasure we need to talk about."

"Okay."

"The selkies said that they've been sent several times into the Atlantic Ocean between Ireland and Scotland. They've been searching for a magical piece of amber that Kismet says she lost in the ocean while trying to escape a pack of werewolves who'd chased her to the Scottish coast."

"What are you saying?"

"I'm saying the woman the Conclave heard was in contact with werewolves in the Scottish woods was definitely your sister. She lied to us. She knows about the missing amber artifact. She is, in fact, the one who caused it to be missing."

26

I WALKED TO the door, wanting to ask Momma and Caedrin about the artifact, but Bryn caught my arm.

"We shouldn't talk in front of Caedrin," Bryn said. "I don't trust him."

"That might be kind of tricky, since it's his house," I said.

"There's plenty of room outside. From what I've heard, the Never stretches for miles to the north and east."

"I'll ask, but Momma may not want to leave him," I said, walking out into the living room.

Caedrin sat on one of the couch swings, and Momma was right next to him. She sat sideways with one bent leg resting against his as she faced him. He held her hand as they talked, their heads close together. I couldn't help myself; I smiled.

Bryn cleared his throat.

"Keep your pirate's britches on," I murmured. "I'm getting to it." I strode to them, standing up straight. "I was wondering if you'd mind letting us talk to Momma alone for a little while about some humanside family business that concerns our aunt Edie."

"If it doesn't concern the fae, the queen won't ask about it. You needn't worry that I'll be forced to tell her."

"Well, I don't know all the particulars of the situation. Could you give us a couple minutes?"

"Yes," he said, giving me a reassuring smile that made me feel better. "I'll see what word's passing through the forest and the village near the castle . . . whether anyone's spotted your cat. Or noted your castle break."

"Try not to be seen," Momma said. "If she orders you in, you'll have to tell her we're here."

"She won't need me to tell her. You can't conceal yourself from discovery. I'm sure dozens of pixies and hobgoblins spotted you making your way here. When she finds out you've left the castle and makes it known she's looking for you, you'll be found."

Momma grimaced and said, "I know. I just want us to have as much time as possible."

Caedrin went out the front door and closed it behind him, but knowing the entire queendom would surround us at the queen's orders meant I wasn't that reassured by having the door closed.

"So, Momma, here's the thing. You know how Aunt Edie's got a body now?"

"Yes. Whose body?" Momma asked.

"My friend Evangeline. You don't know her."

"Evangeline Rhodes? The mentally ill witch from Dallas?"

"Um, yeah. So you do know her. So Aunt Edie's stuck in the headquarters for the World Association of Magic. She's not in a birdcage room, because as far as I know they don't have any of those. But she's a prisoner there, along with Bryn's best friend."

"You didn't say she'd been arrested. What did she do?"

"Nothing. It's not her fault at all!" I chewed my lip. "Though knowing her she'll probably get in a bunch more trouble if we leave her alone there too long." I took a big breath in and blew it out. I explained about being sent to find the amber and how we'd been told Momma or Aunt Melanie knew where it was.

Momma's expression was blank for a moment and then her brows drew together. "I haven't left the Never since I entered it. If I leave, Ghislaine won't let me come back. Witches aren't allowed to come and go. There's concern that one might lead an army inside. It's why the paths are hidden from humans."

I ran a hand through my hair and then tucked some behind my ear. "Bryn and I think it was Kismet who was spotted in the woods and stole the artifact."

Momma pursed her lips. "I believe she was sent out to retrieve an amber, but I was under the impression it belonged to the fae. The rumor was that Kismet claimed she lost it. The queen was furious and had her flogged. It was the beginning of the end."

"Flogged? You mean whipped?" I said with a gasp.

Momma nodded with a grim expression. "Yes, and worse—the queen made Crux do it."

"Why was that worse?"

"Because at the time, he was her boyfriend."

My jaw dropped.

"Well, that explains the animosity," Bryn said.

"Crux is her ex-boyfriend?" I said, still shocked.

"Yes, I am."

All three of our heads jerked to the doorway leading to the hall. Crux leaned against the frame. How long had he been there? And how did he get to be so sneaky? He was as silent as Mercutio stalking prey.

"What do you want?" I said with narrowed eyes. His hands were behind his back. Was that to show us he wasn't on the offensive? Or because he was? Did he have a weapon?

"It's not what *I* want," Crux said, shrugging his shoulders. "It never has been."

"You tricked me into coming here. I'm really glad that Kismet didn't come with me."

"She'll come."

"She will not. She's mad. I was worried, but now I'm glad I don't know where she is. I hope she disappears and you never find her. Flogged by her own boyfriend! No wonder she wanted to get free of this place. It's terrible. You all suck for following the queen's nasty orders."

"If Kismet lost the amber, she did so to spite the queen. That's why she was punished," Crux said. He glanced out the window into the far distance.

My gaze followed his, but all I saw were rustling leaves.

"And she will come, because the Never has the only thing in the world she won't be able to resist." Crux nodded and glanced over. "You."

My insides tightened. I didn't want to be the cause of Kismet returning. "I won't stay here. Let's go, Bryn. We'll go back to the place where we started. I'm sure Zach will head there when he's done at the castle." I wondered again what the Sam Houston he'd gone there for in the first place. Didn't he realize how dangerous these fae were? There didn't seem to be any rules against the queen locking people up for no reason at all. Or trying to put a curse on them! It was a faery tale gone wrong.

I looked at Crux. "Was Zach still touring the castle when you left?"

"No."

"Okay, so he'll be on his way back. Let's go now," I said, catching Bryn's hand in my grip.

"No," Crux said. "He finished admiring the art, but he didn't leave the castle."

"Why not?" I asked, tensing. Would we have to bust him out, too? I should've kept that mallet.

"She wanted him to stay. He's her type."

"She imprisoned him? What kind of room did she have for him? A giant doghouse?" I said, thinking that was where he belonged. I pursed my lips. Zach sure had been flirting up a storm lately with dangerous blond women. Not that it was my business as his ex-wife. But it was my business as his traveling companion.

"She didn't imprison him."

"Well, Zach will leave there soon. If he doesn't, someone will have to go get him. And I'm sure Merc will turn up. He likes to explore, but he usually checks in, especially when there's trouble brewing, which there is." I studied Crux's face and then his shoulders and arms. He still hadn't shown his hands. "Did you tell her that I'm not Kismet?"

"No, because she hasn't asked. My oath is very specific," Crux said.

"Uh-huh," I said. I was curious about the nature of these vows that the fae knights had to make to their power-crazy queen. But I'd get information about the oaths from someone other than Crux. The longer he stayed, the sorer my muscles got from being clenched so tight.

"I obey the queen's direct orders, and I was given one to force Kismet to return to the Never."

"You tried and she got away. You did your best," I said with a shrug.

He smiled. "I did. I thought it would be a bloody battle, and that if she got mad enough, she might kill me. But then I discovered the right leverage to use against her."

I balled my fists.

"Until she returns, I have no intention of letting you leave."

"Yeah, about that," I said, shaking my head. "It's like I told you before: I'm American. We don't bow down to kings and queens, and no one's allowed to lock us up or hold us against our will for no reason. You saw what happened when you tried before. Merc and I kicked your faery butt."

He laughed. "Is that your impression?"

"It's not just my impression. It's what happened," I said, though I knew that things were more complicated than that. "And Bryn trapped you in a circle. Because he's more clever than you are." Probably taunting him wasn't the best strategy, but I was tired of talking.

"His magic doesn't work here, and I don't see your cat anywhere."

I strode to the door. I couldn't stand to be still any longer.

Crux's hands armed with bow and arrow appeared instantly. He aimed at Bryn. No matter how fast I ran, that arrow would be faster.

I froze, my heart slamming against my ribs.

"The more people you have with you, the more trouble you'll be capable of creating," he said.

I realized what he planned to do. "Don't!" I yelled, darting forward.

"Crux, wait!" Momma said.

Crux's wrist cocked at the last second so the arrow went just wide of Bryn's throat. Without missing a beat, Crux loaded another arrow, ready to shoot again. But by then I'd gotten into position between him and Bryn.

"I can wound you. It'll make things easier if I slow you down," Crux said.

"You could do that," Momma said gravely. "But there would be consequences."

Crux's eyes, the color of smoky quartz, gazed at Momma for an instant.

"Not just from Kismet. Caedrin, too," Momma said.

Crux studied me for a moment.

Momma continued in a calm tone. It was like she was asking if he wanted some biscuits. "Caedrin doesn't interfere when the queen orders you to do something to Kismet because he can't. But Tammy Jo doesn't belong to Ghislaine. She's mine. And his."

Crux's eyes narrowed.

"Think things over. Ghislaine's barred the exits out of the Never. Tammy Jo is already trapped here. You don't have to do anything. You've already done it. You've made her the bait. Kismet will either come home or she won't. You don't need to hurt Tammy or her friends to keep them here."

"She's resourceful. Not trained like Kis, but possessed of the same instincts. And of worse. She's dead stubborn."

"Tammy Jo doesn't understand how things work, but we'll explain it to her. Caedrin and Kismet both know you haven't had a choice about the things you've done to Kismet on the queen's orders. But you do have a choice now. Stand down."

Crux's gaze settled on my face. "Will you swear an oath that you won't try to leave?"

"Nope."

The corners of Crux's mouth quirked up. "Do you see?" Crux said, his gaze flicking to Momma for a second.

Momma sighed. "So keep your eyes on her. You can always shoot her later if you need to."

"Momma!"

"Later then. If I need to," Crux said, locking eyes with me.

"Kismet must've been really disappointed when she found out what a jerk she was dating," I said.

Crux lowered his bow. "When she found out? She's always known what I'm like. She's the same."

"She is not."

Crux's smug smile made me want to punch him right in the throat. "Let's see what you think when you get to know her better."

"I probably won't, since I hope she'll be too smart to fall for your tricks."

"She won't fall for any tricks. She'll know she's walking into a trap." He was so sure.

I scowled at him, feeling so frustrated I could scream.

Don't come, Kismet. Stay out there! I'll get myself out of the Never. Don't come!

"You're the one who fell for my tricks," Crux said.

I shot forward and punched him in the face. He shoved me so hard I flew backward. I slammed into a body and hands caught me. I felt Bryn's arms around me.

"Calm down," he said.

Crux pointed at me as reddish-gold blood trickled from his nose. "Impulsive and fearless. That's fae blood in your veins. Feel it?" he asked. "You're one of us."

"Let me go, Bryn. I wanted to break his nose, but it still looks straight to me. I need another try."

Bryn's huff of laughter ruffled my hair. "Tamara, come on. Don't make things worse."

"I wasn't. How can anybody take a knight seriously when he's such a pretty boy? He needs a crooked nose. I was helping," I said, glaring at Crux.

"Let her go, wizard. We'll help each other. I think she's a future assassin. By her logic, an iron scar on her cheek would do her well."

"Future assassin! Listen, you arrogant—"

"What are you doing here, Crux?" Caedrin said, coming in through a tall window that faced the woods behind the house.

The two handsome knights stared at each other. Crux's eyes were darker brown and his hair had fewer streaks of wheat running through it, but they had similar lean, tall frames and long-fingered hands that moved in a flash when necessary.

Sunlight glinted off the blade of the dagger in Caedrin's right hand. Sharp and beveled, it looked like it had been polished that morning.

Crux didn't answer.

"Speak or leave," Caedrin said.

"I'm on the queen's business. Of sorts."

"You've come to escort us to the castle?" Caedrin asked, his voice as hard as the stone floor of the hearth.

"No," Crux said.

"Did she tell you to enter my house?"

Crux folded his arms across his chest.

"You cannot take my life here, but I could take yours," Caedrin said.

Crux uncrossed his arms and held them wide. "As you will, then."

Caedrin sheathed his dagger. "I wouldn't wish for that. But know this: These people," Caedrin said, swirling his finger, "I claim as mine. Any injury you do to them, you do to me. And I'll answer."

"You can't make that kind of proclamation! They're of the human world. The queen hasn't let you take this woman as wife. And she never will. You can't—"

"I can," Caedrin said. "I've been to the oldest archives. A fae knight must offer a first child to the king or queen. But all children that follow with the same woman are his own to claim, be they part human, witch, vampire, wolf, or full fae. And if a knight is willing to forfeit his life for a woman, he can claim her as wife. None can oppose it. Not even the highest lord or lady of the land. Ghislaine may kill me in Marlee's place, but she can't deny me my right to stand in for her in any punishment."

"The wizard isn't yours to protect," Crux said, nodding to Bryn.

"This girl is a knight's daughter and has battled Unseelie fae and killed them. She claims him as hers to protect, and I may do the same."

"Show me where it's written. The queen could challenge that."

"She could. But if you're wise, you won't advise it."

Crux licked his lips. "Time is on your side where experience is concerned, but you've seen me fight. You can't be sure you would win."

"There are three in the Never who might kill me in a fight. You're one of them," Caedrin acknowledged with a nod. "Think that would stop me from trying? I've had years of swallowing my frustration at not being able to protect some whom I would have if the choice had been mine. I would've given my soul for the chance to fight . . . so many times. Death doesn't scare me off. Let one arrow fly into any of them, and I'll show you what it means to love down to blood and bone."

Crux shrugged; then he shook his head. "If someone tasted your blood today, I'm not sure they'd find it to be full fae. How did the humanside seep into you? You never even lived there, did you?"

Something buzzed by me, and I turned, straining my eyes. The pixie moved so fast I couldn't follow its progress.

Caedrin paused, cocking his head. I saw the air blur as tiny wings beat, holding a tiny faery aloft near Caedrin's left ear.

"Thank you, Boislonk." Caedrin turned to Momma, putting a hand on her face. "She's figured out you're gone. No one knows of a passage that can be opened to the paths that lead humanside, but sooner or later the gates will become active again. It takes too much energy to seal them tight enough to keep humans inside. When you near an exit that can be unlocked, any of you will be able to feel it." He swallowed, glancing away and then back. "Maybe you should go," he whispered.

"Maybe. But I'm not."

He hugged her to him and whispered something I couldn't

hear. I chewed my lip and swallowed against a tight throat. Would I have left the Never without Bryn? No way. So could I blame Momma for standing by her man? No, but it sure made my heart ache with worry to leave her behind.

"The thing is," I said in a low voice, "once she figures out that Momma's not cursed, Ghislaine might start trying to curse her again. And all she has to do is ask either of you," I said, pointing to Caedrin and Crux. "Since you're under her thumb by that magical curse."

"It's not a curse. It's an oath. The kind made to a sovereign and homeland. Is there no loyalty and patriotism in your world?" Crux demanded.

"Yeah, we've got loyalty and patriotism, but not some messed-up kind, like here. It's the good kind. The president couldn't make me flog Zach or betray Bryn. Once we're married, Bryn could do any crazy thing he wants to do, even commit a crime, and I wouldn't have to testify against him if I didn't want to. We've got better loyalty there and way better laws. Now, back to what I started to say. If a leader got drunk on power and wasn't being fair to his citizens, in America we'd overthrow him. Now, if Ghislaine has gone power-crazy, you—"

Caedrin shot forward and clamped a hand over my mouth. "Shhh," he whispered harshly in my ear. "No treasonous talk. Not ever. I'm sworn to protect the queen and Seelie court and lands. Ahead of everything else."

My brows scrunched together in a frown, but I nodded.

"I don't think your chosen family's going to last long here," Crux said. "That one's stubborn as a bog, and just as thick."

My middle finger popped up, but Crux didn't seem to understand the gesture. That only made me madder.

Caedrin kissed my cheek gently, his hand still covering my mouth. "It would break Marlee's heart and mine if I had to hurt you. Be careful."

I blinked. He took his hand away, but stood ready to cover my mouth again instantly if I said the wrong thing.

"I'm done talking," I said, making a gesture of locking my lips. "I'd better go," I said, walking to Momma.

"I love you. Be safe," she said, giving me a kiss and a

tight hug. Then she shoved me away from her toward Bryn. "Prove you're more than a prophecy."

Bryn nodded.

I darted forward and hugged Caedrin. "It was real nice to finally meet you, Dad." I hugged him. "If it won't mess up your promise, it'd be great if you could keep Crux from following us."

Caedrin smiled. "Call me that once more."

"Dad," I whispered in his ear. I gave him a quick kiss on the cheek and turned before he could see how watery my eyes had gotten. Bryn and I were on the run. There wasn't time for long, teary good-byes. I bit my lip and grabbed Bryn's hand. "You ready?"

"If you are," Bryn said.

I swallowed hard. "Gotta be." I walked fast toward to the door.

Behind us, Caedrin said, "No, you stay here for now."

"I'm going," Crux said, and the sounds of a scuffle began.

"No," Caedrin said. It was the last thing I heard as we went outside.

27

WE RUSHED AWAY from the house, following the tree line to the path Momma had taken to bring me there.

When we'd walked for about a mile, the whispers of the trees faded to silence. My shoulders hunched, and I jogged away from the forest.

"These trees are loyal to that Colis guy. Let's get away from them," I said.

Bryn changed direction with me, but then he cocked his head and paused. "How about the water, Tamara? I can hear a creek calling to me."

"Yeah, absolutely. Colis is the tree keeper, not the river keeper. Water should be okay, I think. Lead the way."

Bryn pointed, and we started to jog.

"Faster," I said, my skin prickling like static rode the air and would shock us any minute.

"Do you feel that?" he asked.

"Yes," I said, and then a wave of some kind of sharp magic rolled over me, making my breath catch. Because I was already panting from sprinting, it nearly knocked me over. I stumbled to my knees.

Hoofbeats pounded the ground in the distance. Bryn crouched next to me, putting a hand on my back.

"I'm okay," I said, my palms resting on the ground. Fae power flowed through my hands, and I immediately felt better. "How much farther?" I looked up at him. "Till we get to the water?"

He closed his eyes and tipped his head, assessing the water's call, I guessed. "I can't tell exactly," he said.

"They're racing toward us." I rose and started walking. "Let's go as fast as we can."

We jogged through a field of tall wildflowers.

"Almost there," he said, but I knew we wouldn't make it.

Insects or tiny fae buzzed by us. I grabbed Bryn's arm and yanked him down so we were hidden by the grass.

"She only wants me. You stay here. If you get the chance to get out of the Never, you go. I'll follow you as soon as I can," I said.

"What are you talking about? I'm not leaving you here."

"Yes, you are," I urged, giving him a shove. He didn't budge. "I got you into this, and now I want you out of it."

"No way."

"Yes, because I don't want her to see you."

"Listen, whatever happens, we're together. That oath we made, we're connected—for life or longer," he said, grabbing my hands so our rings clinked against each other.

"That doesn't count in here. These are just rings. Can't you feel the difference?"

"I feel a difference, but nothing's changed. Wherever you go in this world or any world, I go as well. I will never leave you anywhere. How can you expect me to? You know if the situation were reversed, you wouldn't leave me."

I bit my lip and tried to lie. "I might."

He laughed. "Be serious."

"Hey, I am very, very serious. I don't want her seeing you. If you won't leave the Never without me, okay. You stay in the water. I'll come find you when I escape again." I pushed his shoulder, but he just quirked a brow. "Listen," I said, changing tactics. "What if I can't figure out a way to escape? If you don't get captured, you can make a plan to rescue me. How about that?"

He smiled, and put his arms out in surrender.

"They're almost here!" I whispered frantically. "Get away from me. Go!"

Bryn backed up, whispering, "Be careful."

"Yep," I said, crawling forward to put some distance between us. When the horses stopped at the edge of the field, I marched out. I shoved my tangled hair back from my sweaty face.

"Hi," I said, waving. "I'm lost. Which way to the castle?"

A group of blond faeries, male and female, jumped down from their horses and surrounded me. Some had bows loaded with arrows, others swords. They pointed their weapons at me.

"Okay, gotcha," I said, holding my hands up in surrender. "Didn't anybody tell you guys that my memory got lost? I'm not fixin' to fight even one of you, let alone all of you at once like I'm in a Jason Statham movie."

Ghislaine rode up on a white horse. She wore a crown of white roses and a shimmering peach dress that flowed around her bare legs. She pointed at three of the fae and then nodded toward the flowers.

"Hey, where are you going?" They disappeared among the blooms. I looked up at the queen. "Where are they going?" I asked, trying to sound innocent.

She ignored the question.

Moments later, they emerged with Bryn. Despite being captured, he looked completely relaxed. I, on the other hand, felt like a jack-in-the-box that was fully wound up. I darted forward and jumped in front of him.

"He's mine," I announced, reaching back to grab his arms. As he tried to move right, so did I. When he tried to move left, I was there before him. He sighed and stopped trying to get around me.

"What do you think you're accomplishing?" Bryn murmured.

I didn't answer Bryn or acknowledge him. "He's mine," I repeated firmly.

"Your what?" Ghislaine asked, looking down at us from the top of her big white steed.

"My everything. My lawyer. My friend. And my . . . my husband."

"Pardon me?" she asked, her lovely almond-shaped eyes narrowing.

"Yep, I married him. We did that in Las Vegas. It's a place with a lot of big casinos and hotels that are based on other places. Sometimes you win six hundred and forty dollars there, and then the next day you lose fifteen hundred, like my friend Kenny. And, boy, is your wife mad, since you swore you were just going to Vegas so she could see Celine Dion sing."

"What are you saying? Are you speaking English?"

"Of course. What else would I be speaking? Anyway, what I was explaining is that sometimes you come home broke. But other times you hit the jackpot. Instead of money, I got this handsome lawyer. And if you get engaged in Las Vegas, you don't have to drag things out. They've got these little chapels where everything's all set. Photographer, witnesses, even Elvis Presley sometimes."

"Your speech is incomprehensible," Ghislaine said.

"Well, I'm—"

"Stop talking," she ordered. "Step aside. Let me look at him." I didn't move an inch. "He's mine."

"So you've said. But you're not free to marry. You're first assassin of the realm. No member of court can marry without my permission."

"Yeah, she can. If she's had a couple babies. Like I did."

"You haven't—What are you talking about?"

"Time moves way different out there. As I'm sure you've heard."

She stared at me. "I don't believe you. You don't behave like a mother."

"Well, I'm not very good at it. Maybe if I'd had a mother of my own instead of getting trained to be an assassin, I would've been better."

"What are their names? Your children?"

I faltered for half a second, then heard myself blurt, "Tamara and Josephine. They're real cute, but they get in all sorts of trouble."

"You never know what they'll say or do in a given situation," Bryn said mildly. "Shakespeare was less creative."

I turned my head slightly and said, "Shhh! I'm handling this."

"Are you?" he asked.

"Shakespeare, we've heard of him. We have his plays. All of them. In the royal library. I enjoy them, but he's not my favorite."

"Who is?" I asked, tilting my head. I would've talked about anything to get away from the subject of my marriage and children.

"Agatha Christie, Oscar Wilde, and Cary Grant."

"Um, Cary Grant was in movies. You've got movies here?"

The queen studied me thoughtfully.

"I thought it was like Excalibur times here," I said.

"Our acting troupes have performed Mr. Grant's plays. I've heard that plays are performed differently humanside now, but I don't know why they've made that change."

"Did Cary Grant write those movies he starred in?" I asked Bryn.

"No."

"Didn't think so," I whispered. "I guess it doesn't really matter."

"You seem to remember a lot about the human world," Ghislaine said.

"Well, I lived there for a while. Married to him," I said, nodding toward Bryn, whom I was still shielding from view.

"Did you see a lot of plays and movies?" the queen asked.

"Um, sure. Quite a few."

"You never liked plays."

"I didn't say I liked 'em all. But what are you going to do all weekend? Sometimes you see a movie," I said.

"I've had some of the pastries you made. You've become exceptionally talented at baking since you left."

"Families get hungry. Gotta learn to make stuff for them to eat," I said, shrugging.

"Separate them," Ghislaine said.

"Hang on," I said, trying to keep them from moving me. I kicked at them, but not all that effectively, since I was trying to stay close to Bryn. When they dragged me away from him, he stood casually still while I struggled until my hair hung half in my eyes and they'd pinned my arms behind me.

"All right," I growled. "I'm done." I settled down and glared at the guy holding a dagger to my throat.

Ghislaine wasn't paying attention to us. She had eyes only for Bryn. Her gaze started at Bryn's hair and finished at his feet, then went the other way.

"You look a little like the portrait we have of Cary Grant."

"Except Bryn is better-looking."

"You also look like a selkie."

"What's a selkie?" I asked, trying to get her to stop looking at him. I'd been afraid of this from the moment I started having visions of visiting Ireland and the Never: This queen would see Bryn and want him for herself. Honestly, I'd been more worried about that than anything. Even getting killed hadn't been as big a concern, which was silly, but there you have it. Faeries are notoriously possessive. Apparently I'd gotten more than my fair share of that fae trait.

Ghislaine's gaze finally shifted to me. "I know everything about Kismet. She does sometimes speak with the accents she hears humanside. She does sometimes seem like a different person for a few days when she returns from a mission. But at her core, she's never been so altered. If she loved a human, she wouldn't bring him into the Never and then try so desperately and feebly to conceal him. Also, she wouldn't love him the way you do. You love the way humans love."

"I'm half human," I said.

"To be sure, you are at least half human. Maybe more. But one thing you're not is first assassin of the Seelie court. Where is she? Where's Kismet?"

"Gone," I said, letting the tension flow out of me. I folded my arms across my chest. No more games. No more fidgeting or posturing. Just one lie that I would tell without flinching. One lie told without hesitation, because it mattered more than any lie I'd ever told in my life.

I locked eyes with the Seelie queen and unblinkingly said, "Kismet's dead."

28

GHISLAINE PALED, HER golden skin fading to ivory as she swayed on her horse. Several faeries darted forward, but she steadied herself.

I glanced at Bryn. He hadn't reacted to my announcement. I'd never been so grateful for his unflappability under pressure.

"Maybe you're telling the truth. But perhaps not. Humans lie. They're notorious for it," she said, dismounting. She flowed forward; it's the only way to describe the way she moved. Her energy reached me a second before her body; it was warm and buzzed like a honeybee. Her feet didn't touch the ground. She grabbed my throat in a supernaturally strong grip. "Where and when and how did she die? If you lie to me, you'll regret it till your last breath."

I knocked her hand away, and everyone gasped. "I don't know who killed her. We were fighting wizards and werewolves in the middle of a rainstorm. She was badly wounded."

"By iron? Was she shot with iron?"

"I guess so. I didn't stop to inspect the ammunition."

Ghislaine exhaled, and the stinging sensation from her essence melted away. Only warmth and light flowed from her in her relief. "She's not dead. You surely mistook her condition. She's very good at surviving. Exceptional at it." Ghislaine said the last line with such conviction, no one would have dared to contradict her.

"She wasn't breathing. She didn't have a pulse," I said. I wanted to go farther to protect my sister. I wanted to claim she'd had an iron bullet or arrow through her heart. Or that her throat had been too badly torn. Anything to convince them that she'd died for sure. If I'd known she wouldn't come to the Never again, I'd have sworn she was dead. But Crux had been so convinced she would turn up. If she did, what would I say? That I'd buried her alive? My own sister?

"Her heart's beating might have been too faint for you to feel. We're not as fragile as humans. Even when there are no signs of life, a faery body can live on, healing wounds that would kill a human, or even a werewolf."

"She's half human. She can die from wounds that weren't made by iron," I said. I'd nearly died from a few wounds that weren't. Of course, I'd also survived and healed things no normal person could have.

"Enough," she said, waving her elegant hand. Her color had returned and heightened. Her flushed skin glowed, creating a halo of light like the sun. She turned and leaped so high it was as if she'd sprung from a trampoline. She landed on her horse without so much as a thump.

My jaw dropped. She could've made a million dollars playing ladies' basketball or as a prima ballerina.

"Bring them," she said.

"Hold your horses," I exclaimed. "I'm not yours to bring anywhere. I'm not Seelie fae. I'm human."

"You're a half-breed, like her."

"Not like her. I'm second-born."

Her eyes flashed furiously, the gold flecks sparkling. The other fae looked at her in confusion. They didn't know the old laws.

"You came into my territory and deceived us. You're half-blooded Seelie fae. I may claim you for the Never as one of us. Or I may declare you a spy from humanside.

Either way, you won't roam free in these lands unless I give you leave to." She looked at her subjects and issued her commands. "Shackle the Halfling. And her lover. Put them behind iron doors and under guard."

They didn't hesitate, and she didn't look back. She turned her horse and galloped away.

I knew one thing for sure: Ghislaine wasn't just angry that her best killer had disappeared. Kismet meant more than that. Did the queen care about her? In a messed-up faery way, had she even loved the Halfling child she'd been given as tribute?

I frowned thoughtfully. Even if the queen did feel bad at the prospect of Kismet being killed, Ghislaine hadn't taken care of my sister when she was little; she hadn't raised her in the castle. She'd put her in foster homes and treated her like a second-class citizen. She'd also had Kismet's own boyfriend whip her for making a mistake on a mission.

My spine stiffened as my blood cooled. I didn't care how Ghislaine felt about Kismet deep down. She'd mistreated Kis her whole life. If I could convince them Kismet was dead and keep her out of their hands forever, that's exactly what I would do. And I wouldn't regret it for a minute.

THE TREES THAT lined the path back to the castle had begun to whisper, which I found comforting. In my experience, silence from trees never meant anything good. I wondered if the spells or magical pact the tree keeper had made with the trees was wearing off. If so, the exits out of the Never might open. Not that it would do us any good at the moment. But I didn't plan to be a prisoner forever.

My wrists were locked together in metal cuffs in front of me, and I sat astride a horse with a fae warrior at my back, who occasionally put an arm around my waist.

"Cut it out," I said, pushing his hand away.

Bryn's cobalt eyes darkened to the color of stormy skies. His hands were bound, too, but behind his back. He was alone on a mount that was being led along the path. I had an intense longing to be on his horse, pressed against him. The black stallion, prompted by Bryn's knee in his left flank, came alongside us. Without hesitation, I swung my left leg up and over, so both legs were on my horse's right side. I popped down to the ground, and grabbed Bryn's thigh to steady myself as I pushed his foot from the stirrup. I shoved my foot in and sprang up. I swung my leg over, sitting behind Bryn and gripping his hands with mine. The whole horse swap took only seconds, which I knew was my body being influenced by the Never and by my sister's skills. I couldn't have moved so smoothly or quickly in the human world. I'm sure if I'd tried, I'd have landed with my butt in the dirt. I hoped that outside the Never, Kismet was getting the benefit of my talents, knowing by instinct how to make friends and how to make pastries and pies. I hoped she was happy.

The knight whose horse I'd been on grabbed the reins of Bryn's horse to keep us from galloping away I guessed.

Bryn leaned back into me, and I rested my chin on his shoulder.

"Hey, there. You okay?" I whispered.

He squeezed my hands. Several faeries circled their horses to stop ours. I tightened my grip on Bryn's hands and leaned closer. It felt immensely better to be touching him. I knew it wasn't just because I loved him. There was something powerful at work. The core of our synergy, I decided. Even though his wizard's magic faded in the Never, it was buried in him and I still reacted to it; like a compass pointing north, I was unfailingly drawn to him. I wouldn't be taken from his horse without a fight.

"She never said we couldn't ride together," I pointed out, watching the faeries intently, waiting for them to grab me. The honey-scented breeze ruffled strands of their glossy hair. Sunlight loved them, making their skin shimmer.

Bryn's skin had a different tone. It was ivory stained with sepia, opalescent rather than shimmery. My arms had the cast of the fae of the land, who looked dusted with gold. The contrast between our skin was striking and somehow right, creating a balance, as our natures did in real life. I'd gotten used to talking with him, especially when there was supernatural trouble. I wanted to be close to him. I also wanted to be alone with him.

"Leave them," one of the fae said.

I sat perfectly still and didn't exhale until they urged their horses forward, and we got under way again.

Bryn turned his head in an attempt to look over his shoulder at me. I kissed the side of his face.

"What do you think? About what I told the queen?" I whispered.

"It'll depend on what happens," he said. Yeah, I knew it would depend on whether or not I got caught telling lies.

A gust of wind carried a richer scent—briny, mixed with sweet. Bryn inhaled. "I want to take you to the water."

"I can't make any sealskin to keep me warm," I whispered back.

"I'll keep you warm."

I smiled and rested my forehead against his shoulder. "Probably you would."

"The selkies don't know what kind of magic is contained in the amber. I think they would've told me if they did. They welcomed me and spoke openly about a lot of things. They're not guarded the way witches and wizards are."

"You sure?" I asked. "Maybe they were pretending to be friendly."

"I don't think so." His thumb rubbed my hand. "It's a tight-knit tribe. Even though I'm many other things, they see me as one of them. I was asked to stay."

I frowned.

After a moment, he added, "I was tempted."

"Faery magic tastes good," I murmured.

"Yeah, there's nothing more beautiful than the ocean."

"What about the night sky full of stars?" I asked. Bryn's celestial magic was a much bigger part of him than his selkie blood.

He glanced at the sky. "I don't know. Ask me again when night falls."

This is how she'll get him, I thought furiously. *She'll use the pull of the sea to make him want to stay in the Never.*

There were a lot of stories of human beings and various other creatures wandering into the land of the fae and never returning. Maybe that's why they called it the Never—because once inside, many never left.

I sniffed the salted-caramel air and narrowed my eyes.

You can't have him, I thought, speaking silently to the sea. Was it my imagination or did the sea answer with a sea-foam laugh?

I pressed my lips to the back of Bryn's neck and licked his spine. His sharp intake of breath made me smile. I blew on the small wet spot I'd left with my mouth.

When he spoke, his voice was low and deep. "Do that again when we're alone. But not until then."

My smile widened. Somewhere in the distance, the sea churned in understanding. I was more than human. The sea might feel cool and silky when he was submerged in its magic waters, but I was pretty sure he found my magic silky smooth, too, when he drowned himself in it.

THE SIGHTS AND smells of the Never continued to be more vivid than anything humanside, and I found myself growing used to them and wondering if I'd miss them if I left.

No, not if I leave! When I leave!

I smelled root beer and gingersnaps. From the corner of my eye I spotted a potbellied faery who looked like Royal, but by the time I turned my head for a better look, he was gone.

I expected the knights to put us in a prison cell or a musty dungeon, and worried that after so many sweet and earthy scents, anything strong and sour would be hard to take, but they led our horse to a stone building that looked like a small castle.

"Fancy for a prison," I exclaimed, happy that the main thing I smelled was baking bread and fresh herbs, rosemary and dill.

After dismounting, we climbed circular stone steps to an upper floor, and our knightly escort pressed a crystal into a groove and turned it. The door opened, revealing a room swanky enough to be in a decorator's magazine. The walls were painted with bright birds and flowering vines. The candleholders and lanterns were gold; the bedspreads and pillows were peach silk. Even the rug was tufted salmon-colored silk. Flowering plants hung from a dozen clear crystal plant holders. In the corner there was a raised tub big enough for three, and mossy plants grew up the steps to it. The windows looked out over the woods and streams.

"Wow," I mumbled as my cuffs were removed. "This is jail?" I dragged my eyes from the room to look at Bryn. "Except for our being prisoners, this would've made a really nice honeymoon suite. Look at all the plants!"

Bryn gave me a wry smile. "Yes, if not for being incarcerated, it'd be perfect."

I walked inside, rubbing my wrists. I turned to say something to Bryn, but realized too late that they were closing the door.

"Hey," I yelled, lunging forward. I was too slow. They'd locked me in alone.

I heard Bryn arguing with them, but the faint voices quickly disappeared.

A moment later I heard them again, suddenly louder and not through the door. They came from over my shoulder. I realized they'd put him in the room next to mine. Near the ceiling there were open windows between the rooms, apparently allowing for ventilation.

I dropped onto the bed and waited. The argument ended with the slamming of a door.

"Bryn, can you hear me?" I said. He didn't answer. I stood under the window and asked again, much more loudly.

"Yes, I hear you," Bryn called back.

"Okay," I said, falling silent again. It wasn't like we could have a private conversation yelling back and forth. I'd wanted him in the cell with me so we could whisper to each other and make an escape plan.

I stared up at the windows and then looked around the room. If I could move the chest of drawers over and stack something on it, I might be able to reach the windows. Then I'd just have to crawl through and drop down. We'd still have to figure out how to escape, but at least we'd be together.

I tested the weight of the chest. It was fairly heavy, but I could drag it. I worked it across the floor. I wanted to hurry. I worried the queen would find some old law or write a new one that allowed her to declare us Seelie fae and under her jurisdiction. If she did that, she could keep us prisoners forever and send knights to hunt us whenever we escaped.

I thought about Kismet. If only I could find a way to warn her not to reenter the Never, I might eventually be able to convince them she was dead, so she'd be free. Would a headstone in a cemetery be enough to fool the queen? We could certainly fake something like that. I chewed my lip. The best way to trick Ghislaine would probably be to get someone she trusted to believe that Kis was dead. Someone who wasn't allowed to lie to her. Could we trick Crux? Then he could report back to Ghislaine and she'd have to take his word for it.

I glanced at the window. This was the sort of thing I liked to discuss with Bryn, him being an excellent strategist.

I heard the door open and close next door.

"Hello?" I called. "Are you still there, Bryn?"

"I'm here. I'm all right," he yelled back.

"Why did they open the door?" I asked.

"I have a visitor."

I grew still. If they hadn't known from our earlier yelling that we were communicating, they did now. So if they didn't want us talking, they'd move one of us to another room. I scowled. It was bad enough we were separated by a wall. It would obviously make my job of getting us out of the Never harder if I had another missing guy to find.

I walked to the wall and put my ear against it. Not surprisingly, the stone wasn't good for hearing through. Was he being interrogated? I didn't worry about that. Bryn was a brilliant lawyer and a stubborn rebel. He'd withstood brutal

WAM questioning where they'd practically choked him as part of the interview. He'd outsmarted them, and I trusted he'd outsmart whatever faery was with him, too.

I paced back and forth, wondering what he was being asked. I hoped he was nice rather than sarcastic. Faeries were wilder than wizards, and more impulsive. Even if they weren't supposed to do something, they might get mad and punish Bryn for being uncooperative or rude.

I really wanted to ask him who his visitor was. I frowned. What if it was the queen? I did not want her alone with him. If she discovered he was an Irish selkie, she might use it as an excuse to claim him for the Seelie. I chewed my lip. I'd had that same thought over and over. . . . What was with me?

I rapped my knuckles against the stone. I couldn't stop myself from whispering, "He's mine." Of course, he and his visitor couldn't hear me, but I'd felt compelled to repeat that aloud. What was going on? The Never had made me paranoid about losing him even before I arrived.

Kismet.

Suddenly I realized it was probably Kismet's knowledge and opinions that were bleeding into my subconscious. She was the one who didn't trust Ghislaine. I tucked my hair behind my ear. Ghislaine had forced Crux to whip Kismet and later to hunt her. Of course, Crux had had to do it because of an oath he'd made before Kismet became his girlfriend, but that wouldn't change how it felt to Kismet.

The jealousy and suspicion that seemed to run as deep as the marrow in my bones wasn't only about being whipped or hunted, though. What else had Ghislaine done with Crux?

Uneasiness gnawed my guts. I trusted Bryn. He was the one who'd pushed for us to be together. I would've taken things a lot slower, but every step of the way he'd done whatever he could to bind us together forever. There was no way he'd fool around with or make a binding oath to some faery queen, no matter how pretty she was.

Trust no one in the Never, Kismet had said.

And Bryn had felt compelled to answer the sea's call by leaving me and going to it. What if fae magic and persuasion were more powerful than he could withstand? He might not know how to protect himself.

I rushed over to the chest of drawers and finished pushing it against the wall. I wasn't waiting any longer. I climbed on the dresser, but wasn't tall enough for me to reach the bottom of the window. I jumped and grabbed the edge with my fingers and dangled.

I couldn't pull myself up by my fingertips. Normally I could manage a couple of chin-ups when I had a firm grip on something, but with my whole body hanging like deadweight it was impossible.

I let go and dropped to the chest, which teetered and then tipped. I hopped back as I fell. I landed a foot from the dresser as it crashed to the floor. Crouched in front of it, I waited, holding my breath. The door didn't open. Bryn didn't even yell to see if I was okay, which seemed an ominous sign.

"Get going," I told myself. I grabbed the edge of the chest and righted it. I puffed with exertion and grimaced at the cracked corners. I kicked the splintered wood away from my feet and then climbed back on top.

I needed momentum. I pictured Kismet leaping up to catch a low-hanging tree branch and then vaulting onto it. We were identical twins. I had those same springy muscles in my legs.

I just needed to get myself going. I hopped up and down until I was breathless with it, and then I jumped as hard as I could. I caught the edge and pulled with my hands as my feet scrambled up the wall.

Rising, I locked my arms and hooked my foot on the ledge. My muscles complained about the crazy stretch, but I ignored them. I reached one hand up and caught the top of the window, which was opened in a slanted position into Bryn's room. I dragged myself up so that my head and shoulders reached the ceiling. Then I leaned my head into Bryn's room.

He stood alone, looking a way I couldn't ever remember him appearing before—dazed. I studied him for a moment. I didn't see any blood dripping from his head. He stood straight, not like someone with a concussion who was unsteady on his feet.

"Hey," I called out in a whisper.

His face lifted to look at me. He held a hand up in greeting, not seeming at all surprised to see me precariously perched on a slender ledge. I reached up to his side of the wall and tried to steady myself as I pushed more of my body through the small space.

"Come over," I said. "I need you to catch me when I jump down. Or at least to break my fall."

He stared at me like I was speaking a language he didn't know. I frowned. As far as I knew there weren't many of those. And, of course, he normally understood English better than most people.

"Bryn, are you okay?" I asked.

He hesitated, then nodded.

"Hey! This is no time for sleepwalking. I'm trying to figure out how to get down from here." I braced myself and climbed forward. Putting all my weight on that frame was a calculated risk. Guess what? It didn't work out.

The window creaked and then gave way so suddenly I didn't have time to gasp. Bryn grabbed me out of the air and pulled me to him, but the force of my fall sent us both to the floor. The glass shattered, but at least we didn't land on it. Shards flew and nicked my legs, but otherwise I was okay.

I sat up and looked him over. "What's with you?" I asked.

He pushed himself up onto his elbows, studying me. "You should be careful. You could've been hurt."

Bryn looked and sounded like himself and I couldn't dispute his point, but there was undoubtedly something wrong with him. I caught his face in my hands and squeezed. "What happened before I dropped in?"

"Let's stay here."

"Stay here?" I murmured, glancing around. There was only one door, which I assumed was locked. "Is there another choice?" I asked, going to the door. I tried to open it, but it didn't budge.

"It's great here. The sights and smells. The sea."

I frowned and cocked a brow. "I don't see or smell anything special right now. And it's not like we can go for a dip in the ocean, since we're being held prisoner!" I clucked my tongue. "What did they do to you?" I marched over to him. "Did you eat or drink something they gave you?"

He shook his head. "It's beautiful here, don't you think?"

"As jail cells go, it's top-of-the-line," I said.

"I don't mean this room. I mean this world. Underhill."

"It's sure pretty," I said, checking his neck and hands for needle marks. Had they injected him with some mind-altering drug? As I leaned toward him, I smelled honey, apples, and hazelnuts. "What's that?" I asked.

"My chin?" he asked, following my gaze.

"No," I said, rubbing my thumb over his lower lip. A sticky residue coated the pad of my finger. "Is that magic lip gloss? Who did you kiss?"

"No one."

"Did someone kiss you?" I asked.

"I didn't return her kiss," he said. "She took me by surprise. But it wasn't unpleasant."

My jaw dropped, and my brows shot up. "Oh, it wasn't bad, huh?" I asked.

"No," he said, shrugging.

For the love of Hershey, I thought, exasperated. "Bryn, I don't want you to take what I do next the wrong way," I said. I wiped the stickiness from his lips, not being too gentle about it. Then I slapped him.

He blinked. "Ow," he said belatedly.

I slapped him again, and this time a pink Tammy Jo handprint bloomed on his cheek.

"Stop that," he said, putting his hand over the hot spot. His tongue slid out to lick his lips, but I grabbed it before it could return to his mouth.

"Nope," I said, pressing my fingernail down to keep him from pulling his tongue back.

"What are you doing?" he said, but it came out all garbled.

"Come with me," I said, pulling him by the tongue.

He jerked his head away, making me lose my grip. Tongues are slippery.

"Do *not* swallow!" I ordered.

"I'll do whatever I want," he said, and that actually made me happy, since he seemed less dazed.

"Come on over here," I said, wetting a cloth in the sink.

"What will you give me if I do?" he asked, looking me over.

My brows pinched together. What in the world? His mood had definitely shifted.

"If you wash your mouth out with soap and water, I'll kiss you."

"What else?"

"Then we'll have to see."

He shook his head. "Not good enough."

I gave him a hostile look. "Come over here."

"Give me a good reason to," he challenged.

"You're not yourself."

"A beautiful fae queen tried to seduce me and I resisted. I—"

"You call going all Zombie Bryn resisting?"

"I deserve a reward," he said, finishing his thought like I hadn't spoken.

I took in a big breath and tried to hold on to my patience. "Come and gargle with some soapsuds, and I'll reward you."

He sat on the edge of the bed, resting his palms on his knees. "If I stay in the Never, will you stay with me?"

"You're not staying here. We're both going."

He stared at the wall, his eyes narrowing. "You don't love me. Not the way I loved you."

My jaw dropped. The way he *loved* me? Past tense? *Oh, hell, no!*

I filled a cup with soap and water and stalked over to him. "Open your mouth."

He only looked at me defiantly. *That sneaky bitch*, I thought furiously.

I took a swig of the water and grimaced, then grabbed his chin. I kissed him, hard, shooting the water into his mouth. My hand gripped his throat and squeezed so he couldn't swallow . . . or breathe.

I spit the water left in my mouth into the cup.

"Spit it out," I said to Bryn, putting the cup to his lips. He gave me a mutinous look, but did so. I returned to the sink and rinsed the cup. I splashed fresh water into my mouth, the taste of honey and smoked hazelnuts lingering. I continued to rinse my mouth until the flavor disappeared.

I turned. Bryn jerked his head side to side, like a dog trying to shake water from its coat. When he looked at me with clear eyes, I smiled. "She had you."

"No," he said. "She drugged me with magic, but it would have worn off. Deep down, I was fighting it."

"Very deep down, apparently," I said.

"I asked her about the amber artifact. She said magical ambers belong in the Never. 'Like all things fae.' Then she kissed me and said, 'You belong here, Sea Foam. You'll stay and convince her to stay as well. She'll do that. If she loves you enough she won't leave you.' "

Manipulative bitch, I thought.

She obviously had her spies working overtime, since she already knew Bryn was part fae. Well, that couldn't be helped. It didn't change anything. I wouldn't let her stop us from escaping.

"It appealed to me," Bryn added. "I'm sure in my subconscious I look for you to make a big gesture to prove how you feel. I had to convince you to date me. I had to convince you to marry me. It was like she knew it."

"She hasn't tricked all her knights into swearing oaths to her by being dumb," I reasoned.

"I didn't kiss her. I think that surprised her."

"Probably so. She's very pretty."

Bryn glanced at me. "You should replace the taste of her on my lips."

"Do you still taste her? Or soap?"

He frowned. "A little of each." He rubbed his face and then squeezed his lips. "It's the worst thing imaginable to lose one's self. A form of dementia really."

The sadness and worry etched on his face troubled me. She had had him . . . well, a version of him. Bryn's brilliant mind had been dumbed down to almost nothing under her poison. It was a truly terrible curse. She doled out her mind-numbing magic pretty casually. I guess she didn't care how violated her victims felt afterward.

I strolled to him and climbed onto his lap, facing him.

"I love you," I said, taking his hand and sliding it under my shirt to press it against the skin over my heart. "With every bit of my heart and every drop of my magical blood. If she wrapped you in chains and dropped you in the ocean, I'd come after you in a submarine. If she poisoned you, I'd beg, borrow, or steal a cure and give it to you." I nodded over my shoulder at the broken glass on the floor. "If she locked you in a room to keep us apart, I'd bust through a window to get to you. I might worry about what will happen to us if we stay together. But I worry way more about how we'd feel if we had to be apart. Don't doubt that I love you enough to do whatever it takes to be with you. You're mine. If she wants me to prove it, I will."

His sapphire eyes darkened. "That was a good speech. It's almost like you've been spending time with a lawyer."

"Thanks." I grinned. "Lawyers are good at talking the talk, but you guys aren't known for being romantic."

"I must be the exception then, since I'm romantic, at least when it comes to a certain redhead."

My hands slid up his neck to his face. I kissed him, slipping my tongue past his lips. I caressed his mouth. He groaned and leaned back, taking me with him.

I reached between our bodies, fiddling with our clothes.

Soon we were naked, lips pressed together, skin sliding against skin.

Things felt different. The wizard's magic that usually crashed over us, heightening every sensation, wasn't with us in the Never. But even though there was a slower build, the passion was still there, still intense. Several times I had the sensation of rocking on the water, like I was on a boat. He tasted of salt, toffee, caramel, and chili powder.

He gripped my hips, and I plunged into pleasure. Then I felt a sharp sensation and a ripple of heat deep inside my belly. I gasped against Bryn's mouth.

He paused. "Are you all right?"

I nodded. "Don't stop," I said, clutching his hips and pulling him.

He smiled, kissed me, and we moved against each other again. Things became faster and more urgent, until we lost our breath and melted into the mattress.

"It felt different without the witch and wizard magic," I said.

"Yes."

I stroked his hair. "Did you miss it?"

"Some. I like when our magic mingles together. It's incredible. But this . . . I could concentrate better. I felt things more clearly. It was just you and me, our bodies and emotions. There wasn't a flood of magic to overshadow us. This felt incredible, too."

I smiled. "Yeah, both ways are good. Like brownies, good with frosting and without."

He chuckled. "It always comes back to food with you."

I smiled. "Yep. Even in my sex fantasies."

"You have sex fantasies? What are they?" he demanded.

"Um, different things, like covering you in chocolate sauce and cookie crumbles. And maybe some strawberries and whipped cream."

He laughed. "I wouldn't say no."

"Maybe on our honeymoon, we should lie under the moon and cover each other with honey. Really make it live up to its name."

"Mmm. That sounds amazing."

I kissed his shoulder.

"If we don't find the amber the Association wants, we're going to run into all kinds of problems," he said. "They'll try to keep us from getting married."

"They're not the boss of us."

"I know," he said with a grim smile. "But might overcomes right some of the time. Underhill is one of the few places Conclave operatives can't reach us."

"Yeah, too bad the queen here is a nightmare." I cocked my head. "There are probably some places in America where we'd be pretty hard to find. The Appalachians, maybe?"

Bryn threw his head back and barked out a laugh. "Nearly a decade studying in the Ivy League, only to end up playing a fiddle and living off the land. That would be an unexpected turn of events." He shook his head. "There would be one upside to that, though."

"What?"

"Edie would never visit."

I slugged him in the arm. "Not nice."

He continued to smile. "I'd go, you know."

"Where?"

"Anywhere you were."

I kissed him. "Yeah, you are romantic. Watch out—they might take away your lawyer card."

"It's not a card."

"Well, whatever it is," I said, sitting up. "Get dressed, Romeo Litigator."

"Litigator. Good word."

I winked at him. "Learned it from Edie. She's good for some stuff." When he didn't move, I tapped his shoulder. "Come on, candylegger. Time to be brilliant instead of sexy."

"Am I just one or the other at a time?" he asked with a smirk, watching me get dressed.

I tossed his clothes onto the bed. "Put those on."

He winked at me, but followed orders.

Bryn, being prepared for trouble, had brought a Swiss army knife and a lighter. While he dressed, I snipped some pieces of fabric and put them into the receptacle in the corner. I lit them on fire and waved the smoke around the room, wrinkling my nose and coughing.

"What are you doing?" he asked.

"I'm escaping," I said. "So are you."

29

"FAERIES DON'T LIKE smoke," I said.

"How do you know?"

"Because I am one." I pulled my shirt up to cover my mouth and nose. "If there are tiny fae spying on us, they'll fly out of here to avoid the smoke."

Bryn took a step back and rubbed his eyes. "Yeah, that's somewhat noxious. I've never had a problem at bonfires. The smell of smoke must be more potent here."

"Yep. And underhill, we're more our fae selves," I commented.

I explained my escape plan, which we quickly put into motion.

I hid behind the door. When the guard opened it to investigate the source of the smoke, I stepped out from behind it and thumped him on the head. Bryn poured water into the garbage to put out the fire before we left, locking the guard inside.

We hurried down the stairs of the tower, but paused at the front entrance when we opened it a crack. I peered out, scanning the courtyard. There were dozens of fae hanging around, sitting on benches, eating fruit and it looked like . . . yes, those were the pastries I'd made. The queen had distributed them.

I couldn't help but smile over the way the faeries seemed to be enjoying them. One of the knights even snatched his friend's popover and darted away with it, laughing as he consumed it before he was caught. The other knight shoved him and complained, but the thieving knight only grinned and licked his lips.

"Zach may not be in the castle anymore, and we're much more likely to get out of the Never if we avoid the queen," Bryn said.

"I won't leave without checking. What if she's got him locked up in there?"

"He should've stayed at the original location. He's not fae. There was nothing compelling him to go to the castle."

I shrugged. "I don't know what he was doing, but we're not leaving the Never without him, so just accept that, and let's make a plan."

"He said he liked it here. Nice weather. Beautiful women. He could do worse."

"He said that?" I said, my brows shooting up. Then I shook my head. "Whatever. I am not leaving Zach with the faeries," I said.

"Why not? As soon as the tree keeper's spell wears off, all the gates on this side will open for Zach. All he has to do is walk out."

"Unless he's chained to a wall."

"I don't think they chain people to walls here. Look how comfortable our prison cells were."

I pinched Bryn's arm to shut him up, and he blinked in surprise.

"Sorry," I murmured. Impulsiveness was harder to resist in the Never. Not that impulse control was ever a strong suit with me. "But have you forgotten that Kismet was flogged?"

He rubbed the red spot on his arm. "I had forgotten, yes, which obviously isn't like me." He frowned. "This place has an opposite effect on each of us. I feel mellower, less sharp. You're more violent."

"Yeah, it's Kis's influence, I think. She's a warrior girl." I tapped my lips. "We need to distract the faeries."

"I don't want to encounter the fae queen again," he said.

My brows rose as I realized what he wasn't saying. Being under a spell that made him feeble-minded had shaken him. He was afraid of losing his smarts and his free will . . . those were the most important things that made him who he was.

"You don't have to come with me."

He scowled. "Yes, I do."

"I will never let her have you. I promise."

"There might not be anything you can do about it."

I squeezed his hand. "Yeah, there will. She'll kiss you again over my dead body." I looked around. "We can't out-run faeries. They're too fast. But I don't think any of these fae in the square were with the queen when we were arrested," I whispered. "What do you think?"

Bryn studied the faeries. "I can't be sure. It's like a Nordic modeling competition. Everyone's tall and blond. Hard to tell them apart."

"Well, we can't stand around forever. It's only a matter of time before the guard in the tower wakes up and starts yelling out the window. Let's just go." I stood up straight and tried to look confident as we strolled across the courtyard. I didn't make eye contact, but I saw heads turn, and eyes followed me. I reminded myself that I looked like Kismet, who'd been gone.

"Where's your bow?" one of the knights called out.

"Safe," I replied without slowing down. I held my breath the last few feet to the courtyard entrance of the castle. We opened it, and I glanced over my shoulder. The knights approached.

I swallowed and then called out in an accent that I hoped sounded like Kismet's, "Did you like the pastries the queen shared? There are more of those at the booth next to Rose-blade's, but not many. As the queen's knights, they'll give you preference when they sell them, but you'll have to hurry."

The knights spoke quickly to one another. All but two of them turned and left for the festival, but one pair followed us into the castle.

"We heard you returned, but that you were in hiding."

"Obviously I'm not," I said, glancing around. "I'm going to meet with the queen." I walked quickly, and when Bryn and I entered the sitting room, the knights stayed outside the door.

"There's another door in this room. C'mon."

"It's insane to waltz in here with no plan. You do realize that?" Bryn murmured.

"Yep, but I gave up on doing the sane thing a couple of adventures ago. You know that."

He sighed but said nothing, because obviously he did know it.

The ground floor was a maze of corridors and rooms. I didn't find Zach in any of them.

"Here's a door that leads outside," Bryn said. "Let's go. If we don't find Zach at the gingerbread house, we'll come back after we've had a chance to put together a better plan."

I shook my head. "He's still here," I said when we reached the grand staircase that I'd climbed earlier in the day to see Momma.

"How do you know?"

I started up the stairs, pointing. Hanging from a loop at the top of the banister was Zach's amulet. It wasn't active in the Never, since it was forged with witch magic, but there was no way he would've willingly left it behind.

"What are you doing?" one of the knights called.

"She gave me permission to come upstairs," I said, jogging up the steps with Bryn.

"No, she didn't," the one with more sharply pointed ears said. They mounted the stairs, too.

I didn't break stride, but I snagged Zach's amulet as I went by. My fingertips burned. When it was under his shirt it didn't bother me, but there was iron mixed with the gold, so touching it wasn't easy. Especially in the Never, where I was more sensitive to iron than ever.

"Smell that?"

"Yes. Honey and ale," Bryn said.

"I didn't smell beer up here earlier. Zach likes it, so maybe . . ." I trailed off as I raced down the hall. I yanked open a fancy door covered in jewels and crystals.

"Stop!" the knights yelled, but Bryn and I dashed inside

and slammed the door behind us. I grabbed the gold rod for barring the door and dropped it into position.

"They can't get in," I said, exhaling in relief.

"And we can't get out," Bryn replied.

I shrugged. "One problem at a time."

I hurried into the suite and spotted a silver tray sitting on a tufted ottoman. There was an empty crystal pitcher that had held beer. There were also sandwich crumbs in smeared dollops of honey and mustard. My stomach rumbled.

We passed through the sitting area and into the bedroom. The large bed was covered in white silk, and lying within the cloud of bedding were Zach and Ghislaine, both naked.

"Are you serious?" I snapped.

Ghislaine sat straight up. "You dare trespass here?"

"Hey, darlin'," Zach murmured sleepily.

"You drugged him, too?" I asked. "That's your specialty, huh? Date rape without the date part?" I demanded. I stalked to the end of the bed and stepped onto another tufted ottoman and then onto the mattress.

"Have you taken leave of your senses?" she asked.

"Nope," I said, and then socked her in the nose.

Her head snapped back from the force of the punch, and she tumbled out of bed.

"Wow," Bryn said. "No supernatural leader is safe when you're around."

"Get up, Zach," I said, dropping the amulet onto the bed next to him.

Zach's denim-blue eyes sparkled mischievously. "A little jealous, huh?" He nodded toward the edge of the bed, where the queen rose like a serpent. Golden-pink blood trickled from her nose.

"Aw, hell, Tammy Jo, you gave her a nosebleed. Here, darlin'," Zach said, shaking his head. He held out his T-shirt to the queen. She ignored it, sliding a dressing gown on, tying it closed, and then taking a square of silk from a drawer. She held it to her face.

I still stood in the center of the bed. Zach pulled on his boxers and hung the amulet around his neck.

"Is that a bite mark on your chest?" I demanded of Zach, and then turned to Ghislaine. "Are you a faery or a vampire?"

Zach rolled to the side of the bed, but when he tried to stand, he wobbled and said, "Hell." He dropped onto the mattress, sitting on the edge and gripping his head in his hands. "The ale here's got a kick to it."

"It's not the beer that has you feeling loopy," I said, climbing off the bed.

To Ghislaine, Zach said, "Come here, darlin'. Let me see your face. You all right?" Zach pulled Ghislaine to him to examine her injured nose.

"Hey!" I said. "Don't worry about her. She's a con woman. You go and wash your own face, especially your lips. And gargle while you're at it. Then finish getting dressed, 'cause we're leaving."

Ghislaine's eyes had a golden glow as she looked at Zach. Faery dust shimmered over his arms and chest, trailing down to the edge of his boxers. For Pete's sake!

"She took advantage of you," I said.

"Is that so?" Zach said skeptically. He ran a fingertip over her nose. "Not broken. It's a little swollen, but it'll go down. How about some ice?"

Ghislaine put a hand on the side of Zach's face. "You're lovely. Run a bath for us," she whispered, pointing to a doorway.

"Don't mind if I do," he said, standing.

"Toss that amulet somewhere out of the way. I'm allergic to iron."

Zach glanced at his amulet, the one that protected him from all kinds of magical creatures in the human world, the one he'd been wearing every day since coming home from his training. He took it off and swung it by the chain so that when he let go it sailed away from him and landed in the far corner of the room, like a used soda can.

I gestured furiously and pointed. "Did you see that?" I asked Bryn, who was checking the room for alternate exits.

"I saw," Bryn said.

"You know he wouldn't do that if he was thinking straight."

"Probably not," Bryn agreed. He opened a pair of doors that revealed a balcony. There was a waist-high metal grate. "There are hooks here for a ladder," he said, stepping outside. He looked around and over the side.

Ghislaine watched Bryn for a moment before speaking. Then she said, "Stop casting about for temporary solutions to your problem. You need to think about your survival. Throw yourself upon my mercy."

Bryn looked at her and raised a brow in question.

"I'm going to have her killed," she said, nodding at me. "Whether you die with her depends upon your actions here and now."

"Did you hear that, Zach?" I called out. "Your new girlfriend is planning to have me murdered."

"How's that?" Zach asked, leaning out the bathroom doorway.

"It's not murder," the queen said. "She attacked me. You saw. That's a punishable offense. The sentence is at my pleasure. And since she's even more reckless than Kismet, she can't be of any use to me. Ergo, death sentence."

"Nah. It was just a punch. You can't go around executing people for throwing a punch. Let the punishment fit the crime, darlin'. Besides, there were some extenuating circumstances in this case. You slept with her ex. If punching the person who slept with your ex were punishable by death, I'd be dead myself."

"Did you punch a royal?"

"I punched a royal pain in the ass," Zach said, nodding at Bryn, who was searching the room.

The light in the room pulsed a silvery pink and for a moment we heard an echo of a knight's voice. "My lady highness, I request permission to enter."

Ghislaine smiled, pulling a cord lazily. Did it sound a signal in the hall? She didn't seem worried, even with three of us in her room. She seemed to be enjoying the show of Bryn stalking around the room, looking for escape aids, and my trying to corral Zach.

"We can tie some sheets together," I said to Bryn.

"Add the dried gardenia petals and silky salts to the water, lover. We can talk about it in the bath," Ghislaine told Zach.

"No, you don't," I said, grabbing Zach's arm to keep him from returning to the bathroom.

Ghislaine stepped toward us, reaching for Zach. My grip tightened. At the last moment, however, she clutched my face and planted a kiss on my lips.

"For the love of Hershey," I snapped, shoving her away. I tasted earthy herbs, hazelnuts, and honey, and the faint metallic tang of blood. I wiped my lips with the back of my hand, but they tingled and my skin shimmered. My heartbeat slowed, the anxiousness of the moment draining away.

Hmmm, I thought. I recognized this feeling. Humanside, when my witch magic was sucked out of me, I became a cool-hearted version of myself. A version of myself who couldn't entirely be trusted.

Hang on, I thought, trying to focus. I didn't want to become more fae, and I definitely didn't want to fall under a spell cast by the queen. A tremor of anger ran through me, but not the white-hot fury I'd felt at seeing Zach in Ghislaine's bed.

I exhaled warm breath through soft lips. I licked them.

For a moment the world shifted with a sharp rocking sensation. I was outside myself, walking through the tall wildflowers. I bent down and examined footprints in the earth, my bow swinging forward, my earrings thumping against the corner of my jaw.

My bow? Earrings?

No, I'm not me.

I glanced at my feet. Kismet's feet. Her tattoos had almost completely faded, but I saw their faint outlines.

"You should not be here," I said.

She looked up, her green eyes flashing despite the darkness around her. "I heard that you were glad I didn't come with you into the Never. I heard that you told her I was dead," Kis said.

"I want you to get away and be safe," I whispered.

"Who are you talking to?" Ghislaine asked.

I blinked, realizing I'd been staring at the wall.

"The selkie's right. There's a way out of the room. Look

up, Tammy. Look up," she whispered in my head. "But don't turn your back on the queen."

I glanced around. Zach had disappeared back into the bathroom. I frowned, stepping away from Ghislaine.

The pounding on the door grew urgent. Knights shouted that if the queen didn't advise them not to, they would break the door down and enter.

The queen smiled, saying nothing.

I looked up. Metalwork and gold leaf decorated the border between ceiling and wall. I followed the pattern around until I spotted the ladder, which was camouflaged as part of the elaborate design.

"Bryn," I said. "Get a chair. I found the ladder." I dragged the ottoman to the wall, and he brought a chair. We climbed and had to stretch to reach it. "It's hanging from small hooks. See them? On the count of three, lift."

"Ready," he said.

I counted, but just as I said *three*, I felt the air behind me shift, apples and honey on my tongue.

Don't turn your back!

I let go of my end of the ladder and twisted on the chair. The dagger grazed my side. I fell sideways, but caught myself on the wall. One end of the ladder crashed to the floor.

Ghislaine drew her arm back and thrust again as I leapt. My knee caught her chin, as I intended, and she fell backward. I'd jumped so high I caught the light fixture and swung from it, landing on the bed in a crouch. I jerked around, ready.

"Holy hell," Kismet's voice said in my head.

"Tamara!" Bryn said.

"You witch!" Ghislaine yelled, rolling onto her side and springing to her feet, the thin blade stained with my blood.

My gaze darted around the room. Where had her weapon come from? Was there another for me to use? I waited for her to attack, but she stood where she was, rubbing her chin, which had begun to swell.

"Bryn, hang the ladder from the balcony. We have to go soon," I said, hearing something heavy thud against the door. The knights were coming, and I had no doubt the queen would tell them to fill me with arrows the second they entered the room.

I rose and walked backward on the bed.

"There's nowhere for you to go," she said. "Your selkie may escape for now, but I won't allow you to leave."

"I'm not asking for your permission," I said, lifting the corner of the bedding.

"What are you doing?" she asked.

"See, how a fight works is your opponent doesn't tell you what she's going to do next," I said.

She grabbed the end of the spread that was at the foot of the bed, but it didn't matter. I stepped onto the part of the mattress that was free of the bedspread and then ran forward. I jumped, she slashed, and the bedspread dropped onto her. I landed, turned, and body-slammed her.

She fell, thrashing, but I rolled her up in the puffy silk comforter like a giant faery burrito.

I pulled hard on the fabric, pressing down on the lump where her arm and hand were trying to rise. I rolled her over and over, pulling the fabric and tucking it tight until she was cocooned inside. I yanked the cord she'd pulled earlier from the ceiling and tied it around her.

Looking over his shoulder, Bryn's brows rose.

"A queen-sized burrito," I said, calmly pushing the hair out of my face. "I am from Texas."

Bryn hooked the ladder on the metal safety grate at the front of the balcony. "Let's go."

"You start down. I'll be right behind you," I said.

"I'll wait."

"No, get moving. We don't want a traffic jam on the ladder." I stalked into the bathroom.

Zach was lying back in the huge tub, suds cresting over the milky water.

"Care for a swim?" Zach asked, taking a swig from a mug of ale. "Or a beer? She's got an ice chest," he said, nodding.

I strode forward and grabbed the mug. I dumped the beer over his head and dropped the tankard. He caught it before it hit the water, blinking through beer-drenched eyelashes. Zach may be only a country boy from a small town, but he's got reflexes that rival those of any supernatural creature.

"There are fae knights about to bust their way in here. If they catch me, they'll kill me, so I've gotta go."

"Go on then," he said. "I didn't tell you to stay."

I grabbed a handful of his damp curls and stared into his eyes. "Get your wet butt out of that tub, unless you plan to be a faery woman's boy toy for good."

He scowled. "I'm—"

I set my foot on the edge of the tub and ran a hand through my blood. She'd gotten me on the side and the calf. I pressed a bloody handprint onto his chest.

"She's not playing. Get your butt moving. Right. Now." My voice wasn't my own. It was cold, almost devoid of anything familiar, even my accent. Across the Never, I felt my sister jogging with cool calculation. There was no fear. She would let nothing stop her until she reached her goal or was dead.

I strode out of the bathroom and grabbed Zach's amulet. He followed me.

"Listen, Tammy Jo, I've got things to do here," he said.

"Yeah, I saw. Bubble baths and beer drinking," I said, striding to where he dripped onto the woven silk rug.

I grabbed the back of his neck and pulled him down. I wiped the queen's gloss from his lips, slapped him, and then pressed a hard kiss on his mouth.

He sucked in a startled breath, and I dropped the amulet over his head. It thumped against his chest as the shimmer of pixie dust faded.

The sound of the bedroom door splintering reached us instantly.

"Time to go," I said, running across the room to the balcony.

30

"THANKS FOR THE smack and the smacker," Zach said, coming over the railing. I was a dozen rungs down. "By her reputation, she's hard to resist, and I should've been more careful. I figured I was still too distracted by us to be really interested."

"If she hadn't used a magical Mickey Finn, you might have been able to resist."

"I'll be damned," Zach said.

I looked up and followed his gaze to the forest and the sea beyond. Mist covered most of the treetops, but four trees rose above it.

"What?" I asked.

He shook his head. "Nothing."

"Look out," I yelled, spotting a pair of knights leaning over the rail from above. I pulled the edges of my shirt out and used it to grip the ladder and then kicked my legs back from the rungs. I dropped at least thirty feet in a couple seconds, my stomach lurching into my throat.

I landed in a mossy clump of dirt, staring up at the sky and Zach's feet as he jumped.

He landed in the pile of dirt and rolled several feet. The knights' arrows struck the ground, having missed us on our rapid and unexpected descent.

I rolled over, catching my breath, and leapt to my feet.

"This way!" Bryn yelled.

Zach and I both ran toward the cover of the trees and the sound of Bryn's voice. Arrows dogged our steps, and one struck my calf. I hissed in pain as I dived past the trunk of an oak tree.

I spit out a mouthful of fern fronds and turned. I took a deep breath and clenched my teeth as I pulled out the arrow. I yelled in pain and fell backward, lying on my back for a moment. The wound throbbed, but I got hold of myself and calmed down. I examined the arrow. Not painted with poison. Well, at least that was something. I got up and limped on the leg. It wasn't too bad.

"I spotted Mercutio," Bryn said. "He's headed toward the water."

"Which way?" I demanded. "Hey," I said, grabbing Zach's arm, since he hadn't waited to hear about Merc. He was already striding away.

"You don't need me to find your cat. I've got something to do myself," Zach said, shrugging off my grip.

"What? What's going on?" I snapped.

"Mercutio went that way, too," Bryn said, nodding.

"Fine," I said, glancing back over my shoulder. "Kismet's inside the Never and on her way to the castle, but I don't suppose we can wait on her."

"I don't suppose we can, considering that the queen's knights aren't likely to give up pursuing us just because we're in the woods," Bryn said.

"Water's your best bet, Lyons. Take her out offshore, where she'll be out of reach. If I see the cat, I'll send him your way," Zach said, and then sprinted away from us.

We followed. In addition to being an avid swimmer, Bryn's a runner. Usually I can't keep up with him. But through the magical forest of the Never, I ran with extra energy, propelling myself forward like I had springs in my legs.

We overtook Zach and kept pace with him.

"Don't come with me. Go your own way," Zach said, panting for breath as we all ran full-out, weaving between trees.

I ignored him. There were things pulling me forward. Mercutio, I thought, and through Bryn, the sea. Galloping horses were heard in the distance, but they didn't drive us to run faster, because nothing could have. We ran as fast as humanly possible and more.

And then we reached a clearing, and Zach and I stopped. He landed on his knees on the ornamental grass. I bent over, sucking air, and held a tree for support. Bryn had run past us, but paused, jogging in place.

I checked my calf. The wound hurt, but was already smaller. The arrowhead had not been iron. They'd have to bring stronger ammunition next time. And probably would if the queen had given the order to kill me.

"Come on, Tamara. We're almost there."

"No," I said, spotting Mercutio circling a giant redwood that looked to be more than three hundred feet tall. At the sides of the clearing there were two other redwoods, each a couple hundred feet tall. And finally at the bottom of the group, the smallest of the giants. It was maybe sixty feet. There was something familiar about the arrangement of the trees. Fanning out from the edges of the clearing were flowering bushes.

"We stopped here for a reason. What's the reason, Zach?" I asked.

Zach ignored my question, but straightened and began to walk around the area, looking at the ground.

The horses were getting closer.

"Come on, Sutton! You're holding us up!" Bryn said.

"Where did her cat go?" Zach asked, circling the tallest tree. Bryn and I followed.

"It's the sunburst pattern," I murmured. "From the castle door and the elevator at WAM headquarters." It was also the diamond. Biggest gem or, in this case, tree at the top of the formation. Two of equal size at the sides. Smallest at the bottom.

Bryn looked over, studying the arrangement of the trees and plants.

Twenty feet from the clearing, Mercutio climbed over uneven terrain and thick foliage.

"There's Merc," I said.

Zach raced into the forest, and we followed.

Mercutio disappeared under the petrified roots of a fallen tree that were blackened and covered on the undersurface with a fine sheen of diamond dust—or so it seemed. Bryn rubbed a finger over the whitened bark and then brought it to his tongue. He tasted it.

"Sea salt," he said.

Zach shoved him aside and climbed down under the roots.

"What are we doing?" Bryn demanded, but I beckoned him to come.

We crawled after Zach and Merc through a tight space. I tasted salt and earth. The musty air under the roots was thick with moisture until we reached the edge of a muddy slope and slid down.

My breath caught at the sudden drop. I landed on the ground in the dark. There was no scent at all and no light. The vibrant world of the Never seemed to have evaporated . . . like we were in a tomb.

"Tamara, where are you?"

I reached back until I found Bryn. We linked hands.

"Zach?"

Zach didn't answer, but I heard him breathing and followed the sound. The passageway narrowed again to a tunnel we had to pass through on our knees.

"What are we doing?" Bryn asked again.

"I don't know."

Eventually a bit of light cracked through the dense darkness.

"I see something," I whispered triumphantly.

When we reached the end of the tunnel it opened into a cave that was lit by five glowing crystals.

The cave's walls were crusted with clumps of salt. Five alabaster pillars stood in a pentagonal shape in the center.

On the top of three pillars, under globes of clear glass, were pieces of amber. Two of the pedestals were empty.

"What is this place?" Bryn asked.

Mercutio stood near the tallest of the five pedestals and yowled at Zach.

"If you touch that glass, Cowboy, I'll run an arrow clean through your heart."

I spun around and found Kismet standing just in front of the opening of the black tunnel. Her bow was raised and pointed at Zach's back.

"What's going on?" I asked. "Don't point that at him."

"Step back, Cowboy. I wouldn't like to kill you here. It would be a lot of trouble to drag your body out. A real nuisance," she added in her lilting voice.

Zach had not moved, but neither did he comply with her directive to back away.

Bryn walked to the closest pedestal. "Don't touch, wizard. I'll kill even you if need be."

"I won't touch them," Bryn said, holding out his arms to show that he planned only to look. He peered through the glass.

I didn't look at the ambers. I looked at my sister.

"Where are we?" I asked.

"The salt hollow," Kismet said. "Just a cave where she hid our treasure from outsiders. She'll have to move them now that your men have been here. Go ahead out, sister."

Zach lifted his amulet off and held it out with his right hand as if to drop it.

Kismet narrowed her eyes.

"Zach, wait!" I shouted as he lunged. He knocked the glass globe off the pedestal with his left hand and brought the amulet down with a slamming force. If Mercutio hadn't leapt through the air and knocked the amber off the pedestal, Zach would certainly have smashed it.

An arrow skewered him in the back, and Zach fell forward.

I screamed and darted to where he lay prostate on the cave floor. "Oh, my God! Kismet, what have you done?"

"Good boy," Kismet said, stroking Mercutio's head as she retrieved the fallen chunk of amber.

Bryn's hand rubbed his chest. "What the hell is this place?" he whispered. "My heart stopped for several seconds when that thing hit the ground."

I realized I'd felt the same horrible deadly sensation, but I'd thought it was fear at seeing Zach fall. He hadn't moved since going down. I pressed my fingers against his neck, relieved to feel his pulse throbbing steadily.

"It's just a cave. A salty hollowed-out hole in the earth. The key is not where we are. It's what this shell contains. The source of all magic is contained in five pieces of amber. Three are here. Two were stolen and are kept humanside." She looked at me. "I thought your ex-husband was on a mission for the witches to steal our ambers. But he has a far darker purpose in mind." She scowled, and then glared at Zach. "He came to destroy them. He wants to snuff out all the world's magic."

Bryn took a step back from the pedestal, shaking his head.

"How could Zach have planned to do that?" I snapped. "How could he have known about this place if Bryn who's studied magic his whole life didn't know about it?"

"I'll take Sutton back through the tunnel," Bryn said to Kismet. "But we'll need a rope to drag him up the incline."

I tested the arrow in Zach's back. The tip seemed to be stuck in his right shoulder blade. I remembered what she'd told us about her arrows, though; they were painted with poison. I grabbed the shaft and yanked. The arrowhead tore a hole in his flesh the size of a silver dollar on the way out, but I didn't care. I tossed it aside, stanching the blood with the palm of my hand.

"Drag him out, wizard. When you've gone, I'll secure the cave and then follow."

"You said there are five ambers. It's one of the stolen ones that WAM wants in exchange for Aunt Edie and Andre then? And WAM won't destroy the ambers, right? They'll protect them. So we could give them one of these," I said.

"No. These three must stay in the Never. Go on now."

"But—" I said.

"I don't have time to explain. Go!" she snapped.

Bryn had grabbed Zach's legs and pulled him toward the tunnel.

"Bryn—"

"No, Tamara. I think we should trust your sister and leave them here."

Zach twisted as he woke. He kicked Bryn's hands away, and then dragged himself to his feet.

Kismet pointed an arrow at the left side of Zach's chest. "If you destroyed them all, you'd kill her, you know. Tammy Jo is a hundred percent magic."

"I don't have to destroy them all. I'd imagine taking out four of the five should do the trick," Zach said. "There wouldn't be enough magic left in the world to cause trouble."

Bryn looked like he could've happily murdered Zach for saying that, but he didn't need to try, because Kismet stood between Zach and the globes that covered the remaining two ambers on the pedestals, her bow still trained on his heart.

"You can leave of your own power, or your dead body can be dragged out. You have thirty seconds to decide," she said.

Zach held his arms out. "I'm going."

I exhaled.

"He'll try to wait for you in the dark. To ambush you. Don't come until I've called to you that he's all the way out and back in the forest," Bryn said.

"Aren't you an apple darling?" Kismet said, flashing Bryn a smile. "But no need to worry. If he waits to ambush me, I'll just kill him where he stands." She shrugged. "It's only that I don't want a body left here. Out there's no trouble."

Bryn nodded and held up a hand to wave farewell. "Once out of here, I'll take her to the sea. There are exits out there, I think."

"Oh, aye. Safe travels," she said, tilting her head. I noted the red dot of dried blood on her left earlobe. She'd taken out the emerald earrings. Anticipating a fight? I wondered.

"Will I see you again?" I asked.

"If I live to see the outside again you will."

I hugged her. "Sorry about bringing Zach in here. And sorry I didn't check to see if you were okay before helping a Conclave witch."

"You should be sorry. Don't do either of those again."

"It was just a mistake, though; you know that, right? And forgive me?"

"I suppose," she said, the corners of her mouth quirking up.

"Okay, be careful," I said, hugging her. I gave her a kiss and then let go. "I love you," I whispered. "Even if it doesn't always seem like it."

I waved and hurried to the tunnel. I held my breath and bit my lip, praying she wouldn't realize what I'd done and shoot me in the back for being more treacherous than a Conclave operative.

I was my momma's daughter. Thanks to a sleight of hand, I had what everyone in the world of magic wanted: one of the almighty ambers.

31

THE FOUR OF us—Zach, Bryn, Merc, and I—left the cave of our own free will. The back of Zach's shirt was stained with a widening circle of blood, but it didn't seem to have affected his strength yet as he hauled himself up the incline and back into the forest.

"We need to try to stop your wound from bleeding," I said.

"I'm fine," Zach said, putting a hand out to ward me off. He scowled, looking at the giant tree roots. He stepped toward the entry to the cave, shaking his head. "We may never get the opportunity to put the world right again."

"The world is right," Bryn said. "Come on, Tamara," he added, grabbing my arm and tugging me.

Mercutio darted around the clearing of tall trees.

"You don't know what you're talking about, Lyons," Zach said. He gestured at the trees. "These trees are like the pattern on the back door of the castle and in paintings in their halls. The tallest tree represents the original magic. Fae magic. The original symbol was a triangle. Fae on top. And to the right a dark stone for werewolves, and to the left a dark stone for vampires."

We jogged deeper into the forest with Bryn leading the way.

"How did it become a diamond?" I asked. "What's the smallest stone for? Witches and wizards?"

"Yes," Zach said with a sharp nod. "The faeries will claim that humans betrayed them, and we sort of did, but not without reason."

"Hang on, Bryn!" I said, grabbing Zach's arm. "We've got to get this stopped or he'll bleed to death."

Bryn paused, frowning.

Zach took off his shirt and I cut it using Bryn's Swiss army knife and then tied the strips together. I made a tight dressing around his torso. He grimaced at the pressure, but at least the wound stopped leaking blood.

"It might loosen when we start moving. Let me know if you feel blood running down your back."

He nodded.

We started off again, and I called for Merc, who'd gotten too far ahead. I couldn't see him. When he circled back, I bent and stroked his back. "Wanna hear about the history of magic? It's about us. Finish the story, Zach."

"The fae like human beings, especially ones who are young and playful or have a certain golden energy, as they call it. Like the legends say, they bring kids and young people into the Never."

"We know all that," Bryn said impatiently. "Get to the point."

"Some humans passed in and out with the fae through the open gates on the solstices. They saw their own world and missed it. But they weren't allowed to come and go freely. Once the faeries claim a human, they feel they own him or her for all time. And they didn't want random humans passing into the Never to suck up its energy. The ambers were once displayed in the castle. A group of former human children who'd grown to be young adults lived with the faery queen. They took two ambers and left the Never with them. It brought magic into the human world. They were the first witches."

"That's why witch magic is the shortest tree or the smallest stone? It's the newest form of magic?"

"You got it, darlin'."

"And if the two stolen ambers are brought back into the Never? The magic in the human world will disappear?" I asked.

"Yeah. You'd be normal," Zach said. "But we don't want the fae to get all the ambers back, either, because then they'd have unopposed magic. The reason they're stuck underhill and can't come into our world easily is because witches, using magic, sealed the outside gates."

"Where did you hear all this?" Bryn said skeptically.

"I trained as a human champion under a descendant of one of the original witches. She believes magic is like chemical warfare: It's too dangerous and powerful. No one should have it or use it."

We were close enough that I could smell the sea and nothing but. I should've been exhilarated, but the trees started to groan and creak, and my muscles grew tense.

Branches swung and blocked our path until we had to slow to walk and climb through and around them.

Flute music floated on the air, and a gravelly voice whispered a foreign language through the forest.

Mercutio yowled and scratched the limbs. A group of branches pinned him to the ground.

"Hey, no!" I said, trying to pull him free.

"Tamara, look out!" Bryn yelled, but it was too late.

A heavy branch slammed into my back and held me down, too. I looked up and saw trees imprison Bryn and Zach. We all struggled and fought, but it was no use.

Finally, I sighed and rested my head on Merc's sleek shoulder.

"Prisoners again! I'm getting so sick of this!"

"HEY, DUDES."

I turned my head as far as I could, pressing my temple against a branch so I could see Oz lying across the twisted limbs to peer down at us.

"Dad has you under his thumbs, yeah?" he said.

"Dad?" I asked.

"Colis the tree keeper is my father. You attacked the queen and—"

"Can you help us free ourselves?" Bryn asked.

"Dude, how do you know that's why I'm here?" he asked.

"I inferred it from your tone. What can you do?"

"I've got a proposition," he said, leaning closer to me and craning his neck so we were practically nose-to-nose. "I'll give you back the already set emeralds. My new price for the second Fozzel you asked for is for you to assist me in my quest."

"Your quest?"

"Aye, to get out of here. To go humanside and see the volcanoes of Mount Doom on a giant movie screen. To go to rock concerts!" He grabbed his T-shirt and pulled it up so I could see the face of Kurt Cobain. "I want to see them play," he said. Then he launched into a pitch-perfect chorus of "All Apologies." With his grungy angel looks and clear singing voice, he made my jaw drop.

"You know Cobain is dead, right?" Bryn said.

"No! How did he die? Airplane crash? They're always falling from the sky, those rock stars. Only fae should fly. We've got the magic for it."

"Um, listen, what can you do to help us?" I asked.

"With the singer dead, there's an opening in the band, yeah? Can you arrange for me to have an apprenticeship? I have the third-best singing voice in the Never, and the other two wouldn't want the opportunity. The first is the queen's lark and the second is a hermit. Neither would venture humanside—"

"Oz! No one will be going anywhere if you don't free us immediately. I'm sure the queen's on her way, right?" I asked.

"Yes, a point for you, Kis. Do I have your promise you'll take me with you? I have my tradesman tools, so no interruption. Everything I need is here," he said, holding up a box with an embossed leather design on the cover.

I had no idea what he was talking about and I didn't care. "Yes, Oz, get us out and I promise to take you with us."

"Gravy," he said. Then he cocked his head, his light brown eyes wide and inquiring. "Did I use that right?"

"Um, I don't think so," I said.

"I mean *it's all gravy*," he said, which still wasn't totally right, of course, but I didn't correct him.

Oz pulled out a flute he'd had tucked into the back of his headband. He played a tune and sang in a foreign tongue to the trees. At first there was only creaking and low whispers from them, but when he added a higher-pitched note to his singing, they suddenly unwound their branches and dumped us on the forest floor. Mercutio yowled and ran forward, tearing off a piece of bark and scoring the tree with his claws.

"Mercutio!" I said, grabbing him and pulling him back. "Don't start a fight with the trees when they just let us go. It's bad manners."

"And lousy strategy," Bryn added.

We jogged through the woods. Whenever trees began to close ranks, Oz played his flute and sang to them, his words carried as whispers on the wind.

We reached a field of dandelions that gave way to a rocky shoreline, but a row of horsemen galloped toward us from the west with the queen in a gown of red rage leading them. A lone knight stood between us and the sea.

Crux held out his hands for us to stop.

"Keep going!" I shouted above the roaring wind and surf.

Oz did. He started down the embankment toward the water, disappearing from view. Zach, Bryn, and Mercutio, however, stayed stubbornly by my side.

The queen's lovely voice rang out fiercely above everything. "Crux, kill the Halfling stranger. The one who pretended to be my assassin when she was not."

From behind me I heard pounding hooves and felt a storm at my back. I glanced over my shoulder, afraid I'd be trampled, but it was Kismet on her palomino. The arrow in her bow was pointed directly at Crux.

I slowed, looking back at him. I'd expected him to pull out his bow and shoot me. The queen had given him a direct order.

He had drawn his sword, though, instead of his bow. I stopped. So did everything, it seemed. Even the wind softened.

He stabbed the ground and then flipped the sword so the hilt stuck into the hole he'd made and the blade pointed up.

My heart seemed to understand before my mind, and my breath caught.

He locked eyes with Kismet and stretched his arms out.

She lowered her bow and opened her mouth. His eyes never left her face as he fell on his sword.

The queen's scream was as sharp as a knife. My hands flew to cover my mouth. Kismet made no sound as her pony flew to Crux and she dismounted.

She dropped her bow on the ground and grabbed him.

"Iron?" she yelled in horror when his blood sizzled on the blade. She dragged him onto his side, withdrawing the sword partway until he grabbed the blade with his bare hands.

"It's no use. I promise."

Tears filled her eyes.

"Why! How could you do it?"

"Death is the only oath breaker. If I had killed your sister, you would never have forgiven me. If you'd killed me to prevent it, you would not have forgiven yourself. This is the best way. Now I am what you wanted. I'm yours above anyone's. And all will know I chose you above everyone else. Even her."

Kismet grabbed her head and made an anguished sound.

"Kiss me as you pull out the blade. Taste how much I still love you."

"You bastard."

"Yes," he said, and laughed. "Like you. Cut of that cloth. If only you weren't. If you'd been full fae you could've challenged her. What a queen you could've made," he said, coughing at the end, and his face contorted with pain. "The iron burns so much, Kis." He panted. "Please pull it out. Steady hand, be quick."

Tears dripped down her face and she kissed him. Her left arm flexed and she jerked it back. The blade slid from his chest on a river of red-gold blood. She dropped the blade and caught him in her arms and held him.

She kissed him again, and when she lowered him at last, his blood stained her mouth.

She grabbed her bow and swiveled to face us. Her green eyes flashed with fury. "Into the sea. Run!" she shouted.

For a second I was frozen, but then I turned and ran. I heard arrows whiz through the wind. I didn't look back. I was afraid to.

Mercutio, Zach, and I rushed headlong after Bryn as he jumped off a cliff that jutted out above the water. I held my breath as my stomach lurched into my throat. A second later I plunged into the fae ocean, my tears mixing with the cool water.

I surfaced, gasping for breath. Bryn caught my hand and called for the others to dive with him.

"There's a waterway, a faery path under the surface. Sutton, grab Oz. When I pull you into it, you'll lead him through. Hurry!" he yelled.

I followed Bryn's gaze to the ledge of the cliff, where the queen's archers were lined up and shooting arrows.

Zach and Oz swam to us.

"Where's Mercutio?" I shouted, but Bryn didn't answer or wait for me to spot him.

"Follow me," Bryn said to Zach, and then dragged me down.

When I thought I'd surely run out of breath and my heart thundered in my chest against my screaming lungs, Bryn kissed me and gave me his breath. Moments later I felt the water shift. It became heavier and colder. A current grabbed us and suddenly we were in a churning tunnel. I felt like a ball shot from a cannon, whooshing so fast even sound couldn't catch up.

I began to feel dizzy, like I would pass out. My belly cramped. The pain was so deep and hard within me I thought I might die.

I lost track of the water, the path, the world.

Finally the waterway released us. We broke the surface

like corks popping from a champagne bottle. The spray was icy cold, but I was so exhausted I almost sank underwater.

Bryn pulled me to him and kissed me, laughing and obviously exhilarated from the journey. He had no idea how close he'd come to losing me and the future we planned.

His black sealskin faded almost instantly, and his wizard's magic poured into us, which rejuvenated me.

We're okay. We made it.

Zach and Oz burst from the water a few feet away.

"Yahoo!" Oz yelled, pumping his fist. His dreadlocks had uncoiled, and his golden hair was plastered to his neck and shoulders and shimmered in the sun.

Zach ran a hand over his face to get rid of the excess water and then turned and swam toward shore.

There was a stone fort to our right and boats bobbing in the water in front of us. People—human people wearing jeans, sweaters, and jackets—came running to the beach when they spotted us. A few of them surrounded something and kept looking down.

When we walked from the ocean, the thing they'd surrounded came bounding down to meet me. I dropped to my knees on the sand and hugged Mercutio.

"You made it! If I've said it once, I've said it a hundred times: You're amazing, Merc. Thanks for coming with me into the Never and for getting out of there alive."

I looked over my shoulder, shivering in my half-frozen soggy clothes.

The friendly Irish people tried to hurry us away from the shore, asking dozens of questions, but I resisted being led to shelter. I smiled at them, but pulled back without answering.

"Let's wait. She might be right behind us," I whispered to Bryn, returning to the water's edge.

"The queen won't kill her. She's too valuable," Bryn said.

"Probably not. But maybe she didn't get caught at all. She said her horse will run off cliffs. She could've followed us out."

"Tamara, she covered our escape. She was pretty far from the water," he said grimly.

I chewed on my lip. "I shouldn't have left her there," I said. "After he died like that."

"She'll be all right. That girl's tougher than month-old beefsteak," Zach said, walking to a pair of middle-aged women who offered him a blanket.

"Yeah, she'll be okay." *She has to be.* "It's just that . . ." I shook my head.

"You're worried about her," Bryn said.

"Yes. Also, I did something. I'll tell you later," I said, glancing at Zach. I didn't trust him with the truth. "Zach, you should get that wound looked at. One of the nice ladies can take you to a local ER. Do you need money to get back to England?"

"Are we parting company?" Zach asked, putting a hand over the back pocket of his jeans.

"Yes," I said. "It's time for us to go our own ways."

Zach's eyes never left my face. "If that's how you want it." He waited.

I didn't say anything more.

"I've still got my wallet. Don't know if my card still works, but I'll manage," he said.

"Bryn, can you give him some of the cash you have?"

"No," Zach said, holding out a hand. "Listen, your aunt Edie's still a priority of mine. I brought her here. Not planning to go back to Texas while she's stuck in London."

"We'll handle that," Bryn said.

"Got it covered, do you?" Zach asked, narrowing his eyes. "Don't need help searching Scottish woods? You don't need a hand defending yourself against wild dogs, huh?"

"Don't worry about wild dogs or anything else. Just go on back home," I said.

Bryn held out a handful of money. Zach shook his head.

"No, thanks," Zach said, then glanced at me. "I'd never do anything to hurt you."

"You already did. You lied. And your mission was more important than me and my family." I shrugged. "Never expected that. But things change. I understand."

"Hey, darlin', you're the one who changed first."

"I know." I swallowed the lump in my throat. "I want to go," I said, looking at Bryn. "Can we?"

"Yes," Bryn said, taking my hand and holding it tight so our rings touched and magic arced between us. I felt another cramp deep in my belly and then warmth all through me.

"Things are real different. Changing all the time," I said.

"Definitely," Oz said, tossing his arms wide. "I made it! Almost didn't. Nearly drowned! But I'm here now." Then, as he looked up, his smile faded. "It's very cloudy here," he said, glancing at the sky. "Is the sun up there? Probably it is. Hey, where are we?" he asked, turning to the people.

"Kinsale," a woman said, surprised. "Did your boat sink?"

They'd asked us that several times earlier, but none of us had answered. Finally Zach did, saying, "No, we jumped from a boat on a dare."

"What? What boat?" the woman asked.

Zach shook his head. "I'm not gonna say."

I don't know if they believed him about the dare or not. I didn't really care.

"Where is Kinsale?" Oz asked.

"Ireland," Bryn said quickly. "We're still in Ireland."

"Ireland," Oz said with a smile at the locals. "All right. I'm the great and powerful Oz," he said, thrusting out a hand. "You've probably heard tell of me. For my first activity, I'd like to meet Bono from the band U2. Would you be cool and introduce me?"

The people stared at him, speechless.

"He's joking," Bryn said, hooking an arm around Oz's shoulders. "This way, Mr. Great and Powerful. Let me explain a few things."

"Oh? Okay, dude."

I stared out at the water, but Kismet didn't emerge. I finally had to admit she wasn't going to.

32

I NEVER THOUGHT I'd be grateful for Bryn's being rich, but his wallet full of cash and credit cards had gotten us transportation to Killarney to get our van full of luggage. We arranged via texts to meet Zach in Dublin just to hand off his bags to him.

We also got a hotel room and a cell phone for Oz and plane tickets for Bryn and myself to England.

Oz got seventeen invitations to be people's houseguest. And that was just in the Dublin airport. He borrowed a musician's guitar and played a version of Eric Clapton's "Tears in Heaven" that made people cry and tip him a pile of money while he waited with us for our flight to board.

He also met a girl who knew Bono's daughter and said she could take him to a party to meet the superstar.

"You're the best," he said, giving the girl a hug. He'd mastered hugging in about five seconds. "But we're going to England. So I guess I'll concentrate on meeting Keith Richards and the Rolling Stones. Keith Richards hasn't died, has he, wizard?" he asked Bryn.

"No, he's alive," I said. "But listen, you're not coming to

England, remember? On account of you don't have a passport?"

"Oh, I'm going. I've wanted to see England for a long
time. The Beatles are from there, you know?"

"Are they really?" Bryn quipped.

I smiled. "Cut it out, Bryn. We'll call you on the cell
phone, Oz. Take a taxi back to the hotel. Your room is paid
for for the week. We'll figure something out after we take
care of our wizard business."

"Go ahead, Halfling. I'm the great and powerful Oz. I
will prevail."

Bryn laughed and was still shaking his head when we
boarded. But five minutes after we sat down, Oz got on the
plane and both our jaws dropped.

The flight attendant had apparently decided to overlook
his lack of passport.

"She can't do that. He could be a terrorist," I whispered.

"I don't know what to tell you. He's the great and powerful Oz."

I spent the flight eyeing him suspiciously. Had he borrowed the queen's magic lip gloss? He didn't appear to have
anything on his lips. But there was no doubt that humans
doted on him.

When we arrived in London, Oz bought black sunglasses
and a charcoal-gray scarf with his tip money. He sold Bryn
an uncut Colombian emerald for seven hundred dollars and
promptly bought a guitar from a man who looked homeless.
Then he bought a leather jacket from a guy with a half-
shaved head.

"Here are your family's earrings," Oz said, hooking Aunt
Mel's emerald earrings into my lobes.

"Hey!"

"I said I'd give those back. The rest of the emeralds I'll
keep for bartering. Thanks for getting me to England. And as
promised, the other part of my debt is repaid. Finished work
on it. You'll see. Hey, I recognize that car's ornamental. That's
a Lamborghini. I'm going to ride with that guy. He'll be able
to introduce me to Keith Richards." He waved and strode off.

"Oz, wait a minute! What do you mean, your debt's repaid?"

But he didn't turn around. He jogged over to introduce himself to the sixtyish-year-old man who seemed to speak only Italian. Oz made a few gestures and the man opened the passenger door and waved for him to get in.

"Do you think he'll be okay?"

"I think he'll be a rock star by Thursday," Bryn said.

"Unless WAM spots him."

"Right. Then he'll be a jailbird. But until then, he's the great and powerful Oz."

WE CHECKED INTO the Savoy Hotel, which is Aunt Mel's favorite. Bryn thought we were going to regroup and make a plan. He didn't know I already had one that I hadn't told him about.

I waited for him to fall asleep, gave him a kiss, and then took a taxi driven by a man named Colin to the World Association of Magic headquarters. He told me about World Cup soccer, which he called football. I confided in him that I'd had to steal from my sister to pay my aunt and my fiancé's best friend's bail, and that I didn't know if my sister would forgive me or whether I'd even get the chance to explain, since she'd left the country and I wasn't welcome in her home.

He said she'd forgive me. Family didn't have a choice about that. I hoped he was right. Kismet was new to families. I wasn't sure how far family loyalty would go with her.

I thought about the rift between my grandma and Momma, Aunt Mel and Edie. "Some families are real good at grudges." I handed him a handful of money and waited for him to sort out the fare and his tip. "I like your money over here. It's pretty," I said. "Ours is plainer. Of course, it's good, too," I said, not wanting to seem unpatriotic.

He gave me back a bundle of bills. "Be careful, Tammy Jo. Not everyone will be honest when it comes to money."

"I know," I said. "But I like to give people a chance to be honest and good. Humanity is attractive. Just ask the faeries,"

I whispered with a wink that left his eyebrows around his hairline.

The outdoor lights of WAM headquarters lit the front entry and the hulking gargoyles. They were just statues after all.

Conclave members acting as security opened the front door, and the president was with them.

"Hey, there," I said, walking right up to him. "Thanks for meeting me so late."

"Where are the boys?" Poppy asked, stepping into view.

"They're safe," I said. "And hi." I didn't shake Anderson's hand. Instead I slapped the amber into it. "There you go. Give me my friends."

Everyone in the lobby seemed to have been struck dumb. They huddled around him.

"It's amber from an ancient tree, certainly." Anderson put on small spectacles and brought the amber practically to his nose. "There's definitely something within it. Wake Basil and Mrs. Hurley. Ms. Trask, you can wait here or go back to your hotel. If this proves authentic, your friends will be dropped off at your hotel by morning."

"I'm not leaving," I said, sitting in a lobby chair.

"Where did you get it? And how?" Poppy demanded.

I folded my arms across my chest and tipped my head back to look at the painted ceiling. "Nobody said I had to give an explanation. All I had to do was deliver it," I said, swirling my hand in a ta-da gesture.

"Answering questions about where it was unearthed should be part of the authentication process. Like provenance for a painting," an operative said.

"That wasn't part of the deal I made." My stomach growled. "I'm hungry, though. For a chocolate croissant, I'll let you in on a little secret."

There were murmurs, and after about fifteen minutes a warm chocolate croissant and a mug of tea with milk were delivered to the lobby.

I ate the entire croissant in four bites and drank my tea. "The truth is, I did something underhanded to get it. And I'm still not sure it was the right thing to do, so I'd rather be boiled in oil than tell you the details. I don't expect Conclave spies to understand my troubled conscience, since you guys don't seem to have consciences at all, let alone troubled ones. Let's just say I'm the great and powerful Tammy Jo and leave it at that."

There was a little bit of an uproar, but I just shrugged. I'd been through too much over the past few weeks to get riled over arguments.

Sure, I'd tricked them into giving me a croissant. Not great manners. But how bad was I supposed to feel? They were the worst bunch of liars I'd ever met. Besides, it had been an emergency. I really needed that pastry. I frowned. Okay, you could take a Halfling out of the Never. But it was going to take more than a day to get the Never out of the Halfling.

I WOKE CURLED in the lobby chair and was informed that the verification of an ancient relic was going to take more than a day. What did I expect, they wanted to know, when I couldn't explain how I'd miraculously found their treasure in a few days after a group of highly trained operatives hadn't been able to find it in two years?

I was trying to decide what to do when Edie emerged from the elevator. She wore a sage-green sweater with a black pencil skirt and green suede knee-high boots. She strode across the lobby followed closely by a man and woman who were dressed like undertakers.

"Hi," I said, standing to hug her.

She smelled like Chanel perfume.

"How come, if you're a prisoner, you've got fresh clothes on and smell real nice? And I'm not one, but I've got crumbs on my shirt and haven't combed my hair?"

She smirked. "I've had lots of practice getting ready after sleeping somewhere other than my own bed," she said with a wink.

I gasped.

"An all-nighter is never an excuse for looking rumpled. Now, I've heard that you brought them what they want. Well-done!" She clutched my hands. "Naturally, they haven't released Andre and me. They're not to be taken at their word. Ever. But we already knew that, didn't we?"

I nodded, frowning.

"So," she said, sneakily pressing a piece of paper into my palm, "we'll soldier on. I need a few more sundries that I forgot to pack. You'll be a darling and run out for me, won't you?"

"Um, I was going to wait for you and then we could all take a cab back to the hotel and leave England," I whispered. My stomach rumbled. "I'm hungry again."

"Shocking," she said dryly. "Take a few minutes to get breakfast. And to run a brush through your hair," she said, finger-combing the strands closest to my face. "Then go on my errand."

I tucked my hair behind my ears with a sigh. "Okay." I stood and shoved the paper in my pocket. I accepted a quick kiss on my cheek.

When I got to the door, the operatives hesitated to step aside. I gave them a hard look. Finally the guy moved and opened the door for me.

I took a cab back to the Savoy. I ate a basket of pastries and fruit and drank two glasses of milk before I brushed my hair and teeth. I confessed to Bryn about stealing an amber and giving it to WAM. He said nothing.

"You mad at me?"

"No," he said. "I'm just not sure about the repercussions of your actions. What if the gates to the Never disappear altogether?"

"That's not possible."

He rested his hands on the table, leaning forward. "We don't really know what's possible, do we?"

"I'd like to know how Kismet is doing. If I could trick the queen into coming out, maybe the Conclave would lock her up and the Seelie world could get a new leader." I glanced through the list Edie had given me. I'd expected to see dental floss or more designer perfume or normal traveling supplies to be on the list. Instead it was a list of witch's herbs. "What in the world?"

Bryn looked over my shoulder. "Valerian, chamomile blossoms, linden blossoms, poppies . . ."

"Those are for sleep. She must be planning to make a potion to knock the guards out, but the ingredients on the bottom of the list aren't for a sleeping spell. Elecampane, dew from a lady's mantle, ginseng, and yerba santa." I narrowed my eyes. "I don't know which spells use these." I shook my head. "I know she wants to have a backup plan ready and I don't blame her. But she's not supposed to need one. We made a deal with the WAM president. God, I hope he's not as big of a liar as the Conclave operatives. An authentic fae amber was supposed to be Edie and Andre's 'get out of jail free' card."

I opened the pouch in my suitcase to put away my hairbrush and found a small leather bag with a dandelion embossed on the front. "What's this?" I asked.

I reached in with my thumb and forefinger and felt a piece of cloth. I pulled out a square of crushed brown velvet. When I unfolded it, I looked down at a piece of amber. My jaw dropped and I lifted it to examine it. It was exactly the same as the amber I'd given to WAM. I stiffened with shock.

"Oh, my God," I said.

"What?" Bryn said, walking over. "Wait, what is that? I thought you gave them the amber."

I raised it and stared, my heart thudding. There were things inside the amber just like in the one I'd given to WAM, a strand of hair and a tiny winged pixie fossilized within it.

"Oh, my God," I murmured again, letting Bryn take it from me. "It's a Fozzel. Oz is the tree keeper's son. Amber comes from the tree's—what's it called? Sap? Resin? He was making art pieces for Kismet to trade. She was supposed to bring him emeralds for making a special piece for her." I clutched my head. "Remember when he gave me back my aunt Mel's earrings? Those were what Kismet paid him for a second special piece, but he didn't want more emeralds. He wanted to come out with us. He told me at the airport that he'd finished his work and his debt was repaid. This is the payment. He made her a replica of the amber she lost. And when she returned to the Never this time, she told him to make her another copy. He must have slipped it into my bag."

"Why did Kismet need copies made of the amber? Do you think she was planning to exchange the replicas for the real ambers? And if so, where are they?"

"I don't know, Bryn. Maybe she actually did lose the original amber." The room was spinning around me in slow motion. "What if, when I picked Kismet's pocket, I didn't get an actual ancient amber? What if the one I gave to WAM is only a copy Oz made for her. A fake like this one?" I sank down to sit on the edge of the bed, feeling so nauseous I thought I might throw up all over the beautiful carpet. I bent forward and rested my head against my thighs, taking some deep breaths.

"It'll be all right," Bryn said, resting a hand on my back and kneeling next to me.

"Do we have any candy left?" I mumbled.

"Here," Bryn said a moment later. I unwrapped a piece of Cadbury Flake. It's a kind of chocolate bar we don't have in America, but should. I chewed and immediately felt better. The sick feeling passed and I nodded.

"Okay, so Edie was right: We need a plan B, because if that amber's a fake, when WAM figures it out we'll be in more trouble than we've ever been in." I rubbed the back of my neck, which was damp with sweat. "Take me to that witches' shop where you were going to get the reference books when we first arrived in England."

"Magic Calling," Bryn said. "Are you all right? Do you need sleep?"

"Nope, I need to get the herbs for Edie. And for us, weapons."

"PLANNING TO ROB a bank?" the girl with the pierced nose and eyebrows asked.

"Um, no," I said, waving away a bug that buzzed by my ear. "Why do you ask that?"

She shook her head. "Thought you were working on a concealment spell." She nodded at the collection of dried herbs and vials of liquid on the counter.

Were some of Edie's list of ingredients for a cloaking spell? So that if she managed to escape, the Conclave operatives wouldn't be able to track her? That would come in handy.

Bryn added three small books to the assortment and paid for it.

We left, and in the back of the cab a small voice said, "Hello, tricky twin. How are you?"

I jerked my head to find Shakes sitting by the back window. The buzzing in the store hadn't been a bug. I should've known!

"I hear you've got two copies of the wolf amber," he continued. "Give me one."

I leaned close. "How did you find me?"

He grabbed a handful of my hair and shook it. "Followed the faery magic. Royal said Kismarley said to look for you in London near the witches' stronghold." He wrinkled his nose. "Cities stink."

"What makes you think I have an amber?"

"You stole the first copy from her in the Never, and the tree-talker faery said he gave you the other one he made."

So the amber I'd taken from Kismet's pocket had been fake. Had she known all along that I'd taken it? Or did she realize it later? Was she furious with me?

More important, what had the queen done to her after I escaped? Had Ghislaine punished her for my crimes?

"Is my sister okay?"

"Tamara," Bryn said, casting a meaningful glance at the taxi driver, who was giving me a funny look in the rearview mirror, since to him it probably seemed like I was talking to my shoulder.

I stared straight forward, but turned my head slightly so I could continue my conversation with Shakes.

"Well?" I said.

"She's sunset, but still golden."

"Sunset? What does that mean? I don't understand faery slang," I hissed in a whisper.

All I knew about sunset was that it came at the end of the day. I didn't want Kismet to be at the end of anything. She was young. She had her whole life ahead of her.

"She's a warrior. One of the toughest ever. Did you expect her to freeze up like a possum? To shake like a deer? To hide like a rabbit? She's Halfling, but she got the brave half of both sides, human and fae. She says the queen broke the sovereign's sacred vow to protect the Never. She called for any full fae not under an oath to the queen to challenge the high lady of the land before the sun next rises."

I gasped.

"What sacred vow did the queen break?" Bryn asked, whispering too.

"She let it slip to the human that the ancient ambers were hidden underground, not even realizing he had a reason for coaxing secrets from her. Then her new lover found the cave and tried to destroy them! If the queen's assassin hadn't stopped him, the light might have gone out of the Never."

"Why can't Kismet challenge the queen herself? She's probably the only one who could defeat Ghislaine."

"Only full Seelie fae can challenge the queen, because, if triumphant, the challenger would rule the Never. The law doesn't allow for a creature of mixed magic to sit on the throne."

"If no one challenges the queen and she stays in charge, can she accuse Kismet of treason?"

"She already has. She says Kismet has the wolf amber and didn't bring it home to the Never. Ghislaine declared that an act of treason. The punishment is death or a lifetime in iron chains. As long as Ghislaine rules, Kismarley will never see humanside again."

I swallowed, biting my lip. "I have to go back."

Bryn shook his head.

"Yes, when Edie and Andre are safe, I'm returning to the Never to help Kismet."

"Good, twin. That's what I hoped you'd say," Shakes said.

33

SHAKES HUNG FROM my purse strap as we entered the Savoy. I kept my arm dangling, hoping no one would spot him. No one seemed to. That's where Bryn's good looks come in handy. When he's around, people aren't going to waste their time looking at handbag straps when they could be staring at him.

In the room, I took the impostor amber from its pouch. Shakes flew over, peering down to examine it.

"Nice work that Osmet does! He's included the body of a fallen fae and a hair of the dog inside. And he's infused some fae magic within. It's a lot like the original!"

"Hair of the dog?"

He looked at me suspiciously. "You don't need to know. You're not trustworthy. Humans are tricky."

"Fae are the tricksters! My sister let me think I stole a real-life amber relic, and I gave it to some witches as payment for our aunt, who's a prisoner."

"Witches," he scoffed. "What do they know of original magic? They won't know the difference!"

Bryn bristled.

"Kismet had Oz make the second replica so we could trick

the witches with it. But who is the first amber for?" I asked. "Surely the queen wouldn't have been fooled by a fake?"

Shakes didn't answer.

"The Scottish wolves," Bryn said.

Shakes put a tiny knife to the pulse in Bryn's throat. "What do you know of it, wizard?"

"Only what I've guessed. Kismet was sent to recover an ancient amber that the wolves were protecting. She stole it, but the wolves have been hunting her ever since. She had Oz make a fake amber to give them, figuring they wouldn't know the difference."

Shakes glared at Bryn. "Sneaky wizard! Quit that cleverness or I'll poke a hole in your dumb blood pipes."

"Shakes, listen, you're not loyal to the werewolves, are you?" I asked.

"To a pack of dogs? No way."

"But you are loyal to my sister, right?"

"To the death," he shouted, raising his arm and then thumping it on his chest. The tip of his blade cut his chin and he yelped. He dabbed his bleeding jaw with his sleeve. "To the death and to the blood," he added. "I'm not pureblood. Royal's from the queen's line, but he's a bastard, too. We're mixed-blood, free fae. We pledge our fealty to whomever we choose. We chose Halfling Kismarley. She's mean, but worthy. That's the best kind of mean."

"Shakes, listen: I can't help Kismet unless I understand what I'm dealing with. You said hair of the dog. The wolf amber is called that because it has a werewolf hair inside?"

Shakes studied me for several moments. "If you're a traitor against the queen, good. If you're a traitor against your twin, I'll make you pay."

"I'm not!"

"You'd better not be," he said with narrowed eyes. He flew up to my face, squeezing my nose with his tiny hands while he peered into my eyes. After a few moments, he said, "All right, then. There are five original tree-stones. Two are pure fae. One is for the Seelie, with a small faery inside clutching a bit of gold. One is for the Unseelie, with a tiny dark faery clutching a chip of onyx. One amber is for the dogs. It has a faery clutching a strand of werewolf hair. One amber is for the undead. That tiny faery clutches a chip from the first vampire's fang. The last amber, the newest, has a pixie who wears a crimson gown that was dyed with a drop of blood from each of the first witches, the traitors."

I nodded, thinking things over. "So the wolf amber contains the magic that gives werewolves the ability to shift. But since they don't practice magic, they won't be able to tell that the faery magic in this copy isn't the original magic that supplies them."

"They won't be able to tell. Dumb dogs," Shakes said.

"So we can use this copy as leverage."

He cocked his head. "What's that? Payment?"

"No, we can use it to barter with the werewolves. They want their amber back. They're really strong and fierce. They can help us save my sister. In exchange for this."

His jaw dropped. "She's in the Never."

"Yes."

"They're not."

"But they could be. I can take creatures in and out. It's the only kind of magic of mine that works right."

He sucked in a breath. "You're crazy, Halfling. You'd try to lead a pack of wild dogs that would like to rip your throat out? You'd try to tame and trick them into being your army, an army that you'll march into the heart of Seelie magic?"

"Um, when you put it like that it sounds kind of—"

"Crazy," Bryn said, using exactly the word I'd been thinking.

"Too right. It's madness!" Shakes shouted, shaking his fist. "And brilliant! I'll do it. I travel with you."

"For God's sake, no," Bryn said.

"I'm sorry," I said, kissing Bryn's frowning lips.

"No," he repeated.

"Let's go!" Shakes yelled, grabbing a clump of my hair and swinging from it like Tarzan from a vine. His insane enthusiasm made me smile.

"The wolves aren't the only part of my plan," I told Bryn.

The room spun suddenly and I almost fell. Bryn caught my arms and steadied me.

"You're not well. You've been dizzy on and off since we returned from the Never," he said.

He was right, but I said, "I'm okay. I just need to rest for a minute."

He kissed me gently. "Your magic tastes different," he said.

I threaded my fingers through his so our rings touched, and his magic rolled over me. He was exactly the same . . . perfect. I felt steadier after touching him.

Merc licked my ankle, looked up at me with his head cocked, and then strolled into the bathroom.

Yeah, a soak would do me good.

"Um, let me think over the details of my plan. Everything is moving so fast."

I SAT IN the claw-footed tub with my chin on the lip, looking up at Merc, who sat on the edge of the sink. The black and white tiles of the floor were elegant and stylish.

Edie would like it here, I thought.

"I don't know what I'm doing, Merc," I whispered. "Going back to the Never, that could be out and out suicide."

Mercutio didn't disagree.

"But what else can I do? Just walk away?"

"How are you?" Bryn asked, pushing the door open. He had a small book with a snakeskin cover.

"What's that?"

"It's a volume I bought at Magic Calling. You know the collection of herbs Edie wants? Some are for a sleeping potion, like you thought. The rest, I suspect, are for this," he said, holding out the book.

At the top of the page there was a sketch of a woman in smudged black ink, and over her image there were three other images done in green, purple, and blue colored pencil. The page smelled like roses and musk, and the spell was for a glamour. It called for all the ingredients Edie wanted, plus a couple of others, vervain and elderberry.

The spell also called for a piece of jewelry to be dipped in the herbs and then topped with salt. The witch dusted her lips with sugar and salt, and then drank hard apple cider and whispered the spell into a flame. The candle's glow would reflect the spell onto the witch when she donned the anointed jewelry, and the glamour would last until she took it off.

"Of course," I said. "I should have guessed. Everyone always says Edie was great at glamour spells. With this kind of spell, she could disguise herself as a Conclave operative and walk out the front door of headquarters without anyone recognizing her."

"And Andre? He won't be able to cast a spell using earth magic."

"Could you write one for him using celestial magic?"

"I don't think they'll let him onto the roof to draw power from the stars. And I'm willing to bet that wherever they're being kept is pretty well insulated, so that unsanctioned spells will be impossible to cast. Andre did tell me that he knows where there are theoretical gaps in security, but he wouldn't try to exploit those on his own."

"I know Edie's probably restless and anxious to get out of there, so maybe she hasn't thought it all through, but that's where we come in. We're going to help her."

"How?"

"I'm thinking," I said.

"You know if she tries and fails, if she's caught, the Conclave will tighten security."

"Yes, but I feel like right now is our best chance. The president is letting me in and out because of the delay in the authentification. People aren't hassling me because they know I'm allowed to be there for hours. I think I can smuggle the herbs in."

Bryn set the book down and sat on the lip of the tub. He picked up a washcloth and washed my back for me. "So, Mercutio, what does Tamara need to tell me?"

When neither Mercutio nor I said anything, Bryn added, "It's all right for her to keep secrets from other people, but husbands and wives should confide in each other. About everything."

Mercutio purred at me.

"Yeah, Merc, okay."

Mercutio hopped down and sauntered out of the bathroom. The water had cooled and it made me shiver. I sat back and turned on the tap for the hot water.

"Come in," I said.

Bryn stood and stripped out of his clothes. He lowered himself into the tub in front of me. I worked up some lather between my hands and then ran them over his back.

"Something has been wrong since I left the Never. I don't know if there was poison on an arrow or the queen's dagger that got into my system . . . or maybe it's the broken connection with Kismet, but I don't feel normal."

"If you were poisoned by the fae, the longer you're humanside, the more likely you'll be to heal."

"Maybe. Too bad I don't have time to wait and find out."

"Going back immediately isn't a good idea. We need to research ways of protecting ourself against fae magic. It won't do your sister any good if we're captured and put under the queen's spell."

"Ghislaine's kissing spell didn't hold me," I said gently.

Bryn scowled, shutting off the tap. The room became so silent that it was hard to bear. "What are you saying? That I'm a liability?"

"No way. Never. I'm saying maybe it's more dangerous for you than for me."

"You couldn't have gotten out of there without me. I took you out on that water path."

"I know. But I also know you're afraid to get close to the queen. I don't blame you. It's okay to stay out here this time."

"You are not going without me," he said fiercely. "And it's incredibly foolish to rush in without a plan."

I squeezed his hands tight. "I can't feel my sister anymore. I have to go back now, when the queen can be challenged."

"Who do you think you're going to convince to challenge her? Crux is dead. Your father swore an oath to protect Ghislaine. Kismet is a Halfling, and Halflings can't challenge the queen for power because they can't rule. Everyone else there is a stranger to you. There is no way you'll be able to get someone to challenge a spiteful and dangerous monarch who's proven she's willing to torture, humiliate, and kill her enemies. What can you possibly think you'll accomplish by going back?"

"That's exactly the reason I have to get Kis out! Or try to."

"Kismet's a spy and an assassin who grew up in the Never. If she can't escape, what chance do you think you have of rescuing her?"

"I have to try."

"No, you don't."

"Yes, I do! Even if I fail, I have to try. Kismet has to know that I didn't abandon her. I have to prove that she's as important to me as everyone else in my family."

"Listen—"

"Nobody's ever fought to protect her, Bryn. She's my twin sister. She came back to get me out. And what did I do? I stole from her and left her." I bit my lip and shook my head as tears welled up. "Even after I'd almost lost her because I helped Poppy before her. Don't you understand?"

"I do. I understand, but your sister is tough. She doesn't need you to rescue her."

"I think she does."

"Listen, time moves differently there. Slower. You can rest and recover. We can spend a week or at least a few days preparing, doing research."

"There are no answers out here. We've read the Conclave's stuff on the Never. We know more than they do."

"Going in blind could make things worse. Give me a few days at least."

"I can't, but you stay humanside. Learn what you can. If I don't return, come after me."

Bryn ran a hand through his hair. "You used to trust my judgment. We worked together. Do I have any say in this at all?"

I rested a hand against his cheek. "I love you more than anyone." I bit my lip and swallowed hard. "I love you more than anybody—I promise. But I have to be brave because I know what has to be done. I feel it."

"You're sure, huh? I hope so, since you're gambling with both our lives."

He pulled back and got out of the tub. As he walked out of the bathroom, I rubbed my eyes. I knew it wasn't fair to drag him back there, and if something happened to him I would regret it forever. But I couldn't leave her underhill alone and a prisoner. I just couldn't do it.

34

BRYN STOOD AT the windows, staring out. He'd dressed in jeans and a thick cable-knit gray sweater. I left him alone for a few minutes after I got dressed, but then I stood behind him and wrapped my arms around him.

He was stiff with anger and frustration, but I held on, talking to him softly, telling him my plan. When he didn't speak, I kept talking, moving on from the problems we'd have to face at WAM and in the Never. Instead, I filled the silence with talk of home, of getting married, of cakes I'd bake him and parties we'd have, of a life we'd eventually get to live. One day real soon, I promised.

He finally relaxed in my arms, resting his forehead against the glass.

"If things go wrong, Tamara . . ." He left the sentence unfinished, but I knew what he meant. He might have a hard time forgiving me.

I pressed a kiss against the back of his neck. "I'm going to headquarters. If I can, I'll help Edie and Andre get out. I'd think that legally, we can defend my doing that, right? The president asked for a magic amber. I gave him one."

Bryn nodded. "But I don't think it'll come to a legal

battle because getting them out . . . Headquarters is very well guarded."

"I know. That's why I'm gonna resort to trickery."

"The Conclave is pretty savvy. There are security cameras everywhere. There are spells to neutralize attack spells."

"You said Andre can disable security."

"Some of it. Maybe," Bryn said. "Definitely not all of it."

"I don't need it all off. What's the one thing the Association must fear more than anything?" I asked.

"Losing the amber they have. If it's truly the source of magic in the world, there's nothing more valuable to them."

"Exactly. And who would they worry would come to take it?"

Bryn stared at me. "The fae."

"Yep. So if a faery were to infiltrate the building, every other thing, including guarding some witches whose crimes were minor and who were probably going to be freed anyway, wouldn't be a priority."

"And what faery is going to infiltrate the building as a diversion?"

"Me. And a little friend with a big attitude."

"You'll never be able to sneak him in."

"We'll manage. Gonna do it the fae way. . . . Gonna wing it." I winked.

He didn't smile. "Be careful."

"I will."

Bryn rubbed his mouth as if to hold back other things he might say. Finally he added, "If you get caught and I have to do something drastic to get you out of there, we'll have to go on the run, you know? That will be the end of living in Duvall. Just so you realize what's at stake."

I caught his face in my hands. "We might do that. Or we might just stand our ground in Texas and beat them with our home-field advantage." I gave him a kiss. "C'mon, Merc; I might need your help," I said, walking to the front door. I gestured for Merc to get in the duffel, which he did. "Hey, Bryn?"

"Yes?"

"I love you."

He nodded.

I stopped at the door, raising my brows and waiting. "Are you going to say you love me back?"

"I don't need to say it. I'm going to prove it by doing the most reckless things I've ever done in my adult life, by accompanying you to Scotland and then underhill. If you don't understand the depth of what I feel for you from that, you never will."

"If something goes wrong, I'll make it up to you."

He didn't answer.

"I promise," I said softly, but a part of me wondered whether that would be possible. My heart ached and I had to bite my lip and force myself to leave the room. What I really wanted to do was to tell Bryn I'd changed my mind and that we could just go home and get married and stop rebelling against the faery monarchy and the witch government. Except that would've meant abandoning our family and friends. So I marched down the hall to the elevator with ten shades of Texas rebel in my Halfling heart.

Getting on the elevator, though, I couldn't help but think that maybe Kismet was right. Maybe I loved too many people too much.

"YOU HAVE TO hack the system and shut down the security cameras," I repeated, whispering into Andre's ear while I gave him a hug. "And you're never allowed to play poker," I added. "Stop making that scared face, 'cause the cameras are still rolling and someone might notice."

"Hi, Evie," I said, moving on. "I brought the stuff from the list. I'm taking over the kitchen so I can drug the president. Think you can glamour Andre to look like him?" I whispered.

Edie's rich, throaty laugh filled the air. "My darling biscuit, I learned a new expression from the young American operative I had sex with last night in the main conference room."

My jaw dropped. "You slept with a Conclave spy in a

conference room? There are security cameras. You could be on YouTube by now."

"What's YouTube? The Internet?"

"Never mind. Listen, this isn't a James Bond movie called *The Spy Who Loved Me*. You shouldn't be sleeping around with these guys. They're killers. Ask Aunt Mel how her affair with Incendio the Conclave warlock worked out."

"Speaking of the warlock that she needed magical earrings to defend against, what are you doing wearing the Colombian emeralds? Those were a gift to your—"

"Cameras!" I hissed.

"Never mind," she added in a whisper, and went on speaking into my ear. "You asked if I could work a glamour on Andre if necessary? That question calls for an expression I learned last night. *Game on.*"

"Oh, my God. Stop talking. I don't want to know any more about that."

"Let's rock and roll, Merc," I said. I grabbed the herbs I needed and left the rest with the Park Avenue Mata Hari.

I got permission from the president to use the kitchen with supervision. The kitchen staff and an operative eyed me suspiciously, but loaned me an oven and a section of counter space. I whipped batter and cream. I also slipped a mortar and pestel in my pockets when the operative's attention was focused on Mercutio. I left the kitchen for a bathroom break and while in a stall ground some smuggled herbs together and put them into a pepper shaker.

When I returned to the kitchen, I filled the cooled pastry shells with cream, and hummed, hoping my plan would work the way I needed it to.

The humid kitchen made Mercutio restless, which was actually helpful, because I watched the motion-activated cameras follow him around. When they stopped moving, I didn't.

I hurried to the dining room, where Andre was hunched over a laptop. He'd sweated through his shirt despite the cool air.

"All done?"

He looked up at me over the top of his glasses. "This is a

huge thing I've done. A greater offense than anything before."
He mopped his damp brow with his sleeve.

"They aren't going to be able to trace what happened."

"Of course they will," he said.

No, they won't. Not if I have my way.

I walked to the window and tried to open it. It didn't budge.

"Those are sealed shut. Even though electronic security
in this block is off, the window won't open."

"Uh-huh," I said, grabbing a chair. I slammed it against the
glass until it broke. Shakes buzzed up and landed on the sill.

"Yahoo!" he yelled, flying around the window frame, but
not entering. Not yet.

"Is that a—Oh, my God, what have you done?" Andre
said, then lapsed into a barrage of agitated German.

"Shakes, you know what to do. It's on the table. Give me
a few minutes." I turned to Edie and Andre. "Aunt Edie, get
moving on your spells. When you're both disguised, just go.
Don't wait for me."

I took the tray of pastries and another of tea I'd brought
from the kitchen and exited the dining room, calling over
my shoulder for them to lock the door behind me.

The experiments to authenticate the amber were taking
place in the conference room attached to the president's
office. I knocked, and an operative let me in after checking
with President Anderson.

My grandmother, a high-ranking WAM administrator
named Basil Glenn, and a couple other wizards who looked
like they belonged in an Indiana Jones movie crowded around
the table. The president, who stood near them, stopped speaking when I entered. In the corner, wearing a red pantsuit,
Poppy chewed bubble gum and pretended to watch me only
casually.

I set the tea and pastries down and started serving people.

"What's she doing here?" Poppy asked.

"I brought treats."

"Don't eat those! Anything could be in them," Poppy
said, stalking over.

I closed my eyes and circled my fingers over the tray. I

grabbed a random cream puff and took a bite. Then I poured myself a cup of tea and took a swig. "Suit yourselves if you don't want to eat."

After a brief hesitation, several of them ate, except Poppy and my grandmother. When no one had a reaction to the food and tea, I smiled smugly. I'd considered putting the sleeping herbs in the cream or drinks, but I thought the Conclave people might be paranoid enough to suspect that and maybe they'd have me act as taster. Also, I wanted to be able to say later that I had eaten and drunk the same things as them. It was what Bryn called plausible deniability.

"So I did my part," I said. "I brought you the amber from the picture. It's time to keep your word. When I leave today I'm taking my friends."

They looked at me, suddenly alert. President Anderson wiped his fingers with a napkin. "We will be done soon."

"Or perhaps we won't. We must be thorough and sure of what we have," my grandmother said.

"Authentication isn't my problem," I said.

"Where did you get the amber?" Poppy demanded. "Did you have it when you left the woods?"

I licked the cream from my fingers. "I'm not telling."

"She is more than she seems. Like me. Don't you see that?" Poppy murmured. "You said the details of where it was found were of critical importance. She should be kept here with her friends until she tells us what we need to know. The guys who were with her should be brought in, too. Give me the go-ahead, and we'll get them."

President Anderson paused thoughtfully.

"Don't even think about it. Just do what you promised," I said.

"We need the details. I'm not planning to lock you up, and I will allow your friends to leave. Eventually."

"That's not good enough."

"You're a valuable asset. Why don't we talk about your future?"

"Why would I want to work for you? When you're proving that I can't trust you to keep your word."

The alarm was like the thump of a bass. It didn't just make a loud noise; it made the walls vibrate and seemed to thud through us. Shakes had flown into an area where security was intact.

I saw a shimmer of light pour from the vent. *There he is.*

I bent my head, took a breath, and held it. Everyone jumped up from their chairs.

"What is that?" I asked.

"There's a security breach!" Poppy said, spinning toward the door. The bass got louder, and I felt the herbs and faery dust blow over our skin. They looked up and around frantically and then they fell, one by one.

I wiped my face and rushed out. Shakes had done a great job with that pepper shaker.

I breathed the untainted air and hurried down the hall.

Metal stairs rattled. Someone was running up or down or both. President Anderson walked into the hall. I looked over my shoulder at the conference room door, which hadn't opened.

"Andre?" I murmured.

The president gave a sharp shake of his head.

Conclave operatives burst from the stairwell. One said, "There's a small faery in the vents. He's probably going to try to reach the vault."

"There are no vents into the vault. And small fae will get trapped in the grids. The charged fields are spelled to smell like honey to them," the other operative said to the fake president.

My grandmother stepped into the hall, carrying a laptop. I realized that she was actually Andre.

"The alarms are loudest up here, sir. Let's move you downstairs until we secure these upper floors. I'll escort you. You, too," the operative said, beckoning me. "Let's go."

I whistled.

He whipped out his gun and pointed it at me.

"My cat's up here. I'm whistling for him to come," I lied. That whistle was for Shakes. It meant he should get out of the vents and the building.

"What's that?" I asked, sniffing. "Is that smoke?"

"Move!" the Conclave operative snapped, shoving me into the stairwell.

A faint German curse reached my ears.

"What?" the Conclave operative said.

"Nothing. I just said shit," I offered.

C'mon, Andre, don't blow it! I thought furiously. My grandma wasn't likely to go around cursing in German.

"Keep quiet," the spy said.

The smoke thickened.

"Mercutio!" I called. "I have to go back for my cat."

The operative grabbed me before I could get through the door, but I spotted Merc. He bounded into the stairwell, swiping the operative's arm as he flew past. The spy grabbed his arm, letting me go. I hurried down the stairs. We were almost to the ground floor when the sprinklers kicked on.

Mercutio yowled.

"I know. It's a mess," I said, glancing at Edie in her President Anderson glamour. His hair wasn't wet. It wasn't even damp.

Uh-oh!

When we poured out of the stairwell, Mercutio, the operative, and I were dripping wet, but the water running off the president and my grandma didn't saturate them.

"What the hell?" the spy said.

I didn't hesitate. I tackled him, making sure his head hit the tile floor. I grabbed his gun, but didn't need it. He was out cold.

"Cover your heads, because you don't look wet," I said. "And hurry!" I yelled, leading them through the chaotic lobby.

"What's happening?" an operative hollered.

"There's an attack on the top floor. Faeries smashed a window and came through. You'll need iron ammunition!" Edie as the president said.

"Second floor," one of them yelled, and rushed into the stairwell. As they went up, we walked right out.

I led Edie and Andre around the corner and then onto the street. I hailed a taxi.

I chewed on my lip. Had Shakes made it out? Faeries never liked smoke. He could've had a coughing fit or gotten lost in the vents. What if he hadn't heard me over the alarms and had gotten caught in one of the grids? I tucked my hair behind my ears.

I couldn't go back for him. If he'd been caught, I'd have to think of a way to get him out later.

I called Bryn. He picked up on the first ring.

"We're out. We need to drop our friends at the airport and then leave London. Could you start packing us up?"

There was silence for a moment as Bryn digested the news. "You did it? You actually got them out?"

"Yes."

"You really are . . . amazing."

"Thanks. See you in a few minutes."

Bryn had sounded so surprised, which surprised me. If he hadn't thought my plan would work, why had he let me go alone?

Realization dawned. He might have considered it the lesser of two evils. If I'd been arrested, the trip to the Never would've been delayed. Presumably he would've come up with some argument or plan to get me released . . . eventually.

Oh, Bryn. Things are never simple, are they?

At the hotel, I paid the driver and we went to the room. As soon as I closed the door, Edie lifted the glamour by taking off her necklace. The spell faded instantly. It was startling to see her and Andre shift appearance.

"Impressive," Bryn said.

"Truly," Andre agreed, blowing his thinning hair out of his eyes. It had been gray and pulled back into a neat bun a moment before.

Edie made a little bow. "What's next, biscuit?"

"You fly back to Texas. Andre goes with you. I have to visit Kismet's hometown one more time."

"I'll come along, just as far as the front gate, in case your dear granny decides to chase after you," Edie said.

I paused, not sure whether to argue. The truth was that if the Conclave chased us to Scotland, we might need help.

And we might definitely need help if the wolves weren't cooperative and decided instead to attack us.

"It'd be safer for you to go home," I said.

"When have I ever been interested in doing what's safe? Honestly," Edie said, mixing herself a cocktail.

"You'll be more helpful sober," I said.

"Who says?" she asked, chugging her drink. She made another, but that one she gave to Andre, who still looked shell-shocked.

"There is no going back. They'll hunt us for the rest of our days," he said.

"Not true. There was no camera footage. No eyewitnesses saw us do anything. Relax. The lawyer will get us off. Won't you, candylegger?" Edie said, sipping a fresh cocktail.

Bryn clapped Andre on the shoulder. "It'll be all right," he said, not convincing anyone.

"Here," Edie said, tapping the bottom of the glass in Andre's hand.

He murmured something in German and then gulped it down.

"Better?" she asked.

"Nein."

"Give it a minute," she said with a wink, and then kissed him on the mouth.

His brows rose.

"Something else to think about," she said lightly. "Hey, where's the cowboy?"

I frowned, noting that she'd thought about Zach right after kissing someone. "I don't actually know. He's got his own agenda."

"And it's reprehensible," Bryn said. "Tell her," he added, zipping his bag closed. "For once your aunt may agree with me about something."

35

EDIE DID AGREE that Zach's intention to wipe out most of the world's magic sucked. She wanted to know whether I believed that Kismet had actually lost the real wolf amber or, if not, where I thought she might have hidden it.

"I have no idea."

"That's too bad. If we were able to offer the Association an authentic amber artifact, things might go better for us," Andre said as we walked through the Scottish woods toward the pub.

"Forget the Association," Edie said. "If we had that amber, the war with the fae could tip in our favor forever."

"We're not at war with the fae," I said.

"You're planning to lead wolves into the Never. You think that'll end in a cocktail party?" she said dryly.

"You must think so. It's what you're dressed for," I retorted, glancing at her geometric-print pewter-and-silver satin dress and heels. Had she packed any jeans at all? Edie might not have worn them in her time, but surely Vangie had had some in her wardrobe.

"Hey, impostor girl, where are you going?" a small voice asked.

I turned and found Royal hovering near my head.

"Hi, there. I'm looking for the werewolves."

"Madness!" He touched down on my shoulder and stood with his chubby arms folded across his chest. "Wait, do you have something they want? Did she arrange . . . ? No, no. She'd have come herself. She'd show off that she could get close without getting caught. Doing it this way, walking right in, you're going to be captured—oh, right now!" He sprang off my shoulder and went straight up in the air.

A group of men emerged from the woods on all sides of our little walking party. Andre muttered in German and raised a hand, ready to cast a spell.

"No, no. Remember we're here to negotiate," I said, pushing his forearm down to his side. "We're here with a proposal."

The young men closed in so they were arranged with two behind us, two on the sides, and two in front, like soldiers.

"Keep walking," one said, and we did.

We were herded into a clearing with a large fire pit in the center. The young man who had shouted at Kismet on the wall in Killarney stood, and the gruff muscular man who was their leader strode around the pit to us. He seemed preoccupied with Edie, who fingered a plant growing within the decaying bark of a fallen tree.

I stepped forward and cleared my throat. He glanced at the others, then back at me.

I explained that I believed they'd lost something important to them, and that if they'd assist us in liberating my imprisoned sister, we'd give it to them.

"No!" Royal shouted. "She'd never trade it back to them! She told the amber bearer what to do. Run, wolf! There are mountains and woods the world over where you could live."

The young guy folded his arms across his chest and shook his head. Had this man been the one who'd lost the amber to my sister?

The leader put a hand on my throat, but he didn't squeeze as he had the first time I'd met him. The other men in the clearing crouched, ready to pounce. Each faced a member of our group, with two on Bryn and me. I suppose I should've been flattered that they thought that in addition to their leader they'd need two more to subdue me.

"I'm not here to cause trouble," I said calmly. "My name is Tammy Jo Trask. I'm visiting from Texas. In America," I said, thrusting out a hand. "I'm pleased to meet you."

The leader blinked. The young man looked startled for a moment; then he laughed. He strode forward and put his left hand on the leader's shoulder and then shook my hand with his right.

"I'm Acton of the Silver Loch Clan. I was amber bearer until your sister relieved me of the honor. This is my brother, Elhard, our chieftain. He would normally be more welcoming, but if we don't get the amber back by Sunday, I'll be punished for its loss."

"What's the punishment?" I asked, grimacing.

The silence that greeted me made me shake my head—something real bad then. "Well, we can help each other. If you don't mind risking your lives to get it back."

"You can't promise them the amber! You don't have it!" Royal exclaimed.

"I know where it is."

"You don't! She'd never have told you!" Royal shouted, thrusting his arms out.

Edie flung a handful of dirt and leaves into the air, whispering a spell. A gust made Royal tumble feet over head and strike a tree. Bryn's magic and two wolves leapt up to grab him, but as he fell, a blur of buzzing fur caught him and dragged him away.

Shakes in his squirrel fur clothes! He got out and is okay!

Elhard nodded in the direction of the fleeing faeries, and several werewolves shifted and burst into the woods in pursuit. Elhard walked to Edie.

"What's your name?"

"That depends. Are you planning to act like a man? Or a rabid dog?"

"Edie!" I snapped.

Elhard tossed his head, his wild dark hair flowing over

his shoulders. "That depends. Are you planning to act like a woman? Or a wicked witch?"

She smirked, her green eyes sparkling. "Evangeline. Evie to my friends. Ms. Rhodes and I'd imagine other names to my enemies."

He didn't smile, but he inhaled in a way that wasn't wholly unfriendly. She interested him; that was for sure. But then, I was just starting to realize that Edie had that same thing Aunt Mel had, where men were concerned: They noticed her and couldn't stop noticing her, even when they wanted to.

"Well, Miss Evie Rhodes, welcome to the Highlands." He turned back to me. "I reject your offer, since it's pretty clear that you don't have the amber. Your sister hid it, and I suspect that that pudgy pixie is the only one besides her who knows where it is."

"Where is your sister?" Acton asked.

"Here," I said, holding out my phone. "This was taken this morning. Look at the date on the paper."

There was a picture of me in the same outfit I was wearing, and I held a copy of *The Times* newspaper with the date showing and the amber resting in my hand.

He enlarged the picture, studying it carefully. The picture had been Bryn's idea, and it turned out to be a really good one.

"That faery might have known where she hid it originally, but I took it from my sister yesterday."

"It rightfully belongs to the werewolf clans of the world. You expect us to negotiate for the return of property stolen from us?" Elhard demanded, a growl rumbling in his chest.

"Well, considering that you stole it to begin with, yep," I said.

"We never stole it. That sacred rock has been passed down and protected by wolf clans around the globe for a thousand years."

"And before that it belonged to the faeries and was stolen by witches."

"That's rubbish!" Elhard said.

"Who's holding your sister prisoner?" Acton asked.

"The faery queen," I replied.

"Her own queen? Why? Has she gone rogue?" Elhard asked.

"I'll go with you," Acton said.

"What?" Elhard snapped, turning his head sharply to look at his brother. "Her own kind have turned against her, likely for a good reason, and it's no concern of ours."

"Yes, it is," I said. "Because part of the reason she's been in trouble with the queen is that she didn't return the wolf amber to the Never the way she was supposed to. And I think there was something else she was supposed to do that she didn't. She was supposed to kill the werewolf who was guarding it. But she didn't. She let you live," I said to Acton.

The words tumbled out of me and I knew they were true. Something had happened between him and Kismet. I could feel it.

"Aye, it's true. She had silver-tipped arrows. She could've used them, but didn't."

"You were wounded. She stole that relic knowing full well you'd be killed at the next gathering when it was discovered that you'd lost it. You said as much under the ale's influence when they took the arrows from your flank," Elhard said.

"She wasn't going to let you die at any gathering, Acton," I said. "She had a plan. It's why she didn't take the amber back into the Never. Deep down she's got a good heart, and she thought you were worth saving," I said softly.

Acton nodded. "She helped me. She got the amber because she caught me off guard and I was already wounded. Some wolf cubs had gone missing. We thought they'd just wandered off and would make their way home, but I came across an ominous combination: the scent of wolf blood and Drakkar cologne. Some vampires douse themselves in perfumes to cover the smell of their dead flesh." He grimaced, wrinkling his nose. "Maybe I should have returned to the pack to gather a force, but I was on the scent of our children's blood; I couldn't turn back."

"You never said," Elhard murmured.

"The boys would've been shamed. They could never have

risen within the clan if it had been known they'd gotten themselves captured and bitten by vamps."

"So the faery caught you after your battle with the vampires? She's got the devil's luck. And his personality. She seized the amber and left, aye?" Elhard asked.

"No. She was on the coven's trail before me. It was a big nest of them. Two dozen gypsy vamps moving fast, feeding off werewolf blood to give them extra power. The fae girl cut their number in half." He rubbed his whiskers and smiled. "As a fighter, she's sublime. Flows like a river. No hesitation. Moves like a force of nature, too, by instinct. They say the fae knights are fast, but that they're like vampires, full of strategy and calculation. Cold-blooded. Not her. Not that I saw. She wasn't blind rage, but she was fury."

"So she's a bonny fighter. And maybe we owe her a debt. But the wolf amber is too dear a price to pay."

"Aye, I know that. I'm sworn to protect it, and if killing her would bring it back, I'd have done it. But so far she's never had it on her. And you know we've searched these woods and much farther. None of us can find it. Maybe it's hidden in the Never. I'll go and see."

"Just like that?" Elhard said. "When they've tricked our cubs into going in and left their bastard changelings in their place? Have any of those pups ever returned? Maybe that girl fought the vampires to steal their quarry for the faeries. Did you ever think of that?"

"No, because she had me incapacitated. She could've taken the cubs if she'd wanted. Instead she ordered the trees to hide and protect us until I was strong enough to run. After she was gone, the cubs didn't wait. They carried me home and said what I told them to say: that they'd been away hunting and they'd found me down."

Elhard frowned. "You should've told the whole truth."

Acton shrugged.

"I've taken a human being into the Never and brought him back out," I said. "Anybody who comes in with us, I give my word we'll make sure he gets back out."

"I'll come as well." It was the werewolf who'd been injured.

I waved at him. "It'll be dangerous. It should probably be men without kids."

The men exchanged glances and smirked. "Then you'd have almost no one to go along. Wolf pups are more precious than the amber, and almost as rare. Every wolf does his best to father as many as possible as soon as the girls will have him."

My brows shot up. "Big families, huh?"

"Not as big as we'd like. Children of magic are rare. You'll know that yourself, I'd imagine."

"Yes," I said. "I've heard that magical lines are dying out. Protecting the ambers is more important than ever, I think."

Everyone was quiet, watching Elhard.

He finally said, "Aye. That's so."

36

WHEN THEY REALIZED that the werewolves weren't going to pin their wings or eat them, the faeries had come back willingly, though they'd stayed out of reach. Royal muttered nonstop that werewolves weren't to be trusted, but Shakes was cheerful about the mad plan to lead them into the Never to rescue Kismet. He showed us the way to the closest gate.

Royal parted company from us then. Shakes said Royal wasn't convinced yet that I was looking out for Kismet's best interests and so wouldn't be joining us on our voyage.

"And he had to move a certain faery artifact, right?" I whispered.

Shakes went stiff as a two-by-four and gave me a sideways glance.

"The reason no one has been able to find the wolf amber is because you guys have been moving it around, leading anyone who searched in magical circles."

"I don't know what you're talking about. But if I did, I'd say that would be a clever plan to keep it out of filthy paws and filthy claws."

I smiled. "My sister is nothing if not clever. Let's hope I'm her twin in that respect," I added.

He grinned and swooped to a row of foxtail plants. I felt the change immediately when I walked by them.

"Here," I said, holding out a hand.

I didn't trust the wolves to be able to stay on the path without my leading them, since they couldn't feel it yet, so we formed a human chain. I noticed that Elhard had a hand on Edie's waist and walked very close to her, while the wolf behind him followed a few feet back.

For her part, Edie either ignored Elhard, threatened him, or laughed her throaty laugh at him. But what she didn't do was push him away. Someone, hopefully not me, was going to have to keep an eye on her from now on. She seemed to attract dangerous men. It was how she'd gotten herself killed when she was alive that first time. I knew technically she'd stolen Vangie's body, but that didn't mean I wanted anyone knocking her out of it by murdering her. And a werewolf kingpin seemed just the wrong sort of boyfriend for her. I wondered if I could interest her in an engineer. Or an accountant. Those guys almost never got into battles with vampires or warlocks. And I didn't think they killed their wives all that often either. I chewed on my lip. I'd have to look into that . . . which professions were the least likely to become murderers? Because something told me Edie was going to push her boyfriends to the limits with her drinking and flirting and fooling around.

We got to the entrance of the Never, and I found the key. I sang and opened the gate. Bryn entered right after me and then the rest of our group. Elhard's nostrils flared and he scowled.

I looked around. No one waited for us. In fact, the path looked barren and deserted.

"What's happened here?" I asked, smelling damp soot. The werewolf chieftain was right. Something smelled off.

Acton bent, pressed the tip of his finger to the dirt, and then tasted it. "Someone's burned and salted the earth," Acton said.

"That doesn't sound good," I whispered.

Bryn looked back at the passageway's gate, which had closed behind us.

"I'll scout ahead," Shakes said, buzzing away.

"Woods," Elhard said, striding toward the trees.

"Wait," I said, turning back to the gate. A metallic tang burned the back of my throat. I looked at the pulverized stone that had been cemented into the wall. It looked unnatural and ugly. I ran my hand over the gate. It felt cold and dead.

No exit here, I thought.

My right foot ached and I stepped back. I knelt and found tiny bits of iron mixed into the burned grass. I touched the ground, and sharp pains lashed my back. I jerked, falling down.

"What was that?" Acton asked, bending to offer me a hand.

"I smell blood," Elhard said.

"Me, too," another wolf man agreed.

"What is it?" Bryn asked me.

I took his hand instead of Acton's, but thanked Acton for the offer.

"Something bad happened here," I said, moving my shoulder. The pain in my back faded as I moved farther from the wall. "We won't be leaving by this gate."

"I can't be any good to you outside the water. We should travel the coast," Bryn said.

"Woods are better for cover," Elhard argued.

"Not in here," Bryn said.

Everyone looked at me, since, crazily enough, even though I was the newest to magic by far, I was the leader. I closed my eyes and inhaled deeply. My instincts had nothing to say, but Mercutio did. His soft yowl made me open my eyes.

Mercutio bounded away, straight toward the rolling hills that led to the castle.

"We're to be led by a cat?" Elhard scoffed, but we all set off after Merc.

When we passed through a field of sunflowers, uneasiness began to suffocate me. Mercutio ran, and we raced to keep up.

By the time we reached a clearing, I was breathless and sweating, but it didn't prepare me for what I would see. Benvolio, the pony, was covered in dried blood and fighting a choke chain around his neck that tethered him to a fence.

"Oh, my God!" I yelled. I jumped over the wood rails as Merc dashed under them. We arrived next to the horse at the same moment.

"Hang on," Elhard said, grabbing Merc. "That horse is agitated enough."

Finding himself in the hands of a dog, albeit a human-shaped one, Mercutio went wild. Ben bucked, choking himself till his legs buckled and he passed out.

Elhard growled, but let Mercutio go.

"Help me!" I yelled, firing my gun at the iron loop holding the chain.

"Lads!" Elhard said, and they grabbed the wooden slat and ripped it free of the fence. In moments they'd pulverized the board so that only a small piece was left attached to the chain. I yanked on the chain to loosen it and then removed it from Benvolio's neck. Mercutio bent his head and rested it against Ben's.

"Come on, Benny, come on," I whispered, stroking his neck.

The horse stirred. Mercutio rushed over to a trough of water and yowled at the guys.

"Aye," Acton said. He jerked his head and another wolf man helped him carry the full trough. They poured it over the horse, washing away the dirt and blood.

I pumped water into a bucket and brought it to Benny, who rose to his feet and then bent his head and drank.

Mercutio circled him and waited.

"You okay?" I asked.

The horse whinnied.

"Did they tie you up 'cause you tried to stop whatever they were doing to her?"

No one moved or made a sound. That horse, her horse, could've been made of stone.

"Or did they hurt you to get her to do what they wanted?" I asked softly.

Mercutio yowled, and the horse's nostrils flared with fury. Benvolio pawed the dirt and threw his head to the side, his mane rustling in the wind.

I nodded. *That damned bitch of a queen.*

"Let's go get Kismet," I whispered.

Benvolio ran forward and jumped over the remains of the broken fence. His cuts didn't slow him down.

We were all armed. Of course, the creatures we'd face would be armed, too, and they'd have the home-field advantage. But in terms of pure will, there was no way they'd have us beat, because I'd never felt like I wanted to kill anyone before. But for what Ghislaine had done to that horse and for what I suspected she'd done to my sister, I wanted blood.

37

MY BARE FEET flew over the ground. The wolves struggled to keep pace with us. I followed Benny to the compound of the Seelie court. Within the courtyard, Crux's body was laid out on a mound that was covered with flowers and plants. Circling him were things that people had obviously left in tribute: crafts of all types, coins, and stones. A length of burgundy-and-gold quilted silk covered him from the chest down. I would've stopped and paid my respects, but Benvolio had galloped back to me when I'd slowed, and Merc had pressed against my legs.

The knights in the courtyard froze when they saw me, until one shouted, "The traitor's twin."

I ran up the bench seat of a picnic table and across the table to avoid them. Benny ran the length of it beside me, and then when I leapt, he was there. I landed on his back and he rushed by the knights, knocking them back.

I heard the growls of the wolf men behind us.

The castle's courtyard door was locked tight. Benvolio rounded and leapt, taking to the air by magic and landing on a balcony, which creaked under our weight. He rammed his head against the doors, but I pulled on his mane to stop him before he hurt himself.

I slammed the butt of my gun against the glass and shattered it, and then carefully reached in and opened the door. Benny walked inside and I had to duck my head. I dismounted, turned, and glanced down. The fight below had turned bloody, and more knights were pouring into the courtyard.

The wolves are good fighters. They'll be okay.

Bryn's and Edie's guns were loaded with iron ammunition, and they weren't hesitating to injure the faeries, shooting them in the legs and taking away their weapons when they fell.

I turned and rushed into the castle. As I raced along the upper corridor, I opened doors. I froze when I found Momma and Caedrin in one. She was shackled to a bed's headboard. He was secured to the wall with iron cuffs.

"What in the holy hell?" I snapped.

"Oh, God, Tammy Jo, you have to get Kismet. She's on the floor below us. Hurry," Momma said.

"I'm going there next. Where's the key?"

"Not here. They've taken it."

"Oh, my God. His wrists!" I yelled, seeing that the flesh under the iron cuffs was blistered and raw.

"His punishment. Kismet incited a riot last night, and the queen ordered Caedrin to kill her. He tried to fall on his sword like Crux had, and Ghislaine went berserk."

I hooked the length of chain over Benvolio's neck. "Can you pull it from the wall, Benny?"

The horse walked forward, yanking the chains and some chunks of wall free.

I steadied Caedrin's hand against the floor and slammed the butt of my gun against the lock over and over until it broke. The jarring of the metal against his wounded wrist made him clench his teeth, but he never made a sound as tears rolled down his cheeks. I broke open the second cuff and took them off.

"It's okay now," I whispered. He rested his head against the wall, panting. "When you're ready, go downstairs. The other knights are distracted. Get out of the compound. Head toward the water. I'll meet you in the clearing where Crux died. You know where that is?"

He nodded.

I broke Momma free, too, and then ran from the room. As I came down the stairs, the queen was coming up.

She screeched like a banshee when she saw me, and her gaze darted to a particular door.

Bingo.

I ran to it, but it was locked. "Benny!" I called. "She's in here."

The horse leapt down from the floor above, landing with a loud clack. He ran forward. Ghislaine flew toward us with a dagger in her hand.

I whipped the gun up and shot her in the thigh. She fell.

Benny slammed into the door, and it splintered. The anguished sound he made upon entering the room made my blood run cold. The smell of blood and earth saturated the air. I strode in and found Kis lying facedown on a mat on the floor. She wore no shirt, and she'd been whipped by someone so viciously that her back was flayed. I could see muscle and bone.

Someone was screaming. I realized it was me.

I felt something sharp pierce my side, and spun. The knife had grazed me. The only reason the queen hadn't skewered my kidney was that Mercutio had jumped onto her back. I grabbed her throat and rammed into her body so hard with mine that we fell to the ground. The dagger clattered away.

I pummeled her, yelling and yelling until I had no voice left. She was strong and threw me off, but hitting the wall didn't stop me. I flung myself back on top of her and fought and fought until she stopped trying to get up. I walked away from the unconscious queen and back to my hurt sister.

"Benny, help me," I said, shaking and sobbing.

Benvolio bent, and Mercutio and I put Kismet onto his back, horizontally across it.

"She's cold, Merc. I can't feel her heartbeat. Nothing," I

said, my voice cracking. "I shouldn't have left her. I should have stayed!" I covered her with a sheet and led the horse out.

He walked slowly now, so as not to jostle her. I was crying so hard I could barely see, but then I heard a little moan.

Alive!

"She's alive!" I screamed.

I grabbed her hand and kissed it. I'm not sure what else happened. Time seemed broken to bits. The next thing I remember was that when we were leaving, I spotted Kismet's bow and arrows lying on an ottoman in the sitting room. I got them and loaded the bow as we exited the castle.

There were dead wolves and dying fae. I kept moving.

Acton rushed over. "Is she badly hurt?" he asked. When he pulled the sheet back and saw her destroyed back, he gasped.

"It's real bad. But she's gonna live. We heal real well. I'm taking her out of this damn place. I'm taking her home with me."

A knight stepped in front of us. I shot him in the leg, and Acton flung him aside.

"Go, Benny. Run to the sea. Mercutio, take him to Bryn. I'll be right behind you."

Mercutio darted around the fighting men and raced away. Benny followed.

"Come on, Acton, get your guys. We're getting out of here."

He howled and called the wolves.

It was a bloody escape, and the fae chased us until something called them back.

We reached the ocean, but Bryn put out a hand. "We can't go this way. The selkies will attack us if we try to reach the underwater path. The queen's orders."

Kismet stirred.

"Give me your shirt for her," I said.

Bryn started to pull his off, but Acton was faster.

"Here," he said. "I'll help you." He lifted her, and I put the shirt over her head and slid it down to cover her, grimacing at the way her blood oozed, saturating the back of the shirt.

"If I'd had an iron blade, I've have run it through Ghislaine, death sentence or not," I murmured.

"My apple darling," Kismet murmured, clearly half out of her head from shock. She tried to reach for me, but her fingers missed. I clutched her hand and held it.

"I'm here. I'm right here."

"I felt you come into the Never. Held on so I might see you."

"You're going to more than see me. You're going to take magic from me. Take my strength to heal. The way you gave me yours when I was hurt. Hurry up now."

"See," she said, her head lolling against Acton's shoulder. "As good as a pack member. Halfling fae, but not half sisters. Whole sisters."

"Yes," I said. "We're going to be one. And then we're going to split the magic between us in a different way."

"Oh, aye? How's that, Tammy, love?" she asked.

"You'll see. Just go along with me, all right?"

"Sure, anywhere. Let's run away to the sun," she said.

"Oh, hell!" I said, spotting the queen on horseback. She was battered, but upright and clearly out for blood—mine. A dozen knights rode behind her, armed with bows.

"Take some of my strength," I said to Kis, and put my cheek to hers. I closed my eyes and whispered into the wind. Nothing happened, though, until she opened her mind to me. Then I felt that I was lying across Acton's arms. And my back wailed with pain. It staggered me and I fell to my knees, blinded by the terrible sharp ache that seemed to swallow my whole body.

It eased some over the next few moments, but I couldn't get comfortable. My back was on fire. It hurt so badly! My stomach cramped and I thought I'd throw up, but the sickness faded and there was strength at my core. A deep magic endured.

Kismet's color was better, though. Not golden, but not as pale as a vampire's either.

"We may have to go into the water!" I yelled. "We need to get out of here and onto a path. Kis, where's the closet one?"

We were almost within range of the queen's archers, but Kismet still seemed too dazed to understand my question.

"Andre, Edie, come with me," Bryn said. "See that? Feel its pulse?"

"I do! What is it?" Edie asked.

"A chunk of volcanic rock that juts up from the ocean floor. It doesn't seem to be a true part of the Never. I can feel my wizard's magic stirring from there. We may be able to cast from it. Stay close to me and use your guns against the selkies only if you have to. It's not their choice to attack us."

"Wolf, come closer," Kismet said, looking more clear-eyed. She tugged on Acton's neck to bring his ear close. "There's a faery named Royal who lives in your woods. Tell him I said to invite you to the bastard's banquet."

Acton smiled. "That's the code phrase, aye?"

"Yes, he'll know what to do. He'll give it back to you."

"We thought your sister had it."

"She did, too. She has one . . . not the original."

"He likely won't trust me. I'll need you there to convince him, so you'll have to stay alive. Try, aye?"

She didn't respond, but steadied herself, breathing deeply.

Bryn helped Andre and Edie swim against the current to the rock, which was farther offshore than the path had been. He dragged them up onto the slippery surface.

A shadow surrounded them like storm clouds. Sleek seal flesh bobbed in the water as three selkies approached.

Kismet pulled herself up and locked eyes with Acton. "You're a pretty animal, but even with a faery's bird bones I'm too heavy to ride a wolf. Help me onto my horse."

He lifted her and set her on Benvolio. She bent down and grabbed my forearm. "A boost for her, amber wolf."

Acton cupped his hands. I stuck my foot in them and hopped up. I glanced back at the water. Edie was shooting into the ocean to drive the selkies back. Bryn and Andre were back-to-back, mouths moving, casting spells at the fae. Some horses reared up, their riders falling to the ground.

"Benny, do what you do best," Kismet said. "Run with the wind."

Benny bolted along the shore. The queen and several

faeries changed course to chase us. Others continued to the shore and the wolves.

"Bryn!" I yelled.

He heard me and looked over. I beckoned him and he dived into the water.

Edie, who must have been out of bullets, dropped her gun and straightened to take Bryn's position on the rock. She and Andre flung magic, and the wolves shifted, crouching and growling. More horses bucked, but others barreled forward fearlessly.

I shot at our pursuers until my gun was empty as well.

"Switch," Kismet said, bringing her legs up and then standing on Benny's back. She turned to face me and I held her thighs to steady her. She let her arrows fly, skewering the riders one after another. She deflected the arrows that nearly hit us. It was like a circus act.

I felt a ripple of cool air, and then an arbor appeared on the beach about forty feet in front of us. Vines hung from the top of the arch, and hooked to it was a brass key.

"Here comes a gate!" I yelled, glancing at the water's edge. Bryn emerged onshore and sprinted toward us, his skin sleek and black. Edie and Andre were still on the rock in the water, so we couldn't leave, but I at least wanted to get onto the path where Kismet and I would be part witch. If I could get Kismet out, it would be one less person to rescue and hopefully she could draw more magic from me to heal herself.

"Stop them!" Ghislaine screamed.

The key was out of reach, but Mercutio streaked by.

"Fly, Merc!" Kismet shouted, grabbing my hand and stretching it out. Shimmering gold burst from my fingers, and when Mercutio leapt, he rose thirty feet and caught the dangling key, tearing it from the vine.

He landed and circled to us. He jumped again, sailing over our heads. I reached up, and he released the key. I plucked it from the air. A pair of crossed chains appeared, forming an X in front of the arbor. A padlock hung from the center, connecting the chains.

Benny galloped to the arbor and stopped. I bent forward, shoved the key into place, and turned it. Unhooking the lock and dropping it allowed the chains to separate. Benny walked under the arbor and through the gate.

Bryn and Merc skidded in just behind Benvolio.

We all panted for breath. I jumped down from the horse and went to Bryn. I took his face in my hands. "Draw off my witch magic so I can heal and move faster."

He whispered a spell and drew the magic into him. I felt my heartbeat slow, my senses sharpen.

Kismet had dropped down to sit on Benny's back. She slumped forward, exhausted from the exertion of the trick horse riding when she was still weak from blood loss and shock. Adrenaline could take a person pretty far, but it always ran out eventually.

I bent down just as Ghislaine flew into the passage. Her horse slammed into Bryn, and he flew backward, landing hard on the path. The sharp pain in my head left me dizzy and disoriented for a moment.

The queen leapt down, screaming, and swung her arm. The dagger came at me, and I rolled away just in time. Ghislaine rushed toward Kismet. I kicked the queen's leg, and she buckled, but her incredible power blew around us like hurricane winds.

When she lunged again she pinned me to the ground. It took all my strength to stop the dagger from plunging into my chest. But I couldn't hold on. I brought my knee up hard and struck her in the chin.

I scrambled to my feet.

"Ghislaine, stop this. My sister hasn't done anything to you."

"She's Seelie. She's my subject. She turned my knights against me. That's treason! To fall on their swords rather than keep their oath? No talent or training, no matter how great, is worth that. She's staged her last rebellion. So have you."

The blast of magic from Bryn hit her in the back, and she staggered. She flung herself forward, though, and I didn't move fast enough. The blade cut into me, skidding off my rib. My breath ran out of me in a rush and I landed on my knees.

Bryn grabbed her by the hair and yanked her back, hitting her with magic, but on the faery path his power wasn't at its full strength.

I turned to Kismet. "You're as strong as the queen. She's got more control, but you're tougher. When she tried to bespell me with her kiss, you overcame it."

Kismet said, "I'm so tired." Her legs shook from the effort of staying upright.

"Trade power. Trust me. It's the answer," I said, grabbing her shoulders. I kissed her on the lips and felt her magic mirror mine. "Witch only in me and fae only in thee. Sisters forever. You'll rule in the Never," I whispered against her lips. I sucked her witch magic into me and felt her draw my faery magic out.

The unfurling of the magicks was like being turned inside out. We fell apart, screaming and writhing in pain.

"They're killing each other! Yes, destroy each other, you nasty Halfling creatures. Twisted and traitorous!" Ghislaine swung her elbow back into Bryn's stomach as he tried to hold her from behind.

He lost his grip and, free of him, Ghislaine jerked forward and spun to face Bryn. She thrust the dagger, cutting so deep into his thigh that the knife struck the bone and gashed it.

He dropped to the ground, grabbing his leg and grunting in pain.

I felt his injuries sharper than ever because we're connected by witch magic and my fae magic was gone. The queen's dagger must have been enchanted.

Her magic flowed outward, and I knew she was coming for us. For Kismet and for me. The queen's fury tasted of bile and reeked of honey and rancid butter.

I staggered to my feet and turned to run, my back to the queen. Kismet was in front of me, and she darted toward me.

"Drop!" Kismet yelled, grabbing my arm and jerking me down.

I landed on one knee.

"Boost me!"

I don't know if Kis said the words aloud or if I just heard them echo in my head. My body understood before my mind. My cupped hands rested on my thigh. Her right foot landed in my palms, and I shot up as she did, lifting her light frame, which was already springing.

She flew over my head, and I watched her.

Her hands caught Ghislaine's dagger arm as it swung down to impale me in the back. Kismet's momentum dragged the fae queen backward, and they tumbled out of the passage. I turned and rushed after them.

In the Never, Kismet rolled away from Ghislaine and flipped backward in a handspring.

The queen flew forward and planted a kiss on Kismet's mouth as she passed. The shimmer of the drug on Kis's lips caught the light like ground gold. Kismet froze, her eyes wide, and then her stare turned blank.

"No!" I screamed. Maybe Kis was too weakened to resist the queen's magic this time.

"Yes!" the queen yelled in triumph, and made her final rush.

I leapt forward, but I wasn't nearly fast enough. I was just a witch without magic in the Never. Unarmed against a Seelie queen in her own domain, I was nothing.

"Kismet!" I cried as the queen barreled toward her and leapt into the air.

At the last possible moment, Kismet's eyes grew sharp.

A trick!

Kis bent backward so far she was parallel to the ground. And she had an arrow clutched in her hand! The queen's momentum carried Kismet.

With the flick of her wrist, Kismet made the arrow rise and point up at an angle, like Crux's sword in the ground.

The queen screeched, but couldn't stop. She landed on it. One end drove into the ground, the other into the queen.

The arrow went straight through her chest, the tip emerging from her back. Her eyes widened with shock, her beautiful face contorted with rage.

The wind roared; the sun blazed; the ocean churned.

The knights rushed forth.

"No," I yelled, blocking Kismet from their arrows. "She's not a Halfling! She's not. She's full fae now. I'm full witch. She challenged the queen and won."

"It's all right, Tammy, love," Kismet said, pushing me aside.

She faced the Never. There weren't only knights now. Thousands of Seelie fae who lived underhill had come to see the battle and to help contain the witches and wolves who'd stolen into their homeland.

"I'm Kismarley, former Halfling and former first assassin of the Seelie court. I accused our queen of treason for telling a human spy the location of the ambers that sustain the world's magic. I asked any full fae brave enough to challenge her for power to do so. In the end, I was the Never's champion. I claim the right to rule this land and all of you." She stretched her arms out and whispered in an ancient language as old as magic itself.

The power of the fae queen circled around her, gilding Kismet in bright gold. The red in her strawberry-blond hair drained away, leaving her golden blond.

My body felt tired and heavy, and I sank to my knees.

"Long live the queen!" Caedrin called, going down on one knee.

"Long live the queen!" others yelled, bowing before her.

Kismet waited and then nodded. "You honor me. Your trust in me will not be misplaced. I will take us back to the way we were meant to live and be. The Seelie fae were once a source of light in the supernatural world, a wonder for all to behold. We will be that light again. This is my promise. My solemn vow."

The faeries cheered. I spotted Edie and Andre, who were soaking wet and bleeding from some scratches, but otherwise seemed unhurt, despite being in iron cuffs. How had they gotten from the water to the gate? Had the selkies overpowered them and turned them over to knights on shore? Or had they swum to shore and been caught?

"Kis," I whispered, nodding at Edie, Andre, and the wolves who'd helped us and were also surrounded and subdued.

Kismet scanned the area and then all around, to the water and the land and the castle in the distance. My heart thumped, waiting. She and Elhard were enemies. What if she didn't let the wolves go? I'd given my word I wouldn't leave without them.

Kismet's steady gaze came to rest on the fae knights. "Release the witches and wolves. Let them take their wounded and dead and leave our lands. There's no more war with them this day. And, Caedrin, go and get the captured human and release him into their custody. The wolves will see him out for me."

Captured human?

I was shocked a few minutes later when Caedrin brought a bound and bruised Zach to the path.

Acton and Elhard each took an arm and pulled him to the gate and through it. Edie and Andre shuffled after them, leaving the Never.

Kismet stepped forward and hugged me. "Witch or no, you're my family forever. I'll see you again," she whispered.

I hugged her tight and kissed her cheek. "I love you. Always."

I cried a little as I turned to leave, but I forced myself through the gate again. Bryn stood on the path with an arm around Andre's shoulder for support.

"Is your leg broken?" I asked, hurrying to him.

"No, it'll support my weight. It just hurts."

I hugged him.

"Are you all right?" Bryn asked. He'd seen me wounded plenty of times, but I think he sensed that this time I'd been changed forever.

"I'm okay," I said. "We all are."

EPILOGUE

ON MACON HILL, the magical tor in my hometown of Duvall, Texas, there stands a chapel. From its roof, I've shot at werewolves. Within its walls, I was betrayed by a beautiful witch. Sitting outside it, I cast an astral projection spell that landed me in bed with Bryn for the first time. And that didn't even begin to cover the times I'd lain on the grass next to it as a little girl, coloring or writing book reports.

I had a feeling that from now on, however, no memory would be more vivid than the one we were making. At the front of the chapel, Bryn, my future husband, waited for me.

Oz played "The Way You Look Tonight" on guitar. He was one of three Seelie fae in attendance. My sister wore a green dress and was my maid of honor, much to the gossip and annoyance of my best friend, Georgia Sue, who thought she should've had the job. I didn't even try to explain that if someone had to be jealous, it was better that it was Georgia Sue than Kismet. Georgia Sue would whisper and complain behind my back. Kismet wouldn't do that, but she might bump off a matron of honor to get her spot.

Caedrin and Momma escorted me in, one on each side,

both smiling. They exchanged little glances with each other, and I thought they might be next to get married.

Edie and I had forgiven Zach, but he hadn't forgiven himself for not being able to destroy those ambers. Also, he didn't want to see me get married to anyone else. So my best guess for where he was at the moment was in a bar getting drunk. Edie came, under protest. Mercutio wore a black tie instead of his collar, and he stood with Andre and the other groomsmen.

I wore a dress of pale gold and a gold-and-emerald comb in my upswept hair. Johnny Nguyen and his vampire boyfriend had styled me up like a movie star headed to the Academy Awards, but my feet still wouldn't last long in the fancy high heels.

I waved to my friends and family. It looked like all of Duvall had turned out. Plus we'd had some unexpected foreign visitors, including my grandmother and the president of the World Association of Magic. Aunt Mel was flirting with him, and Edie was distracting my grandmother by pretending to do hexes. At least, I hoped she was pretending.

My grandma and Basil Glenn had declared the amber I'd delivered to be authentic. I'm not sure whether they knew they were lying or not. The werewolves had the real wolf amber back and were guarding it with their lives.

The dustup at WAM Headquarters was blamed on fae warriors and greatly downplayed. My name was never mentioned. Bryn and I decided that the WAM administration didn't want it known that an untrained witch with malfunctioning magic had brought WAM headquarters to its knees and walked out the front door with two of its prisoners in a plan that was executed in seventeen minutes, with eight of those being time spent eating pastries with the president. A story like that might encourage others to follow my lead. Plus, I don't think the president wanted me to be in trouble. He seemed to like my pluck.

Bryn and I had talked it over with the fae guests and had convinced them to try to act like they were just regular folk, not regular Folk. The fact that the whole town was resting on the territory of enemy fae was a concern. I sure hoped no wars would break out before people got to have cake. I'd made it special.

My magic was different after having come back from the Never. We weren't sure if that was because the change in Kismet and me was permanent . . . her magic being all fae and mine all witch now. Or whether the change was because I was pregnant and that threw the magic out of balance. Yes, when we'd made love in the Never we'd made a baby. That was why I'd been dizzy and sick at first after coming home. When I got back to America, though, I felt strong again. I decided the baby wanted to be a Texan.

I didn't want to find out too many details about the new little life inside me, though, so it might be a boy or a girl. It might be one baby or, in the family tradition, twins. One thing was sure: Bryn and I were thrilled. He claimed he didn't even care if the baby's magic was all screwed up, but I knew it wasn't true. He'd been to the witches' bookstore in Austin and had gotten a whole collection of baby books. *Baby's First Spell. Larkspell Lullabies. Enchantments for Infants.* It was silly, since as far as I knew none of the witches in my family or his ever got their powers as babies, but the books sure were cute. And I liked seeing him happy and excited.

Kismet took her place at the front with a satisfied smile. Momma and Caedrin sat in the first row with Aunt Mel and Aunt Edie. I strode to the front, giving Merc a wink, and stopped next to Bryn.

Johnny fixed my train, and I heard him sniffling. He's sentimental, like most folks in Duvall.

When the ceremony started, I reached over and laced my fingers through Bryn's. I knew it wasn't really time for us to be touching yet, but I was a little nervous, and that jolt of shared magic calmed me right down.

He glanced at me out of the corner of his eye.

"This ceremony is just a technicality anyway. We're already for life or longer," I whispered.

"I know," he said, looking back at the preacher, but whispering to me. "But I like for things to be legal. I'm a lawyer, you know."

"Are you? I sure wish you'd told me that sooner. Marrying a lawyer, what a mistake this could turn out to be."

He winked at me. "I love you."

"We're not at that part yet."

He smiled.

"But if we're doing things out of order, which we usually are . . . I love you, too."

The preacher paused, waiting for us to settle on down. I zipped my lip and stood up straight, but I didn't let go of Bryn's hand. Maybe I never would again.

I heard rumblings behind us. And was that a growl? Had the Texas werewolves who had a grudge against me shown up to tangle with the Highland werewolves who'd come to visit?

For the love of Hershey, I hoped not!

"May I continue?" the preacher asked.

"You can sure give it a shot," I said. "That's really all any of us can do in this mixed-up life. If you want some of the Chambord torte wedding cake, though, I'd recommend that you hurry things along."

I guess he did want to try my famous torte, because he finished the ceremony in record time.

So, yes, when the next magical battle breaks out in Duvall, Texas, I'll face it as Mrs. Tamara Josephine Lyons.

But just so you know, to my friends, I'm still plain old Tammy Jo.

JENNA REITGARTEN IS awfully lucky that my witch genes are dormant, or I'd have hexed her with hiccups for the rest of her natural-born life. She stared at me across the cake that had taken me thirty-six hours to make, a cake that was Disney on Icing, and shook her head.

"Well, it's a really pretty cake and all, Tammy Jo, but it's got too much blue and gray. It might be good for a little boy, but Lindsey *just loves* pink—"

"The castle stones are gray and blue, but the princess on the drawbridge is wearing pink. The flower border is all pink," I said, tucking a loose strand of hair behind my ear.

"Uh-huh. I'll tell you what. I'll take this one for the play-room. I'll put the other cake, the one with the picture of Lindsey on it, in the dining room. And I can't pay two hundred thirty dollars for the castle, since, after all, it'll be a spare."

"Why don't I just sell you the sheet cake?" I asked, glancing at the flat cake with the picture of her three-year-old decked out in her Halloween costume. Lindsey was dressed, rather unimaginatively, in a pink Sleeping Beauty dress.

"And what would you do with this one, honey?" Jenna

asked, pointing at the multistory castle, complete with lake-front and shrubbery.

"Maybe I'll just eat it."

She laughed. "Don't be silly. Now, you'll sell it to me for a hundred thirty dollars or I'll have to complain to Cookie that you didn't follow my instructions, and then—"

"I followed your instructions," I said, fuming. "You said 'think fairy-tale princess.' Well, here she is." I flicked the head of the sugar-sculpted princess, knocking her over on the blue bridge.

Jenna gasped. "I've had just about enough from you," she said, standing the princess back up. "You know we order once a week from this bakery for our Junior League meetings. Cookie will have your hide if you lose my business."

Cookie Olsen is my boss, and "Cookie" fits her like "Snuggles" fits a Doberman. As a general rule, I don't want Cookie mad at me, but I was in the middle of remembering all the reasons I don't like Jenna, which date back to high school, and I really couldn't concentrate on two annoying women at the same time.

"You can buy the sheet cake, but you can't have the castle cake."

She huffed impatiently. "A hundred seventy for the castle cake, and that is final, missy."

I'd never noticed before how small Jenna's eyes were. If she were a shape-shifter, she'd be some kind of were-rodent. Not that I'd seen any shape-shifters except in books, but I knew they were out there. Aunt Mel's favorite ex-husband had been eaten by one.

I come from a line of witches that's fifteen generations old. They've drawn power from the earth for over three hundred years. Somehow I didn't think Jenna would be impressed to hear that though.

Jenna flipped open her cell phone and called Miss Cookie. She explained her version of the story and then handed the phone to me.

"Yes?" I asked.

"Sell her the cake, Tammy Jo."

"No, ma'am."

"I'm not losing her business. Sell her the cake, or you're fired."

"Yes, ma'am," I said.

"Good girl," Cookie said.

I handed the phone back to a very smug Jenna Reitgarten.

"Bye-bye," she said to Miss Cookie and flipped the phone shut. She dug through her wallet while I put the castle cake into the box I'd created for its transport. I took out the sheet cake, which was already boxed, and set it on the counter.

"That'll be forty dollars," I said.

"What?"

"Cookie said I could either sell you the castle cake or get fired, and I'm going with option B. A cake this size will feed me for a month," I said. "Longer if I act like you and starve myself."

Jenna turned a shade of bright pink that her daughter Lindsey would have *just loved*. Then she tried to reason with me, and then she threatened me, waving her stick arms around a lot.

"Sheet cake, forty dollars," I said.

Her complexion was splotchy with fury as she thrust two twenty-dollar bills at me. "Lloyd won't hire you. Daddy uses him to cater meetings and lunches. And there are only two bakeries in this town. You'll have to move," she said.

"Well, I'll cross that drawbridge when I come to it," I said, but I knew she was right. Pride's more expensive than a designer purse, and I can't afford one of those either.

Jenna stalked out with her sheet cake as I calculated how long I could survive without a job. I'm not great at math, but I knew I wouldn't last long. *Oh, to heck with it. Maybe I will just leave town.* If Momma and Aunt Melanie came back and found me gone, it would be their fault. I hadn't even gotten a postcard from either of them in a couple months, and the cards that came were always so darn vague. They never said what they were doing or where they were. I really hoped they weren't in some other dimension since I might need to track them down for a loan in the very near future.

* * *

LIKE MOST GHOSTS, Edie arrives with the worst kind of
timing. It's like getting a bad haircut on your wedding day,
making you wonder what you did to deserve it.

There was a strange traffic jam on Main Street, and as I
was trying to get around Mrs. Schnitzer's Cadillac, Edie
materialized out of mist in the seat next to me. It certainly
wasn't my fault that it startled me. I rammed the curb and
then Mrs. Schnitzer's rather substantial back bumper.

I held my head, wishing for an ice pack or a vacation in
Acapulco. Then I got my wits together and moved my car into
the drive of Floyd's gas station and out of traffic. I grimaced
at the grinding sound I heard when I turned the wheel too far
left. I hoped the problem wouldn't be expensive to fix, given
my new unemployed status. With my luck, it would be. Maybe
I could just avoid left turns.

Mrs. Schnitzer didn't bother to get her Caddy out of people's way. She slid out from behind the wheel of her big car
and sidled up to mine. She wore a lime green polyester skirt
that showed off her own substantial back bumper, which,
except for the dent, matched her car's perfectly.

She asked me a series of questions, like what was wrong
with my eyes (plenty, since I can see Edie, my great-great-
grandmother's dead twin sister), was I on drugs (not unless you
count dark cocoa), and what did I think Zach would say when
he found out (which I decided not to think about).

Edie was decidedly silent in the copilot's seat. She was
dressed in a black-sequined flapper dress, which is a bit much
for daytime, but I guess ghosts can get away with some
eccentric fashions, being invisible to most people and all.

"Here Zach comes now," Mrs. Schnitzer said, beaming.

"Great," I mumbled and checked my rearview mirror.
Sure enough, a broad chest of hard muscle covered by a tight
white T-shirt was approaching.

Mrs. Schnitzer said, "Tammy Jo ran right into the back of
my car. And I've got to get home to get ready for the mayor's
party. I don't have time for this nonsense today, Zach."

In other words, "Deputy Zach, straighten out your flaky ex-wife." I clenched my teeth, resenting the implication.

He played right along with her. "You go on, Miss Lorraine. I'll deal with this."

She wiggled back to her car and drove her dented bumper off into the sunset. Zach tipped his Stetson back, showing off dark blond curls and a face that incites catfights.

"Girl, you're lucky your lips are sweeter than those cakes you bake, or I'd have revoked your license a long time ago."

I'd had a fender bender or two in the past. Mostly, they weren't my fault.

"Edie showed up—"

"Tammy Jo, don't start that. It still chaps my ass that I paid that quack Chulley sixteen hundred bucks to get your head shrunk, and all I got for my trouble was a headache."

"I told you it wouldn't work."

"Then you shouldn't have gone and wasted my money. Now listen, I'm busy. You go on home and get ready for Georgia Sue's party, and I'll talk to you there."

"We're driving separate?" I asked. Zach and I have an on-again, off-again relationship, but we were supposed to be on-again at the moment, as evidenced by the fact that he'd slept over the night before last and I'd made him eggs and bacon for breakfast.

"Yeah, I'll be late," he said. "I was at TJ's house when they called me to give them a hand with this. Longhorns were on the thirty-yard line. You believe I'm out here today?"

On game day? Frankly no. If there's no ESPN in heaven, Zach will probably pack up and move to hell. The fact that he forgets our anniversary and everybody's birthday every year, but has the Longhorn and Cowboy football schedules memorized as soon as they come out is just one of the reasons our marriage didn't survive. Another small problem was the fact that I still believe in the ghost sitting silently in my passenger seat, and he felt a psychiatrist should have been able to shrink her out of my mind with a pill or stern talking-to.

I looked around at the traffic jam as Zach examined my front end. "So what's going on here?" I asked. He didn't answer, which is kind of typical. "What's happened?" I repeated.

He looked at me. "What's happened is you crashed your car, which means I'll have to call in another favor to get it fixed. Unless you've got the money to pay for it this time?"

Now didn't seem the right moment to mention I'd gotten fired. "I'm going home," I announced.

"You think you can handle it?" he asked, his lips finally curving into that sexy smile that could melt concrete.

"Yes."

"Good. Gimme some sugar." He didn't wait before stealing a wet kiss and then sauntered off just as quick.

"Hi, Edie," I said, as I maneuvered back into traffic. "I really wish you wouldn't visit me in the car."

"He still has quite a good body."

"Yes."

"Are you together?"

"Kind of." Like oil and vinegar. Mix us up real good and we'll work together, but sooner or later, we always separate.

"So it's just sex," she said, voice cool as a snow cone.

I sighed. "You shouldn't talk like that."

"He is forever preoccupied and yet often overbearing, an odd and terrible combination in a man. It wouldn't matter so much if he could afford lovely make-up gifts, like diamonds."

"Can we not talk about this please? I've had a rough day."

"I heard you quit your job. Well done."

"I didn't quit. I can't afford to quit. I was fired."

"That's not what I heard."

"Well, what did you hear? And who from?" It unnerved me that there were ghosts that I couldn't see strolling around spying on me. Did they watch me in the shower? Did they watch when Zach parked his boots under my bed? I blushed. Edie noticed and laughed.

I stole a glance at her exquisite face. With porcelain skin and high cheekbones, she was prettier than a china doll. She wore her sleek black hair bobbed, either straight or waved, depending on her mood and her outfit. Her lips were painted a provocative cherry red today. Rumor had it that Edie had inspired men to diamonds—and suicide. It was generally accepted in my family that one of her jilted beaus had murdered her, but she never shared the details of the unsolved 1926 New York homicide of which she'd been the star.

"How are you?" I asked.

"I'm dead. How would you be?"

I opened my mouth and closed it again. I had no idea. Was it hard being a ghost? Was it boring? She was very secretive about her life, er, afterlife.

"What made you visit today?" I asked, still trying for polite small talk.

"I heard you showed some backbone. I decided to visit in the vain hope that you might be turning interesting."

I frowned. Edie could be as sweet as honey on toast or as nasty as a bee sting. "I'm so sorry," I said. "For a minute I forgot that this isn't my life. It's your entertainment."

Her peridot eyes sparkled, and she favored me with a breathtaking smile. "Maybe not so vain after all. Did I ever tell you about the time I stole a Baccarat vase from the editor in chief of *Vanity Fair* and gave it as a present to Dorothy Parker? I liked the irony. He fired her, you know."

"Who was the editor?"

"Exactly," she said with a smile. "Getting fired isn't such a bad thing. You just need a present to cheer you up. As luck would have it, one is on the way."

"One what?" I asked, peering at her out of the corner of my eye. She couldn't take a corporeal form, so there was no way she could pick something up from a shop or even call into the Home Shopping Network, which was really a very good thing. From what I knew of Edie, she had very expensive tastes. There was no way in the world I would have been able to pay for any "presents" she sent me.

"What's this?" Edie asked as she moved through the passenger seat to the back.

"A cake," I said.

"It's a Scottish castle. Eilean Donan. Robert the Bruce still visits there. You're such a clever, clever girl. Only you have the bridge a bit wrong."

"I've never been to Scotland. It's just a castle I made up."

In the rearview mirror, I saw her tilt her head and smile. "Did you see it in a dream perhaps?"

"A daydream," I said hesitantly.

"It's about time, isn't it?"

"About time for what?"

"I'll see you later." She faded to mist and then to a pale green orb of light that passed out of the car and was gone.

I was happy that she'd liked my cake, but troubled by what she'd said. I was afraid she was thinking, as she had before, that I was finally "coming into my powers." She'd proclaimed as much on other occasions and had always been disappointed. No one in the history of the line had ever had their talents appear after the age of seventeen. Here I was twenty-three years old now; I knew I was never going to be a witch. In a lot of ways, it was a relief. Magic had always tempted my mother. She'd mixed a potion to help her track down a lost love, and she hadn't made it home to Duvall in more than a year. Finally her twin sister, Aunt Melanie, had gotten worried and had gone after her. Now who knew where they were? And what about Edie? She was said to have had remarkable powers, but they hadn't saved her life, had they? They may even have drawn something evil to her. Magic was dangerous, and I was glad I didn't have it. Really, I was.

LIKE A LOT of things about our family, our home is more than it seems to be. From the street, it's a Victorian cottage that yuppie couples find quaint and offer us lots of money for. But that's because they can't see over the big wooden fence. The backyard hides a darkly shaded Gothic alcove with a collection of brooding gargoyle statues and a garden of poisonous plants and plenty of stuff for potion-making. It's the kind of place where Edgar Allan Poe would have felt right at home but that I try to avoid except for an occasional round of fertilizing. You'd be surprised how well witch's herbs respond to Miracle-Gro.

I was relieved to find a package on the front step. My

friend Georgia Sue had remembered to drop off my Halloween costume for me. I was going to be Robin Hood this year,
and had already been practicing getting my long red hair
squished down under a short brown wig. I scooped up the
box and went inside, only to remember I had left the cake in
the car.

I zipped back out and retrieved the cake. As I set it on the
countertop, I noticed that the light on the answering machine
was flashing and pressed the message button.

"Tammy Jo, it's me. I dropped off your costume. I thought
you were going to be Robin Hood, honey? Well, at least it's
blue and green, and those are good colors for you with your
hair. But hoo-yah, I don't know what Momma's going to say.
And Miss Cookie. Tongues will be wagging. You know how
the ladies of First Methodist are. Katie Dousselberg still
hasn't lived down singing that Britney Spears song on Talent
Night . . ."

I scrunched my eyebrows together, advancing on the box
suspiciously. Georgia Sue's voice kept going. I love her dearly,
but she's the sort of person who can't see why anyone would
say in one sentence what could be said just as well in three.

"Did you hear about the sheriff's house? There was a
crazy traffic jam on Main, Tommy Hilliard said. If Zach
told you anything, you better call me up. I want to have the
best gossip tonight. I am the hostess, after all. Don't hold
out, sugar. Call me up."

I peeled the wide cellophane plastic tape off the box and
peeked inside, blinded for a moment by the reflection of a
million little sequins.

I pulled out the gown, which had some sort of stiff-spined
train and a plunging neckline that would embarrass a Vegas
showgirl.

"What in the Sam Houston?"

I shook out the dress and realized that the back was a
plume. In this costume I would be something of a porno-
graphic peacock. I tilted my head and wondered how I'd gone
from a sprightly Robin Hood to this. Then I remembered
Edie's comment from the car. She'd sent me a present.

Our town, Duvall, Texas, prides itself on having all the things that the big cities have (on a slightly smaller, but still significant scale), and one of our residents, Johnny Nguyen Ho, had created diversity for Duvall in several ways. He was our Vietnamese resident, our community theater director, and our not-so-secretly gay hair salon owner. Recognizing his talent for costume-making during his early play productions, most people in town sent him orders starting in February for their Halloween costumes.

Johnny Nguyen, in addition to his other considerable talents, fancied himself a psychic. And crazily enough, Edie had found a way to be partially channeled into his séance room, a spare bedroom he intermittently converted for this purpose by using a lot of midnight blue velvet and a bunch of scented candles from Bath & Body Works.

As I looked at the dress, I clenched my fists. There was no time to get a new costume, and I could not skip my best friend's Halloween party.

"Edie!" I called, wanting to give the little poltergucci a piece of my mind. But Edie is not the sort of ghost to come when called.

"Edie!" I snapped, as a new thought occurred to me: Liberace had had less beadwork on some of his costumes—how much would this upgrade cost me? I didn't need to be psychic to have a premonition of myself living on peanut butter and Ramen noodles.

If Edie could hear me, she ignored me. "Typical," I grumbled. One of these days all the people and poltergeists who didn't take me seriously were going to need me for something, and I just wasn't going to be there—or at least I wasn't going to be there right away.

Of course, my day of vindication would likely be sometime after Sheriff Hobbs, a serious churchgoing man, arrested me for indecent exposure. He'd probably give me a stern lecture on how short the path could be from poultry to prostitution.